WE Blend slow-burned its way into my heart with a perfect mix of sweetness and tension.

Music is the backbone of this book, and El's way of seeing the world through chords and melody made for an immersive experience I rarely see in young adult books...It is remarkably well written, with a refreshing dose of bantering and cuteness. Now, my only wish is to read the sequel to this incredible series, because I can't get enough of WE. -PA

Wil and El friendship will forever be unmatched.

I absolutely love a good friends to lovers book and this just scratched the spot. – TM

Grab your copy and let them take you on their journey.

This is their story and will pull the reader in as well. They have the talent to make it and their own reasons for fulfilling the dream. – EP

I AM SO EXCITED TO MEET THEM BOTH, AGAIN!

A New Adult romance, a sweet and clean, slow-burn romance, a cute couple, and a passionate female character. There's no more saying to describe how much I love it. – S

Fun, sweet, a romp.

Like dessert with no calories! Love this author. -CM

Catchy idea caught my attention, good story kept it!

I don't normally leave reviews but I really enjoyed the contradictions between the different sides of the characters. Finding good three-dimensional characters who make you want to like them isn't easy, but this author did it and did it well. -WW

My Fav Kindle Vella YA Romance

Took a chance on this story and didn't regret it. Hooked me from chapter one. El's way of hearing the world is cool. Didn't expect Wil to not be American. Searching a way to get to his rockstar father sucked me in. These two are so cute together. -A

Kept my interest from the very beginning.

This is a thoroughly enjoyable read from the first word. The characters are believable and engaging. I really enjoyed reading it. -N

Even Better Than Expected!

I had seen this story pop up on the Top Faves for awhile, but it stayed on my to-read list. It took me a few episodes, but then I was hooked! I needed to know more about these characters. I also find it interesting that this story was created by two authors. -CV

WE BLEND

A NOVEL

WILLA DREW

Grab a coffee, turn on your
favorite tunes, and
fall in love with Wil & El.

WD

MOVING WORDS PUBLISHING

Published by: Moving Words Publishing

www.movingwordspublishing.com

Cover: Books and Moods

(@booksnmoods on Instagram)

Artwork: María Peña

(@me.me.pe on Instagram)

Printed in the United States of America

ISBN: Paperback 978-1-957897-02-8

First Edition: September 2022

Join the mailing list for updates and follow Willa Drew here:

www.willadrew.com

If you enjoy this book, please consider giving it a review, so others can enjoy it as well.

CONTENTS

Falling for the Rockstar's
Daughter Series, Book 1

A NOVEL

WILLA DREW

For our fathers
William and Andrew

ONE

El

FAME FOLLOWS ME EVERYWHERE.

Not today. This morning I'm invisible. Everything is going according to plan and twelve hours crammed upright in an airplane seat were a small price to pay for my freedom. London commuters rush by on their way to work as I stroll back to my hotel sipping my average cup of Joe. No bodyguard in sight.

A smattering of paparazzi in front of the marble staircase sends my heart beating faster. No. They can't know I'm here. Can they? I tug the brim of my baseball cap. I look nothing like myself. Maybe I should've picked a smaller hotel, but the Four Seasons is where Dad always stays. Lots of celebrities choose it.

I rush past the cameras and try not to groan at how long the doorman takes to open the wrought iron doors. Inside the hotel, it's quiet and calm. Made it.

"Melodie." I hear my name ring across the gleaming two-story lobby.

A shiver shoots up my spine. "Dad?"

I look over to the plush maroon couches arranged in a semi-circle, and sure enough, there's Bill Rockerby. Stepdad to me. Rocker to the world. That's who the press is here for. He's not even hiding his rockstar status, decked out in black leather like he just walked off the stage after one of his concerts. Except he's walking toward me, his mouth pressed into a thin line, the look of disappointment I dread souring the handsome face lots of women, and men, drool over.

"What are you doing here?" I stumble over my words.

"The better question is, what are you doing here?" His voice is low and tense.

"I—" I don't have a comeback. Truth: I'm supposed to be in New York on a shopping spree, chaperoned by my mother-approved cousins, not in this swanky hotel in London.

His hand is on my arm. "Not here." Amber eyes dart left and right and back again. "People are listening." Dad's always paranoid about the press, especially in Europe. He corrals me toward the elevator, presses the call button, and we stand in awkward silence as we wait.

My mind races between two thoughts. Was it Bailey or Zoe who spilled the beans? 'Cause they were supposed to cover for me and not fold less than twenty-four hours into my escape. We have a pact: provide alibis for each other when we need to escape the parental cages, but their end of the bargain is harder to uphold. And I've never left the country by myself before. Zoe asked me five times if I was sure about the ruse.

More important: How do I get out of this?

There's a soft ding, probably a D-flat but the pitch is off a hair, and the gold doors slide open. I jump in first, hit the button for my floor; Dad follows close behind. More silence, like the pause between songs on a playlist. The doors close, and the elevator jumps to life.

"Your mother is sick with worry."

Slash. His words are tiny shavings of metal cutting at me. He knows my weak spot. Making Mom anxious, given what she's going through, is one of the worst things I could do. I squeeze my teeth together and don't reply because I've never learned to lie. My parents' publicist keeps trying to coach me, but the closest I can get is to omit the truth. Ask me a direct question, and I'll blabber, but I can't tell Dad about why I'm here.

"You can't silence your way out of this mess. Is it Dillon? I called him as soon as your mother got the alert on her credit card about the hotel charge." The elevator is playing a Muzak version of Justin's *Holy*, and my ears want to bleed. "He pretended he hadn't heard from you—better at lying than your cousins."

Mom's card. The receptionist said they had to have one in case I have other charges but promised they won't use it as long as I pay cash. Months of saved allowance was just enough for a ticket, three nights at the hotel, food, and paying for recording my music video. I'm not staying at this chain anymore. All the talk about keeping their clients' confidentiality, and they sell me out to my parents within hours.

"Talk to me." His voice softens a bit, and he angles his body toward me. "I might be forty-two, but I remember what being young and in love was like. I thought you were over him. With him back in England, you stopped pining for the asshole, pardon my French."

Dillon. Right. If I agree I'm here for Dillon, Dad might not dig deeper. My plan might still have a chance. "I thought I loved Dillon." It's true. I did think that. I don't anymore, but I let Dad draw his own conclusions. I keep squeezing my teeth. I can do it. Don't say anything, don't say anything, don't say anything.

"And what was your thought process? Fly across the ocean, profess your love for him, and hope, what? That he'll ditch his new job and come back to the States for you?"

New job? Is that why he left? He didn't offer me an explanation when he sent me his "I'm sorry, I can't do this" text.

I don't trust myself to speak, so I shrug instead.

"It's been six months."

The elevator doors open, and I trudge to my room, push the heavy door, and sink onto the king-size bed, leaving the chair by the desk for Dad to sit in. The calm gray-blue hues of the room cool the emotions circulating between us.

"You know you don't have to lie."

I want to scream "I do. You won't let me do anything otherwise."

"You know we love you."

"I know." This one's no lie. If anything, they love me too much. So much, there's no room for anything else.

"And that we do these things to protect your privacy. To keep you safe from another paparazzi-triggered breakdown. Can you blame your mother for wanting a semblance of normalcy for you?"

"Nope." After what happened to Papa and me, I can never blame her for wanting to keep me safe. But I don't have to like it. The bubble-wrapped life is smothering me. Sometimes I feel like I can't breathe between the rules, the bodyguards, and the ever-narrowing circle of things to do or people to do them with. Probably not a good time to bring up my complaints. Today, I need all suspicion away from the true reason I'm in London. And it isn't Dillon.

"I'll call your mom while you pack, tell her you're safe. The pilot's getting the jet ready for us."

"But . . ." If I don't show up to my meeting with Mr. Astor tomorrow, I'll lose the fifty percent down payment I transferred. "Can I at least go talk to Dillon?" I run my hand through my hair, find the familiar strands that always feel different, out of place, and pull, causing just enough pain to distract me from spilling the truth. The pain merges with the cloud of cutting metal of Dad's words.

"Why do you want to go down that road?" Dad puts his Doc Martin on his knee and shakes his foot. "No. You're not leaving this room until I escort you to the plane. It's nonnegotiable."

"But, Dad—"

"Melodie." He touches my hand, and I stop with the hair.

I focus on my tennis shoes and not on the buzzing shrapnel in my chest.

"Look at me."

I do as he says, because I'm a good girl.

"Leave it be."

Damn. There is no getting out of this. I'll have to message Lenard Astor and figure out a way, another time we can find two days in his schedule. Even if I do lose part of the money, I'll make it up with several months' of my allowance, if I buy nothing at all.

"Oh, and since you insist on being treated like an adult, it's time you took on some adult responsibilities. How about getting a job?"

"This again. I don't even have a high school diploma. How would it look if your stepdaughter asks 'do you want fries with that' for a living?"

"I wouldn't mind as long as you're happy."

He always says stuff like this. Cares almost too much. Unlike Mom who loves me but uses the tough-love parenting style. Nice or not, my music is my priority. "How can I be happy doing that when what I'd make at such a place is pennies compared to my allowance."

"Your mother wants to cut off your allowance as well."

"She can't. I have expenses." The metal ball of doom swings on a chain, and I cling to it, not wanting to wreck my plans.

"Really?" His bushy eyebrow performs that sky high thing it does when he's being sarcastic. "We pay for everything."

"I need clothes."

"You have two walk-in closets."

"I was going to buy a new keyboard."

"What's wrong with the one in the studio?"

"That's yours."

"I have a solution. Why don't you come and work for me at Rocker, Inc. Nadine needs help in the back office. It'll give you some work experience and you can help discover the next *it* artist."

I don't want to discover them, I want to *be* them. But I need the money to start again, and working for my stepfather isn't the worst thing in the world. "What's the starting salary?"

He smiles for the first time. "You make it sound like you're doing me a favor here and not the reverse. I'll pay you the same as I'd pay anyone I'd hire to do the job. And no special treatment. You'll be like any of my other employees."

It's not as if I have a lot of choice here. "Fine."

I grab the suitcase Mom gave me for my eighteenth birthday and fling the lid open. I stuff the ten outfits I brought for my stay into it and hide my sheet music under the top dress. My independence day's gone. Guess it's back to the US for the Fourth of July.

"This is ridiculous." The bright yellow Louis Vuitton with my initials monogrammed in blue, MVR for Melodie Vella Rockerby, mocks my ruined dreams with its bright cheer.

"You running away is what's ridiculous." His phone dings an F-sharp, and he answers.

"Yes. I'm with her. Yes. Safe." I can feel his eyes on my back as I snap my suitcase shut. "I told her the terms. Love you too."

He puts the phone down and gets up. "I have to go make an excuse to the press. They spotted me at Southend when I landed. Wait for me here. Hotel security has someone by your door. Don't even try talking to them."

The lead ball drops from my chest into my stomach at the sight of the security guard when Dad leaves my room. I grab onto the doorframe and take a moment to survey the hallway, looking for possible escape routes.

"Get inside and stay there." Patience is no longer in Dad's voice, and I want to scream. Instead, I slam the door.

The heavy metal doesn't connect but bounces off the fingers on my left hand, still clutching the white casing. I jerk them toward me and watch the indentations on the index and middle finger bloom pink. At the sight, the numbness disappears, replaced by blinding pain. The scream I've wished for erupts from my lungs. I suck air and glare at the places where the edge of the door tore through the skin. It doesn't look that bad. That's when the throbbing begins, and I can barely hear Dad barking orders at the guard to get the hotel doctor.

This is not how I imagined my first jail break would go.

Two

Wil

I HAVEN'T BEEN IN LA for more than five minutes, and he walks right by me. So close, I can almost smell his designer cologne. A few steps, and I could slap him on the back, assuming I could get past the security detail.

My father. The rockstar.

Bill Rockerby strolls through the airport, his entourage carrying bright yellow luggage like little ducks in a row, while I stand here at baggage claim waiting for mine like a normal person.

Is that his stepdaughter in the back? She sure lucked out when her mother remarried, getting a rockstar as her new father. Some tossers get all the breaks. She doesn't look happy about being home. One hand sports a splint binding her fingers together. Did Daddy's little girl's vacation get ruined? Poor her. Not.

The sunglasses that hold up her red hair surely cost more than my entire wardrobe. Her signature streak falls on the left side of her face. If not for that shock of white, from this close she looks more like a girl next door than the glossy spoiled brat in the pages of the magazines Mum used to bring home from the clinic. Without the makeup and the posh clothes, her beauty shines. Not my type, but plenty of people would love to have someone like her as their arm candy.

Whispers start around me, and phones turn in their direction. Some brave souls take a few steps to get closer, others shout about getting a selfie. Rocker and Melodie keep walking. We're nothing but an annoyance to them. They could've smiled, waved, but no, not rock-n-roll's elite. They press on with sour faces and disappear from view.

"I almost touched him," a bloke in denim overall shorts and flip-flops gushes to the girl next to him. American fashion is not something I'll ever understand.

I unzip the inside pocket of my GOODBOIS messenger bag, the one nice thing I own, and get out the small notebook covered in black faux leather. With a pop, the pencil snaps out of the elastic holder, and I jot down:

Annoyance on the clean face or a perfect smile on a glossy page
sound of flip-flops on a linoleum floor
Almost. Always almost.

Notebook safely tucked away, I roll up the sleeves of my dark green shirt. Mum's been supplying me with the pocket notebooks ever since I started writing up the ideas that pop into my head on my hands and arms. There's a drawer full of them at home and two more in my pack that, with any luck, is not lost. I shift the beat-up guitar case from my feet and onto my shoulder and walk closer to the conveyor belt.

Time to let Mum know I've arrived. I connect my phone to the free airport Wi-Fi, pull up WhatsApp, and type "I'm here." She'll relay the message to Opa, who doesn't get the whole text-message thing. I can hear my grandfather grumbling, "Why can't you just pick up the phone?" Even though it's midnight in Bremen, I get a barrage of messages back. Mum should be sleeping, she needs it, but I type back some deets.

The LAX Airport Shuttle bus goes to the Transit Center, where I catch the Number 3 Big Blue Bus, which gets me to Westwood for fifty cents. My kind of price. I get off and make sure my backpack doesn't hit anyone when I turn—the top part is higher than my head, and I'm taller than most men around me. A short walk, and I arrive at the UCLA campus. It has people, but it's quiet, unlike the one I just left. Had to bail on the rest of the semester for this, but I'll be back in time for the October session.

There are a few people around, and I catch the eye of two beauties lying on a blanket on the grass. They both smile at me, and I make sure to return the gesture. I may be here for serious business, but that doesn't mean a fella can't have fun in the process.

Part of me can't believe my luck in getting into the program. I applied to the Starlight Future Filmmakers Foundation's annual film competition as a laugh. I never thought I'd get a call for the audition. The committee gave me the option to fly in or do it over Zoom. Yeah, 'cause I have the dough to drop on a trip to LA for a bloody interview. Harder to turn on my charm over the internet, but I made it work, and here I am—an almost-all-expenses-paid trip to the U.S. of A.

Checking in to the dorms is the simplest thing I've done today. Let the free ride begin. After the airfare, the credit card I usually only use for emergencies is almost at its limit. Finding a job will be one of the first things on my list. I stick my key into the door but before I turn it, the pale wood slat opens, and a bloke with a buzz cut smiles at me.

"Welcome, bienvenidos, bienvenue—all the languages I know."

"Willkommen," I say.

"Ah, isn't that what they say in Germany?"

"Yup. Born and bred there, so I can vouch for that."

"More of us internationals." He scratches his head. "What's with the British accent?"

"That's ten years learning English at school in Bremen plus summers with family in Sussex."

"Willkommen then, Mr. German."

"It's Wil Peters actually."

"I'm Mateo. Mateo Gallardo." He opens his arms and steps away, so I can enter. The common room isn't a fancy resort, but the light is good, and we're far away from the stairwell. In the middle there's a pair of brown leather couches separated by a low glass table, dominated by a flat screen TV hanging on the wall. Pushed up against the window is a wooden table with six matching chairs. Home sweet home.

"You're the last to arrive, so the only bed left is in my room." He points to the second door on the left. "Me and the other dudes were about to head out and grab some grub. Wanna join?"

I want to drop my stuff and take a shower, but some food wouldn't be bad either. "Sure. Any idea where I can get a SIM card around campus?"

"I'm your man. I scouted all the things we're going to need in this country."

"Including a grocery store? The website said there's a kitchen I can use on this floor." I've learned over the last year living on campus how much Mum did for me. First time I did laundry, I washed my clothes in one load. I still have the shirt that used to be white and is now a combination of gray and splotches of blue. Cooking is another thing I had to figure out.

"You're ambitious. It's just for three months. One thing my mami never let me do is cooking. I already miss her empanadas."

Mateo shrugs as he follows me into the room we are to share. Why do the people who design dorms lack imagination? They're all the same. Two single beds pushed against opposite walls, one night table, and what I presume is a closet the size of a coffin.

I drop my backpack on the bed and prop my guitar in the small space against the wall.

"You here to make a movie too?" Mateo sits down on his bed.

"Yeah, I'm the sound person."

"Way cool." He taps his chest. "Set designer. I'm on the green team."

"Green?"

"Each team has a color. Don't worry." Why would I worry? "You'll get one at the orientation session tomorrow. We can go together in the morning. Already checked out the building."

Seems my luck is holding. Mateo is doing the heavy lifting.

I hang up a classic white long-sleeve shirt Mum snuck in that raises the number of clothing items I brought to eleven. My side of the room looks spartan compared to Mateo's, who on his twelve-hour drive from Mexico brought twice the stuff I had in my old dorm room at uni. I'm particularly impressed with the precise placement of the array of multicolored pens and pencils he's using to draw something in a large notepad. He catches me eyeing them.

"Tools of the trade. I always sketch by hand first."

Day one in the States rushes by in a blur of dropping more money on my credit card. I thought the giant Coke I drank with my first American burger would keep me up but incessant yawning reminds me I've been awake for twenty-four hours.

When I get back from the shower, the bedroom is empty and quiet but for the laughter filtering from the living room where my new flatmates are gearing up to play a video game. I set my alarm for five a.m. so I can fit in a quick workout before orientation. The gym on campus even has rowing machines, so

I can keep up with my crew in Berlin. They'll be rowing on the river daily. Can't get out of shape.

Exhaustion seeps out of me into the mattress, and I stare at the curtains filtering thin pinpoints of light through the top. I'm here. If Opa's right, I'll figure out a way to meet Rocker. I've come the farthest I've ever been from home to talk to the man. And for Mum, I'd go around the world in a rowing boat to improve her health.

The rockstar can spare the money, go without another car or a house in Fiji. It's not like he had to pay child support for eighteen years. What I need is a fraction of what that would've cost him. I'm not looking for a father. Opa filled those shoes for me, but Rocker should help. Mum's done everything for me, her only son. Even if I am just the product of a one-night stand, I'm the only blood offspring that wanker has in this world, and I'm ready to use that fact.

I'm not going home empty-handed.

THREE

El

THE DANG SPLINT PROTECTING my injured fingers gets stuck in the sleeve of my turquoise dress shirt, and I have to rethink my outfit. No sleeves. I move the hangers in the silver section around until I spot the vintage Paco Rabanne metal chain halter I kept after the *Rock Squad Magazine* photoshoot for Dad's kids charity fundraiser. The cold links were my armor against the photographer's words telling me where I should stand and what my face should look like. I hang it back up. That is Melodie Rockerby's outfit, not El Vella's.

What will El wear? My stage name is my nod to Papa. Technically, it's still my name, the Rockerby added when Mom married Bill Rockerby. He sat me down and asked if I was okay with him adopting me, explained he never had any kids of his own, would never replace Papa, but he wanted us to be a family. It's not like I could say no. True to his word, Bill, Dad, has always treated me like his, and I do love him. I know I'm lucky, but Rockerby is too famous, too recognizable. No one outside of the opera world will know the last name Vella, which is perfect. I need them to see *me*.

I tuck my hair behind my ear. What would I wear if I didn't have to think about the tabloids and eventual comments on social media? Something comfortable, because tonight's gonna be tough enough without having to worry about my clothes; something I can keep my cool in, because I'll be sweating all over; something I can sit down in without worrying about showing my underwear.

My last vacation in Malta with Papa's family, I went shopping at the local market and got the most comfortable moss-green palazzo pants that sorta looked like a long skirt, along with a simple white tank top. My arms glide through the holes and my heartrate slows a bit. Memories of the sun and the simple conversations envelop me, offering support. There's something about clothes that sets my mood, and I've found the right ones for El Vella's first stage appearance.

"Are you ready?" Sven asks from behind the closed door. "We have to leave in five." My friend is less than pleased with me since Dad reassigned him from lead bodyguard duty to my personal babysitter. I lucked out, though. If Dad only knew the messes Sven cleaned up for me. There's no one I'd rather have by my side day and night.

Am I really doing it? Stepping on a stage, however small, and not fainting from the greedy eyes trained on me, ready to judge my every wrong word, false pitch, awkward movement? My hands shake when I open the door and follow Sven down the stairs, panting a little too hard. Not good signs, but I have to ignore them. We sneak past the theater room where Mom and Dad are binge watching some historical drama about a queen.

"And where are you going?" Mom's voice stops me in my tracks. I'll need a better route next time.

"Ice cream with Zoe." I've already texted my cousin to cover if my parents get nosey.

"And Sven?" Mom turns around and sees my human shield looming behind me. "Be home by midnight."

I hurry down the hallway before she changes her mind.

Sven opens the back door of the light blue electric Rolls Royce Dad got for my required bodyguard to chauffeur me around, and I slip in. The door clicks shut, surrounding me in silence. Almost. My ears are ringing. My personal Superman jumps in and starts driving us to downtown LA.

Outside the tinted windows, the sky deepens into a purple haze as day morphs into night. Time for my transformation as well. I pull out my phone and follow the instructions on the YouTube video I've watched a hundred times. I finagle my shoulder-length auburn hair into flat twists and cover them with a wig. The platinum locks are longer than my real hair and feel odd falling over my shoulders and down my back to my waist. A little shine on my lips completes the look.

"You are not allowed to go into the actual bar." Sven repeats the instructions he gave me twice before, ignoring my new look. "All the performers under twenty-one have to stay backstage."

"I know."

"I've checked out the place, and I'll be in the back, the left corner closest to the hallway that leads backstage. It'll take me maybe thirty seconds to get to you if you are recognized."

"Left back corner. I got it."

"And you're not talking to anyone but me and Pauline, the manager. You're there to get that job, not have fun at a bar."

"Aye, aye, captain."

"Not funny, Melodie. You don't have to do this. We can turn around and go home." He stops at the red light and looks over his shoulder at me. "There are other ways to get money. Let me help you for once. I'll get a loan and give you the cash, and you'll pay me back once Mr. and Mrs. Rockerby reinstate your allowance."

"Which, according to Mom, is never."

"They're still angry. Give them time."

"I'm angry too."

Sven does his silent listening routine.

"If I'm doing it, and dammit, I am doing it, I'm doing it on my own. I'm not the useless, spoiled baby they think I am. I might not have a formal education"—I air quote the words—"but I had the world's best tutors. Taking the GED seemed more trouble than it was worth. Not like university has ever been in the picture." I sit up straighter, raise my chin, and meet Sven's eyes in the rearview mirror. "But I know a lot about music, and I can earn my own money, live my own life, and be my own person. I don't need them as much as they think I do."

Even though I booked Mr. Astor's last available session in November, my down payment is gone, and the salary at Rocker, Inc. is a start but it's not going to get me the amount I need to cover the cost. Zoe felt bad about the London debacle and offered to make up the difference. After I refused to accept her money, she pulled some strings and snagged me a spot in tonight's open mic competition. The winner gets paid to perform at the Devil's Martini's coveted Saturday night showcase.

This gig alone won't cover the whole sum, but it'll make a big dent. If my plan is to become a singer, why not start now? I've spent enough hours practicing in my room and Dad's home studio to stand a chance. If I win, I prove to everyone I can earn a living with my music.

We enter through a side door of the Devil's Martini, and a preppy young woman in glasses, who looks more like a librarian than someone who'd work at a bar, shoves a clipboard my way.

"Write your name here. You're number five." She hands me a sticker with the number hand-written in red marker. "Are you performing too? Or just the boyfriend?" Her eyes survey Sven's solid body from head to foot, and I swear the top of her cheeks pink up.

"Friend. Audience." Sven gives his standard just-the-facts reply. .

"Oh, straight through there, then." Her cheeks are definitely pink when she shows my fair-haired "friend" the way. "And you go left." She switches to me. "You get one song. Hang around till the end, Pauline'll talk to you about the gig if you win. And don't try to butter me up, I'm not one of the judges. Break a leg."

The door slams behind me. She glances at Sven one more time and aims her smile at the next person. We head past her, and I take the door to the left that says, "STAGE. STAFF ONLY," and Sven gives me a thumbs up as he heads up the long hallway and into the bar. I wipe my sweaty palms on the sleek silk crepe of my pants.

The stage is my friend. The stage is my friend.

I'll get on it even if I have to ask someone to push me out. Recording a video for my EP won't happen if I can't perform in front of a crowd. Doubt this dinky bar will even have more than twenty people here, but as long as it's more than zero, it won't be easy.

I knew this day was coming. I just didn't expect it to be this soon. I thought I'd have time. Shoot the video, send it to some producers, make a whole album before I had to perform in front of real live people.

Twenty minutes later, the open mic competition begins, and Jeremiah is not here. My feverish texts go unanswered, and although they have an extra keyboard and a couple of guitars I could use, my broken fingers will take at least five more weeks before I can start using them again. This is what Jeremiah is for:

study the music for my songs, bring a guitar, and accompany me. Now what do I do?

I walk up the hallway to the bar area, peek from the door into the room, and scan the place. Jeremiah is steps away, beer in hand, sitting at a dark wooden bar talking with some guy. That jerk. He shouldn't be drinking before we perform. He should be backstage rehearsing, or at least have the decency to answer his phone. I'm not letting him screw this up for me. Google informed me both Dasher and Carlee Waters had their break after winning the open mic competition here. Maybe El Vella can be next.

"Jeremiah," I shout across the room. "Jeremiah, over here."

Jeremiah looks up and meets my eye. Shit, shit, shit. He can barely focus on me. How much has this dufus had to drink? I look at my phone. Our slot is in ten minutes. How can I sober him up? I look for Sven, but he's far off, the librarian's hand on his impressive bicep and his attention on her blazing cheeks and not the bar I'm not even supposed to be in. I don't need him to show up, scare Jeremiah, and end this night before I even get a chance. One eye on Sven, I slink over the black floor to Jeremiah's barstool.

"Jeremiah?" The way his body sways when he moves his head kills any hope of him being my hands today.

"Elllllllll." The happy drunk sings my name. I could kill him. He's no use to me in this state. I side-eye his companion who's drinking . . . water? Odd.

"Meet my new friend. He'sss from Germany. How cooool is that?"

I don't have time to meet people. I need Jeremiah to sober up. I don't have a choice.

"Hey, I'm Wil." I turn to him because my parents taught me manners. His one-sided grin is certain to score, but it's not going to work on me. I'm here on a mission, and it's not a random hook-up with a hot stranger. This is the one time I wish Sven were by my side, so I could get him to remove this playboy. I flick my gaze to Sven to reassure myself he's there and if I scream his name, he'll run over and rescue me.

"Hey. Um, can I talk to Jeremiah? In private."

Light brown, almost golden eyes examine my outfit, the ends of my hair sweeping my hip bones, the exposed skin at my neck, and finishes the round with my face. If I weren't already hot from nerves, that stare would've gotten me there. He's cute, jet-black hair flopping all over the place in that boy-band-wannabe way. He reminds me of someone, but I can't quite put my finger on whom. I shake my head. I have bigger problems.

"Could you please give us some space?" I take one step closer, as if I can intimidate him into vacating his spot.

"Not sure it's smart for you to be next to him before your turn on stage." Wil nods at the number five sticker on my shoulder. His accent is decidedly British. Didn't Jeremiah say this dude was from Germany? Or is Jeremiah too drunk to know the difference between the two countries? "He might just chuck up all over your pretty clothes and ruin your performance before you begin. How about I keep an eye on your boyfriend, and you can talk it out after you're done?"

"No."

"No?" His thick dark eyebrow climbs up, and a smile returns to his face. Maybe it is working on me. Would've worked if I didn't have a drunk Jeremiah and my dreams riding on the line.

"No. He's not my boyfriend. Who has time for that?" Why am I telling him I'm single? Need to focus. "I hired him to play the guitar for me." I raise my splinted fingers and shove them in front of Wil's face. "See?"

"Well, that clears that."

If I expected sympathy from this dude, I didn't get it.

"I don't do the girlfriend thing either. Not planning on starting it now." He licks his lips like I might be his next meal. "Jeremiah might have difficulty standing up, so playing an instrument is bloody unlikely."

"Dammit." I know the guy is right.

We both turn to regard the hoodie-clad Jeremiah, currently staring into his half-empty beer glass as if the golden liquid has the answers to every mystery in life.

"What did you say your name was?" Wil's molten stare focuses on my eyes then my mouth, as if he were ready to catch whatever tumbles out next. And I wish I were here for fun. Hot, kiss-worthy fun.

"El. El Vella." My voice sounds raspier than normal.

His eyes flash back to mine. Something switches in them. He re-surveys me, and his demeanor changes. The relaxed flirty vibe drops as fast as the last note of Dad's latest hit. He loses his smile, the fire in his eyes gone, and for reasons I can't understand, I miss it already.

Wil leans in like he's going to kiss me, his fiery breath tickling my ear instead. Is this his signature move? Is he going to ask me out? Would I say yes? Goosebumps run down my arms, and my heart rises to my throat.

"I know who you are."

Four

El

I REACH FOR MY hair. My hand brushes against the long strands of the blonde wig, concealing my identity. My heartbeat is tapping out the baseline of the Tings, Tings, That's Not My Name in my ears. He can't know who I am. Can he?

"As if." Even I don't believe my words, they croak out so weak. I step away. I need air.

"The wig is a nice touch. Hiding your . . . signature hair is a good idea. But you look better as a ginger."

Shit, shit, shit. He does know who I am. That's it, I'm outta here. I'll find another way to make the cash. Not even bothering to say goodbye to Jeremiah, I turn and bolt toward the exit.

There's a hand on my arm. How dare he? No one touches me. My bodyguards never let anyone get near enough to try. Dillon had to sneak handholding in the elevator. But the hot librarian is all over Sven, and he has no idea I'm not backstage. I should've listened to him, texted Sven to look for Jeremiah.

I scan the bar. What if this dude says something, and everyone here figures out who I am? It'll be the scene in Neiman Marcus all over again. All I wanted was to try on some dresses with Zoe, be normal, but one person posted my location and suddenly, there were cameras stuffed in my face as I tried to leave the store. If that happens, they won't let me take part in open mic. They'll think it's rigged in my favor. This day is getting worse by the minute.

"Let go," I hiss.

And he does. I take a step back at the lack of pull.

"Don't worry. I won't tell anyone."

"Why not?" I gotta stop this blurting around him.

He looks at the crowd, shrugs, and cocks his head to the side. "Not worth it."

The hairs on the back of my neck stand at attention. Everyone wants something. It's a fact.

"What is?"

Those big eyebrows knit together. "What?"

"What's worth it?"

His eyebrows relax, and a different smile from the sizzling one earlier touches his full lips. He could be a villain in a movie. A beautiful, dangerous being that offers deals to young virgins for the price of their soul. At least I'm not a virgin anymore.

"I'm not drunk, and I play guitar. Rather well, I've been told."

"Oh." I follow his drift. "How much?" He gets I'm asking about the money.

"What did you offer Jeremiah?"

"Two hundred for today and twenty-five percent of any future profits until my broken fingers heal."

He stretches his hand my way. "Fifty percent of what you get, and I think we have ourselves a deal."

A deal I don't want, but I'm minutes away from my slot, and I don't have any other options. Sven can knock a man's teeth out with his fist, but he has no idea how to play an instrument. If I abort this mission, I might as well give up and become the corporate drone my parents want me to be.

I grab his hand, and the heat of his palm brings back the fever from earlier. I'm hot again, but now it's all below my waist. The asshole knows how to work his charm.

"It's a deal. But you only get paid after each performance. My mother didn't raise a fool."

Our hands are linked and although there's no blood oath or metal branding my skin, his palm sears mine. I should pull it away, but I don't. His almost yellow eyes seem to have a film of smoke in the darkness of the hallway.

"Don't get your knickers in a twist. It'll be fun. And when you're a big star like your daddy"—he says, *daddy*, with an exaggerated American accent—"I'll get to tell my friends I got to play with you before everyone else catches on."

He hasn't even heard me sing and already jumped to the conclusion I'm good. I'm not even related to Rocker by blood, and still everyone assumes I have talent. I want to punch him in the stomach. Or the face. And I don't need Sven to do it for me.

But I don't. I squeeze my teeth together and force myself to be calm. Just like I do when I wake up from nightmares. I focus on the blue squiggle zigzagging through Wil's T-shirt, pushing all thoughts out of my head except for one: I need to sing.

"Do you have a guitar?"

The playboy vibes are back, light dancing in his golden eyes. He holds up a finger as he backs away. I watch him head over to Jeremiah, place a hand on his shoulder, and the two engage in a quick conversation. Wil dips behind Jeremiah and pops back up, acoustic guitar in hand.

I don't know if I'm relieved or scared. He's silver-tongued, that's for sure. Now I'm thinking about his tongue. And lips. And eyes.

He swings the strap over his shoulder like he's done it a million times before.

And his broad shoulders.

He's taller than me, at least Dad's height, if not more. I envy the ease of the motion, his familiarity with the guitar. My hand itches to get back to playing. It's different from piano and what started as a way to bond with Rocker has turned into a love for the instrument. I love how the strings feel under my fingers, the vibration of the wood pressed against my body, the music ringing through it.

"So, what are we playing?"

I walk down the hallway to door labeled, "staff only," and he follows.

"Do you know *The Only One* by The Troops?"

The first few chords of the song strummed on the guitar are his answer. I can't help but smile. This could work.

"Good. Wait here." I turn toward the stage.

Wil mumbles, "Someone's a proper madam."

I ignore it. Five minutes on stage, and my video shoot is still possible. If I sing in front of strangers that long.

I check in with Pauline, confirm the pronunciation of my last name and our time slot, and head back to Wil. He's leaning against the wall, guitar pointed to the ground, scribbling something in a little black book. Rare to see someone writing—I use the notes app on my phone—not that I write much. The words never come out of my head the way I feel the music.

"We're up next."

Will tucks the book in the back pocket of his jeans. "Great." He's cool, oozing charm, and I'm not the only one who notices. The couple of girls who're still backstage, waiting for their turn, can't keep their eyes off him.

"Follow my lead."

"As you wish." His eyes twinkle. They twinkle, dammit.

"You've got the deal. No need to suck up. Let's go win this thing."

We step toward the stage as the older man playing the piano finishes the final notes of his song. My hand aches. The crowd offers a halfhearted round of polite applause as he takes a bow and walks out of the spotlight. Pauline nods at me as she grabs the single microphone on a stand at center stage. The cold sweat from earlier returns, and my ears are ringing again. I swallow, trying to relieve my throat, which has gone dry.

"A big round of applause for Jim Sawyer." Pauline checks the piece of yellow paper in her hand. "Next up, we have a newcomer to the Devil's Martini. Put your hands together for El Vella."

There's a huff from behind me. Maybe I should've included Wil's name in the introduction. I was so focused on myself I didn't even think about it. Didn't even ask him his last name. So unlike me. "What's your last name?" I wait for his answer.

"Peters."

Pauline's waving us on stage. I take a deep breath and plunge into the bright lights. This is it.

My ballet flats scuff along the well-worn wood of the stage as I make my way toward the microphone. I can already feel the heat of the three spotlights pouring down on me. I look out at the front row, where a couple is whispering to each other and pointing at me. People are everywhere I look. The bar did not appear this full when I was out there dealing with Jeremiah. Some conversations continue, and my chest is ablaze with anxiety. I clutch at the microphone and pick out a few seemingly friendly faces to focus on.

"Hello, everyone." My voice is timid, and I hate it. I clear my throat and try again. I can do this. I have to do this. "I'm El Vella, and this is Wil Peters." I point to Wil, and he acknowledges the crowd like he's used to being on stage. Maybe he is. The ease with which he's been strumming the guitar doesn't disappear. It magnifies, like the stage is a second home for him.

With a nod from me, Wil dives into the intro. The first line is coming. I take a steady breath, ready for El Vella's big moment.

And nothing happens. The first words of the song I know by heart remain lodged in my throat.

FIVE

Wil

ALL I WANTED WAS a beer, and instead I got the break I needed.

What is it with this country and its bloody stupid drinking age? I've been sipping on beer legally since I was sixteen. Thought I might convince some girl to buy me one, but instead I met this bloke, Jeremiah, crying in his beer over the fact some girl just broke up with him. Sucker. Letting himself double dip and worse, grab feelings.

But Jeremiah's foolishness is a stroke of luck for me. He's drowning his broken heart in the piss of at least his fifth pint of Busch. One taste of it, and I knew I'd be sticking with water. How is that liquid passing for beer? I shouldn't be cursing the drink that got me here. My luck has never steered me wrong. Coming to this bar with a fake ID was brilliant, and now, here I stand on stage with Melodie Rockerby. Or should I say El Vella? What kind of name is that?

The stage is different from my usual DJ setup or the street corner I busk at with my guitar, but the anticipation of performing for others fuels me. It's the best drug, and my mind makes the switch into performance mode.

El nods at me to start, and I dive into the intro. I've played this song a hundred times in my dorm room, on the street, on my turntables, can play it without thinking. It's all gushy words about finally finding the one that completes you. Such bullshit. But the girls love it, and it works for me.

Intro over, the first verse starts. Except El doesn't move. Lips pressed together. She doesn't sing, which is the whole point. I play through the line and start again. Still nothing. So, I do what I must and step up to the mic and sing the lyrics.

You are a thief, and you keep stealing
What new trick will you be revealing . . .

She jerks away from me, like a scared rabbit. I get the feeling she wants to run. The first time I spun at the club, I almost puked. There are some mavericks out there who jump on stage, and it feels like a second home right away. But for me, and most performers I've worked with, it takes loads more. Time, practice, the experiences of forgetting the music, lyrics or doing a completely wrong thing, even losing the audience's attention. I learned how to notice what works and what doesn't, and how to adjust it the next time I played. And I got used to the nerves.

Now I can DJ and pick up girls at the same time. Mum raised a talented boy.

Wide eyes study me as I finish up the first verse and head to the pre-chorus. Am I going to have to sing this whole song myself? She'll have to pay me double for that. What the hell is she doing up here if she can't sing? Or is she afraid? I almost laugh at the irony. The daughter of two of the world's most flamboyant opera singers, stepdaughter to the stage-humping Rocker, and she has stage fright?

Shite. I'd love to amuse myself at the pop princess's expense, but I need this to work if I'm going to use her to get to Rocker. I turn to her, raise an eyebrow and mouth, "naked." Imagining the crowd without clothes made me laugh every time I tried it, unsuccessfully. I have to break her stupor. She stares at my lips then turns pink. Her mouth closes, and her eyes beg me for something I'm not sure I can give her.

I start the chorus and angle my body, so she has to look at me and me only. How can I get through to her? My hands are busy with the guitar. I do the next best thing I can think of: I bend down and touch my forehead to hers, telepathically telling her we're in this together.

I've got you. Sing.

And she does.

Her voice comes out timid and soft, barely there at first. I offer her a smile, and the timbre tightens, her voice louder as she gains confidence. There's an ethereal quality to her singing voice. I lower mine to let it meld. It works. Our voices blend together, creating a new sound. I don't understand it, but it feels right.

The chorus ends, and I don't know what to do. Do I keep singing or will she take over? I separate our heads so I can catch her eye. The blue irises shine in the spotlight, an electricity there. It's like she's talking inside my head, saying "I got this," so I let her sing but stay right by her side, almost touching.

I'm still here.

I continue our wordless communication.

In case I need to jump in.

I don't need to jump in. She's . . .

Amazing.

Never breaking eye contact, I smile, and she does too, and the room brightens. It's like she's singing to me, no, for me. Her voice is clear and powerful. I almost forget to keep playing, sheer muscle memory taking over as I strum the chords of the song. The stupid song takes on new meaning when she sings it. The melody in tune, just the right amount of vibrato. At the crescendo, she belts out the line about wanting to be the only one, and the idea doesn't sound that absurd anymore.

Her voice reminds me of when I heard a live concert for the first time—the chords, the beat, the words connecting with some part of me no one gets to touch. Immersing myself in the song, surrounded by it, the direct contact with a human voice in front of me, against my body, inside my head, moving my blood.

On the chorus, I join her. We get into a groove, and our voices blend. I didn't think the feeling and the sound could get better;

it does. The microphone is the only thing between us. Our mouths are inches away from it. Inches away from each other. For the last line of the chorus, she puts her hand on my shoulder and closes her mouth again. I get it, and I sing the last verse.

I thought she needed me to take over, but she didn't. As soon as I begin, she starts echoing some of the words, as if we are having a conversation, as if both of us are complaining about our stolen hearts. And then it's over. There's a moment of silence, both of us sucking air in and blowing it out in sync, as we try to get our breath back. Her small smile grows into a huge grin, and I bathe in the light of her exuberance. El Vella takes over the space, Melodie Rockerby nowhere in sight.

At first, I don't even hear it. It's just the two of us in this secret pocket of light, surrounded by darkness. The audience doesn't exist. A sharp whistle cuts through the air, and the applause pierces our bubble. It's thundering.

Six

El

WE WAIT.

We watch our competition.

Wil drums triplets against the cover of the tiny notebook, his thigh, the top of the guitar. I hear The Beatles' *Come Together* in the rhythm of his fingers. I wonder if he realizes it.

The final contestant is a willowy girl about my age with flaxen hair in a braided crown around her head, and a pale beige guitar with daisies on the strap. She rocks to the slow beat of the classic Simon & Garfunkel *Sound of Silence*, strums and sings, her voice soft and husky.

"That's a Fender, probably a custom one. Why are all the money bags trying to get a spot here?" Wil's question hurts. He's most definitely including me in that statement.

"A couple of famous artists got discovered here. A&R folks sometimes attend."

"A&R?"

"Artists and Repertoire. They scout talent for record labels."

"Like, they come in person? Is that even a thing anymore? Isn't everyone discovered on SoundCloud or YouTube?"

"Yeah, that works too. At Rocker, Inc. they listen to music, scour clubs, monitor social media, read music blogs, and a bunch of other stuff when they hunt for promising artists."

I got the spot here only because Zoe pulled some strings. No one knows I'm Melodie, but Pauline must have some inkling I'm not without connections. Her waiting list is hundreds of wannabes long, and I couldn't wait months until it would be my turn. Better get my rejection now and see what else I can sell without Mom noticing. Or I might have to take Sven up on his offer of lending the money. After all, getting him and his brother, Trevor, to Comic-Con last year was one thing; this year, I won't even get to go with them.

"Good to know." Three fingers cascade in rapid succession, and if I didn't know better, hadn't seen him flaunt his skills, charm the backstage gaggle, who are, for frigging sake, our direct competition, I'd say he's anxious? The tiny notebook is open again, as he transfers the nervous energy onto the page. The lines fill up with large letters slanted right, but I can't quite read what they say. He stands up, returns the book and its mysteries to his back pocket, and resumes the tapping, now a soft staccato on his black jeans. I shouldn't enjoy the crack in his oh-so-cool demeanor. Maybe the creature has a soul after all.

That's not fair. The guy beside me is very human. I bring my uninjured hand to my forehead, as if it can be a stand-in for his touch, the one that lingered on my skin even after he stepped away and made sure I was good to carry on. He's just a random guy at a bar, yet my nerves disappeared with him around—the last thing I expected. Not that I expect much from people. I don't meet many. That sounds wrong. I meet far too many people, but none I get a chance to get to know, never mind trust.

The usual entourage rarely admits new people, most of them family or close work friends of my parents. They've always been there, acceptance born of years spent together. It's how Dillon and I met. Dillon was the backstage kid of a celebrity joining on tour.

What happened between us in that hotel room was inevitable. I said yes to prove to myself I'm a grown-up and in control of my body. I craved to feel the bubblegum sweetness of the instant attraction they wax on about in songs. Dillon and I had a spark, and his familiarity with my lifestyle were the right ingredients for Melodie Rockerby's boyfriend. And yet.

Maybe choosing Dillon as my first was a mistake. Or maybe I'm immune to human touch.

Wil stops drumming. He clenches and unclenches his fists and lays them on his knees, palms up. I see the calluses the guitar strings formed on them, so much like Dad's. Six inches away from me and somehow, he's too far. I crave the connection we had on stage, so unexpected, so unlike anything I've ever had with anyone.

Is that what it feels like when you meet the person you're supposed to perform with? Dad told me when his band got together, they went through various members until they found the right five, where their talents gelled and what they created on stage was not a product of one voice, a guitar, a bass, the keys, and a drum. They were a band creating magic. He tried to explain the link they formed as performers, as writers, as composers, how one starts and the other finishes a phrase, a note, a melody. I didn't get it. Not until I stood on that stage with Wil by my side. It was exactly that. Magic.

How can that be? The physical pull, the mental clarity, the security of his body, shielding me from the invisible stares of the audience—how could a stranger deliver what the twenty-three guitar players I interviewed before settling on Jeremiah, failed to do?

"Why are you so calm?" Wil whispers the words my way.

"Am I?" He's right, I am. It's not like me. Yet, knowing it worked is almost enough, a prize I didn't expect. I shrug. "I guess we've done all we could. My worrying now won't impact the judging. Fate and all that." Winning is more important than ever, but it's out of my hands.

"I hear you, but I prefer to make my own fate."

The audience applauds, and it's loud. Louder than for us? It's a close call. It's the first time I hear the audience respond to someone with an equal measure of enthusiasm as they did for us. Doubt in the power of us creeps in, and I join Wil in fretting about the outcome.

Pauline runs over to us. "Come with me now." And she strolls onto the stage.

Wil's quick to follow, and I do the same, my legs wobbly, aware of every squeeze of my heart, every pump of blood through my veins.

The stage glows. The girl with the Fender, Pauline, and Wil all look at me as I swim through the surrounding air that's getting thicker by the minute. I find the gold of Wil's eyes and pretend he's the only one waiting for me. I follow their beacon, and when his arm touches mine, I slide my gaze down his body and to the floor. I find a fleck of glitter ahead and zero in on it, as if I'm trying to keep my balance during a yoga pose.

"We, my dear audience, have a tie." Pauline shouts into the microphone I don't think she needs. She's loud enough for her words to carry to the far wall of the bar and bounce back. "Looks like I need your help to make the final choice."

Pauline pauses, and the crowd cheers, a couple heckles of, "Tell us what's going on already," fly our way.

"We need you to clap, shout, whistle, and you get my permission to be as obnoxious as you'd like. Show us which one of these fine contenders you'd like to serenade you every Saturday for the next three months." Pauline looks at the girl. "The raspy voice of a diva, Marina Baylee, or the full of feels vocal gymnastics of Wil and El."

Out of the corner of my eye, I see Marina step to the edge of the stage. Pauline gives a signal, and she turns and waves, all wispy and delicate. The crowd roars. The repeat of the whistles, a woot, and "Marina" assault my ears. They are all around me, hitting my skin like mosquitoes, biting and stinging. My stomach drops. She's won.

The noise dies down, and it's our turn. Wil moves away, toward the people surrounding us, but I don't move. Can't. We've lost. I see Wil's chest reappear in front of me. "Get ready," he whispers.

Ready for what? Our loss? His hands are on me, around me. He lifts me up and cradles me in his arms. And it begins. Applause. Whistles and woots. Out there in the dark, a low chant starts, rolling like thunder toward me, toward us. Screams of, "Wil, El, Wil, El" merge.

Pauline holds her hand to her ear. "Am I hearing WE out there?"

"WE," soars from every corner of the bar. Wil's beaming at them, and I'm watching the fire of his eyes ignite the crowd then shift to me. I hold his eyes, even when they get closer. Closer. Closer. His face is an inch away. His lips are an inch away. What's he doing? I can't breathe.

His forehead touches mine, and the people lose it. It's pandemonium, and if Pauline's telling the truth, we are not the losers. WE are the winners.

Seven

Wil

THERE'S NO WAY I'M letting the folk singer win, no matter how hot she is.

The applause swells, and someone starts chanting "WE, WE." It takes me a moment to realize it's the first initials of our names. Wil and El. Pauline blended them together. Cool. If they are screaming our couple name, they are hooked. All WE need is to ham it up a bit, remind the crowd of our performance, and we'll have this in the bag.

The shouts wash over me, a music of their own. It's steady, but it's not enough. I meet El's eyes. In this light, they are almost cobalt. Wide and curious. Not a calm ocean or a stormy sky but the color of the center of a flame, pure fire. That's exactly what they need, what I need. I lean toward her and her bare lips, the gloss she wore earlier on stage worn away. They look so soft.

She parts them, and a piece of me that should not be affected stirs. What does she taste like? What could it hurt to try? Bet the crowd would love it. The crowd.

This is about winning. Winning this competition. The excuse I need to see her again. My way to Rocker. The whistles escalate, the crowd eager to see us kiss. Delayed gratification is so much sweeter. What if? I change my trajectory by a centimeter and touch our foreheads together, reminding the crowd of what got them so mad for us in the first place. The magic is back. I breathe her fire in and push the one inside my chest into her. The place where our skin comes together burns me. The audience erupts, but I don't care.

"Wil and El it is. Congratulations to our sweet couple and come back next Saturday to see more of them."

Pauline whispers something to Marina, and the self-proclaimed diva throws a look our way and says, "Congratulations."

I did it. El and I did it. WE did it. El moves in my arms. I should put her down. In a minute. The audience needs to see us for a little bit more. They want WE, and we want them to come back. WE does have a ring to it.

"Are you going to put me down?" El asks.

"I thought you'd never ask." I set her feet back onto the wooden slats. We stand facing the crowd, our arms linked, and the burning I had in my forehead before moves to where we touch. It's not a fluke, but I can't let it mess up my plans. The reason I'm in LA is to get to Rocker. And she's my ticket to see him. Her stepfather. My only father. The high of being on this stage is messing with me. I step away to put some distance between us.

"WE love you," I shout at the crowd. They eat it up. Gotta acknowledge the adoring fans.

We follow Pauline backstage, and I keep a couple of meters between us. The farther I am, the less likely I am to want to take her hand and lose focus.

"You need to be here by eight. It's a forty-five-minute slot. Send me your set list for approval each week. Need to make sure your songs don't clash with the headliners'." She looks between me and El to assure we understand her. "Aside from that, it's up to you, as long as you bring whatever the hell you roused the audience with tonight. The hotter the better. Make them thirsty, and I can sell more drinks. That's your job. Got it?"

"How much are you paying?" This gig wasn't intended, but the cash will be a bonus to this plan of mine. Maybe I can afford more than ramen noodles for dinner. Or good beer. El shifts her feet beside me. Hey, princess, I'm half the act, I get half the profits. I'm sure you can afford it. Whatever it is we have on stage, money is money.

"Hundred and fifty plus ten percent of the drinks for that hour."

I do the math. If I can load the place up with Starlight Future Filmmakers Foundation folks plus whoever else on campus I can pull in, I could make a hundred a week—not bad for an hour's worth of work.

My phone vibrates the double tap. It's Mum. I catch El's eye and shake the phone. "Gotta take this." I leave her to seal the deal. Surely, she can manage that part alone.

"Mum, everything okay?" I press the phone against my ear.

"Yes, luv."

I unclench. No matter how many times we message every day, I'm always dreading the call—that something has gone wrong. I'm not a momma's boy, but she and Opa are all the family I have. All the family I thought I had for nineteen years. Mum never talked about the man who knocked her up. Opa never had a good word to say about the "sperm donor." Both told me he wanted nothing to do with me, so they wanted nothing to do with him. Until Mum got sick and Opa told me the truth.

"Opa insisted we call. I'm not interrupting anything, am I?"

I find a quiet corner by the door. "No. Just having a drink with some mates."

"Oh. Well, we won't keep you from your fun."

She doesn't hear my "it's okay."

There's a rustling noise, and Opa's gravelly voice is in my ear. "Want an update . . . on the competition." I know what he's really after. An update on our plan.

"Working on it."

His voice lowers. "Your mother's out of the room. Tell me. Did you go to Rocker, Inc. yet?"

"Yes—" I start to tell him they turned me away, no getting in without an appointment, but Opa's never been a patient man.

Or a good listener. Years of working construction damaged his ears along with his body.

"Good, good. Did you see him?" Even though I'm not in the room, I can see the sneer on Opa's face. When he told me about the one-night stand, how Rocker abandoned Mum after she told him about being pregnant, he pounded back shots of schnapps and spat out the details. To say he's not a fan of Rocker is an understatement. Then we came up with our plan. I'd fly here, confront the sperm donor, and get the money to help Mum cover the cost of the biologic drug for her rheumatoid arthritis if she can get into the program. The steroids and conventional disease-modifying antirheumatic drugs stopped working, and this new option could be a gamechanger, but it's so expensive the only way to get it is to pay out of pocket. The plan sounded simple, sitting in the backyard of our semi-detached in Bremen.

I look down the hall at where El is talking to what can only be described as a modern-day Viking, just missing his horned helmet and in a black suit rather than chainmail. "Not yet. I'm working on it."

Opa's voice rises an octave. "Glad to hear it." Mum must be back in the room with him. "Keep up the good work."

I mumble a thanks in return. Mum comes back on the phone, tells me she loves me, and we hang up. Words are crawling across my brain again, and I need to write them down. I reach into my pocket and pull out the book. It's half full already.

Hospital vs. Krankenhouse

Place for visitors vs. a house for the sick

Words matter

Unsaid words matter too

"Whatcha writing?" El's words make me jump.

"How much I'll be earning from this sweet gig. Half the fee still sounds fair."

Her face sours, the eyes from earlier dark and stormy. "That's robbery, but Pauline wants us both or no deal."

After my help, she actually asked? The balls on this princess.

"Don't look so crushed. Not like you need the money. Is sharing the stage such a big deal?" I hold up my hands like I'm under arrest. "I'll back off if you want the spotlight."

"Of course, you assume I don't need money."

"What? Your parents cut you off?"

Her face freezes.

Bloody hell. She's on the outs with Rocker? That's not gonna work for me. "What happened?"

"Like I'd tell you."

I cross my arms and lean back on the wall, as if I don't have a care in the world. "Maybe I need a little persuasion to come back next week."

"You'll get paid."

"Of course, you assume I *do* need the money." I throw her words back at her.

She sighs. "Fine. I need cash to fulfill a commitment at the end of October. And I have only myself to rely on. Sharing this gig's money with you puts me further away from my goal."

"Couldn't you sell a couple of your dresses, or some jewelry?"

"I technically don't own much. Mom has my stylist catalog everything of value I wear. If something goes missing, how would I explain that?"

"Champagne problems." Poor rich princess.

"You don't get it." She crosses her arms on her chest and tries to give me my own don't-care look. "I'm not going to spend my breath explaining my life to you. If you don't want to do this, I'll find another way to earn the rest of the money."

Eight

Wil

WELL, THAT'S NOT HAPPENING. My shoulders tense. I've pushed this far enough. Fun time is over. If she can get me in front of Rocker, I can play nice. I drop my arms and push myself off the wall. "No need to get all pissy." I hold out my hand. "Partners?"

Her hand is light in mine. "Partners." A quick shake, and it's gone. But her smile lingers, making her relief obvious. El better work on her acting skills along with her stage fright.

"It's settled then. Can I have your number?"

Her eyelashes flutter. "You want my number?"

Even in the low light of the bar, her eyes burn me. I remember the liquid fire of them going through me on stage. Maybe that's how she looks at everyone. "To rehearse."

"Oh, right." She reaches into the pocket of her pant-skirt outfit and produces a phone with a crown and a flag design on it.

"Some designer brand?" I point at the cover.

"It's the crest of Malta."

I take the phone from her hand. Of course, it's the latest model. I open the contacts, type in "Wil the guitar player and DJ of your dreams Peters" and my US phone number. I send myself a message and hand her the phone.

She looks at my name on her screen, and a smile comes back to her face. "Your self-esteem is impressive."

"Not the only impressive thing about me." I get a hold of my tongue before I cross into the flirting territory, because I'm not going there. I'm using her. That's all.

"And do I get a chance to create my name?"

"Haven't you done it already?"

The light in her eyes dims.

"Hey, stage names are a thing. No judgment here. I sort of get El from Melodie. And Vella's your father's name? Or was it a stage name for him too?"

"Vella was my Papa's last name. It's common in Malta." She points to her phone. The cover makes sense now. "Papa died. Dad, Bill, he's my stepdad."

"Sorry about your loss."

"Yeah, thanks." She fidgets with the ends of her wig. "I have to take off. Can, um, can Sven and I give you a lift home?"

She shoves the thumb of her uninjured hand over her shoulder at the pale-haired Norse titan about my height but built like a fridge. Of course, she has a chauffeur. Probably came here in a stretch limo. It's going to save me some bucks on a rideshare. *Why not?*

"Sure."

It's worse than a stretch limo. Out in the parking lot, Sven opens the door of a powder blue Rolls Royce that screams ostentatious rockstar. *Fuck me.*

El climbs in and slides across the back seat. I give silent Sven a nod, like the one he gave me when El introduced us, and enter the world of luxury. First time for everything. The door shuts without a sound, blocking out the traffic from the nearby street, encasing El and me in silence.

"Water?" A tall cylinder that looks like a test tube with a silver top sits in her hand. Of course, she drinks designer water—good ole tap water far too simple for her.

"Thanks, but I actually care about the environment." I pull out my reusable steel flask and wave it in her face, dent and all. It's been with me through rowing competitions, drunken parties at my dorm, backpacking across the Scandinavian peninsula, and I'm not wasting cash on a new one, even if I can after we get paid next week.

"Um, actually"—there's a confidence in her voice we could've used back on that stage; she matches my tone—"we bottle this ourselves at home. Well, Marta, our housekeeper, does. We have a reverse osmosis system that converts rain into potable water."

I open my mouth to say something smart—not quite sure what—when Sven lands in the driver's seat and demands, "Where to?"

"Corner of Sunset and Bellagio."

"You go to UCLA?" El studies me.

"Are you surprised I know how to read and write and everything?" She shouldn't assume I'm dumb because I'm poor.

"I wanted to go there but . . ." Her eyes fall to the floor, and the long strands of the wig she's still wearing cover her face.

I want to spit, "Daddy wouldn't pay the bribe," but something stops me. "I'm not a student. Just staying on campus for the summer. The Starlight Future Filmmakers Foundation paid for it."

"Starlight Foundation?" She pulls at her hair. The almost white strands slip sideways and reveal auburn hair wound in tight twists. She begins taking pins out, and her shoulder-length wavy locks burst around her face. It's Melodie Rockerby again. Kinda. Without the makeup and the fake hair, she looks young. Innocent? Pretty.

"It's a non-profit. They support the arts."

"Interesting." She folds the wig up and places it in a blue bag at her feet. Her elbow brushes against my jeans. A scent that reminds me of the school break I spent on an island in Greece fills the air. Sizzling days in the sand, air fresh and clean, the sun beating down on my skin, everything relaxed and carefree. I inhale. "What do you have to do with it?"

"They hold a competition every year. A way for amateurs to get into the film industry. The jury selected me to come to the US to participate."

"You're a director?"

Of course, she thinks that. "Not my deal. I'm into music."

"Composer?" She looks at my hands.

"Sound engineer. I choose the music, record the audio, edit the sound. Without me, the movie is just moving pictures."

She untwists the silver cap of her special water bottle. "That sounds"—I hold my breath, waiting for her to piss on my craft—"incredible. You control the tempo of the story."

"In a way." I've never looked at it like that, but I guess that's what I do. "There're ten teams, and the winners usually get job offers."

"So, you want to stay in the US?"

"No," I scoff.

The water bottle she was lifting freezes in her hand.

"I mean, maybe. I haven't thought that far ahead."

"No plans for the future?"

"I'm more of an in-the-moment kind of person." I catch Sven's eye in the rearview mirror checking me out. "Carpe diem, and all that."

El takes a sip of water, long and slow. I watch her delicate neck move with the motion. How can her taking a sip of water make my mouth go dry? She catches me watching, and I turn to look out the window. What the fuck is wrong with me?

How hard is it to find something else to focus on? I search the car, direct my eyes down, and see her blue bag.

My luck struck again. I never told anyone at the Starlight competition blue is my favorite color, so when I found out I was on Team Blue, I took it as a positive sign.

I check my phone and see a string of messages. The latest is from our director.

NStavros: Are you drunk? Need you alert for the brainstorm tomorrow.

Nick's one to talk. With all the rules, instructions, and constant reminders, I'd say he's the one who's drunk. On power. The bloke seems decent, has a couple of documentaries under his belt, and maybe he has an eye behind the camera, but he lacks life experience. Never even been out of the United States. Backpacking alone teaches you a lot about living.

Me: No, boss.

Not yet. The night is still young.

I scroll through the messages of the other team members' answers to my invite to join me for a pint. I catch up on what I missed when I was on stage.

SConor: Working.

Of course, Sarah can't come. How does the girl have a life? She's always running to her job, our sessions, writing her own screenplay, and trying to fix everybody else's problems.

BSato: I don't put that poison in my body

Blimey, I asked her, no, them—need to remember to use their pronoun— to come for a drink, not join a cult. A simple, "No, thanks," would suffice. But Bri's always the first to overshare. Didn't need to hear the full resumé of every play they designed a costume for either.

NStavros: How'd you get into a bar?

MGallardo: Party happening at the dorm. Come join.

And, of course, nothing from Riyaz. He can't be arsed, but he makes up for it with the pictures he's created of the few scenes we've managed to hammer out.

I sneak a glance at El. She has what looks like a mini tart in her hand.

"What's that?" I point at the pastry.

"Butter tart." She breaks the little cup in two and offers a half to me. "Want some?"

"Is it sweet?"

Her eyes sparkle like Mum's do when it snows on Christmas morning. "Absolutely."

"Ah, no, thanks. Don't do sweet."

She shrugs. "You don't know what you're missing. Marta whipped up a fresh batch this morning."

"Bottles rainwater and bakes from scratch? Marta sounds like a talented woman."

El smiles; my sarcasm flies over her head.

I catch Sven's glare in the rearview mirror. He didn't miss my dig.

My phone vibrates.

NStavros: Change of location. Tomorrow's extra meeting is now at Sarah's apartment. 1859 Rose St. Apt. 5a

Better than the noisy coffee shop Nick works at. Free coffee last night didn't make up for the ukulele album the manager pushed everyone in the place to buy. No one could hear the song I played over that disaster. Plus, the girls at the next table laughed at Bri and Nick acting out the dialogue Sarah wrote for the love scene.

I need to find a job myself. This gig with El will bring in some much-needed cash. Need to cover all the surprise extras in this country, like sales tax added at the register on top of the price, tipping, and the cost of health insurance. The trip to the grocery store nearly bankrupted me.

I send back a thumbs up.

NStavros: 2pm sharp. Everyone.

I shove my phone in my pocket and watch the city that's temporarily my home whip by. The familiar sights of UCLA greet me. Much faster by car than on the crowded bus I took to the bar earlier.

"We need to talk about next week." El breaks the silence. "Pauline wants a set list."

"Can we do that later?"

"Right, not a planner." She licks the last of the sweet treat off her fingers.

Oh, I have plans.

NINE

El

WIL GETS OUT, BUT the scent of freshly washed cotton lingers in the leather interior.

"You have his number?" Sven asks.

I watch Wil walk down a path toward a pair of squat gray buildings, probably the dorms. Another part of life I'll never get to experience.

"Um, yeah."

Sven's XXL palm reaches into the backseat "Give it to me."

"Why?" I hold my phone against my chest like it's the little stuffed lamb I used to take everywhere as a child.

"I need to check him out."

"Not this again. Trust me, he's not going to kidnap me and keep me in a cellar somewhere."

"I trust you."

"I sure hope so. If he kidnaps me, you can turn on that app you made me download—TrackerTime." Sven insisted on some way to find me if I "get lost" during a shopping trip in New York last year. It makes him feel better even if he'll never need it.

His military stare barrels down on me. "How do we know he didn't plan this? That guy could have liquored Jeremiah up to take his place on purpose."

When Sven completed his eight-year service with the marines and first joined Dad's bodyguard detail, this would've been enough to bring me to tears. Not anymore. Sven and I have been through too many secrets and adventures together in the past two years for me to take it as anything more than an intimidation tactic.

"C'mon. That's crazy. Not everyone has a hidden agenda."

Silence. I know this is his job and all, to seek out the bad, protect me from it, but this is taking it too far. I can tell a guy in a bar who happened to be in the right place at the right time from a scammer or paparazzi out to use me for their benefit. If anything, I'm the one using him.

I could repeat this spiel to Sven a million times, make a scene, but I need him on my side. On our side. There's nothing incriminating he'll find on Wil. Why waste my energy?

I open my phone, pull up Wil's info, and pass it over to Sven. He taps away on his phone, hands mine back to me, and starts the journey back to Malibu.

"You aren't going to find anything." I will my statement to be true.

"Better safe than sorry."

Sven's life philosophy summed up in four words. I should get him a T-shirt printed with that phrase for his next birthday.

"You need to live a little. You're either working, working out, or saving Trevor." I mean it as teasing. "Maybe you should ask out that girl from the bar."

Sven doesn't say anything, but the streetlights speed by faster. Pushing the limits with speed is the only time I see a crack in Sven's composure. I get it, I love to drive fast as well.

"I saw you two. She was definitely interested." Another nudge in the right direction, and maybe Sven can finally get a girlfriend. "What was her name again?"

"Lisa."

I raise my hand to cover my smile. "Right, Lisa. Did you get her number?"

"Maybe."

"Good for you." I reach forward and slap him on the shoulder. "I bet you didn't even notice when I got on stage."

"I saw."

"So . . ."

"So, what?"

"Well, since you heard me tonight . . ."

A nod. He's going to make me say it.

"What did you think? Of—"

My skin tingles at the memory of the dozens of eyes trained on me and the words I've practiced over and over in my bedroom ringing through the air toward an actual audience. The thrill of doing it, of my voice connecting with the crowd. The inspiration to echo Wil's version of the chorus at the end. My voice matching his to create something new, something different.

"—of my singing?"

Sven catches my eye in the rearview mirror. "I've never seen you happier."

And I have no doubt he's telling the truth because I haven't been happy lately. But I intend to be again.

I shower off the grime of the bar, put on my go-to comfortable PJs, and creep down the stairs into the kitchen. My stomach no longer in knots, I can't ignore my hunger. The butter tart was my treat for getting up on stage, but now I need real food.

The fridge is packed with plenty of options, but I search for something quick and easy. On the second shelf I find a container with what looks like Marta's famous stuffed peppers. Perfect. I grab a fork, put two halves plus some extra sauce on a plate, and stick them into the microwave.

"Really, baby girl? All those cooking lessons, and you can't warm up the leftovers on the stove?" Mom tightens the belt of her silk robe above the barely there slope of her belly.

"At midnight?"

"Don't remind me." She sleeks my wet hair off my face and yawns. "I need pickles. Do we still have some?"

Mom opens the fridge. "Thank God for Marta and her gift of clairvoyance. I was tossing and turning and couldn't get pickles off my mind. Got to satisfy the cravings." Without closing the door, she opens the jar and inhales one green spear then another.

The microwave beeps and jolts her out of her pickle-induced trance. She moves to the chairs at the end of the counter, and I follow like the little chick she thinks I am. Me with my stuffed peppers and her with a rapidly emptying jar of pickles.

"At least I'm not craving meat, like I did when it was you in my stomach. I couldn't look at vegetables." She sets the jar down on the black marble countertop and stares lovingly at the remaining pickles.

"You told me."

"Let your mother reminisce."

My peppers combine the briny flavor of pork and beef with the sweetness of the vegetables. Marta makes the tomato sauce herself. "I still love meat."

"You've always been my carnivore." Mom pats my hand, careful to avoid the splint. She knows better than to hug me. Fewer and fewer people touch me as time goes on. I made an exception for Dillon. And Wil. I press my other hand to the spot where our heads touched.

"Headache?"

"Just tired." I can't look at her. I know what I'll see. My migraines subsided over time, but Mom is always searching for a sign of one, a reason to smother me some more. This baby has turned her protective dial from medium to extra high.

Her hand goes to her stomach. "I worry about you. It's my right as your mother."

"I know."

"You would tell me if anything was wrong. Right?"

I nod. Mom's always on the lookout for what's wrong, never interested in what's right. At least, what I know is right for me. I tried talking to her, explaining what creating music means, but she only sees the harm my dream of singing might cause.

Over and over, I've heard how it takes many years to make it. She started when she was four and practiced ten hours a day and only had her big break by accident. When the star soprano of the production of La Bohème came down with tonsillitis, Mom, the understudy for Mimi, lucked out and finished the season in the lead role. After that, the offers rolled in.

"I'm here to listen. No matter what happens." She pulls a bottle of water out of the fridge, pours two glasses, and places one in front of me. "You know, I always have time for you."

Ah, Mom's other warning when I say "What if I make it?"

Time.

Her argument that once a singer gets noticed, their time is not their own. Life on the road means missing family, friends, holidays, and any semblance of normal. She wanted another child, a baby brother or sister for me, but her schedule never gave her a free moment.

"You do. I was lucky to have you as a mom, and that little one"—I pick up my glass of water—"is lucky too." The cool water slips down my throat and stops me from adding more.

She puts down the pickle in her hand and rubs her belly. "All these tests, I couldn't even fly to England to get you."

"I know." And I'm glad it was Dad and not her.

"But it looks like both the baby and you are fine."

She glances at my splint again.

"I'm fine, Mom. I really am. This"—I lay my unharmed hand over hers on her stomach—"is what should be your focus now. I can take care of myself. Maybe I should look after you for once."

Mom's eyes light up, and for a moment, I want to tell her about tonight. Have her be proud I got up on that stage and sang in front of a crowd at last. Tell her I understand now why she did it night after night, years of performances that dragged me around the opera houses and concert halls of the world trailing after her. But I don't. I stuff the last bite of pepper in my mouth to stop it all from spilling out. Someday, Mom. Someday you'll have a reason to be proud of me.

"We're a family, baby girl. We look after each other."

"So, this is where all my girls are." Dad strolls into the kitchen and puts his arm around Mom.

She brushes his bangs out of his eyes. "Antonio needs to clean this mop up."

"But I love it when you run your fingers through my hair."

"He leaves plenty for me to hold on to."

I groan. "I shouldn't be hearing this."

"According to you, you're all grown up." With exaggerated moans he plants one on her. Mom plays along and wraps her hands around his neck.

"Get a room."

My words only egg them on. Will I ever learn? "You win."

He lets go of Mom and looks at the remnants of our meal spread out over the counter. "Did you save me anything?"

"You snooze, you lose." I tap my fork on the empty plate. Not quite a B-flat but close.

A deep chuckle echoes through the room and distracts us as he steals the last spear.

"Oh, my pickle." Mom frowns at the empty jar.

"Did you really think I'd deprive you?" He hands the pickle over to her.

Mom takes a bite, grins, and offers the last piece to Dad, who bends down and snatches it up.

"I'll leave a note for Marta to get more tomorrow." Dad crosses to the chalkboard in the corner, erases jar, and adds case beside the word pickles. "Anything you want, Melodie?"

"All good here." I'd like my allowance back, so I don't have to sneak out and play at a bar with a cocky German dude. But that's not happening.

I put my empty plate into the sink for Marta to deal with in the morning. My heart swings between love and sadness, the bittersweet moment I've been waiting for is here. The IVF finally worked and Mom got the present she's been trying for since Dad and her got married. Another baby to love and spoil. I stayed with her during the first trimester as promised. Things are good now. She no longer needs me to be by her side. My chest warms at the thought of a new family member. Will his eyes be blue like Mom's and mine, or will he inherit Dad's golden stare? A new future is waiting for us, and I can't wait to meet my only sibling.

TEN

Wil

THE PATH FROM THE road where El dropped me off takes me
through the modern blocks of Hitch Suites. The cool night
air is full of campus noises. Eleven on a Saturday night, and
no one is asleep around here. I hear the low thrum of basses
from the open windows, and laughter spills and chases me as
I run up the stairs to my building. It's more of the same on
my floor—except louder. The dorms are not only temporary
home to the international participants of the Starlight Young
Filmmakers Competition, but a popular place for youth from
all over the world to come experience LA in summer on the
cheap.

I open the door to our common living space, and a cacophony
of music and chatter vomits onto me. It's packed. A smell of
stale beer mixed with weed reminds me of my dorm in Berlin. A

switch flips in my brain. This is where I belong. Not in the back of a posh car with a pop princess.

El's world is not my world. I take in the crush of bodies, shorts, tank tops, and skin everywhere. These are my people. And I just might score that beer I went to the bar for in the first place. Should've known there was gonna be a party, and that means alcohol. I'm not the only one Mateo directed to the bloke on the first floor, who made the fake IDs like hotcakes.

"The prodigal son returns." Mateo waves me over to a makeshift bar the table has become. Pushed against the wall, it sports beers, giant red plastic cups I do not plan to use, tequila, vodka, an array of two-liter soda bottles, and a cute brunette's ass. Ass on the table is not something I thought of before, but the view of it against the array of alcohol would appeal to most adults with a pulse. Beer can wait.

"What have I missed?" I shout into Mateo's ear, my eyes on the face of what turns out to be a worthy accompaniment to that ass.

"More of this?" He gestures at the room. "A little less drunk than now, but that can't be a bad thing. I didn't expect you back so early. The bar a no-go? Or did they figure out your ID was a fake?"

"No worries, they barely looked. It's a long story." And I'm not planning to tell it to Mateo. "More importantly, tell me who's the cute ass on the other end of the table." I point to her with my eyes.

"No idea. I'm bad with names. She came in with some girls from the dorm across campus." He leans in. "And that girl looks too much like my mami to be interesting."

"Well, my mum is tall and fair, so a short, curvy brunette is right up my street."

"If you need an interpreter, I'll be happy to help, mein freund."

In the last week, Mateo prodded me for a dozen German words a day, and the rate at which he's retaining them is absurd. Apart from my native German and English, which is sort of a must at school, plus the summers in Sussex, with Mom's cousins, where I picked up the cooler English vocabulary, I know a little pick-up Spanish, French, Italian, and Portuguese. I can order a beer or find a bathroom, and that much took me years. I know how hard it can be to learn a new language. Mateo is a freak of nature. He'll probably speak fluent German by the end of the program at this rate.

"Good to know. But I think I can handle it." I slap him on the back and focus on the beer in front of me, selecting a can with German colors. I can always flush it down the toilet if it's a match to the Busch disaster. The brunette is alone, watching the smaller group attempting to dance to one of the worst mixes I've heard in a while.

"Wanna dance?" I raise an eyebrow at her and point to the impromptu dance floor with my unopened beer.

The smile she gives me signals she approves. Like I knew she would.

"Sure," she says.

This is better. Back in familiar territory where my pick-up skills shine. I don't dance, but the DJ in me feels the beat, and all I need to do is move my body enough to appear I know what I'm doing. We wind our way through the swarm of sweaty bodies and face each other in the tight corner with the other "dancers."

My body relaxes, and we join the crowd in a familiar routine of push and pull, the silent question and answer of seduction. I don't have to think twice, my glances are automatic, my slight touches practiced and performed a hundred times before.

Her response gives me the go signal. Yup, she looks like someone who'd be down with my "not seeing the same girl twice" rule. No drama, no promises, no expectations. We get what we want tonight and don't have to worry about tomorrow. Simple. Not like—

"What are you thinking about?" She has to lift her lips to my ear.

"You." Simple and straight.

"Good." She squeezes my arm. "How long are you in LA for?"

Information she doesn't need to know, as we won't be seeing each other after tonight. "Not sure. You?"

"One more week, and then I move on to San Francisco."

I step closer and touch her cheek. "My room is down the hall. Shall we?"

"Lead the way." She grabs my hand. I tug her back through the masses to the table, pick up my beer, and get us to my empty room within a minute. With a click, I lock the door behind us. I hope Mateo saw I pulled the girl and finds a place to spend the night.

"Is this yours?" She gives a tentative strum to the strings. I wait for the heat to rise in my body, but it's been a long day and an even longer night. I need to get my hands on her to wake myself up.

"I'm Valentina." She places her palm on my arm, initiating the skin-to-skin I desire.

"Wil." I give her the English version of my name everyone here knows me by. Wilhelm is the way Mum and Opa refer to me when I'm in trouble. "Is it okay if I kiss you?" No matter how many looks she gave me, I need to be sure we're on the same page. That she wants me to do this.

"You better." Our lips meet. Hers are cool and sticky. No alcohol on her breath. Probably drinking one of the sodas. Fanta? Or maybe that's her lip gloss. Its artificial sugary flavor makes me want a beer even more. I close my eyes and run my hand up into her short hair. Why isn't this working?

Her lips leave mine, and I look into eyes that are not the color of the ocean. This is not what I want anymore. "Hey. Sorry. I don't actually think I'm up for this. Maybe next time?"

"Next time?" Valentina crosses her arms. "Am I not good enough for you?" She's speaking louder with every word, and I glance at the door. Where is Mateo when I need him?

I paint on the penitent little-boy smile that usually gets me out of any situation. "Sorry. I changed my mind."

"Changed your mind?" Her hands are waving in the air now. "Can't even get a proper lay in his city." She spies the beer can and grabs it. If the beer gets her out of here, she can have it. "Next time, pick a decent beer, loser." Instead of heading to the door, she skips away, landing close to the narrow dorm window. Maybe she's not as mad as I thought, and we can share the beer.

Her arm rises, and she hurls the black and gold tallboy at the window. The can flies through, shattering the glass.

"What the fuck?" This isn't even my house.

"Well, Wil, if that's your real name. Have yourself a great summer. I know I will." As she flings the door open, she flips me the bird.

I stand, beerless and dumbfounded, with a gaping hole in my window letting in the noise of the parties outside. That's what I get for being honest with a girl. We haven't fucked, but she fucked me over good.

Eleven

El

WIL THE GUITAR PLAYER and DJ of your dreams Peters: I have
a proposition.

I almost spit my coffee out on the pristine black marble coun-
tertops Marta polishes daily. That name is not staying in my
address book. A few taps, and it's now Wil the cocky German.
Is this more flirting or does he need something from me? Either
way, I'm not interested. This is a temporary business partnership. That's if we can tolerate each other long enough to get
back on stage.

Maybe once my fingers are usable again, I can persuade
Pauline to let me perform by myself. Just the thought, and my
pulse jumps at my temples as the fear of being alone on stage
tightens my throat. I put down my trembling coffee cup and
close my eyes. I sang on stage on Saturday. The memory calms

my nerves. I did it then; I can do it again. I don't need Wil. He's not the only guitarist in LA.

Me: A bit forward, don't you think?

Wil the cocky German: Only caring for your best interests.

Me: And how would you even know what those are?

Wil the cocky German: We need to rehearse, and I found us a place.

Why does this sound like a trap? I look across the kitchen island to where Dad is feeding Mom cubes of watermelon. On stage he's this sex symbol, struts his stuff, whips up the crowd, but the real Bill Rockerby is addicted to baking shows and anonymously donates ten percent of his concert earnings to feed inner-city children.

Too bad Wil isn't more like Rocker. I look at his last text. We do need to rehearse. I can always say no.

Me: Okay.

Wil the cocky German: You are dripping with enthusiasm.

Me: Just tell me what it is. I don't have all day.

Wil the cocky German: I'm going to ignore that. My idea is .
. .

I wait for the next message, but it doesn't come.

Me: I'm not begging.

It's easier to lie when it's a text. I'm dying to know, but I have some self-control.

Wil the cocky German: On campus. I got us a room at the Music School.

He so does not get it. Life is simple for him. I chew on my cereal.

Me: Even if I could persuade Sven to take me there, I have this face that tends to get recognized in public.

I pull on the familiar colorless strands that showed up after Papa's death. It's not unheard of after a traumatic event like our accident. Over the years, I considered dyeing my hair to get rid of the white streak everyone in the media comments on. Zoe thinks if I go for the sun-kissed look and try blonde, I'd fit in with the California crowd more. I can't do it. I'd look too much like Mom.

Besides, I like my hair: the color, the texture. Mom says it comes from her Scandinavian heritage, but Papa always insisted redheads ran in his family. So, I keep my natural shade and the pale waves. The hair reminds me of Papa. My dyeing it would be like letting the past slip away. With my memories fading, what will I have left of him?

Me: The bar is one thing, but I can't just walk across campus. Someone will recognize me. One post on Twitter and my parents will be all over me, never mind the press. I won't ever get to leave the house again.

Wil the cocky German: Sven might be the muscle, but I thought you were the brains of your duo.

Wil wouldn't say that about Sven's duties in the marines or his IQ, if he knew the man. I don't know what Sven did because he won't talk much about his time in the military. And good thing Sven isn't monitoring my messages.

"Haven't seen that smile in a while, baby girl." Mom's voice and her hand on my shoulder almost make me drop my phone into the bowl of milk and cornflake crumbs. "What are you madly texting about?"

Damn. I can't tell her about Wil. Or how we met. "A new musician I found." I hold my breath, hoping she can't spot my non-answer.

"Oh. Going to be a star?"

"I think so."

"Scouting new talent. You have a good ear. And good taste." Dad puts his empty plate in the sink. "Excited about your first day?" Dad looks at me with such hope in his eyes.

I shrug. "Dunno. Will people take me seriously, being the boss's daughter and all?"

"That's why you're starting in the back office. Nadine doesn't care who your parents are. She appreciates hard work. Impress her, and you'll make your mother and me proud."

That will make you proud, but you dismiss my music. Wait until you see what I can do.

My phone buzzes.

Wil the cocky German: Looking up "brain" in the dictionary? *winky face*

"We should move." Dad grabs a kombucha from the fridge and twists off the top. "I have a nine a.m."

"Five minutes." I pop off the stool and run up the stairs to the safety of my room.

Me: I'll figure it out. When?

Wil the cocky German: The studio can be ours every week-night after seven. That's when the last class ends.

Sounds too good to be true. Sven and I go running most nights between 7:00 and 9:00. This could work.

Me: And how did you get so lucky?

Wil the cocky German: Do you really want to know all my dirty secrets?

I lie back on my bed. This dude is so full of himself.

Me: Only if they have to do with me.

Wil the cocky German: Don't say I didn't warn you.

I'm not going to follow his bait.

Me: We need to decide on the songs for Saturday. What other songs do you know?

Pauline needs to approve our set, and maybe Wil is a one-trick pony. It can't hurt if I find out what he can do with those hands.

There's no quick comeback. I pull out the outfit I obsessed about last night. First day at the new job—wanna make a good impression. I've been to Rocker, Inc. a million times before but never beyond the lobby and Dad's office.

Wil the cocky German: Send me yours, and I'll send you mine.

His nickname is proving to be highly accurate.

Wil the cocky German: Ideas.

Right. He does think I'm stupid.

Me: Late for work.

I've no time to deal with his childishness.

Wil the cocky German: You work?????

He could've added another question mark to show his opinion of how I spend my days. Not that he's too far off, but I'm no longer a drain on society. How many people can say they have two jobs?

Me: Yes. I don't sit around texting all day.

Wil the cocky German: Where?

Me: Rocker, Inc.

He doesn't need to know it's my first day.

Wil the cocky German: I thought you needed money. What am I missing?

Me: Long story.

Wil the cocky German: I've got time.

ME: I don't.

Wil the cocky German: Text later?

I'm looking forward to it.

"Melodie, we need to leave," Dad shouts from the stairs.

Me: Gotta go.

Wil the cocky German: See you at 7, Cinderella.

Sven drives us past the UCLA campus and parks the car in the lot next to a three-story building with Rocker, Inc. in black plastic letters on the side of the brick facade. At night, it lights up in a flurry of colors. I much prefer that version. Dad heads to the elevator and pushes the button while the security lady, whose badge reads Sandi, makes a badge for me.

"Come by my office at 6:00, and we'll head home together." Dad gives me a smile and disappears in the elevator.

"Ready to meet Nadine?" Sven puts the lanyard with my new badge over my head. Melodie Rockerby, printed in the biggest possible letters, will make sure everyone in the building knows who I am. Who am I kidding? They'll know it, anyway. As if they haven't been briefed and warned about me.

"How about a tour of the office first?"

Anything to delay meeting my boss. Sven takes me past the shared kitchen, the workout room, the lounge, and we take the stairs to the second floor. Four recording studios line the hallway.

"Can I take a peek?"

"Sure." Sven opens the door to one that lacks the red sign, and it's not occupied. Now, I'm in heaven. It's twice the size of Dad's version at home and split into two rooms. One's full of the sound boards I'm used to, but the other is massive, a stack of music stands, mic and guitar stands stacked against one wall, a piano on the other. I could get used to this. I can imagine myself cutting my album here after the music video Mr. Astor is going to make for me hits it big and Mom and Dad can't deny my talent.

"It's ten to nine." Sven waves me out of the studio.

"Five more minutes. We have time."

"Early is on time, on time is late. Let's go." Another Sven-ism.

Up to the third floor I trudge. The only floor I've spent time on. Dad's office is not a place I need to see again. We continue to climb up to the fourth and final floor, and my feet in my three-inch heels are letting me know they are not happy with these many steps.

The open floor space we enter is bigger than I expected. The roof slants over the six people typing away at the four shared desks under the skylights. The walls, desks, and cabinets are white, but the teal accent wall and little teal spot lamps give the space a little spark. A compact girl in a dress that would fit in on a fashion week catwalk pushes off the long desk on the left side of the room, and a smile half her size spreads across her face.

"You're here. Hi, I'm Nadine." Three short bursts of B-flat from her desk interrupt her. Nadine holds up a finger and puts a headset on. "Yes? Coffee?" Nadine's almond eyes focus on me. "Send it up to the fourth floor."

Sven clears his throat. "I'll be at the security desk downstairs. Let me know if you need anything."

Part of me doesn't want Sven to leave. How pathetic is that? "Okay."

"I got her." Nadine directs her hundred-watt smile my way and waves at her colleagues behind her. "Welcome to the inner sanctum of Rocker, Inc. Let me introduce you to everyone, and I'll show you where you'll be sitting."

I place my bag on the corner of the desk by Nadine. Sharing a space with my supervisor . . . Awkward. After a barrage of introductions, I retain the web designer's name because he'll be showing me how to resize images for different social media platforms. At least I'll get to see the artists unlike my main task—stuffing folders with promotional flyers, posters, and contact lists.

"Knock-knock." A familiar voice sounds behind me.

"Place the coffees over there." Nadine unlocks the drawer and pulls out a jar stuffed with dollar bills, and fishes out a five.

"Oh, thank you." I know the voice because it's Zoe's.

I intercept Nadine's hand. "Don't bother. This is my cousin. Zoe. She's just bringing me coffee. She's not a delivery person from Blend. No tip necessary."

"Not necessary, but always appreciated." Zoe threads her fingers through mine. "Can I steal her for a sec? I'll bring her right back. Promise."

Nadine looks between us. A wrinkle appears between her eyebrows, no smile in sight. "Five-minute break. My favorite drink is pumpkin spice latte. Just FYI, in case you decide to interrupt another workday."

We hide in an alcove I spotted on the way in.

"So, first day . . . what are we thinking?" Zoe hands me my coffee.

"Nothing. I've been here for less than an hour." The smell of the caramel in my cappuccino and my cousin's concern uncoils the tightness between my shoulders. My phone dings. "I better put it on mute. Wouldn't want Nadine to think I'm not serious about this job."

A notification on my screen catches my eye.

Wil the cocky German: I can't make the rehearsal tonight.

Great. We haven't even started, and Wil is bailing.

"Bad news?" Zoe peers at my face.

"You have no idea." I put my phone on mute and stuff it back into my pocket. My shoulders stiffen, and the familiar weight of failure settles in my stomach.

"I will when you tell me about it."

I usually tell Zoe everything. She and Bailey are more than cousins. Their mothers are sisters of Mom's, so I get a certain amount of freedom with them because they're family. If Mom knew half the things Zoe got up to, she'd never let me near her. "The gig at Devil's Martini that I won thanks to you—"

"You're welcome. You'll be repaying me by wearing one of my dresses to whatever event you go to next that's full of press."

"I'd like it to be when I pick up my Grammy for the best new artist of the year, but that's not going to happen if this jerk doesn't show up."

"And the jerk in question is?"

"Wil. The last-minute replacement for my guitar player I told you about?"

"Ahh." Zoe takes a sip of her coffee. "I didn't realize you were seeing him again."

"I'm not seeing him. I'm rehearsing with him." The caramel's sweetness fades, and the coffee's bitterness coats my tongue. "Or at least I was."

TWELVE

EVERYTHING IS FALLING APART. Bri and Riyaz are not talking to each other. Nick, the supposed leader of this Blue Team, is looking scared as shit, which is quite the feat considering he towers over everyone, even me. And once again, his "friend" Sarah is late. I've seen the hungry looks he throws at her when he thinks no one's looking. The only person he's fooling is himself. Car trouble's her latest excuse. Like she's never heard of taking a taxi.

If this movie ever gets made, it'll be a miracle, never mind winning the Starlight competition.

"It has to be on the beach." Riyaz rams his finger into the board, where he's taped up a series of drawings of our lead characters. "We have no money for a romantic setup, and the beach during sunset is free and screams romance. I don't get why this is even a discussion."

Someone found his voice. Who knew a sunset and a beach would bring out the passion hiding underneath his silence? "Beach waves crashing will be an interesting sound challenge, but I'm up for that. Can't we do it not on a Saturday?" Sunset in LA in July is exactly when I'm on stage with El. I can't fuck either one up.

"It has to be Saturday, that's nonnegotiable." Nick pulls his top-priority card. Now, he grows a backbone.

I watch for the three little dots. Is El going to answer my text? Probably too busy ordering underlings around Rocker's production company. Nepotism is one way to build a career.

"She would never wear that to the beach. It won't work." Bri's voice squeaks, and a red flush sweeps across their face. Part of me thinks Riyaz irritates them on purpose.

"Sorry, I'm late." The cocktail server and wannabe screenwriter has arrived. We're saved. I pull out my notebook as Sarah steps between our warring wardrobe expert and set designer.

"I didn't sign up to babysit you bunch." The two of them look at the floor. Scared babies. Good on Sarah. At least someone's size clearly doesn't matter, because I do bicep curls with weights bigger than her.

I scribble:

Cinderel

El

Not lying

Independent of size

The power is perception

I glance at my phone again, even though I didn't hear the double note ringtone I chose for El last night. It's two pulses for Mum, so I always know if she sent a text.

"I told them—" Nick's voice joins the peacemaking mission.

Does he know he looks at Sarah with those puppy dog eyes? So whipped.

Two dings.

Princess: Bailing already?

I stop tapping my fingers on my leg. That snark of hers is a welcome sight.

Me: You wish. Drama over here in film town. Can you do Wednesday?

Princess: You? Drama? Can't see it.

Princess: I have a life too. Plans.

Right. Shopping with her girl squad. Why do women shop in groups?

Me: Can you try? I'll make it up to you.

Princess: ???

Well, that got her interest. Whatever are you thinking, princess? I should toy with her a bit.

I type "I'm open to suggestions" but I come to my senses before I hit send. What am I thinking? I delete that.

I have an inkling of what the girl wants.

Me: A sweet treat?

Princess: Butter tarts?

Me: That gooey pastry from the Rolls?

Princess: *heart emoji*

Never heard of them until I saw one in her hand. No clue where to find one, but I'm sure Nick or Mateo can hook me up.

Me: Deal.

"Wil, what d'you think?" Nick and the others are looking at me. Shite. Time to turn on the charm. I shrug. "I'm good either way."

Sarah rolls her eyes and turns to Nick. "You decide."

Princess: Wednesday it is.

Things always go my way.

Two sticky concoctions sit in a bag hanging from my wrist. El's request wasn't as simple as I thought. Neither Nick nor Mateo had any idea what I went on about. It was Sarah who, shocked that butter tarts aren't a thing either in the US or Europe, directed me to a specialty store that carries the typically Canadian treat. LA is a land of immigrants, and I now believe one can find absolutely anything here. Even butter tarts.

A coffee warms my hand, and I lift my shoulder higher to prevent my guitar from sliding off. The smell of the caramel macchiato alone can keep me awake. Five minutes till go time. The phone in my hand buzzes. Not El's two dings. I still check.

Nick: Did you eat the quiche like I told you?

Me: Threw it into my stomach instead of the bin. Thanks for the tip. And for the job.

Nick: Stop thanking me already. You're an hourly employee now, not part owner.

Even though Nick's not pulling his weight as a director, I owe him for setting me up with some shifts at Blend. The coffee shop is pumping gallons of their signature house blend into little lime green cups, and their pastries aren't much worse than what Mum makes.

Me: Thanking concluded.

The campus is busier than usual. A warm July evening is the reason everyone seems to want to be outside. There's a gang of students on my left playing catch. I scan them to see if Valentina is among them. No such luck. After campus police showed up on Saturday, I had the pleasure of receiving a bill to replace the broken window. Like I have five hundred dollars sitting around. Last time I checked, my bank account was less than a hundred. The first paycheck from Blend comes in ten days. Unless Pauline pays us after every performance, I'll need to find another way to keep me afloat. Not the first time in my life. Nothing I can't handle.

A cute girl in a baseball cap and matching bright pink tank top that highlights her perky chest power-walks down the path, the bag on her shoulder bouncing off her hip. Not bad, not bad at all. She has definite potential. Not the curves of Valentina but the pale skin of her bare legs kinda glows in the long rays of the golden-hour sun. I spot the monster of a man beside her and look away. Not messing with a girl with a boyfriend. Wait. The boyfriend. Was that Sven?

I turn back to the pair, who are closer now, and there's no mistaking Sven, even though he's also dressed in shorts and trainers. Did he grow more muscles since I last saw him? His legs are like tree trunks. I take another look at the girl. At El. It's her all right. She raises her injured hand and waves at me.

"Sorry I'm late. There was an accident on Sunset Boulevard."

"You're just in time." I move the coffee to my other hand and hold up the bag with the butter tarts. "A few more minutes, and I would've had to eat these all on my own."

Her blue eyes sparkle at me. "Are those . . ."

"Yup. A promise is a promise."

She holds out her hand. I pull the bag back. "Not so fast. Rehearsal first, treats second."

El exaggerates a pout. It looks cute on her. I glance at Sven. "What's with the getup?"

Sven's eyebrows try to merge into a unibrow. He doesn't understand my question. "Sven and I run most days."

Do they now? "By the ocean?"

El's smile wobbles a bit, and Sven steps closer. "Griffith Park. More hills."

Explains the tree trunks.

"Sven's going to lap the campus while we practice." She steps away from the big guy and looks back at him. "I'll text when we're done."

"No more than an hour."

El raises her hand in a horizontal line over her left eye in a salute. "Yes, sir."

I expect Sven to be mad but instead, the corner of his mouth twitches before he turns and jogs away. The girls playing catch all watch him as he passes by. Some men too. Does El ever look at the giant like that?

"Shall we?" I don't wait for an answer, pull on the door handle, and hold it open for her. I think of Opa's comments on California girls as I check out El's butt in the shorts. Such a different look from the bar, more approachable. Just another girl on campus.

"Hey, Frank." The old man is reading a book at the desk in the vacant lobby. I pass him the coffee. "As promised. Room three still available?"

"Sure thing, kid." He smells the cup, puts it on the counter next to him, opens a drawer, and fishes out a silver key attached to a white label with the number three printed in black on it. I place the paper bag on the desk, unroll the top and pull out one of the butter tarts. "This is my friend El. She asked I bring this treat for you to say thanks for letting us use the room."

Frank licks his lips, and I know my instincts were right. Of course.

"Yes, Frank. We appreciate this."

"Anytime. You two kids have fun." We are the only ones at the bank of lifts. I press the button for the third floor, and the doors close. Only the hum of the lift motor and the hint of sunscreen is in the air between us. I shift my weight to my right foot to create some more distance in a shrinking space.

"You make friends everywhere you go?" Her voice reverberates off the steel walls of the lift.

"What can I say? I'm irresistible."

"That's one way to put it."

With a shudder, the lift comes to a stop and the doors slide open. I cross the hall to the double doors opposite, insert the key and with a click, it opens. I step into my own personal heaven.

This room isn't as big as the main room, but the walls are alive with a mosaic of wood and soundproofing materials. I pull out my phone and take a snap.

"What are you doing?" El's voice is cold.

"Taking a pic for the gram. My friends at home have been asking for pics of what I do here." I take in her wide eyes. Geesh, overreact much?

"No photos of me. Ever. Understand?"

"Don't worry, princess. I won't out you."

She pouts but not in a good way this time. "I know you think I'm being—"

"Bossy?"

"I was going to say picky. But you don't know what it's like. There are people who would pay a lot of money for a picture of me. Here. Looking like this. It would be a story."

For a moment, I consider it. Could one click of the phone in my hand really solve all my current money woes? Maybe. But it'd blow my chances with El. I mean, my chances to use El to get to my father.

I walk over and show her the picture. "See, just me and the studio." She watches as I type, "Home Sweet Home," in the caption. "So, no tagging you in the post, I assume."

"I don't have Instagram."

I blink at her. "No?"

"One post taken the wrong way, and it's a public relations nightmare. Easier just not to have one."

Damn, is she not allowed anything normal? Lightness fades, and my empty stomach churns. I never considered what life is like for the child of famous parents. When Opa told me Rocker was my father, I was mad at Mum. The life we could have had. Instead of scraping by on second-hand recording equipment and our little semi-detached house, I imagined living in a mansion and every toy I wanted at my fingertips. I never considered the strings attached to being rich and famous.

Maybe things worked for the best, not having Rocker in my life. I got a normal childhood and don't have to worry about cameras in my face.

THIRTEEN

El

I DON'T KNOW HOW, but I successfully lie to Wil. Well, it isn't a lie—Melodie Rockerby doesn't have an Instagram account. I have one under a fake name. But I'm not telling him that. I don't trust him that much.

Still, his question hits me hard. I've been concentrating on writing my song, securing a date with Mr. Astor to shoot my video, saving the money to pay him. I didn't think about promotion. I'm so used to minimizing being in the public eye, I forgot no one knows El Vella. Maybe I should set up some social media accounts to generate buzz.

Wil tunes his guitar, strumming the opening chords of the song we sang at the Devil's Martini. I'm instantly back on the stage, and my pulse quickens. "The G is a little flat."

Those bushy eyebrows rise in doubt, and he hits the G note once, twice. The eyebrows fall, and he nods his head. "You're right."

"I have an ear for these things."

He looks at me like he wants an explanation.

"It's like the world talks to me through music. The elevator hummed at a B-flat."

"That's sick. Do you hear words too?"

I shake my head. "Melodies, chords, pitches, yes. Words are harder. They're here"—I point to my temple—"but I can't get them out onto the page."

Sharing this secret shame of mine with him doesn't send me into a panic. First, following Mom and Papa on performances, and then becoming part of Dad's touring routine were part of the reason I never went to school. Tutors also helped me find ways around words when they didn't want to cooperate. They slide around the page; the letters get mixed up. They won't listen to me.

"I see words everywhere," says Wil. "They materialize before I even know what they are there for. Music is more of an artistic expression, something I can control, shape, and alter."

"I'd love more control. But when I feel it, the music, it's like a crack, it reshapes." Words fail me again.

Wil strums a cord and moves into a progression I recognize. The song about change.

"The erosion," he says over the melody he's now picking with his fingers on the strings. "A powerful force that reshapes the familiar world around us into a universe previously unknown or only hinted at."

How did he know? The cocky jerk from the texts falls away.

"Do you know this song?" he asks.

My singing along with him is the answer. And it's here. The odd harmony of his instrument and mine concoct a narrative that's better than anything my words would have expressed. I use the other artist's words and melody to share a dark corner of my soul with this stranger standing across from me.

"You do have a gift." His eyes catch mine, and the shaky feeling I get when I step on stage returns. I'm shivering. Maybe it's the air-conditioned room combined with me not wearing much.

"You okay?" Wil slides his gaze to the goosebumps covering my arms and legs. "You're freezing."

He looks down at the same black T-shirt with the blue design he wore on Saturday.

"Hang on." He moves the guitar to his back and grabs the messenger bag he put on the floor earlier. He takes out a long-sleeved thermal shirt with a bright gold and blue circle emblem on a red and white background that reads "SV Energie Berlin."

I pull it on and sniff at the smell of coffee.

"I wore it at work earlier."

"Better to be warm and smell of coffee." I point at the emblem on my chest. "What's this?"

"My rowing club back in Berlin."

He lifts his palm up to my face, and I see the calluses I noticed earlier. "I assumed those were from the guitar."

"A bit of both. These"—he takes my hand and runs it across the pads under his fingers, rough and hard—"are from rowing. And these"—he moves the tips of my fingers against his—"are from guitar."

The casual way his hand is guiding mine across his palm, tracing its hills, peaks, and valleys, the contact of his warm skin against my icy one, brings warmth into my core. I start to melt. Icy-hot. Too comfortable.

"So, you run?" I see his Adam's apple bob as he swallows and looks at my legs. His shirt falls lower than the hem of my shorts, and it appears as if I'm wearing the jersey and nothing else.

I snap out of whatever trance I've been in and slide my fingers out of his.

"Like I said, almost every day." I grab my phone and pull up the music for the first song of the set we agreed to try today. "We have forty-five minutes left. Better get started."

We have five cover songs selected to play on Saturday when my phone buzzes again. It takes a second for the emotions from the last song to settle. For me to come back down to reality. For El to return to Melodie.

Sven: You're late.

Me: There in five.

"Your jailer summoning you?"

"Why don't you like Sven? He's a good guy. A really good one, actually."

Warmth seeps out of Wil's face. "Good guys are overrated."
His guitar goes into its case.

"Sven takes care of me. Mom forbade me to be out of his
sight." I shove my tablet into my bag, missing the music already.
"If my parents find out, Sven will be out of a job. He's doing me
a favor. Us a favor."

"I haven't said anything to his face."

"I'd rather you not say anything behind his back, either. I'm
Team Sven all the way. Got it?" Anger flickers in my chest.
Damn fingers. Four more weeks, and I can get rid of this jerk.

I tug on the hem of Wil's thermal, trying to peel it off me.

"Keep the shirt. You can give it back to me on Saturday."

"No." I succeed at pulling the garment over my head and hold
it out for him. "I don't need charity."

Wil huffs and grips the sleeve, careful not to touch me. "Way
to confuse charity with friendship. Did your parents forbid you
from having friends too?"

"I have friends." A fire ignites below my ribs.

"What are their names? And relatives don't count."

Well Zoe and Bailey are out of the running. I still have Sven
. . . Heat rises from my chest into my cheeks. Why is he right?
Why are we even talking about this?

"The way you push people away"—he stuffs the shirt into his
messenger bag—"you make it fucking hard to be your friend."

"I'd rather have one good friend than several fakes." My
phone buzzes against my butt. I know it's Sven. "The world is

full of impostors." I don't wait for Wil's reply and head for the door.

"Wait."

Is he going to apologize?

I turn to find the paper bag with my butter tart in my face. How foolish of me to think he'd be sorry for his words, consider anyone's feelings but his own. I snatch the bag from his hand and walk out of the room, choosing the stairs rather than wait for the elevator.

"You're welcome," echoes down the hall toward me. I clench my teeth at the attitude wound up in those two words and resist saying thank you.

Sven's sitting on the low wall outside the door. He advances and looks me over. Checking for wounds? Signs of torture? He'll have to look at my pride to see the damage Wil's words did to me.

"Let's go." I storm down the path to the car. Sven opens the back door for me.

"Shotgun?" I smile a sad smile at him.

"Melodie."

I wave the bag with Wil's treat inside. "I have a butter tart. I'll share." Sven plays a good game, but he likes sweets as much as I do. Bear claws are his favorite, but we've shared many a butter tart. His eyes betray the calm he is exuding.

"Don't get used to it." Sven opens the front passenger door, and I rest my sweaty back against the soft warm leather, placing the bag on the console between us.

Sven gets in but instead of starting the car, he lifts the bag with the dessert, takes a tablet out of the console, and after typing something on it, passes it my way, keeping the food on his lap.

"The dossier on your singing partner."

I scan through about five pages of information, including a photo of Wil's driver's license.

Wilhelm Peters, nineteen years old, birthdate September 4, born in Bremen, Germany. Citizenship: German and British.

Hmmm . . . explains why his English is so good and his British accent.

I read on.

Son of Hanna Peters, a clerk at a plastic surgeon's office, no husband on record. Wil's father is not listed. Known residences: Bremen, a two-bedroom duplex. Lives with his mother and grandfather, Sebastian Peters, retired construction worker. During the last school year lived in Berlin: university dorms. Student at Berlin University of the Arts, Sound Engineering. On the university rowing team. Reported income as a DJ. Has multiple social media accounts. The visa to stay in the US was sponsored by Starlight Future Filmmakers Foundation. The competition began the first week in July and will conclude at the end of September.

I turn off the tablet and pass it back to Sven. "Didn't take you long."

"He checks out." Sven puts the tablet away and places the bag with the butter tart back between us. He starts the car and pulls out of the lot. "No red flags."

"Good. No hidden agenda." I stare out the windshield as we sit at a stoplight. "I'm still getting rid of his ass as soon as this stupid splint is gone."

"You'll need physical therapy after."

"Really, do you have to be so logical all the time?"

"Yes."

I can't help the grin. "The gig is only until November. Worse comes to worst, I can tolerate him that long."

"Is he at least a decent guitar player?"

"He's annoyingly good. Does the report say where he learned to play?"

"Isn't it something you can ask him?"

I pick up the bag, pull out the tart, break it into two and hand half to Sven. "I could. But . . ."

"I'll take care of it." Sven pops the whole thing into his mouth. "Is there anything else you want to know?"

I run my finger along the gooey inside and suck the sweet essence off my finger. I like to savor each portion of my favorite treat. "Find out where he works."

The sugar hits the roof of my mouth, and I try not to groan. Damn this is good. And damn Wil Peters.

FOURTEEN

Wil

THE ONLY REASON I'M still awake is my scheduled call with Opa at eleven p.m.

It's going to be eight a.m. on a Saturday for them, and Mum will be having her monthly breakfast with Heidi and Anna. Those three have not missed their breakfast dates in the ten years since I've known them. Came to our house when Mum couldn't stand the thought of going to a restaurant when her arthritis flared up, and she had to go through another round of medication that left her nauseated, sensitive to light, and with a compromised immune system. Now it's six months later, and the side effects were worth it. The medication seems to be paying off, and she's started venturing outside, before the next flare-up puts her back under house arrest.

The light in our room is on. At least I won't have to tiptoe around a sleeping Mateo.

"You made it. I thought you forgot." Mateo puts down his phone and looks me over. "Um, you're changing right? You smell of coffee. Pre-caffeinating before we party?"

The party. Shit, I forgot. Working at the coffee shop is harder than I thought, definitely not like in the movies.

"The party, right." I drop my bag on the floor. "Slipped my mind. The shift was insane. Never worked so hard for so little."

"I did offer you other options to pay your bills. Every new fake ID customer you bring gets you ten percent of their fee." He glides his hands along the freshly edged line in his hair. Must be nice to have time and quid to go to the barber every week. "Or you could DJ some parties and turn up the heat. I'll pay cash. No one will have to know."

"Trying to stay above board here, as much as I can." Mateo seems to have his fingers in a lot of pots. Some I don't think I want to be part of. "Blend only pays minimum wage, but I get to eat any leftovers after the shift. Day-old scones never tasted so good."

He shrugs. "I'm not going to beg. If you ever need more cash . . ."

"I get it" I put my phone on the charger and flop on my back on the covers of my unmade bed.

"Think I'm gonna bail." I give him my please-forgive-me smile, which has a nine-out-of-ten success rate.

"Your loss. Don't wait up." Mateo gets up, grabs a jacket off the back of his desk chair, and slams the door behind him.

Mateo is right. I do smell like coffee. I need to clean up. In a minute. I'll just lie here first. It's been a while since I've been dog tired.

My legs and back ache from standing at work so much, my eyes are sore from staring at the screen mixing the sound in the latest scene we shot for *Indigo* over the last two days, the only working title the team agreed to. Going from Team Blue to *Indigo* was not a far stretch. My eyes close, and thoughts float in my head. Coffee shop. Rowing machine. Frustration. El's face. The tarts in the case beside the register that keep reminding me of her. Stop.

I sit up and rub my eyes. She didn't even thank me for the butter tart. I had to go clear across town on two buses to buy the fecking thing. If not for Rocker, I'd be dumping her ass and working on the film with Nick. Find another way to get to my father. But El's my best bet. Eyes on the prize, and winning the Starlight competition is not why I'm here.

I'm freshly showered and shaved. I open my bag and take the rowing thermal I left there since El wore it on Wednesday. It stretches tight across my chest, while on El it hit her thighs right above the knee and teased her legs every time she moved. Stop.

I roll the sleeves, sit down at the desk, and press call. It rings and rings and rings. Maybe I'm not talking to Opa today. There's a beep, and Opa's face appears on the screen. He waves at me, and by the way his mouth is moving, I know he's talking.

"You're muted." I point at my mouth. Opa's eyes shine bright when he hears my voice, and his lips start moving faster. "No, Opa. I can't hear you. You need to click on the microphone button." I point at my ears and then at the camera.

Opa's mouth stops moving. His forehead zooms toward the camera, and I can see his salt-and-pepper hair he keeps as trim as Sven does his.

" . . . stupid contraption. Why can't he hear me? Where's the volume on this damned thing? Why can't people just pick up the phone—"

"Opa, I can hear you now."

"Oh." The hair and forehead retreat, and Opa's tight lips tell me everything. "You look like you've had a twelve-hour shift hanging up drywall."

"Close. Worked on the soundtrack for the movie till lunch, then a full shift at the coffee shop, and hit the free weights before our call."

"Good, good. How's California?"

"Haven't seen much of it."

"I haven't raised you to be a complainer. Do what needs to be done and come home." Opa's voice is always like steel, but today it's extra. Is it Mum? Or something else? "I'll find a job with my old boss for you."

"It's not as easy as you think." How much do I tell Opa? He's used to taking a hammer to smash through the barriers in his life. But I can't deceive the man who raised me. Lying to Mum is hard enough.

"Excuses. You went to his office, you talked to him. What did he say?"

"I didn't talk to him. I got as far as the lobby. Security won't let random people in. And when I asked to make an appointment with him, they laughed at me."

"And what did you do? Did you tell them you are his son, and he has to see you?"

I try to keep my face calm. I have practice at it. Club managers snarking at me when I ask for the money they promised. Redhead rich girls bossing me around like they own the place. "Making a scene with the staff didn't seem like a good idea. More likely to land me in jail, and then I'll have zero chances of meeting Rocker."

Opa does not hide his disgust when I use my father's stage name. His face pinches, and I half expect him to spit like he does on the construction site. "Excuses is all I hear. What are you doing then? If you can't see him, come home. It's not a vacation. Your mother misses you." It might be me, but I feel his "I miss you" left unsaid.

"I miss her too." I don't tell him I miss him as well. I miss home. My friends. My life. Everything was easier in Germany. Sure, I didn't have money there either, that never changes, but it wasn't such a struggle. Everything is expensive here. Different. Harder.

There is good here, though. I lucked out with Team Blue. Same with my roommate. And then there's El. I can smell the scent of her on my shirt. Reminds me of the beach. Of red hair in the back of her car. She's . . . Singing with her the other night, I thought the magic of the bar might be a one-time thing. But . . . I don't know. It was even better, more. Every song she met me toe-to-toe with her tenacity, strength, charm. It was addictive. Like . . . Stop.

"I'm doing this for Mum," I remind Opa. And myself. "I have another way."

"Why does this sound like you are not sure?"

"I met Rocker's stepdaughter."

"Did you ask her? Did she say yes?"

"It's complicated." I go for it. I need to talk to someone about this. Need someone to tell me this is the right thing to do. "She doesn't know I'm his son. But she works with her dad. At his office. She'll get me in. Introduce me to him." I can't say his name.

"You are so much like your mother. Zero planning. Hoping you'll figure it out when the time comes. You've been there for weeks already. Don't waste time. Get that girl to introduce you to the scumbag."

He's right. Getting to Rocker is my priority. If it comes down to it, I'll have to ditch Nick and the crew tomorrow night. I have to make nice with El. I have to show up at the Devil's Martini for our gig. Let Team Indigo make some decisions without me.

"I'll get it done." I breathe a lungful of air and hope the weight on my chest gets lighter. It doesn't. "How's Mum? She sounded cheery, but you and I know she's good at putting on a happy face, so we don't worry."

"She's holding her own. Misses you but is proud you got into that competition. Keeps telling everyone in town, as if they care. She's sure you'll become a big shot in Hollywood. The stories she spins make it sound like you've made it. Like your name will be on the movie poster with Brad Pitt." Opa hasn't been to the movies in a lifetime. He thinks Sean Connery is still James Bond.

"They don't put sound engineer's names on the movie posters."

"Don't tell her that."

The conversation loops and after a couple more of Opa's rants about technology, my inability to plan, and Mom's delusions of my grandeur, we agree to have another call next week.

FIFTEEN

El

I STARE AT THE black chalkboard covered in red and blue lettering advertising the Devil's Martini's specials tonight. Their house nachos are half-price until nine. I could order a plate to drown my sorrows.

Or to throw at Wil Peters.

If he ever gets here.

We are on stage in five, and he is a no-show. I check my phone again, but there hasn't been a text since his last one twenty minutes ago:

Wil the cocky German: I'll make it.

To distract or to torture myself, I take a peek into the bar. Last week's standing-room-only feel is gone, but with half the tables full, there are plenty of people for me to freak out about on stage. I should tell Sven to go join them. But keeping him in the wings gives me a better chance to remain calm and sing when Wil's irresponsible attitude leaves me to perform a cappella. On a stage.

What the hell am I going to do if he doesn't show? I look at the lonely mic standing solitary on the worn hardwood floor. I knew I couldn't trust him. The only person I can rely on is me.

Pauline comes up behind me. "Where's your better half?"

"Running a little late." Shit. I need to learn to lie.

She presses her lips together, the friendly smile she greeted me with when I walked in half an hour ago nowhere in sight. "But he'll be here, right? I booked you both."

"He'll make it." I quote Wil's text.

She walks away, and I lean against the wall, close my eyes, and repeat over and over in my head, Everything's going to be fine. It's a trick I learned after Papa died. Fake it till you make it. The excitement I've felt since morning about performing tonight, proving to myself I can do this job, has disappeared, and the old familiar self-doubt has settled in my bones again. Who am I kidding? I can't go on that stage alone.

No. I can't think like that. I-don't-care-about-any-one-but-myself Wil Peters will not determine my fate. If I have to, I'll sing every song a cappella. I've seen Mom do it. It was impressive. I can be impressive.

"He's here." Sven put his hand on my shoulder, and I follow Sven's eyes to find Wil charging down the hall, guitar case in hand. "Told you I'd make it." He smiles, and I want to hit him.

"Where the hell were you?"

"Wow, chill." The guitar case lies open on the floor as he kneels down beside it. "I'm here. That's all that matters."

"No. That's not the point. You can't just waltz in here two minutes before we have to be on stage and expect me to be fine with it. I don't work that way."

"Look, princess."

"Stop calling me that." The term of endearment that sounded like the best music in Papa's voice is like an insult when Wil says it.

"No? Would you prefer spoiled brat, rich girl, or privileged? Which one is more precise for you?" He slams his guitar case shut and brings his face closer to mine. "Some of us have to actually work." He's no longer shouting. The cold calm wrenches my heart even more. "We don't have Daddy's money to live off."

"Oh, get over yourself." I search for my white strand to calm me down, but my fingers brush against the synthetic strands instead. "Money doesn't solve all problems." He knows nothing about my life or my parents. It couldn't bring my Papa back. It won't make Mom worry less about me. It can't make my parents believe in me the way I want them to.

"But it helps. I don't see you struggling."

He should thank my therapist and the media training for the calm-and-collected Melodie Rockerby the world knows.

"You want to play pop star, but I have real problems. Shit to deal with." He runs his hand through his thick black hair. "I'm in a foreign country, everything is so fucking expensive here, I have to replace a broken window at five hundred dollars, even though it was not my fault, and my visa only lets me work on campus. Even if I was allowed to get another job, between school, filming sunsets at 'the perfect time,' the shitty job I'm grateful for, and pleasing your perfect ass, I'll run out of hours. I'm here, and I'm doing the best I can."

The dam breaks, and Wil the cocky German slips away, and a boy emerges. More human than he has the right to be. I'm supposed to be angry at the jerk, but his words wreck me, and I want to hug this boy, tell him everything's going to be fine.

"I—"

"I busted my ass to get here for you. For you. The least you could do is give me a break when I get here—on time."

"Ladies and Gentlemen, put your hands together for WE."

A burst of applause, and Pauline is waving us onto the stage. Wil pushes by me and into the spotlights beyond.

Hug and then punch him. I watch the boy who was yelling at me moments ago smile and play happy for the crowd, fanning the flames of their good mood, acting for the audience. I've been so wrapped up in my problems that Wil's side of the story didn't cross my mind. He doesn't make it easy, hiding under his mask of I'm-so-awesome. Guess we're both wearing disguises.

I step on the stage, determined to push the drama out of the way. We can't get fired on our first night. I need this, but Wil needs it as well. He says he's doing it for me, but he needs the money too.

I take the mic off the stand, wait for a wave of nausea to cover me, or for my body to ignore the commands my brain sends its way. "Good evening." The words leave my mouth, and my voice doesn't even shake. "Thanks for that great welcome." I lift my eyes and scan the tables and the bar. My chest tingles with anticipation. I'm scared, but I'm also not afraid. "That's Wil"—I point at Wil, who's strumming his guitar, his back turned to the audience—"and I'm El." Wil was supposed to deliver the punchline we practiced on Wednesday, but even though he looks casual and cool, the guitar is off. I can hear the flat G again and see him trying to fix it, not paying attention to me. "Wil and El, the two halves of WE."

Tepid applause follows. Wil would've done a better job. It was supposed to be his role, but I have to buy him more time to fix his guitar. The G is still flat.

"Anyone in the house from last week when we won the open mic contest?" I grit my teeth as Wil over tunes the G, now too sharp. There's a spattering of "Yes" and "You were awesome" from the crowd. I walk over to Wil and place my hand on his arm, willing him to understand I'm buying time, no need to rush the tuning. Hard eyes watch me through slits then soften by a shade.

I turn to the audience. "Well, thanks for coming back. We have a great set planned for you tonight." The G is still sharp. I squeeze his arm, and Wil throws me an I-know glare. Shit. I'm not the words girl, but I have to keep going. "Before we start, did you know the Devil's Martini's famous nachos are half-price until nine? Wouldn't want to miss them." I shoot a glance back at Wil.

He rolls his eyes. I should stop expecting a "thank you" or an "I'm sorry" from him. The G is now perfect, and my stomach uncoils. Time to get this show on the road. Instead of his usual playful plucking of the strings, Wil peels off a harsh collection of chords. A woman near the front squishes up her face.

There must be a way to fix this, shift Wil's grumpy mood. Grumpy. Perfect.

"You'll have to excuse *my friend* Wil here. He's a bit grumpy tonight." I turn to him and mouth "Lighten up."

But Wil isn't looking at me, his eyes are on the audience. "And *my friend* El here is a bit uptight tonight." Out in the crowd someone chuckles. "I mean, it's Saturday night." Wil finally moves his head my way. "We're here to have some fun, aren't we?"

Message received. I match his stare and place a hand on his shoulder. "Oh, I can have fun." I expand my ribcage and belt out the opening line of Queen's *Somebody to Love* in his face, giving Freddie Mercury a run for his money.

Wil's eyes widen at the onslaught of my voice. A sly grin spreads across his face as he picks up on the last G I'm holding, matches it with his perfectly tuned guitar, and runs with the melody.

It's not the song we planned on opening with. This was supposed to be our swan song, ramping up the crowd for the headliners to come. But it works. The audience cheers. I turn to them and pour the emotions I can't find words for myself into the songs. I give it everything I have, Wil right beside me.

WE are back.

"Me-e-e-e-e." The last line of Taylor Swift's *ME!* hasn't even finished, and the crowd is howling and whistling. In a flash, our time on stage is up, over far too quickly. My fingers shake as I return the mic to the stand. My cheeks burn, and my blood whooshes in my ears. That was the best performance of my life. I've never thought singing would turn into a race of words, melodies, heartbeats, glances between Wil and me. Every time I was sure we had reached our peak, Wil revved his guitar and showed me there was another height for us to conquer. There is no stopping WE.

Wil grabs my hand as we take a bow and run off stage. I can't stop smiling, my body light and alive. I could do another set, two more sets right now, right here. I catch my partner's eyes and see my joy reflected in them. He had as much fun as me; I know it. I squeeze his hand.

The anger of the fight from earlier is gone, but I haven't forgotten the sentiments he shared. "Wil, I—"

"I'm sorry."

There must be a shift somewhere in the universe because the high-and-mighty Wil just apologized to me.

"It was a shitty day."

"You don't say."

"Yeah."

"Tell me about it."

Wil's eyebrows merge into a questioning line.

"Seriously. You're not alone here. You have me. I know lots about being alone in a foreign country. You can tell me. Vent to me. I've been told I'm a good listener."

He shakes his head. "It's nothing."

Not this again. We're back to water-off-a-duck's-back Wil. A girl could get whiplash. "The film's not going well?"

There's a pause. I want him to talk to me, say something true, real.

"We're behind schedule." Wil puts his guitar back in its case. "We don't have a theme song. Or even a title for the thing. It's a mess."

"That's shitty." I wish I could do something, but I don't have any skills, any way to help.

"There's my dynamic duo." Pauline interrupts us before I can come up with anything better. "You rocked out there." She puts her arms around us, and I resist pulling away. She's just being nice. I have to get used to this. "Want a soda or something while I tally the till and get you your money?"

"Can I have a beer?"

I whack Wil in the stomach. My hand meets a surface that hurts my fingers. "Sodas would be great." Pauline squeezes my shoulder before she heads into the main bar area. There's a wooden bench against the wall, and I nod at it, asking Wil to join me.

"You got a job?" Sven already told me he works at Blend, but I'd rather hear it from him.

"Had to. The scholarship only covers the basics, and apparently that doesn't include food." Wil leans his guitar case against the wall beside him. "Nick works at a café on campus, and he got me in there."

"Is it Blend?" The coffee he gave Frank was from there. "It's close to Rocker, Inc. I get my iced cappuccino, two shots, with cashew milk, a pump of caramel, two pumps of vanilla, poured, not shaken, and a mint leaf from there. Dad loves their matcha lattes."

Wil keeps his head down. "I hope you tip well. That's quite a special order. Matcha latte is easy. Guess he doesn't pick them up himself."

"You'd be surprised. He loves going to 'normal' places if he can. Where do you think I got my disguise tips from? But when that's not an option, we place a delivery order."

"Blend doesn't deliver."

"For Dad they do. He most certainly tips well. Nadine does, actually. She's my boss. She's the one who rules the tipping jar."

The fingers of Wil's left hand tap against the wood we're sitting on. The rhythm is getting faster. The performance is over. We did great. What can he be stressing about? And the tapping tells me he is. The one giveaway his poker face can't cover up. I'm about to ask what's wrong when Wil's drumming halts, and his cocky grin reemerges as if it never left.

Sixteen

El

My second week at work I'm upgraded to ordering lunches for the musicians that are recording at Rocker, Inc. today. The tipping jar is still with Nadine, but she promises I'll work my way to it, like it's an honor I have to earn. The best part of the day was when I went to clean up the lunch leftovers and stayed in the studio to watch the sound engineer at work. Until Nadine came to get me. If life at home under Mom and Dad's supervision can be stifling, my day at the office offers less privacy.

It's Marta's day off, and when Mom and Dad have a last-minute Tuesday night dinner to attend, I ditch my usual takeout. Alone at the house, I'm in a mood. A creative mood. The success of our second performance at the Devil's Martini brought back the inspiration I needed. I scan the fridge, freezer, and pantry, and all the ingredients I need for fish tacos are there.

Lucky me. I pull the tilapia out and turn on the oven. The tune for a new song loops in my head.

Plucking the melody on the piano with one hand is painstakingly slow, but when the new song keeps rolling through my head, there's no stopping it. I have to let it out of my mind and hear what it sounds like in the world. It's good. Damn good. I place the fish on the baking sheet, season it, dot it with small pieces of butter on top, and put it in to bake.

Torn cilantro leaves and mashed avocado go onto a plate together. I hum the tune. My voice and the piano bring it to life, but it needs a strong guitar solo. I plug in the food processor, missing the weight of my chef's knives in my hand. I look at my fingers. Two more weeks until the splint comes off. Red cabbage whirrs as the machine comes to life. I take the colorful strips out and place them beside the rest of the ingredients. There's no harm in asking.

Me: A favor?

I put the phone down and start on the creamy sauce. I manage to measure sour cream and mayo into the bowl when I hear a text come in.

Wil: Good evening to you too.

Now he pretends to be a gentleman.

Me: I thought we were past the niceties.

Wil: Could've told me earlier. I've been on my best behavior for no reason.

Me: I have a serious question.

Wil: . . .

Me: If I send you ten bars of music, could we record them tomorrow?

There are no dots or answer from Wil, and I go back to humming and squeezing limes, mixing the lime juice with the creamy base. A dash of sriracha, and it's perfect. Tangy. Smooth. A tiny kick at the end. What's left? Tortillas. Flour, salt, water, olive oil. I check on the fish. Plenty of time. I cover the dough and set the timer for ten minutes to let it rest. My phone buzzes.

Wil: Back. Sure. Was grabbing dinner.

Me: Dinner time here too. I'll show you mine if you show me yours.

I shouldn't have said that.

Wil: How could I resist such an offer?

A photo of a plastic cup with dried ramen noodles and some red and green bits I assume represent an attempt at vegetable matter fills the screen. It looks sad.

Me: That's it?

Wil: There's a shared kitchen here, but it's not what I'd call gourmet. This works.

Maybe I should pretend I'm eating something crappy too. The timer for the fish beeps, I take it out and look at the shiny golden fillets. The aromas of the ingredients mix in the air and remind me why I asked Mom to hire a chef to teach me to cook for my sixteenth birthday.

Me: Give me fifteen.

There's enough dough for eight tortillas. Once both sides are light brown, I take one and put some pull-apart fish into it, red cabbage next, cilantro and avocado go on top. Some crumbled Cotija cheese and a drizzle of the spicy creamy sauce. My photo doesn't do the fish taco justice, and sending it to Wil makes me a bit uneasy. I have the real delicious food here while he has to subsist on dried noodles. I hit send.

Wil: Does a chef cook for you?

Not technically. Marta makes most meals. Although she's not a chef, she's an excellent cook, and her skills in the kitchen are why Rocker hired her, but she's our housekeeper. I can safely say no, and it'll not be a lie.

Me: No.

Wil: Your parents made this.

Me: Nope. I did.

Wil: Right. You don't have to lie to me.

My taco beckons, and I take the first bite. The warm tortilla, crunchy cabbage, aromatic cilantro, creamy avocado, salty cheese, and the expected spicy notes of the sauce create a heaven of textures and flavors in my mouth. I bite again. Maybe pursuing cooking as a career didn't end up being my thing, but this taco alone is worth the year I spent in the kitchen every day.

Me: I never lie.

Wil: That's a lie.

He manages to win an argument when I know I'm in the right, but I'm not letting it slide. I might not have the right words to fight back, but I have a way to prove I didn't lie. I stuff the rest of the taco into my mouth, build another one for myself and pack the rest of the food away into glass containers.

My tacos will do the speaking for me tomorrow. I bet he'll change his tune when his stomach is full of something better than ramen. Show is better than tell.

I pull up Zoe's Snapchat.

Me: Can we pretend I'm out for dinner with you tomorrow?

"Come talk to me," trills three times in Zoe's voice from my phone, and her face fills my screen. I accept the call.

"Dish." Zoe sounds like she's on speakerphone.

"Where are you?"

"On my way to drop off the samples. To the stylist who commented on my IG. Remember our Nieman Marcus disaster?" Like I could forget the paparazzi incident. "She's interested in the rest of my collection."

"Congrats. That's major."

"We'll see. But we're not talking about me. Dish already."

"It's Wil." Fed and contented, I wander out of the kitchen and out onto the side deck, avoiding the balcony with the direct view of the ocean.

"As in your Wil?"

"As in Wil the guitar player. He's not my Wil."

"Semantics." I hear a loud off-key D-G-B of her horn. Wouldn't want to be the car in Zoe's way. "What did he do this time?" She shouts over the noise.

"He thinks I'm lying about being a good cook."

"Doesn't he know you don't lie?"

"I keep saying it, but he's not believing me." The sun is low in the sky, and I remember Wil's words about filming the perfect sunset. I must ask him about it. "So, I have a plan."

"A plan?" Zoe whistles. "I live for plans. Are we stuffing him full of delicious food and making him beg for forgiveness?"

"Something like that." I like the visual. "I'm going to feed him dinner tomorrow night. My fish tacos."

"Melodie's famous fish tacos? Can I have some too?"

"Not this time. I need to pretend I'm having dinner with you, while I'm with Wil."

"Pretend? Again?" There's a pause. Did I lose her? Being inside her convertible is always fun, yet the wind makes a phone conversation difficult. "When do we get to have a meal together? I haven't seen you in person since your first day at work." The traffic noises don't cover the notes of disdain in her voice. "Do I need to learn to play an instrument? How long does it take to master a tambourine? I've always thought I'd look good with one of those in my hand. And a peasant skirt, of course. They're coming back into fashion now—"

"Zoe, stop." I shut my eyes and remember the breathing technique my therapist taught me after Dad's death. Mom was happy something other than the pills tampered my erratic emotions. I let the air in.

Zoe follows my command. In the quiet, the crashing booms of my heart slow against the counter melody of the ocean. I breathe out. I open my eyes. Zoe's just messing with me. "You know I'd love to hang, but for once I'm actually busy. Like running across the four floors at Rocker, Inc. from nine to six and rehearsing with Wil at night busy."

"Whoa. You're not messing around this time, are you? This music thing sounds serious. Like you actually believe in yourself."

"Shut up." I do feel different. Maybe it's because of winning the gig at Devil's Martini. I'm certain this plan will work. Shit, plan. "Way to take me off track. I'm not calling you to have a heart-to-heart about my music career. I need you to cover for me tomorrow night. Say, till midnight? Can you do it?"

"Can I do it?" She pauses again.

"Zoe . . ."

"Yeah, I can do it. But on one condition. I want a weekly lunch with you."

"Lunch is doable." Half of the office works from home on the last day of the week. "Can we meet Fridays?"

"For you—anything. I'm dying to try the new Japanese fusion place at The Grove. Have you heard of it?"

"No deal." It's not like I can just walk into a restaurant, sit down, and eat. "Can't you just bring takeout to the office, like you did with the coffees?"

"You owe me, remember?" Zoe's right but doesn't mean I have to like it. "I'll get you a beanie, and a crop top and you'll look like any other rich teenager who hangs there."

"Thanks, but I . . ." My hand is twirling the white strands that make me instantly recognizable. "It's complicated."

"Nonsense. That's not the kind of place anyone would expect you to go to." The click-click of the turning signal on Zoe's end matches my heartbeat as I imagine being mobbed by paparazzi with wasabi on my chin. "Stop freaking out already." Zoe's always had a sixth sense about what's going on in my head. "We're going."

"Yes, Mom."

"That's a low blow. I'm the one pushing you to go out, not locking you in."

"Funny." I chuckle.

"I'll text you when I'm heading home tomorrow, so we can show up about the same time, in case your mom checks with mine." I hear her slam the door of her car. I better wrap this up.

"She shouldn't, but good thinking." The sky around me is gray-black, the air cooler. The sun is gone, and I head back into the house.

"I'm not just a beauty," says Zoe.

No, she is not. She's the one who knows me. The me I am when no one else is in the room. I'm lucky to have her.

SEVENTEEN

THE LIGHTS IN THE studio are off and when I flip the switch on, El shield her eyes. Nothing changed in the space, but it reminds me of how we left things last time. She pulls a roomy jean jacket around her. No need for my sweater today, I guess.

"The sheet music you sent was a bit challenging." I spot a container she places on the table. "What's that for?"

"I'm bribing you with food." I stare as she opens the lids of several square boxes. "My famous fish tacos."

"Did you really make those?"

"I did. I had to sneak out Marta's insulated food carrier to keep the fish and tortillas warm, so they are not going to be as good as yesterday. Freshly cooked is always the best. Maybe one day—if you're nice."

The warmth in my chest mirrors the warmth of the food she's opening. "Maybe?"

"Today, it's the best I can do." She waves me over. "Dig in. It's good. Unless you don't like fish or food." Wrinkles dance at the corners of her eyes.

"I like food. All food." I pick up a real china plate, not paper like I've been using for days, and load two tortillas. A bunch of the filling spills out before I manage to bring the concoction to my mouth and take a nibble. The fact the tacos smell delicious doesn't mean they'll taste that way. I don't want to spit El's creation out in front of her.

"Mmmm." There's no need. I dive in for a second bite and savor the ingredients. "You're not lying. It's good."

She makes herself a taco. "I told you. I never lie."

She brought me food. Something Mum used to do when she drove up from Bremen to visit me in Berlin. She'd bring me home-cooked food, and we'd eat it together, catch up, laugh, and feel at home in my narrow single-bed dorm at uni. The recording studio is twice the size of that cell, and I'm certain no food is allowed here, but, bloody hell, I almost feel at home.

"Thank you." I shove the last of my taco into my mouth before I say too much.

She puts her plate on the floor we're sitting on, swallows the food she was chewing, and wipes her lips with a cloth napkin she brought alongside silverware and white plates with gold trim. "My pleasure." And I believe her. I believe she cooked this simple but delicious meal. I believe she's changing my mind about who Melodie Rockerby is.

"Might be best if we don't tell Frank we brought food." The warmth in her eyes dims. "But I won't say no to more dinners together." Because I like food. And the company is not bad.

The air in the studio grows heavier. She looks down at her empty plate and tugs on her white streak. Without a hat and with her hair loose, it's impossible to miss. Her hair hangs down and shields part of her face. She's bundled up in a jacket and leggings, and her neck is the only part of her body, apart from her head and hands, I can see. What would I have thought of her if I met her like this? Another student on campus to complain about the class load to over coffee. We could've played some music, hung out at a party, lounged on the grass in a park and talked, or went to a beach for a swim.

"Do you still think you could do it?" she asks.

"Do what?" Her face turns back to me, waiting for my answer.

"Play the guitar part I sent?"

Oh, that. I turn off the picture of El and me running through the shallow waves and splashing water on each other. "Yeah, I practiced a bit, but it might need several takes." I scramble back to my feet and take my plate to the bag she brought it in.

"Just put it in." She's up as well, and I help her close lids on now-empty containers and pack up the soft-sided cooler.

"Should we run through our set changes for Saturday or your hard stuff first?"

Her hand hesitates on the zipper of the cooler. "Could we start with my song?"

"Your song? You wrote it?"

She stuffs her hands into the pockets of the enormous denim jacket she's wearing like armor. "Don't sound so surprised."

"I'm not. Makes more sense than the cooking."

She chuckles. "I can do both. And I can do other things too. I'm not helpless."

"I believe that too." The light pink of her lips draws me in, and every word she says takes shape, because it comes out of that mouth. How come I've never noticed how much she articulates her U?

"You okay?"

I swallow and find her eyes. "Aces. D'you have more of the song for me to listen to?"

"Hold on." She fetches her phone and brings it to me. "I have some of the melody on the piano. It's simple." She holds up her injured hand as her excuse. "It needs more layers. And some words."

The song draft she turns on for me is wistful at the beginning, El's quiet contralto gives me goosebumps. The tempo changes, and it brings hopeful notes and an anthem-like quality when she reaches the end. She's right, the guitar will bring in the rhythm and upbeat quality to the second part of the song, bringing it to life.

"Do you have the piano-only part?"

She does and at first, I fumble through some of the fingering. We try again, and together we work through the parts that are not working like she thought they would. I could do so much more with this if we had my laptop with us. She shows me what she was thinking for the drums and maybe pedal steel. We make notations on her tablet, record new takes, and bounce off ideas for tweaks we can do next week.

"I like the new ending." El's eyes burn with a fever of creating something where there was nothing before. I recognize it and let myself feed off her passion.

"How many have you written?"

"Oh, my first one was probably when I was ten." A shadow crosses her face but doesn't linger. "Mom and Papa started me with piano lessons when I was what, gosh, five? I love having every note right there in front of me. It's like I can see the melody calling to me."

Before me is the El I'd kill to see more of. Her hands move in quick jerky motions as she talks, animated and alive.

"And then Mom married Dad, and I was around his guitars so much, I picked one up. He's still teaching me when he has time. And now a bit of drums, bass, and ukulele. None very well, but I love picking up new toys, as Mom calls them. I even own a harpsichord. The first thing I bought when we moved into the house we live in now." Did she breathe at all during that torrent of emotions? She can hardly sit still, and I find myself infected by her vitality. "Do you play other instruments too?"

"Just the guitar for me. I can pluck some stuff on the piano but never had formal lessons or access to one. Self-taught. Partially why I love sound engineering so much. I can create the sounds I can't play myself. Still gives me a chance to put the music and combos I come up with into a solid form. You know?" I'm rambling, but El nods and smiles in agreement.

"The power must be awesome." El gets it. Being at that board is a bit like playing God. "I'd like to try it. I can set up the stage and fix some technical stuff. At seventeen, I went on a tour with Dad. Mom took a month off to join him, and there was no way she'd leave me home alone. So they decided I'd be helping the roadies. For real. It was eye opening." El draws an exaggerated circle with her good hand.

"So many people work backstage getting the instruments set up, the stage ready, the packing and unpacking, lights, pyrotechnics. But sound level check was my favorite part. I think that's when I decided I want to do this music thing. For real." She finds my eyes and plays with her hair again. "Funny. They partly did it to show me how hard life on the road is and how much work it is. And it only made me want it more."

"Fools. They don't want you to follow your passion?"

"Kinda. They understand music is it for me. I shared my songs with them at first but stopped after they figured out I wanted to perform them. They, Mom mostly, has this idea that I can't handle the pressure of being 'the talent,' that it would corrupt me or something. Dad won't talk about it, but at the start of his career things got pretty wild. Wilder than the stories the public knows."

I might just have an idea how wild. What would El do if I told her my secret right now? Probably run away from me.

"As an option, Dad suggested producing. But that's his passion right now, not mine."

"It's a safer option."

She sighs and lies down on the floor of the studio, as if all that talking drained her. "I love the acoustics in this place. This is the perfect spot." I watch the girl I thought stuck up and snobby relax on the polished wood. "Can I tell you a secret?"

Didn't expect that one. "If you think you can trust me."

She turns her head to the chair I'm sitting in. "With this one. I have many. Baby steps." She grins and pats the spot next to her. I leave the chair behind and join her in the middle of the room. "And stop looking at me. Close your eyes. And I'll pretend I'm not waiting for you to judge me." I do as she asks. "I'm going to shoot a video."

I open my eyes to look at her.

"Hey, no peeking. I'll tell you when I'm done. Then you can open them."

I close my eyes, settle back, and concentrate on her voice. It's smooth like butter.

"Yeah, so the plan is to create a music video for a song I wrote. I have Len Astor booked to film it. Do you know him?"

With my eyes closed, I have no idea if she can see me, but I suspect she's watching me. I nod. Len Astor has made ground-breaking videos for years. His *Lines and Lights* masterpiece he shot for Cassie Leopold is a classic.

"That's what the money is for. He's coming to LA in November, and I've booked time with him."

I don't open my eyes but say, "That sounds expensive." Bollocks, did I just piss on her dream? "But sick. And can I open my eyes now?"

"Not yet." I feel her hand on mine. "I screwed up. Got caught when I went to London to shoot it the first time. The whole thing imploded. I missed my chance. Now I need permission to leave the house, and my parents foisted Sven on me. At least he and I have history. The break I got"—she chuckles—"was me breaking my fingers. It distracted Mom and Dad from guessing the real reason I was there."

"What did they assume?"

"They think I was there to see . . ." El pauses too long. ". . . a friend." I've been around her enough to know when she's self-editing. Finding another word to replace the one she wanted to say.

"What's his name?"

There's a puff of air that ruffles my hair when she laughs. I knew it, she's watching me. "Dillon."

I'm glad Dillon is a continent and an ocean away. And I get to be in this room, on this floor with El.

"And now Sven is my constant companion, I have no allowance, and Dad made me work at Rocker, Inc."

Her fingers are cold, and I wrap my palm around them, pushing my warmth to her. "So, you're earning your own money for once." She starts pulling her fingers away. "Sorry, that didn't come out right. You're earning your own money. Good for you." She stills her fingers, and they relax.

"You can open your eyes now."

I do, and I find her staring at me, our linked hands form a bridge between us. I hold her gaze, and she doesn't look away. Princess has problems of her own. "Will you sing it for me?" My voice breaks at the word sing. She can't play it for me.

The corner of her mouth twitches. "If you want."

"Please." Her hand leaves mine. She takes out her phone, finds the song, puts the speaker between us, and hits play.

The first chords draw me in; the progression establishes a moody but positive vibe for the song. When she starts the first verse, I focus on the timbre of her voice, low and full as the words form a string. That rush I get on stage starts deep inside me.

I'm not getting the meaning yet, but it's an interesting start. It rolls into the first round of the chorus, and she soars on a long high note, leaving me wanting to hear what's next. Her vocals on the second chorus are even stronger. Why am I not connecting to it? The song wraps up with a strong steady rhythm of a hopeful promise.

The room falls silent. It stretched between us until she breaks it with a whisper. "What do you think?"

How do I tell her this? Do I tell her?

"Wil?"

"I loved the music, but the lyrics are terrible."

Eighteen

El

Laughter bubbles up in my chest. His face. Priceless. I let the giggles escape, and his eyebrows go up. I bare my soul to this guy, and he tells me my words are terrible. No one would ever say such a thing straight up to me like that. He could be a little less blunt, but then again, I get enough of fake suck-ups around me.

"No, El. I'm not saying it's bad. It really is a beautiful tune, and I love the concept. The words though. They—"

"Suck. So you said."

"I believe my exact words were 'the lyrics are terrible' but 'they suck' hits the spot." Wil shifts his body onto his side so he's facing me, leaving me nowhere to hide. "What were you trying to say there? What's the story?"

"I don't want to live my life in fear and bubble wrap?" No idea where that came from. I've never said it like that before.

"Even these words are better than 'I'm not into this.' What is the 'this?'"

"Like, what they see on the screen is not me, it's what Dad's publicist created. Even you call me that. And I'm not."

"Not what?"

"I'm not a princess."

Wil's eyes brighten, and he sits up. "That's your line. Instead of 'I'm not into this,' sing 'I'm not a princess.'" I match his pose and try the line, the words fit the beats, and it's like they were always meant to be there.

"It works. Go on?"

"It's your song. Talk to me." It's the words I said to him in the bar the other night. "What's the beginning about? I did not get that at all. Like at all, at all."

"I want to say how I got here, to the Bill Rockerby's step-daughter everyone knows. From a kid who traveled the world with her opera singer parents, to losing Papa, to becoming Melodie Rockerby, the calm-and-collected magazine-posing socialite, I believe is what they call me."

"Hang on." Wil walks over to his messenger bag and takes out the black notebook I'd like to flip through one day. He's back by me, scribbling away. "Okay. I got that part. Sounds like cool and collected is not what happens when you aren't on display. What happens behind the closed doors?"

"I cry. I lie on the floor like this. Crumpled. Or I think a million thoughts. Imagine myself in a life where I can walk out my front door without the press following me and do the normal things kids my age do. Instead, I smile at the ever-present group of paparazzi camped out by the exit of our driveway, pretending everything is okay despite what's really going on. And that's the image the world sees." I can hear his pencil scrape the surface of the page.

"Floor. Crumpled. Press. The world's eye," Wil whispers as he continues to write. "There's something there. Let's see. I don't have the first line yet. Something about you changing yourself, reorganizing. We can work on that."

I watch Wil, and I can almost see his brain spinning. It's kinda mesmerizing. And he said "we." I never thought about a writing partner, but it makes sense.

"Maybe 'followed the demands of the modern press.' We need ten syllables there." How's he doing this so fast? "Or 'I would much prefer simple life with less' or 'ignoring the signs of my own distress.' Nah, that last one isn't flowing. Would you try singing the first two?"

The new words fit my tune better than what I had originally, but Wil's not happy. He keeps scribbling, giving me options and changing the lines, sometimes one word at a time and sometimes throwing a brand-new verse at me. I've never seen a person so concerned with fine-tuning and looking to stuff two or three layers of meaning into one phrase.

"What about 'portray' there? It has a double meaning."

"That's perfect." Wil's knee bounces, but it's not the nerves this time. He's excited. About my music. About our words.

"Come talk to me, come talk to me, come talk to me," blasts across the room in Zoe's voice. Wil turns his head, looking for the source of the noise.

"It's my cousin." I grab the phone and answer. "What?" I whisper but make her understand I'm not pleased with her call.

"It's midnight. I've shopped, had dinner, ate ice cream, and watched a movie. If you still want to fly under the radar, you need to wrap it up with your lover boy and get the F home. I'm not driving around LA in the dark anymore."

"Midnight?" I glance back at Wil.

He pulls out his phone. "Bloody hell. It's midnight. I'm opening Blend at six a.m."

Bloody hell indeed. "Thanks."

"Anytime, cuz. I'll expect a full report Friday." She hangs up.

Wil's messenger bag and guitar hang over one shoulder and Marta's container across the other. "Ready?"

I'm not ready to leave. I'd much rather stay and keep the flow going, but Zoe's right. This is just the beginning and getting Mom suspicious is not in my best interest. I nod at Wil.

Sven and Frank stop talking the moment they see us come out of the elevator. Sven says nothing, takes my bag from Wil's shoulder, and inserts himself between Wil and me in the process.

Wil grins at Sven and holds out the Blend bag I didn't get to explore. "Don't forget these."

Sven snatches the bag. I mouth "thank you" as my bodyguard starts moving to the doors, and I have to walk in front of him, the mass of his body directing me away from Wil.

"I'll text you the words," he shouts to my back. I raise my uninjured hand and give him a thumbs up. I can't wait to get his texts.

The sushi restaurant Zoe has been talking about turns out to be a tiny place with a black shiny counter raised above a long bar and five tables along the opposite wall. White faux leather covers the seats, and lights on long, thin stems hang to almost eye level throughout the space. Behind the bar, chefs are combining strips of seaweed, rice, vegetables, and fish.

"Reservations under Zoe."

A server dressed in black nods and leads us to one of the tables. No heads turn as we walk. No hushed conversations or phones pointed my way. My back is stiff, and I can't believe this is going to work. I stay alert in case I have to use that back door Sven informed me about. One of the reasons for my daily jogs is to leave anyone chasing me in the dust. It's hard to run and film at the same time.

"I've heard we have to try the omakase. And I hope the pickled veggies are good here." Zoe opens the menu. "I could eat just those alone as a meal. Remember how I ate a whole tub of Mormor's pickled cucumber agurksalat last summer?"

"Maybe I can get Mom here." Her pickle obsession has reached new heights, and we stock a variety of options at home now. She even tried pickled watermelon.

"Still can't believe you guys are not going to Norway this year." Every summer, our mothers' families vacation together at Mormor Nilsen's estate in Norway where we spend long days and short nights full of song and conversations. "But we still have two lunch dates until I leave, and it's on my calendar the week I'm back." Zoe wags her finger at me as if I plan on bailing on her.

"I'll be here ready to catch up." The server brings us our waters, a metal tea kettle with green tea, plus two stoneware mugs without handles. I trace the design of the white cherry blossoms painted on them. "I didn't think Mom was serious, but apparently I only accrue"—here's a word I never thought would come out of my mouth—"one day off per month. No vacation for me for a while. How do people do this?"

"I hope I'll never know." Zoe flips to the next page of her menu.

When I agreed to Dad's plan, I didn't expect to miss visiting both sets of grandparents. After Norway I always get to spend at least a week in Malta. Mom's concession to Papa's family. She can't bear to go there; too many memories, she says. Papa's family never approved of Mom, and they silently blame the extravagant lifestyle Mom and Papa led for his death.

Besides my grandparents, the best part about Malta is how tiny it is. Hardly any press, and I get to be myself, a teenager living the simple life. I miss strolling along the main street of Marsaskala, sitting in their converted palazzo, the bitter taste of my glass of Kinnie mixing with the salty homemade ftira as they tell me stories of Papa as a child.

Zoe closes her menu and pushes it off to the side. "But that's not what we are here to talk about. How's week three at Rocker, Inc. been?"

"I now know there are sixty-four stairs between the first and fourth floor. The elevator is so slow. My Yeezys are getting a workout."

Zoe claps her hands in glee. "Nothing like toned legs to show off the shoes I've planned for your Grammy red-carpet walk."

"Right, that favor I owe you." My phone buzzes on the table.

The server returns. "Are you ready?"

"Could you order for us?" I ask Zoe.

"I know exactly what to get us." She turns her smile to the server, and I check my phone.

Wil: I have an idea how we can both get some cash, but it's not exactly above board.

I fight a smile.

Me: Are we reselling leftover Blend pastries on the black market?

Wil: No. But that's not a bad idea.

Wil: Busking.

"Sorry?"

"I was saying, how awesome I was to suggest this weekly lunch." Zoe's beautiful face glows with enthusiasm. Her olive complexion is flawless, like she's stepped from the pages of a magazine. My phone's buzzing again.

"Sorry. I just need to check this." I lower my gaze to more messages from Wil.

Wil: All we need is your voice, my guitar, and a hat for people to put their monetary appreciation into. It's easy.

Me: Have you done this before?

Wil: All the time back home.

Me: What if I get recognized?

Zoe wiggles her eyebrows at me. "Who's more important than me?" More eyebrow wiggling, like she's suggesting I get two scoops of ice cream and the chocolate sauce.

I almost don't want to tell her. She'll get the wrong idea. But I tell her everything. "Wil."

"Knew it." She sits back as the server sets a plethora of plates in front of us. I take in the rainbow of fish and vegetables in the middle of the table.

My phone buzzes again. "You start." I motion for Zoe to eat.

Wil: Jeffery Bell played in the subway for hours and nobody noticed him.

Damn. He knows Jeffery Bell.

Wil: Your wig and your costume worked the other night.

Me: In the dark bar. Not sure the wig will work in daylight. I can't just start singing on the side of the road. One post on

Twitter and my parents will be all over me, never mind the press. I'll never get to leave the house again.

I can't be considering this. If I hide my hair and wear something unlike my usual clothes, it might work.

Wil: Hair dye?

Men. They have no idea.

Me: I'll figure it out. Maybe.

Wil: When can you escape?

Right. Escape. I look up at Zoe and catch her staring at me. This worked out. Thanks to the Tracker App, I'm Svenless for an hour as long as I get back by one and stay within the two-mile radius. I pick up my chopsticks and move a few of the closest pieces of sashimi onto the square plate in front of me. I add a small dot of wasabi to the first one, fold it with the wooden sticks in my hand and pop it in my mouth.

"So, are you dating now?"

I nearly spit out the fish at Zoe's question. "Dating? How did we go from singing to dating in that drama-infused brain of yours?"

"Um, in my world if your face lights up every time you get a text from a boy it's about more than just singing."

"It's not."

"Dating or singing?"

"No, no. He's just a friend." Way to jump to conclusions, Zoe.

"If you say so. What does he want this time?"

"He wants us to busk." I place another nigiri roll in my mouth. The salmon melts, the wasabi burns, and I don't know if it's because I'm having a normal lunch in a normal restaurant like a normal person or what, but this is the best sushi I've ever tasted.

"Like sing on the street for money?"

"Exactly like that. Can you imagine a worse idea?" I point to the hair under my beanie.

Zoe taps her hot-pink nail on her lower lip. "You singing on the street. I can see it. I think it's a great idea. And I like this Wil person."

"You two need to do it then." The wasabi burn moves from my tongue to my throat. They'd look perfect together. "You can wear your highest heels around him. He's at least as tall as Dad."

"Show me a pic."

"Don't have any."

Zoe drops her chopsticks. "No selfies?"

"Nope."

"Can you at least describe what he looks like?"

"You know I'm not good with words."

"I'm not asking you to write me a song. Give me something. Hair color? Eye color? How many abs does he have?"

I tilt my head and try to stare Zoe down. "Playing guitar doesn't require him to be topless." Topless Wil. Another image I didn't need in my head. How do I describe Wil? "Black hair. Light brown eyes. Normal lips."

"What the F are normal lips? You are bad at this."

"I told you I was."

"Fine. Tall, dark, and handsome. Is that fair?"

I nod.

"Nothing I would say no to. Is he model material?"

"He sure thinks he is." And judging by the stares the girls give him at the bar he's not wrong. For once.

"His looks and guitar playing. Your voice . . . You're sure to rake in the dough."

"What about my looks?"

"Your goal is to try and hide those. Maybe show off those toned calves instead." A familiar dare-devil light sparks in her eyes. "Oh, I have the perfect dress for you to wear. They'll be lapping at your feet and won't notice your hair or your face. Or your family connections. My disguise for you worked today. No one here has given you a second glance."

I look around at the other tables, packed with people eating and talking. And not caring about me at all. Maybe Zoe is right. If I can go undetected in the restaurant in the middle of LA, maybe I can busk as well. I answer Wil's waiting text.

Me: Lunch?

Wil: I can swing that.

Me: Where?

Wil: You in?

Me: Where?

Wil: Westwood farmers' market. UCLA campus. Far enough away from the crowds but busy.

Me: I know it.

The location is perfect: a quick walk from Rocker, Inc.

Nineteen

"What are you wearing?"

El's lips twist at my words. At least I think they do. It's hard to see it under the purple boho hat that's pulled down so far I can't believe she didn't bump into the flower or fruit stands on the way here.

She stops in front of me, and the couple following behind her split to walk around us. The farmers' market at lunchtime proves to be busier than Blend is in the morning. Students run between classes, people in business clothes peel off any suit jackets to get a direct hit of the blazing California sun. "It's the only hat I had appropriate for the street."

Aren't all hats appropriate for the street? Her fashion choices and mine have less in common than mine and Opa's. I grab the brim.

She clutches my hand to stop me. "Don't."

I can't resist. I want to see those beautiful blues. I pull the hat up.

Ah, there they are. Her eyes flit left and right as she searches for evidence that someone has recognized her. I lean in and whisper in her ear. "No one's looking, not a princess." Except me.

"But they're going to."

"Fine." I take the sunglasses that hang off my T-shirt and put them on her. She smiles. I don't. Part of our magic when we perform is when we talk without talking, through our eyes, reading each other's thoughts. But if the glasses make her feel more confident, their placebo effect is worth it. "Better?"

She adjusts the shades. "I guess." My aviator frames complete her look. There's one problem. Her mouth is now the focus of her face, and I'd love to know the flavor of the gloss making them shine.

"C'mon." I stop staring at her lips. "I found us a good spot." I lead her deeper into the market and point at a bare space between a specialty jam stand and a vendor selling freshly squeezed juices. "Now, we just need your hat." I pretend to go for her hat again.

"Wil." She giggles, and I like how carefree she sounds.

"Fine, fine." I grin back at her. "We'll catch our tips in my guitar case." I place it on the ground before us, flick open the latches, and pull out my guitar, leaving the case open. "Do you need to warm up?"

"Nope. Been humming all morning. Nadine thinks I'm in a great mood."

"How can you not be? You're ditching lunch to spend time with me." El hits me in the arm, and I pretend like she really hurt me. A woman in a skirt that drags along the pavement gives us a look like we are her misbehaving children. I resist the urge to stick my tongue out at her. "Okay, okay. Wanna start with Pink's *Cover Me in Sunshine*?"

El looks up at the sky. "Looks about right. Let's do it."

Half an hour later, the alarm on my phone buzzes in the middle of Queen's *Somebody to Love*. El has a small crowd gathered around us, swaying, smiling, kids dancing, some phones are out recording us and taking photos of the sign Mateo made: WE — find us at Devil's Martini every Saturday at eight p.m. An Instagram account is next, but not without talking to El about it first.

She's lost in a song beside me, and the audience claps their hands, taps their feet, and one bloke in the back attempts to sing along with us. Not happening, mate, she's my singing partner. We finish the song, and the group breaks into applause. "Thanks everyone. That's it for us today, but we'll be back."

A disappointed "Aww," comes from the back, but others drop coins and even a few dollar bills into my guitar case. The sun is blistering now, and I'm looking at the fresh juice beside us. Can we spend some of the money we just made on ... anything? My bottle sits empty on the ground. The water would've lasted me through the whole hour, but that was before El started taking sips and finished the whole thing.

The crowd disperses, and someone slow claps. I look up to see Nick's face smirking at me. "I came by to see what all the fuss is about." He reads the sign. "Explains why you made Sarah drive like a maniac on Saturday."

I give him a "shut up" look that he chooses to ignore. "El, this is Nick. He's the director of the movie I was telling you about."

El waves at Nick. I expect her to clam up, but she doesn't. "You're the one obsessed with sunsets."

Didn't think El had the sassy comeback in her. Nick does that goofy confused look. "I might've ranted a bit when I nearly missed the start of our gig."

"Oh." He scratches the stubble on his face and sucks air through his teeth. "Had to pull rank. But now that I know the reason, I'll try to keep Saturday nights free." He crosses his arms. "You two are great."

I bend down and start sorting the money. "Thanks." El and I speak at the same time, in sync even after the music stops.

"Wil tells me you write your own songs."

I groan. Is El going to be upset? "Did some humming of my own during my morning shift. Might've bragged to Nick a bit about our writing session."

"You? Bragging? I don't believe it." El's voice is back to the happy joking tone.

Nick covers his mouth, but his laughter rings across the market. "Oh, man, she knows you well."

Nick has no idea how right he is. In the last three weeks, El's learned more about my true self than some of my uni friends did last year.

"El." Nick has his puppy dog look he uses when he wants something or wants to get away with something. I step closer to El. He's not going to ask her out; he's too head-over-heels for Sarah. So, what is this about? "Any chance you'd be interested in writing a song for what could be the next Oscar winner?"

El does clam up this time. Nick has gone too far. "I think she's too busy, mate."

"Wait." El turns to me. "Not so fast. Your friend is asking for help."

"My friend is over budget and looking for free talent." After a rocky start, the crew pulled it together and things are starting to roll, but we're short in a couple of areas, and copyright music costs.

"It's not always about the money, Wil. I'll do it if you do it with me."

"Really?"

"Yes. Is it too much? Will you have time?"

"I'll find the time. Helping the movie and writing with you? It'd be fun." The mini brainstorm the other night had me buzzed for days. Glad it won't be a one-off.

"Perfect. It's settled then. You'll write and record a song for *Indigo*." Nick leans in. "That's the name of our film."

"Oh, now I'm recording it as well?" El says it with a smile, and if she weren't wearing my shades, I'm sure I'd see her eyes shine with excitement at the prospect.

"Seems only fair. With a voice like that, you have to record it." Nick rubs his chin.

She stretches her hand to Nick. "It's a deal."

Nick shakes it. "I'll see you later. We can tell Sarah and the crew together."

With Nick gone, El turns to me. "So? How much did we make?"

"Fifty-seven dollars and ten cents."

"Oh." She sounds disappointed.

"It's great for our first time. People will get used to us, and we'll have regulars. Plus, we might see some of them at the bar, which means we get more money from Pauline for the drinks they buy. Let the time work its magic."

El takes off my sunglasses and hands them to me. "Thank you for these. And for all of this." She swivels her head around the market. "You're helping me more than you know."

"Thank you for being my friend." I put the shades on in time to break the moment, before I say another dopey line swirling in my head.

The walk to Rocker, Inc. takes all of five minutes and is full of El's humming and bad beatboxing on my part, trying to imitate what the drums track will sound like. I look at the building of glass and brick. Is Rocker in there, surrounded by his gold records?

"Does Rocker, Inc. own the whole building?"

El nods. "My favorite place is the second floor. Where the recording studios are."

"Is that where you work?"

"No, I'm up on the fourth with Nadine and the other back-of-fice folks. Dad and his partner are on the third."

Good to know. "And Sven?"

"He hangs out at the security desk mostly, when he's not doing rounds." The hulk wasn't in the lobby the last time I was here. But his colleagues politely asked me to leave, and then escorted me out after I insisted on a meeting with Rocker.

Here I am again, at his doorstep, but no closer to talking to him after weeks in LA. Opa's words resurface in my head. I shouldn't be wasting time writing songs, enjoying myself, forgetting the real reason I'm in this country. Acid eats at my stomach, and I can't meet El's gaze when she says goodbye.

The moment El disappears, exhaustion seeps in. I'm hot, hungry, and sweaty. And my plan of going to the gym before joining the film crew in the afternoon loses its luster. Some food, a cold shower, and a nap are the new marching orders.

I move the guitar case to my back and return to the market. The booth with gyros looked good, and it's okay to spend some of my busking earnings on it. It's a celebration. My phone rings as I reach the market, and the +49 country code sends my heart into overdrive. One o'clock here is what, ten p.m. at home?

"Mum?" I press the phone to my cheek, hoping she can hear me over the noise of the market.

"She's asleep." Opa's voice is a whisper, and I plug my other ear with my finger, straining to hear him.

"Speak up. I'm outside. What's going on? Is she okay?"

"Why wouldn't she be?"

"No emergency?"

"What? Why?"

The person at the food cart hands me my gyros and the soda I'm splurging on. I juggle the items and the phone and look for a spot to put down my guitar. "Opa, you're calling me out of the blue. I thought something's wrong."

"That's what you get for forgetting to call me and me having to try and catch you between whatever full life you have in Hollywood land."

The tension of Mum possibly not being okay fades, but my shoulders ache at Opa's words. El would understand. "What's going on?"

"Absolutely nothing. And that is the problem. I'm home alone all day. I fixed everything that could be fixed in the house. Your mother is always at work for hours or at physical therapy. My friends are dealing with their grandchildren, and I'm bored. Maybe I should go back to work. Part-time. What do you think?"

A couple leaves a bench in the shade, and I jog over and set my stuff down. "Opa. What about your heart? You can't have another heart attack. I need you to look after Mum."

"I'm not talking a construction site job. A handyman maybe."

"Is it boredom or is this about the bills again?"

"Both. But—"

"I'll take care of the money part. And I can send you some today. I have a couple hundred." That money was supposed to go to Mateo for spotting me the cash to pay the university for the broken window. Do I want to know where he got it from? I do not, and plausible deniability is better than satisfied curiosity. Any time an unfamiliar face appears at the door of our dorm, I make sure to leave them alone and stay out of earshot.

"That'll help, but—"

"I'm working on it." I look at the spot where El and I performed less than a half hour ago. The gyro doesn't look as appetizing anymore.

Opa rumbles some more about finding a part-time job of his own and agrees to go to bed. I pull out my bank account and transfer all the money from it into Opa's. I check the cash in my pocket, left over from busking. I have $18.72. I'll get my cut of the bar money on Saturday. It's plenty to last me until then, but it's going to be ramen for dinner again tonight.

TWENTY

El

THE WALK TO THE studio to meet Wil has become one of my favorite parts of the week. But not tonight. My stomach hurts, and I consider going home. Canceling.

I see Nick, Wil, and a tiny girl with golden hair chatting it up in front of the rehearsal hall, calm and collected like they belong there. My mouth goes dry, and my confidence in my songwriting abilities plummets. I shouldn't have said yes. I've never written on demand, or with a group. Maybe the vibe Wil and I had last week was a fluke. Opening up to him was one thing. Sharing myself with two strangers is so far out of my comfort zone, I can't even see my comfort zone anymore.

Wil sees me first, and his smile lessens my doubts. If he's taking care of the words part, I can take care of the music part.

I catch Sven's eye, and he swerves and takes the path that goes around the building.

"I hope I brought enough food." I smile and move the bag from my hands onto my shoulder.

"No one told me there'd be food." Nick rubs his hands together. "We're supposed to be doing you favors, not the other way around."

The girl rolls her eyes. "Don't mind Nick. He's going through a growth spurt."

Nick casts his eyes to the ground but smiles.

"I'm Sarah, by the way. The screenwriter."

I hold out my hand. "El."

Sarah takes it, and when her eyes meet mine, the hairs on the back of my neck rise. She knows who I am; I'm sure of it. I do my best not to run.

"Nice to meet you, El. Appreciate you helping us out here." If she recognizes me, she doesn't let on. My heart starts beating again, and my feet move forward. "And nice of you to make us dinner."

"I can't be the only one eating." I don't want to single Wil and his financial troubles out.

Frank greets the four of us with a quizzical twist of his mouth. "Are there going to be six of you next time?"

"This is for you." I take a brown paper bag from the soft-sided cooler. "Egg salad sandwich."

Frank sticks his nose inside the bag. "Mmm. The smell of my childhood."

Wil and Frank do the food and keys exchange. "Let me know if you need a bigger room," Frank whispers.

"Sure." Wil gives Frank the key back and receives a new one.

"Top floor, second door on the left."

The studio is bigger with a full engineering booth, and Wil beelines to the myriad of knobs, buttons, and sliders. "I can do some damage with this." He sounds like I did as a kid when Mom and Papa got me the giant dollhouse for my birthday.

I slip my phone into the zip pocket of Wil's bag like I did earlier at the farmers' market for safe keeping. Onto the table by the door, I put the bowl with chicken orzo salad, half a loaf of pre-cut twelve-grain bread Marta made yesterday, and a container with egg salad.

"Shoot. I forgot my water bottle."

Nick piles the egg mixture onto the bread and spoons the salad next to it.

"I lived off these and peanut butter sandwiches when I first moved to LA." Sarah hands Nick a napkin, and he smiles again.

"Wil, are you eating with us?" He lifts his head and with visible effort, detaches himself from the board. He piles the chicken orzo salad onto his plate. "I'll finish this." He eyes the bowl with the egg salad.

"We could share. Half each?"

Wil shrugs. "Okay."

We eat in silence, and I manage a few bites before my mouth goes dry with anticipation. A piece lodges in my throat and sends me into a coughing fit.

"Here." Wil offers me his banged-up metal water bottle.

I cough a couple more times into my elbow. The water doesn't taste much different from the purified stuff Marta bottles for us. "Thank you."

"Time to get to work, people." Nick's plate is empty, and he looks at the rest of us, still playing with our food.

"Let me wash my hands, first." I head to the washroom.

Sarah follows me. "I'll come too."

In the solitude of the bathroom Sarah asks. "Does he know?"

I freeze. "Does who know what?" Please, please don't recognize me. I can't lose this.

"Wil. Does he know you're Melodie Rockerby?"

I close my eyes. It's ruined. Over. I got too comfortable. Too trusting. The food sours in my stomach. I hate being right. The weight of being recognized drains the high of writing with Wil.

"Hey, hey. Don't freak out. I won't say anything to him."

"He knows."

Sarah's eyes widen. "Oh, you think I'll screw you over? I guess that's fair." She grabs a paper towel from the dispenser and hands it to me. "Listen, I have no idea what you've been through, but I do know about fighting like hell to follow a dream. I respect it."

"Are you going to tell Nick?"

Her eyes soften. "Oh, honey. I have to. I can't lie to him. But trust me, Nick is familiar with fake identities, and he'll keep your secret."

Familiar with fake identities? That should scare me off, but I must be losing my mind because I trust her.

Back in the studio Sarah leans into Nick. I'm not sure I'm okay with her telling him my real identity, but it's too late to stop this. I've come too far now and already decided to work with Wil's friends. Over time, Nick probably would've guessed on his own.

"No fucking way. Melodie Rockerby? Like *Rocker*—Rockerby? *Born on the Wrong Side* Rocker?"

Wil looks at Nick, Sarah, and me. He looks at me as if he'd done something terrible. Guilt etched on his face. "Blimey. Did I say something?"

"She guessed."

"Sorry."

Wow, two apologies from Wil, and this one wasn't even his fault.

"I didn't think. So stupid. I'll fix it."

I put a hand on his arm. Gosh, he's warm. How does he do that? It's freezing in here. "Sarah promised they'd be cool. I can trust her, right?"

Wil glances at Sarah, who's singing the chorus to Dad's signature song with Nick. They look so cute. "I'll say one thing about Sarah. She's real. If she says she won't say anything, I believe her."

She turns my way. "Have these two idiots even told you what the movie is about?"

"Nope." I shake my head.

"Figures. It's a love story between two college students who meet at a coffee shop in a bookstore called 'Indigo,' It's a Canadian bookstore chain. I'm from Toronto, in case no one mentioned that, either."

I shake my head again and catch both guys rolling their eyes in mock despair.

"Essentially, our hero woos the girl with lines from his favorite books. The girl is not into nerds, but he wins her over. When he earns a scholarship to study in England, she tells him he can't miss the opportunity." Sarah pauses to make sure I'm following. I nod for her to continue. "Five years later, he's back in Canada on a book tour for his debut novel, the story of their relationship. She surprises him by showing up at the signing, and they reunite. He moves back to Canada to be with her."

"Oh, I like that. And the song?"

Nick pipes up. "It plays over the scene when she tells him to leave. We"—Nick steps closer to Sarah—"were thinking something about letting go of the person you love because it's in that person's best interest." He looks down at Sarah. Not puppy dog eyes this time, they're soft and sincere. "Even if it hurts you."

"Do you have any lyrics yet?" I ask Wil.

"A few ideas." He walks back to where he dropped his messenger bag, takes his black book out, and heads back to us when a double beep of a phone stops him in his tracks. His body tenses. "I have to take this." He reaches back into his messenger bag, pulls the phone out, and answers. "Hallo."

His eyebrows merge, and for a moment, I'm worried. He says something I don't understand. That was not English unless my ears are broken. More rapid sounds from Wil. The hard H, the soft SH, the different way he says R. They mesh into a tight string of harsh yet soft sentences. Wil's face loses its edge, and a gentle smile rests on his lips when he's listening to the other side of the conversation. Another Wil appears, and I don't know what to call him. His expression is almost tender. He catches my eyes on him and walks away into the room with the soundboard.

Sarah and Nick are having a whispered conversation, and I know they're not trying to exclude me, but they are not paying attention to either Wil or me.

"Sorry, Mum's checking in." Wil's back. And it's the Wil with the British English accent I'm used to. The one I know best. The facts from the dossier Sven put together on him are in my head: lived with his mom and grandfather, went to a university in a different city from them. Wil the son is what I saw earlier. He never talks about his mom. Or grandad. Or his life in Germany. It's not like he's hiding it, but I rack my brain for anything Wil told me about himself. I know he was on a rowing team back home, only because of the shirt he let me wear the first night we rehearsed.

"Everything okay?"

He nods. I search for something to say. "I bet she misses you. My mom would have a fit if I moved across the world."

His lips curl into a smile. "It's not so bad. Not much different from when I'm at uni. Except for the bloody time change, and I can't come home for Sunday roast."

The food thing again. Did Wil have enough for dinner tonight? I'll have to make more next time. Maybe I can bake something tonight when I get home and bring it to him when I see him at lunch tomorrow? "Your mom a good cook?"

"The best. Opa says she could win *The Great German Bake Off*, but she doesn't want to enter."

I like hearing him talk about his mom. "Why not? Sounds like fun."

Wil's face shifts, the light in his eyes dimming. "No time." He picks up his little black book. "We should get back to this." He begins rifling through the pages.

"Here it is." Wil scoots next to me; he extends the black book my way with a page open to a series of words and phrases. They crawl up and down, sideways. The angles of his letters spike up, as if written with force and little care. I try to concentrate, make them stay still, but they jump around, and I can't make out what they are. I see the words, but there are too many of them all at once, attacking me with the lines and curves that don't form meaning.

"Would you mind reading them?"

Wil's eyes meet mine. Checking in. He shoots a glance at Sarah and Nick, who are staring at me too, now. Wil taps his nose, as if he's pondering the question, then grins, bumps my shoulder with his arm, as if this is some inside joke and nothing is weird about my request. "Sure thing." I lean into him and put my head on his shoulder in thanks, our telepathic conversation complete. "I'm thinking 'go away' should be in the chorus, but we need four syllables there."

"Go far away?" I look up at him.

His index finger points my way. "That'll work." I watch him write the phrase down, and I can see the words I told him appear on the page.

"Hey, before we get too far, could you play the melody for us?" Nick wags his finger between Sarah and him. "Wil hummed it earlier, but Sarah's not heard it at all."

I shift away from Wil and the solid warmth of his shoulder. "I have a track on my phone, or I can sing it live."

They glance at each other. "Live?"

So, I sing. The ta-da-da on the verses and o-o-o-o on the chorus. Wil picks up the guitar and joins me. On the second chorus, he adds his voice to mine in a counter melody we haven't discussed before. The room fades away, our shared energy tickles my skin, and I can sense the inspiration wrapping around us. We riff off each other and fall through the cracks into another dimension, the one where WE was born and where parts of Wil and parts of me blend into a new powerful heady mixture I can't get enough of.

TWENTY-ONE

Wil

OUR USUAL SPOT IS taken by a balloon artist. Kids flock to him and shreds of popped balloon animals litter the walkways between the stalls. I always come early enough to stake claim to this somewhat shady spot between two tents. El's fair skin is a sunburn waiting to happen. This location also has great foot traffic from the customers who stop and listen.

The only other option is in the center of the market where three rows merge and form a little plaza. The challenge is that there is nothing in this space to go behind us. We'll be surrounded by people, and playing in a circle adds a level of difficulty I'm not sure El will be interested in. I walk over and put out the portable amplifier Mateo found for me for free. I take the microphone stand out and assemble it. Over the last couple of weeks, we've collected a lot more equipment, and it helps us not strain our voices or get lost in the hubbub of the market.

I place them far enough apart to create space for El and me to have some room to move. This is the way she walks to get from Rocker, Inc., and I see her before she notices me.

"El," I shout and wave at her. She looks in my direction and changes course to join me in the center. She's wearing a wide-brimmed hat I imagine millionaires wear by the poolside or on Italian yachts. One floppy beige side droops and covers part of her face. I'll be the only one baking in full sun in the middle of August in LA.

"Why are we playing here?" She can't be angry at me.

"Our normal spot was taken. It's either here or we skip to-day."

El tucks her phone into the pocket of my bag for safekeeping and takes her microphone out. "We are not skipping." It's hard not to smile at her determination.

It takes us a couple of songs to get used to the new arrangement. I ham it up when I don't have a singing part and move closer to her, doing my best sidekick routine. Mostly, I give her the space to shine, to take over and cover the chatter of the shoppers with another verse. I spot a few familiar faces, our regulars, including the bloke who was there the first day and likes to sing along.

Everyone is swaying to the music, eyes on El, as she claims center stage. She takes full advantage of her wireless mic, skims the edge of the crowd gathered around us, bending down to the kids and giving her long floor-length skirt a swish. It's like she's done this before.

We sing one more song after the alarm goes off for El to go back to the office. I want to keep going, especially with this crowd that's eating up the music and tossing money into my guitar case, but we can't risk Sven getting suspicious. Him not knowing what El is up to during her lunch hour is more important than the extra ten dollars we can get if we keep playing.

And once again, my minutes with El draw to a close. Snatching an hour at lunchtime during the work week to sing here and another on Saturday nights at the Devil's Martini is not enough. Nick and Sarah took over our Wednesday rehearsals, and I'm fed up with sharing El's time with someone else.

El dismantles my mic stand and folds it so it fits perfectly into my duffle. "Are Sarah and Nick coming tonight?"

"Only Nick can make it. Sarah's working. And you know Nick the control freak. He can't not be there when you're recording." I tally up today's haul. It's bigger than it's ever been at the other location. Maybe my luck has kicked in again.

She hands me my water bottle. "I washed it. Thanks for lending it to me."

"Keep it. I got a new one." I hold up a new bottle with SFF for Starlight Filmmakers Foundation in large letters on it. "Can't believe the competition is almost over. We're near the finish line. And your song will get us there."

"I hope I don't mess it up." She adjusts her hat, looking like she's about to jet to a tropical island.

"You won't. I'll be there, and you know the vocals like the back of your hand."

She looks at her splinted fingers. "I'm so ready to get this off."

"We'll have to celebrate."

"I'll celebrate by playing on the piano with two hands. Never thought I'd miss the hours of practice." She adjusts her hat. "And I'm sure I'll have to build new calluses for the guitar. I forgot what the strings feel like."

She'll play with both hands. And on a guitar. Is that a hint? She won't need me anymore? I snap the lid on my guitar case with more force than I intended.

El's hand lands on my shoulder. "How about adding a dueling guitars bit to our act? I might even let you win."

She's not giving me the slip after all. "Not sure there'll be any 'letting.' I'm that good."

"Excuse me?" A tall woman in a farmer's hat with a clipboard clutched under her armpit waves at us. "You and I need to have a talk." She pulls the clipboard out and clicks the end of a ballpoint pen in her hand. "I'll need your information: names, email address, a phone I can reach you at."

El and I look at each other.

"I wrote down that your group name is WE, and you are El and Wil, and I hear you play at the Devil's Martini on Saturdays." She smiles, and though uncertainty about her request remains, she loses a threatening quality. "It would be great if you could commit to a set schedule for the market as well. We have a roster for the weekends, but weekdays are such a hit and miss."

"Are we in trouble?" El asks the question that's on my mind.

"Trouble? No, dear, not at all. We love having musicians here, and you two sound like you're going far. I guess I was hoping you can come for longer than an hour?"

El digs into the pocket of my bag and gets her phone out. "Maybe ninety minutes?" She starts typing with one thumb. "I really have to run." And she runs, more like jogs, to the exit.

The woman shoves the board to me, and I put down my email and phone number, leaving the spaces for our last names blank.

El holds the note, and I resist the urge to turn up the gain. It's at the perfect level for this song, but I know I could amp it up, have her voice blast through. But that's not what's right for this portion.

Nick sits to my right, his elbows on his knees, chin resting on long fingers steepled together. He looks as enthralled as I feel. Watching El sing, being in her presence is awe-inspiring. I can see the superstar she's going to be one day. Can't believe I'm lucky enough to be able to record this. Record her. Be with her.

Her voice fades, and silence creeps into the studio. I hit pause on the recording, stop, and ensure it's uploading to my phone.

"Is it okay?" El's voice is small, timid, the opposite to the powerhouse that was coming out of her mouth moments ago.

How can she doubt herself after a performance like that? My skin is still covered in goosebumps.

"Okay?" Nick rises to his feet. "That was fucking amazing." No need to turn up the gain on his voice.

El looks at the floor. Weeks of performing at the bar and busking, where the crowds get bigger and bigger, and the beanpole's compliment flusters her. Her parents really did a number on her. Did Rocker have a hand in this? If so, Mum did the right thing keeping me from him.

The beanpole picks up his backpack, slings the navy sack over his shoulder, and holds his hand up for a high five. "Good work, little buddy. I gotta go pick up Sarah from the club. Talk later." I hit his hand and watch as he walks over to El, offers her a low five and exits.

"Do you want to do another take?" El's voice rings through the booth.

"Do you?"

"Well"—she twists her hair around a finger—"I thought I kinda nailed it on that last one."

"I agree. Nick's right. It was amazing."

"Cool. I guess that's it then." She looks at her watch. I glance at my phone. There's still twenty minutes left before Sven comes to pick her up. I don't want her to go.

"Hey, what about we take a run at your song for the video?" Her head pops up. "I'd love a crack at mixing it. I mean, Lenard Astor will do a professional job but . . ."

"You're a professional."

"Thanks for the compliment, but hardly. Still learning here."

"Everyone has to start somewhere." She offers me a small smile. "Maybe you have fresh ideas."

I chuckle at the thought. How is it she can have such confidence in me and not a shred for herself?

"Let's test that theory. D'you have your music?"

"Always." She digs in her bag and pulls out the now familiar tablet. I leave the sound board, join her in the studio, and take my usual spot on her left. She scoots closer, her hip brushes my finger, and I shove my greedy hands in my pockets, settling for the scent of the beach that is El. How long has it been since it's just been the two of us? No crowds, no fans, no friends. Just El and me. Together.

She unlocks the tablet, and it comes alive in her hand. The notes and lines on the screen are the key to how she interprets life. What a privilege to be included in this secret world of hers. If only her parents knew what hides behind that locked screen. Once Lenard Astor makes her video, they won't be able to deny her talent.

"I added the new line you suggested." I try to focus on the words standing out in black and white below the familiar bars of music that accompany them, but I'd rather look at her.

Because Wednesdays I can see the real El. No disguises, no wigs like at the bar, no fashionista outfits like at the farmers' market. The simple T-shirt, shorts, and running shoes are her. It's just El. Here. Now. No princess or rock star's daughter. Just a girl with hopes and dreams.

"Perfect, don't you think?"

I swallow. "I do."

Twenty minutes pass in a blink, and it's time to go. I put my stuff into my bag when my phone buzzes with the Indigo group chat.

Sarah: Did you ask her yet?

El's packing up her tablet. I gather my things and walk toward her.

"So—" Why's my voice shaking? "Nick's got the first cut of the film done. The team and a few of our friends are getting together to watch it. And, well, you're part of the team. Wanna come?" Smooth, Wil, real smooth.

She stops at the door; her bag is over her shoulder, and the back of her head moves as if she's about to turn, but she doesn't. "Oh. Um. When?"

Blimey. I hate how everything has to be scheduled, approved. I want to grab her hand, run out of this building, and do something ridiculous. Go down to Santa Monica pier, eat ice cream, ride the stupid Ferris wheel without her disguise or a bodyguard. How can she stand this? For the second time today, I'm glad Mum kept me from this life.

"How about next week?"

"Next week Zoe's in Norway. Can't pretend I'm out with her. I'll have to make a deal with Sven."

We don't need a babysitter, but if it means more time with El . . . "Sven can come too. And we'll do it here. Frank told me there's a small screening room in the basement."

She does a one-eighty, and her eyes betray her excitement. "Really? They wouldn't mind me crashing your screening party?"

"Mind? It was Sarah's idea to have you watch with us. She insisted." And I want you there. "Say you'll come."

Her lips turn up, and I know I've won. "I'll be there."

Twenty-Two

El walking toward me in the late afternoon sun is maybe my favorite part of the week. I can stare and admire for a long time. The whole evening stretches before us, and I have no idea what to expect. What food will she bring this time? Her long dress hugs her curves, the canary yellow color stands out against the green shrubbery lining the path. It's a shame her fiery hair has to be locked away under a hat. Today, it's a narrow-brimmed white faux-straw Panama hat paired with large sunglasses that cover half her face.

Sven doesn't run away this time, no nighttime jog. He's joining us for the show. The button-down shirt barely contains his muscles. Nice effort. The Hulk cleans up well.

I slow clap. "Sven, my friend, no short shorts today?"

"Don't push it." His shoulders drop a millimeter lower, confirming he gets my joke. Maybe we can be friends.

I don't have my guitar tonight, no need, as we are watching *Indigo*, but I wouldn't deny her a butter tart. I hold out the bag from the only place in LA that sells the treats. "Put this away before Nick sees it. He'll charm you with those puppy dog eyes until you share with him."

She throws back her head and laughs so hard her hat starts sliding off, and she barely manages to grab it. The little pull inside me I got the few times I really made her laugh tugs so hard it tears through the layers of obligations, money problems, and the need to stay on track. I burst into laughter alongside her because she's infectious. And I can't protect myself from her anymore.

"Puppy dog eyes. So true." She checks the area around the door. "Where are the others?"

"Everyone's already here. You're the last to arrive."

Her expression changes, mouth curving in the opposite direction. "Am I late?"

"No, right on time." I open the door for her, nod at Frank on the way. El stops at his desk and pulls out a small red and white container. He winks at her. This is new. Frank's a winker now. El changes people. Makes everything brighter.

We take the stairs down to the basement, and I miss another one of our rituals. The few moments in the lift. Sunscreen and the beach invading my senses. My weekly hit.

The screening room seats twenty people in four rows of five plush red seats. Our group takes up half the place. Besides the *Indigo* crew of Sarah, Nick, Riyaz, and Bri, Sarah's roommate Siobhan is here, and I couldn't not invite Mateo. He's competition, but no one on the crew objected to my roommate tagging along as well. Both teams' films are done. Not like he can steal it and submit it to the judges instead of theirs.

"Feck Me, aren't you a fine fella? Use those muscles for good, do ya?" Siobhan shakes Sven's hand. For his part, the Viking scans her from toe to the turquoise hair piled on top of her head in some messy ponytail, and I think I see his mouth twitch. It's the most emotion I've ever seen from the man. Don't blame him, the girl has all the right stuff in all the right places. And she knows it.

Sarah greets El with her usual warm smile but doesn't hug her. Our screenwriter is in tune with El, like she understands El doesn't like hugs or physical contact in general. I leave El in Sarah's safe care while I introduce Sven to Nick, who's in the small room behind the projector.

There's a commotion, and I can't see El for the crush of people around her. Both Sven and I jump.

"What is it?" Bri holds their phone up high, stands on their tiptoes, and snaps pictures of El swarmed by the ravenous gang. I want to tell Bri to stop taking photos, but that's even riskier. No way to explain why. The snaps are bound to surface on her Instagram. Would anyone suspect? I look at my princess. Her sunglasses are off but she's not wearing any makeup and the boho-chic outfit gives her a soft romantic look, a polar opposite to the glossy Melodie Rockerby. Only those in the know would.

"I brought popcorn, of course." El's pulling more of the red and white containers from her bag and passing them around. The smell everyone associates with the movies fills the air.

"Bang on." Siobhan grabs a red and white container, cracks open the lid, and tosses a few of the white puffed kernels into her mouth.

"I brought toppings too. There's sour cream and onion, cheese, and dill pickle. Had to sneak that one past my mother."

"Why?" Mateo asks.

El raises her hand to her mouth like she's said a swear word in front of her grandmother. "She's pickle obsessed lately."

"Pass the cheese," demands Riyaz.

Sarah pats El's shoulder. "This is wonderful. Thank you."

"Thanks for inviting me."

"We wouldn't have it any other way. You're part of the team."

Siobhan slings her arm around El. "Honorary member, just like me. I provide moral support, and my living room has been their script room for the last two months." Sarah pulls her roommate away from El. "What, I had to miss The Bachelorette Reunion special because of you tossers. I should get credit."

"Yes, yes, Siobhan, you're already in my acceptance speech."

"Before or after your gran?"

"Ahem." Nick's voice cuts through the chatter, and we all turn to look at him. "If you'll kindly take your seats, the show is about to begin."

"Dramatic much?" Sarah rolls her eyes at her friend's snarky remark. Sven and I bookend El as we walk down the aisle to take our seats. I'm not going to get a minute alone with her tonight. At least the hulk of a man doesn't try to sit between us but lands in a seat on the other side of El. Siobhan plops herself down beside Sven and for once, I'm glad the busybody is here. Maybe she can divert his attention.

"Notice anything different about me today?"

I study El. The dress hits her ankles, hiding her slim legs, so that can't be it. No way she cut her hair. I move to tug the hat off to confirm the halo of red with its signature white streak is still intact when she raises her hand to stop me. Her pale white hand. I blink, look at her other hand, a shade darker. "Your fingers. No more brace?"

"Yup. Came off this afternoon." She beams at me. My hand goes for the fingers, curious, but then I pause. Will it hurt her? "They need physical therapy to regain their strength, but you can touch them."

Her delicate hand appears vulnerable without the splints I've seen protecting it. I reach out and run the pad of my finger from her wrist up to the tip of her index finger. Her skin is cool, soft, and I can't stop. I continue over her nail, over and onto the bend of the index finger, down into the hollow between it and the next one. She turns her hand over, and I make it to the tip of her middle finger.

They are just fingers, and they should not make me feel like, what? Like I have a right to do this. Like touching her sends my blood boiling, spreading the heat across every limb. Like I'm running a fever every time she's close, every time our bodies come in contact I need a cold shower. A series of cold showers. And she stays cool when I combust.

The lights flick off, and the screen before us comes to life with an old-fashioned film countdown from ten. I place each of my fingers against hers, and she doesn't move her hand away. Mine is so much bigger; her fingers support mine. My breath catches. Why is she not pulling away? I find her face and can see the reflection of the numbers descending in her eyes. She points to the screen with a soft jut of her chin. "Aren't you supposed to look at the screen?"

I swallow and shift in my seat to focus on the reason we are here, resting my arm on the padded bar between us, where El's arm sits. Our skin touches: elbows, wrists; my palm lies on top of hers, and she still does not pull away but moves her elbow toward her body, giving me more room on the armrest. Space away from her is the last thing I need. I lace my fingers through hers, tug her back to the middle, and lean in to whisper in her ear, "We can share."

The actors on the screen are no longer the theater geeks I spent the last eight weeks recording with. The bookstore is a perfect backdrop to the quotes he peppers his speech with. The orchestration I put under some of them brings elegance to the scenes and underlines the romantic feel Nick insisted they lacked on their own. I notice a couple of places where I need to clean up the tracks but don't go to my black book. That'd mean letting go of El's hand, and I'm keeping it as long as she lets me. Whatever fluke keeps her fingers between mine, I'm not messing it up.

The dark night of the soul scene, as Sarah insisted on calling it, comes, and Nick was right. The bright day, the liveliness of the lead's face contradicts the words she says, her sending him away. And that's when El's voice weaves its way to the background first. The couple faces off, their eyes speak to each other, and El sings what they think. What we in the audience don't want them to agree to. They are meant to be together. Not apart. El's hand slips out of mine. I turn to her.

Her eyes are full of tears. She's covering her mouth and wiping the liquid that keeps rolling down her cheeks. Despite a sniffle, she remains glued to the screen, where he doesn't turn away as he walks backward to the door. Their eyes still locked, still carrying on the silent conversation Nick captured by moving between their perspectives.

The only sound is El's clear voice; the haunting music pours into our ears and souls. The final few soft notes of the piano, the last phrase promising to never forget, never regret, kiss the air, and then it's gone. He's gone. She's gone. There's a lump in my throat. I don't want him to go. The sadness they feel we feel too, seeping in and taking hold. The bittersweet moment of hearts tearing to let the other be what they are meant to be. I am not going to cry.

The screen fades to black. A moment of silence, an eternity for us to adjust to the new reality. A world where love doesn't win, doesn't conquer all, doesn't survive.

A sunrise, and the screen fills with energy again. Life moves on, the characters grow up, change, evolve more than they wanted to. I miss El's voice already, I miss her hand more. I don't watch the screen, only see Nick's brilliant cinematography through El, can't stop staring at her. Her reactions tell me the story of the movie better than if I watch it again.

Lines form on her forehead. She's breathing fast, and I want to reassure her everything will work out. Tell her there'll be a happy ending, love will conquer all. But I resist and let her experience the years apart.

Relief flushes through me when I watch her see the main character hand the love of her life the book containing the story of their passion for him to sign. I'm rewarded with a smile: small, but hopeful. She can see it now. The possibility. The hope. The smile grows, and her forehead relaxes. My heart expands with her joy. The corners of her eyes form creases as she can't stop smiling when together, they walk through the same door that separated them five years ago. In that moment, we all believe in true love.

The credits start, and El turns her beaming face to me. "Thank you."

"What for?" I whisper back.

"For letting me be part of the magic."

TWENTY-THREE

El

THE LAST OF MOM'S four suitcases make their way out to the waiting SUV. You'd think she was leaving the house for a couple of months and not a long weekend.

"Maybe we should stay." Mom canceled all her performances and has not been farther than Orange County since the last in vitro treatment was successful. Four months in the same place is a record for the woman who dragged me around the globe, a new city every couple of months.

"Dad wants to treat you, Mom. He has everything planned to the smallest detail." He's been talking my ear off about this place for weeks now. We brainstormed resorts for a getaway close enough to LA they could drive, but far enough it felt like a vacation. The retreat he settled on caters to expecting mothers. Dad thinks of everything.

"It'll be great. Just you two, pampered in your private abode. The seven-hour drive is worth it." She purses her lips, and I know what she's worrying about. "And it's near Tucson if you need any medical attention. You can't cancel." I'm trying not to be obvious, but I'd like the house to myself. Three days without my parents breathing down my neck . . . heck yeah, I want them to go.

"The resort has a no phone policy, but I'll try to sneak mine in. But if I can't—you call them, and they will find us. And I told them to wake us up or interrupt any session we're in if you need anything." Mom's holding my now splint-less hand between both of hers, her eyes inches away from mine, as if she can engrave the information in my brain with the laser beams of her eyes.

"Mandy emailed you our schedule. And I keep reminding your mother you don't need a babysitter. Just a bodyguard." Dad winks at me as if he is funny.

I hold up my phone. "Got it. Promise to call if I stub my toe." Dad smiles, and Mom bites her lip. I rub her arm. "I'll be fine. Don't worry. You focus on relaxing, enjoy this babymoon before Alfonzo comes." It's our new game, coming up with uncool names for baby boy Rockerby.

"Good one." Dad offers me a high five. I jump up and tap his hand.

"You two are incorrigible."

"I'll make it up to you, love, say, with a foot massage to start. We'll see where that takes us." Dad gives Mom a kiss that offers me a clear idea of what he's imagining as the follow-up.

"I'll make sure to scrub my brain of that image the minute the door closes behind you."

Dad gives me another wink that apparently no woman can resist and puts his arm around his wife, tugging her toward the door. "Let's hit the road. Don't want to miss the dinner I have planned for us."

The best way to take my mind off my parents' activities in the back of the SUV is talk therapy, and Zoe's been after me for two weeks.

Me: A run at Runyon Canyon?

Zoe: Call it a walk and I'm in.

Me: We'll pick you up in an hour.

Zoe: Not even asking if I have plans?

Me: Do you have plans?

Zoe: Does scrolling through Pinterest for inspiration count?

Me: Fresh air will do you good.

"You have two songs now?"

Zoe stops and stretches her left leg. Even two meters away I can feel Sven tense up. He does it more than usual on these runs with my cousin. Well, a fast walk at best. Today, it's more of a stroll. Sven likes Runyon Canyon because the up and down terrain gives us a challenge. But not when Zoe's with us. My personal Superman starts running on the spot where we've stopped.

"Well, one is mine and the other is a collaboration. *Our Lines* is for the movie."

"But you wrote it." I open my mouth to protest, but she cuts me off. "Yes, yes, you wrote it with Wil, but the point is you're creating music. Not just singing covers anymore."

I never thought about it that way. The only melody I could set words to before was the song I planned to record with Len. I've always had music in my head which I picked out on the piano, but the words, they stopped me. They never felt real. The things I've written with Wil, they have weight, they're solid. I'm not playing around anymore. I'm creating songs. "Yeah. And I want to do more."

Zoe lunges at me and wraps me in her arms as I let only her. She jumps and squeals in my ear. "This is exciting." After eighteen years of this, you'd think I'd be used to it. I jump with her. It is exciting.

Sven sprints a hundred meters ahead, turns, runs back, and repeats the loop.

"People are looking." A lot of famous people run these hills, and it's an unwritten rule that everyone has a certain amount of anonymity. Aside from sometimes hanging out at the main entrance, the press basically stays out, and you rarely see someone snapping photos.

My cousin gives me a squeeze then releases me. "Let 'em." She beams back at me. "Wow, I go away for three weeks, and it's a whole new Mel. Will you write a song about me?"

I laugh. Zoe pouts. Sven sweats. I wind my arm through Zoe's to propel us forward. "I'll think about it."

"Yes." She pulls her fist down in a pumping motion. "It has to have a kick-ass beat. No sappy stuff for my song."

"Noted. And I don't write sappy stuff."

"Um, I beg to differ. Remember, I've heard your stuff. 'I want to taste sweet freedom somewhere else.'"

I groan. That was bad. I can see the difference so clearly now. Wil took that line and spun it into gold. "Well, that line has changed a bit. It's now 'One way or other, I'll leave your palace.'"

"Oooh, me likey. Actually"—she meets my eye—"it's really good."

A warmth spreads through my chest. I've never sought my cousin's approval. She has her fashion obsession, and I have my music. Unlike my parents, Aunt Patti supports Zoe's dreams, going to the ends of the earth to get her a bolt of fabric or accessory for the latest outfit. She's brilliant. I like every post of hers on Instagram and even copy her now and again when it's something tamer than her usual flamboyant style. She made me a beautiful dress for my last birthday that I haven't had the courage to wear yet. I'm proud of her. I just never thought she could be proud of me.

"Melodie, we should move." Sven's impatience is showing.

"Why don't you"—Zoe adjusts Sven's baseball cap—"do a loop around the park, and Mel and I'll meet you at the west entrance?"

To my relief, Sven nods and takes off without a word.

"I thought he'd never leave. Now, we can plan for the party on Monday. Your parents don't come back from that spa place in Arizona until Tuesday, right?"

"Zoe, I don't know."

"Oh, Mel, come on. The place will be basically empty. Marta's leaving for her niece's wedding. Give Sven the day off, and we're golden. I'll only invite a few friends. Ten tops." She squeezes my arm. "You could invite Wil."

"I'm sure he has better things to do."

"And you know this how?"

"He's a student. And he works." How do I get out of this? I love my cousin to bits, but I'm not ready for her to meet Wil yet. I want him all to myself a little longer. Once he sees her, I'm sure she'll try to pick him up, or vice versa. They have a lot in common: outgoing, fun-loving, self-centered. They'd make a cute couple.

"Fine. It's settled. You're inviting him."

The entrance is up ahead. I can get out of this conversation when Sven returns. "We'll see."

"You know I always get what I want."

"Well, not always. Remember when you were into unicorns, and you wanted one for your birthday party?"

A grin splits Zoe's face. "And Dad brought home that horse wearing a horn strapped to its head with a sparkly purple headband."

We burst into thirteen-year-old-us giggles.

Too absorbed in the joy of laughing, too wrapped up in my thoughts of parties with Zoe, too comfortable. I let my guard down. I don't notice him step toward me.

"Melodie, are you excited?"

Twenty-Four

THE COFFEE SHOP IS buzzing with people. All summer, Saturdays have been manageable, but with the school year ramping up there's been little down time. Everyone needs their caffeine fix. I have to keep pushing away the lines itching to escape from my brain until I can get a minute to write them down in my notebook.

"Extra hot cappuccino with a shot of vanilla." Nick shouts the order of the last customer in line.

The espresso machine hisses, and I feel my phone vibrate against my leg. It's not the double buzz buzz of Mum or El's text, so I don't bother with it. I hand the final cappuccino to the Instagram-star-in-training who was checking me out, long raven hair falling in ringlets around her face covered in too much makeup. The phone buzzes again and again. I wipe off the film of milk from the frother's nozzle and toss the rag in the bin. My pants continue to vibrate. Whoever it is, they are impatient.

With no line for a moment, I pull out my phone. A string of notifications shows up on the home screen.

Melodie Won't Face the Music

Rockstar's Daughter Refuses to Comment

The alert I set up for anything to do with El is exploding. On the last one, there's a frozen picture of El with a microphone stuck in her face.

Watch Melodie Rockerby's Reaction to a Question About Her New Brother

"I need five," I tell Nick.

"Sure."

I slip into the back room, close the door to drown out the chatter of the café, and tap on the video.

The screen comes to life with a laughing El walking along a dirt path, a statuesque girl with straight brown hair in tow. El's red strands are held back by a white headband, and she's wearing that tight hot-pink tank top I like. I smile at how relaxed she looks.

The camera shakes as the owner runs toward El, breaking the idyllic moment when he shoves a microphone in her face.

"Melodie, are you excited?" the voice off camera yells at her.

She jerks back, and I see the concern in the creases marring her forehead. "Sorry?"

"We heard the good news. Are you excited about being a sister?"

Her mouth makes that little O I like causing when I mess with her. But it isn't so cute when someone else is doing it. I want to swat that microphone away. Her friend has the same idea and pushes El forward, out of the line of the nosy reporter.

He isn't giving up that easily but jogs alongside El. "Is Rocker excited to get a son to carry on the family name? Are you being replaced?"

Where the fuck is Sven? He's supposed to protect her from these leeches. Her friend is trying to shield El, but she doesn't have the right body build for it. "No comment," comes from the brunette. El needs the Viking; he'd squash this scum like a bug. And his camera friend too. I want them squashed.

"What do you think about having a brother?" another voice chimes in.

The reporter's question hits me. Brother?

My heart vaults. No, no, no. We're not related. The word sounds wrong. Off. Not possible. My pulse seconds the worry in my brain. There's no way they could've realized who I am. El can't find out this way.

I look around the dark storeroom as if a paparazzo might pop out and ask me a question as well. My blood is pounding in my ears. My vision blurs. I collapse on the crate by my feet. How did they find out about me? It's not possible. No one knows I'm Rocker's son except Mum and Opa.

The video doesn't stop. "How's your mother feeling? The baby's due in December, right?"

The brother they are talking about is not me. I exhale to slow down the throbbing in my temples. My cover is not blown. The pounding in my head subsides, and I can see the full picture. They are asking El about her mom. Sylvia must be pregnant.

"What would your father have thought?" The reporter keeps shouting his questions. My next breath comes out as a snicker. Rocker gets the son he actually wants.

Big blue eyes fill the camera as it zooms in on her, wanting a reaction. What an arsehole, asking about her dead father. If she wanted to say something about him, she would've done so already, but every interview I've seen where they tried to get El to talk about it, she never said a word.

The only information about his death seems to be the original account of the boating accident in Italy, with pictures of Lake Como full of whitecaps. Or images of Sylvia dressed in black, devastated and being consoled by her sisters at the funeral, no El in sight.

The shot goes dark as a massive chest steps into the frame. Sven. What took him so long? "Melodie is not talking to the press today. Back up." At last. Shouldn't he have been there to begin with?

I breathe again as the camera cuts off with El climbing into the back of a silver SUV. She's safe, and the reporters can't touch her now. I look at the timestamp of the video: posted twenty-two minutes ago. Texting El is a need and not a rational thought.

Me: You OK?

No response.

Me: I saw the video.

Nothing.

Me: That reporter is a wanker.

Why isn't she answering me? I drum my fingers against the phone. I must know if she's okay. Of course, she's okay. It was just a reporter asking questions—not that bad, but that look on her face. I've never seen her look that way. I've seen her nervous, angry, but never scared.

I check my phone again. Still no answer.

There's a knock on the door, and I jump.

"Wil, need your help out here."

Hot steam and sticky syrup fill the next few hours, but not in a good way. The stream of customers at the café doesn't let up until my shift ends. I send another text to El asking if we are still performing tonight. Nothing comes back.

After my shower, I try again.

Me: I'm headed to the bar now.

Silence.

The Devil's Martini is already busy when I arrive.

"Daylight saving time isn't until November." Pauline looks at me with suspicion. I couldn't stand another hour at the dorm.

"Better early than late, right?" I put my messenger bag and my guitar by the chair I can monitor the door from.

"As long as both of you are here before your set time."

I give her a confident nod when I'm anything but. The look of permanent self-assurance is a trick I mastered a long time ago.

My outside may fool Pauline, but words of worry about El strike at my brain. I get my notebook out.

Paparazzi.

The life with a camera on you.

Brothers not brother. Fathers not father.

Public eye.

Every time the door opens, I raise my head, only to be disappointed by El not entering the backstage lounge, a churn in my stomach. But I keep looking. She'll show. She has to. This time, the door opens and it's not El, but it's a familiar sight. Ten minutes before eight Sven fills the doorway, barrel chest blocking out the hallways behind him. I stifle the urge to shove him aside. Is El with him?

A lifetime later, Sven moves and a pale girl with long blonde hair walks in. El. She's here. Dressed in the familiar outfit of green pant-skirt thing and the white top, she reminds me of the first night we met, and the look of frozen panic in her eyes matches the one she had on stage that day. My presence reassured her then, maybe I can do it again. Not hugging her takes more of an effort than it should.

"Hey."

"Hi." Something's off with her voice, and it sends chills up the back of my neck.

"I've been texting you all day."

Her eyes widen. "Oh, sorry. I had my phone off. I . . . I . . . Paparazzi. It was—"

"I saw. It was all over social." Her eyes fall to the floor. I step closer. "Are you okay?"

"Sure."

I don't believe it. "We don't have to do the gig."

Her head jerks up. "You don't want to?"

"No. I mean, yes." What's wrong with me? Words never fail me. They are my shield, my sword, my magic wand. They're something I can always count on. I take a breath. "Miss basking in my weekly dose of adoring fans? Never."

They almost fail me tonight, but what I manage to say is enough to produce a weak smile on a too-white face of the girl my fingers long to touch. Waiting until we're on stage is too far in the future because I need to know she's okay. "Your wig is . . ."

Her hand brushes the synthetic locks. "What?"

I reach out and stroke the blonde tresses, skimming my thumb along her forehead. There's nothing wrong with her hair, but the excuse works. I draw it out, running my thumb down her face, along her cheek, and back again. "You sure you want to do this?"

She nods.

Sven coughs.

I pull my hand away.

On stage, once again we are in another world. It's like out in the dark, past the spotlight, the city might be invaded by aliens, and it wouldn't matter. Our two voices blending here and now is the life I want to live. When the set ends, I grab El's hand and raise it above our heads before we bow. I've done it a million times, but this time I don't let go, and she doesn't pull away. We walk hand-in-hand stage left and over to Sven, who stood there the entire performance.

"We should go for ice cream." No idea where that came from.

Sven shakes his head. "Not tonight." Now, he decides to do his job.

I open my mouth to object when El releases my hand and steps away. "I should go home. Marta almost caught us sneaking out."

She walks away, and I let her. I have no choice. No claim to her. I'm just a guitarist she pays. And even that'll be ending soon. I can't expect her to confide in me.

When I lie in bed unable to sleep, I imagine an alternate universe where there are no secrets between us. Where we can talk the night away. Just us.

TWENTY-FIVE

THERE'S A KNOCK AT my door.

"El, I made breakfast."

"Come in."

Marta shoves open the door with her foot and bustles into my bedroom with the wooden tray usually reserved to deliver soup when I'm sick. Our housekeeper is a firm believer in sitting at the table to eat, and you have to be on your sickbed to get a bowl of ice cream in bed. She places a feast before me: eggs, bacon, waffles, preserves, whipped cream, syrup in a tiny glass jar, mini brioche, grapefruit juice, a pot of tea, and my favorite cup and saucer. It has pink flowers and raised bumps like lace in the fine-bone china that feel like my own personal brail when I run my fingers over it.

"Marta, you didn't have to."

She sits on the end of my bed. "You didn't eat last night. I'll not have your mother come home to find you wasting away. She'll dock my salary."

It's our long-standing joke. Mom adores Marta. Has since the day Rocker introduced them. She's been his housekeeper since the beginning of time. Or at least since he got famous enough to afford a housekeeper. If there is anyone in this country who has job security, it's Marta.

I feign a smile. Marta doesn't buy it. "I think I should stay here this weekend."

"No, you can't. You bought those tickets months ago. I know how much you've been looking forward to your niece's wedding. You have to go."

"I don't want to leave you alone."

"I'm not a kid anymore. I'm an adult. I think I can manage a few days by myself." Marta doesn't look convinced. "I've got that new Cole Sprouse series to binge. You'll be bored stiff."

Marta purses her lips. "Promise me you'll eat properly." She eyes my untouched breakfast.

I pick up a brioche and stuff it into my mouth. "Every bite," I say with my mouth full. She shakes her head and pushes herself off the bed. One down, two more to go.

With a cup full of tea, I grab my phone from the side table and text Zoe: The party is off.

Zoe: Figured as much. Wanna come over here?

Me: Paparazzi are camped out at the end of the driveway. No escaping them.

Zoe: I hate them.

Me too, Zoe, me too.

Zoe: Consider coming over. Please.

Me: I'll think about it.

I will think about it because I know I'm not doing it. So, it's not a lie.

The mostly empty tray in hand, I make my way downstairs, handwash my dishes, and leave them in the rack to dry. I steel myself for my next task. Sven.

I find him swatting away at the stuffed red bag hanging in the gym off the bungalow where he lives with the other security team members. His punches remind me of the staccato beating of my heart when the reporter accosted me in the park yesterday. "Shouldn't you be leaving soon?"

"Not going." Another punch. This one sends the leather swinging so hard I think I hear the hook squeak in protest.

I sit down on a flat piece of equipment covered in red leather. "You have to go."

"Nope."

This man is so stubborn. The bag in front of him is more movable.

"I'll stream BTS at top volume all day."

"I have ear plugs."

"How will you hear me cry for help when the press breaks down the gate?"

Sven grabs the bag and squeezes it. "Not funny, Melodie."

"No, it's not, Sven." I elongate his name. "It's stupid for you to cancel. He's depending on you."

His arms freeze in the air. His mouth moves, and I know he's grinding his teeth, caught between two worlds, not knowing who to protect, who to disappoint—me or Trevor. Sven grabs a towel, wipes it across his barely sweating brow, and ice-blue eyes find mine. "I don't want to leave you alone."

"I want to be alone. Please." His shoulders slump. "Or I won't make red velvet cupcakes for your DC Comic Club bake sale."

"You wouldn't."

"Try me."

Sven attempts the stare, but I'm immune today. His brother needs him.

"You go with Trevor to visit his father, and I'll make a double batch."

"With cream cheese icing?"

"Is there any other kind?"

An hour later, Sven speeds down the driveway. I refuse to think about the reporters camped at the gate.

And I'm alone. Finally.

My phone vibrates in my back pocket. If it's Mom again, I swear I'm ignoring it. I glance at the screen and smile.

Wil: Can you chat?

Like he's ever asked me that before.

Me: Yup.

Wil: I have a new line of lyrics for Don't Give Me Comfort.

Straight to the point. That's more like Wil. No coddling me or treating me like a baby the rest of this house still thinks I am. How can I not adore him for that?

Me: Really? Spill.

Wil: I need to show you in person. Can you come to the studio today?

And I'm a prisoner in my own home. Again.

Me: Sorry. Can't escape.

Wil: I'm off today and tomorrow. Any time will do. The studio isn't booked. I checked.

I hate to disappoint him. I could take the car. Nope. Pointless. The reporters would follow me. Even in a disguise. They followed Marta to the grocery store once like I was hiding in her trunk. Ravenous when they think there's a story.

Me: Reporters at my door. Can we do it over video?

No dots. Maybe he's mad.

Wil: Not the same.

I stare at the screen. Possibilities swirl in my head. Maybe instead of a party with Zoe and her friends, I can have a party of two. It's not a bad idea. Might even be a good one. Will take my mind off yesterday.

I tap my teeth. Would I dare? I don't let my fear stop me. My fingers shake, but I keep typing.

Me: Come here.

I expect a denial, a suddenly-I'm-busy message. His response is instant.

Wil: Send directions.

The lock on the sliding glass doors leading to the pool offers a soft click. I pause and wait for a security guard to shout, "Who's there?" but everything is silent. The new guy Sven insisted stay here is camped out by the front gate, monitoring the paparazzi and making sure none of them decide to scale the fence, which happened before.

I run down the side of the yard, past the grotto with the hot tub, and don't stop until I'm in the trees. The side yard is not in direct line of sight from the guard booth, and I'm being extra cautious, but if I manage to get Wil inside the house, we can relax. I find the latch. The gate between the Menkens' property and ours doesn't have a lock, and if Sven knows about it, he never bothered to rectify the situation. It's not like they are in Malibu much these days; weekly staff visits is all the traffic I see. I skip along the fence and find the gate that opens to a private trail that runs between the properties and leads to the beach.

The hood of Wil's red hoodie is pulled over his head, and he's got his aviators on, his guitar case in hand, and the familiar messenger bag across his body. If he thinks he'll be less conspicuous wearing a long-sleeve outfit to the beach, he needs to take some notes from Dad's book. He should've worn swim trunks and a towel to blend in with the sun bathers. An image of Wil in swim gear overlays the Wil in front of me.

"Nice day for a break-and-enter."

I stand in the shadows and wave him into the laneway. He jogs by me, close enough I catch his fresh cotton scent. I trace my steps back, and Wil follows me. Grass and leaves crunch under his feet. My back's to him most of the way as I scan the property, just in case. I slide the door and stop to direct him in first. The billiards room is a recent remodel, and the acrid smell of fresh paint lingers.

"Who plays?" Wil touches the green felt and walks around one of the two tables.

"Dad. He's not bad."

He moves his guitar to another shoulder and raps triplets on the wood side. "Is he here?"

"No, he took Mom away for the weekend." Wil's hand clenches into a fist. "You're safe. You'll remain my secret."

Wil hits the wood and doesn't meet my eyes. "Hmm." The guitar shifts on his shoulder again, and he keeps his eyes on the colorful balls in the triangle in the middle of the green.

"I have something to show you."

I lead him past the sauna, the gym, movie room, down the stairs, opposite the wine cellar, and push the door into the room where I spend the most time after my bedroom. I step into the center of my dad's personal studio and twirl around. "It's not as spacious as the one at UCLA, but it does the trick."

Wil takes off his sunglasses, and I watch him absorb every detail of the room. What is just another space to some must be a picture of wealth to Wil. Because it is. Dad spared nothing. The

5.1 control room has stands with guitars and basses, shelves with keyboards arranged like museum pieces. The walls have built-in speakers around us, and the ceiling has special sound-absorbing tiles, so even if a party were in full swing, no one outside this room would hear a note.

"Can I go in?" Wil points to the glass doors in the isolation booth. "Does he? Do you use it much?"

"Might be the most used room in the house." The bright space has a glass wall that opens to the opposite side from the one we came from; some lawn and more trees are a calming view. "I've even fallen asleep here. After I cried my eyes out when the lyrics got worse and worse with every try. The crumbling on the floor? It's this floor I was talking about."

Wil looks at the wood surface covered by rugs and then up at me. There's something in his expression. Pity? I'm not sure. He's so un-Wil today. No, that's not right. He's Wil, just not the cocky Wil I often see. I wish we were on stage and I could read his mind.

"D'you want to hear what I have?"

Right. This isn't a courtesy visit. How could I forget? "What d'you need?"

Wil takes his laptop out and plugs it into the system, as if he's been here before. "It's a rough draft, but I laid a metal peel under your voice, like you asked. The harpsichord recording you sent follows the chorus, and you were so right. It does make it more fairy-tale–like. Supports the princess line in a way I'd never thought of."

The music saturates the studio, and I don't hate my voice. The words are crisp, fast, and run together like they do inside my head. When the verse ends, Wil pauses. "You like?"

"Keep going." I sit on the chair next to him.

"This is the rough part. I still don't like the words. But when I saw the, ah, paparazzi chase you yesterday, I had an idea." He pauses. "Stop me if it's too raw or you're not comfortable with it."

I lick my lips. "Go on."

"What if before you get to 'It awakes the pain from my past,' you talk about no matter how the paparazzi are part of your life, and even though you know how to protect yourself from them, their words still cut you." He looks down at the laptop and his voice gets quiet. "I didn't get it until I saw them hurt you yesterday. If you want, we can find the words for that."

"But I don't have the words."

His fingers press into the wood on either side of his laptop, turning white at the tips. "Am I right? Did they hurt you?"

I close my eyes. This is for the song. I have to try to make him understand. "This time. Yes. Sometimes their questions are harmless, easy to avoid. But this time." I open my eyes, and he's looking at me.

"This time?"

"He asked, 'What would your father have thought?' They know that hurts."

Wil puts his hands in the pockets of his jeans. "Why?"

I search for a way to explain. "It's like Mom is cheating on him or something. Dad, Bill, no, Dad. He is my dad. He tries to do, *does* everything a dad should. But he's no Papa, that's what I've always called my father, but he is still Dad." The words keep coming. "He loves me and takes care of me. Not like a stepdaughter, he never uses those words, he treats me like I am his daughter. Flesh and blood."

I step closer to Wil. "And when the reporters try to make Mom and Dad's marriage this ugly thing, a betrayal, it's like spreading small words like crumbs. Pesky little things that aren't hurtful on their own, but if you walk barefoot and unprepared, they lodge under your toes, and it's all wrong." Wow. How did I say that and not stumble?

Wil's not writing, his black book lies closed by his laptop. I wait for him to reassure me. To tell me the right phrases, the words the song is lacking, like he always does. To be my words, to dive inside my mind and come up with the perfect way to express the imperfect emotions of my broken self. He doesn't.

The tune of this part of the song finds its way to my lips, and I hum it on repeat. Then words like cards slide into the beats. Crumb. Succumb. Across my lane. Dust. Past. The rhymes pop, and I sing.

"But I still succumb
To the little crumb
Right across my lane.
Smaller than the dust
It awakes the pain

From my past."

Wil's head snaps to me, golden eyes ablaze. "That. Sing that again."

Twenty-Six

Wil

A GOOD DAD. ROCKER can't be a good dad. He has to be a
selfish buffoon, who treats his stepdaughter like Cinderella and
Rapunzel mixed together. All the rules, the restrictions, the not
listening to what she wants, protecting her like she's made out
of glass, making her pick a career that is a guarantee instead of
letting her chase her dream. That's . . .

I expected to meet Rocker today. Confront him here. Reveal
who I am, get what I came to this country for, and be done.
Fulfill the mission. Make Opa proud. Get the money for Mom's
experimental treatment. It would've been a perfect ending to my
stay in LA. No need to take the semester at UCLA as an excuse
to stick around. I don't need to wait to find out who won the
competition I never needed to win. Go home, see my friends,

drink beer legally, eat Mum's cooking, get back to rowing. Stop lying.

Today, I came to say goodbye to El, to get my money, and get my life back.

Plans change. People change too. And the changes I see in El make me want to stay and see where she will go. Be part of it, in some way. She has the words. And she might know it now.

"Want to hop into the isolation room and give it a try?"

She smiles a coy smile. "You want to use my words?"

"Most definitely do."

She skips to the booth. Like a schoolgirl. Her bare legs, long and lean in the tight white shorts she's wearing. The lightness around her crashes into the heaviness in my chest, and the storm of my disappointment at not meeting Rocker calms.

We record the new words. And some of the old ones. El runs through the whole song and every take she loses herself more, connects with the words. Even though I helped her write a lot of them, they grab my attention, hurt me when they should, lift me up when I most want them to. This Lenard fellow might be the lucky one. Getting his hands on this song. On El singing this song. It's a golden goose, and I'll make sure El knows it.

"One more time?" El's heard the last remix twice already.

"Sure. Last one. I'll send it to you, and you can send it to Mr. Astor. You're ready."

"You think?"

"I know." I catch the time on my phone. "And I need to head back. It's getting dark."

"What?" El looks at the floor-to-ceiling windows of the studio as if she hasn't noticed the sunset. "What time is it?"

"Almost eight."

"Oh." One of her hands dives into her hair. "Wanna stay? Spend the night?" She points to the floors above, her face lit up with confidence.

I don't know how to react. What exactly is she offering me? What do I want her to offer? With anyone else there'd be no hesitation, but with El my body is screaming yes, while my mind is telling me to shut this down.

She rocks on the balls of her feet, and her eyebrows knit together. "Sorry. I mean, I can make dinner, at least." She's looking everywhere but at me. "I also have this other song I started and a tune I had from before I met you that could use some words. And no one is here tomorrow. And you said you were free, and if you don't have anything to do—"

This offer I can accept. "Dinner would be great." I stop her torrent. "And maybe a bathroom break?"

"I'm such a terrible host." El jumps to her feet. "Follow me." I get up and start closing my laptop.

"Leave it here. It's just you and me. We can get it later."

Just you and me. I've spent hours locked away in the recording studio at the university with El. We've spent hours today together in this room, and those are the words that push me across an invisible boundary. If I weren't hyper-aware of her presence before, I am now, and maybe staying for dinner is not a great idea.

"Let's go upstairs. You can use the restroom by the kitchen while I see what I can come up with to feed us." The pep in her voice is too dear for me to spoil. My stomach grumbles in agreement.

The stairs land us in the living room with not one, but two pianos and a panoramic view of the ocean. It's stunning. What's up with the universe shoving romantic sunsets over the ocean in my face? I walk over to another floor-to-ceiling window, and it's better than the one in the recording room where we could only glimpse the promise of the ocean. Here it stretches to infinity, like our own personal slice of sea and sky. Like my insides, it's not calm.

I can't hear it, though. Soundproofing here is as good as in the recording room. These windows must've cost a fortune. I turn to El, who stays in the hallway, not joining me to enjoy the panoramic view. Living here it's probably part of the everyday, not noticeable. We get used to the good in our lives. Take so many things for granted. I've learned my lesson. I'm not letting my life pass me by.

On my way back to El, I can't resist running my hand across the light brown instrument. The eight thin bowed legs look like they can barely hold up the ancient artifact. The open lid displays a baroque pastoral scene in muted colors. Unlike a piano, it has two short, stacked keyboards that give it a compact look.

"You found my harpsicord." She bounces on her toes.

"The line from your song?" I thought she bought the sound off the web, not played the real thing.

"That very line."

I touch a key. A grainy note pierces the room, grating on my nerves. I abandon her treasure and admire the black grand piano twice the size of the harpsicord. Way to make a big room look small. "You really need two pianos?"

"Not mine. Papa's wedding present to my mom." She turns her chin away from the window. "Are you done playing with my toys, or do you want to eat?"

If the view was the best part of the living room, the sheer grandeur of the kitchen is its selling point. No windows, as it's in the middle of the house and backs to a den sporting a view of the hill the front of the house sits on. But you could film *The Great German Bake Off* in here and have room to spare. Mum would love it. Gleaming, white cupboards, black marble counters, stainless steel appliances that I have no idea what they do. There's a coffee machine in the corner that looks more expensive than the ones at work.

"The half bath is this way." She points farther down the hallway and continues into the kitchen. I guess I'm on my own. The bathroom is the third door down after a laundry room and a library with bookshelves going up all the way to the ceiling.

I walk into a space the size of the dorm room Mateo and I just vacated. He moved into the frat house, and for a fee they are letting me stay for what I thought might be another week or so. Unless I sign up for the class on compression, limiters and gates Mateo's been pushing me to take.

Here I am. Back at the beginning. Finding a way to Rocker. Two months, and I'm no closer to meeting him. I can hear Opa's words in my head. He's going to expect progress tomorrow, but I have nothing to report.

I wash my hands at a sink the cost of which would probably cover Mum's first treatment. I can't rifle through Rocker's house and steal enough stuff to get Mum into the experimental treatment program the insurance wouldn't cover. Can I? One guitar might cover all her expenses and then some.

A collage of Rocker at various concerts runs up the wall on both sides of the vanity. I look at his image and at myself in the mirror. I've avoided this, comparing myself to him. I zone in on one in his younger days, on stage, guitar in hand. No matter how much I hate it, he can't pretend I'm not his son. We have the same eyes, the same jet-black hair, although mine is straighter, the heavy eyebrows, the chin. I have my mother's full lips and her softer nose, but the rest is Rocker's face. Even the angle at which my shoulders and neck meet are a carbon copy.

El has an array of vegetables out, taking up a corner of the king-bed-sized island. She hums a tune I don't recognize, and I'm drawn to her, curious as to where it's going. I sit down on the bar stool across from her.

"Want a beer?" She winks. Once again, El surprises me. Mateo and I have used the fake IDs a number of times, hit a few bars or brought beer back to the dorm, but I have yet to stumble on a good beer since I've arrived in this country. Unlikely my luck is going to turn here, but I'm not saying no to a free beer.

"Sure. Don't wanna check my ID? I'm a year away from the legal drinking age in the US."

The knife halts mid-chop. "A year? You're twenty?"

"Tomorrow."

"And you were going to tell me when?" Hands are off the knife and on her hips.

"Wasn't planning on telling anyone here. Never been big on birthdays."

"Don't you want to have a party? Presents? I could've talked to Sarah. The crew would've made a big deal out of it."

"Not really my thing. At home, Mum makes me blueberry muffins, and we'll have them for breakfast."

"Well, this definitely calls for a beer." Her red hair sinks under a counter, and I hear the familiar clink of glass bottles being moved in what I assume is a drinks cooler. I shake my head at the luxury of having a fridge just for beer and wine. "Helles or Beck's?"

"Beck's. No questions."

A green bottle with the red label I've spent hours peeling off at home until I can do it all in one go—considered a lucky sign—appears, and she pushes it toward me. "Glass?"

I twist the cap off and take a swig. "Hmm. No. Your parents won't miss it?"

"Dad's a German beer connoisseur. We stock it en masse. This one won't be missed." Rocker is everywhere, yet nowhere when I need him.

"You not having one?"

"I'm a lightweight. One of those"—she points at my beer with the thick knife in her hand—"and you won't get dinner."

A tipsy El. The thought brings a smile back to my lips as I bring the bottle to them. That might be fun. "What are we eating?"

"It was a toss-up between roasted potatoes with sautéed vegetables and grilled chicken or poached egg over asparagus and fingerling potatoes. Chicken sounded like a better match with the beer. But I can switch."

"I'll eat either one. The only home-cooked meals I've had since I got here are the ones you bring. I might never again buy pastries for myself, though: too many day-olds from Blend. Eating it for breakfast, frequently lunch, and sometimes dinner is enough to turn one off even the best croissant or muffin."

Her eyes flicker to my stomach and immediately flee, as if she's not allowed to look at me. "No soft middle yet, but only because I need more calories than pastries offer." I pat my flat stomach.

"Good to know." Sliced potatoes slide into a bowl, get doused in olive oil, and she sprinkles them generously with salt and pepper. Like a pro, she coats them in the slippery mixture, spreads them on a baking sheet, and puts them in the oven on the wall behind her.

"Mum wants a wall oven. Bending down has been hard on her. She'd be impressed with your setup."

"Marta's setup. Dad had her work with the designer and pick every knob, tile, and appliance. He spends hours watching Marta cook but his execution is lacking. Dad goes from mixing up tablespoon and teaspoon to mistaking salt for sugar. Mom is more concerned with the dining room where the food ends up and lets Marta rule the kitchen." El chops and chats like it's second nature. "Mom's only request was this bar area, so we all have a place to sit and watch Marta work her magic. It's family sport. Marta is a saint for putting up with us."

I don't want to hear about their cozy dinners where someone else feeds them because they can't bother to learn the basics the rest of us have to. Yet I can't help saying, "Sounds like you're all pretty close."

She stops cutting the carrots and meets my eyes. I have to work not to look away. "I guess." She finishes with the carrots and moves to the courgettes. "How about you? Is it just your mom and you?"

"Opa too. My grandfather. They live in Bremen. That's where I'm from."

"Mom and I were in Munich and Dresden when I was"—she looks up at the ceiling—"eleven, I think? With no school year, time kinda mixes for me. Is Bremen near there?"

"No, it's more north. Near Hamburg."

"Oh, like where The Beatles played?" I nod. "Dad's a big Beatles fan."

I take another sip of my beer.

"Do all Germans speak perfect English?"

"Some do. My grandma was British. Mum sent me to visit her cousins every summer. I think she needed a break from me. I don't remember the time I didn't speak English."

"Brothers or sisters?"

"No. Only child."

She opens a cupboard, and I lose her face for a bit as she searches for something. "What about your dad?"

Twenty-Seven

I CHOKE ON MY beer. Her innocent eyes stare into mine. Is she testing me? What gave me away? She lives with the man, after all. Has access to the pictures in the bathroom daily. El blinks, waiting for my answer, and the sincerity of her question becomes evident, her concern for me, her honesty. El wouldn't deceive me.

Why did we have to meet this way?

"Oh, sorry. Didn't mean to pry."

Every moment between us is tainted by the secret I'm keeping from her. The secret kept from me. It weighs on my soul, on my heart. She's going to find out soon. When I finally do meet Rocker, get what I need and leave, will he tell her? Will he do it at this kitchen counter? Will he hold her hand?

For a moment, I consider telling her . . . everything, the truth. Get it all off my chest, come clean. Dispel the black bile of all the lies I've been carrying around. I could explain why I'm here, not just in this room, but in this country. Would she understand?

It's an insane thought. She'd kick me out, never talk to me again. Then I'd have no way to finish this. No, I can't tell her. I shake my head.

"It's not that. He's . . . not in the picture." What do I say? He screwed my mum and ghosted her. You're living with him. I'm so sick of the lies.

She's got her hand in her hair, twirling the single white streak. Bloody hell, now I've upset her. Being here, in his house, seeing the life I could have had is screwing with me.

"Do you like spicy food? Marta has a great rub for the chicken, but it has quite the kick."

Saved by the spice. "Yeah, I can do spicy."

"Dad and I can eat the spiciest thing on any menu, but I can half the amount. It'll still burn."

"I'm good. Don't change it for me."

She rubs the mix over the chicken then washes her hands. "Don't want any of that to get into my eyes."

"At least you have both hands again."

"Getting there." She opens and closes the fingers on her left hand. "The physical therapy is helping. Another month and I'll be good as new."

The chicken goes on with a satisfying sizzle. The smell of meat and spices fills the air. My stomach reacts, and my mouth waters. When was the last time I ate?

She reaches for a small pot.

"And what's this for?"

"Just some rice. Nothing fancy."

The rice and chicken should not make me salivate like I am. She pulls out a bunch of green leaves. I get off the barstool and walk over to her.

"Here." I hip check her away from the sink. "You cooked. The least I can do is wash some lettuce." I get one of my favorite things; a look of surprise lights up her face. I feel better when she smiles. Like what I'm doing isn't wrong.

She turns over the chicken, stirs the rice, and by the time I finish assembling the salad, the timer beeps.

"The chicken is ready."

"Can we eat out by the pool?"

El's face pales. "Can't. The, um . . ." Her gaze falls to the floor. "Press are everywhere today. They'll get photos."

It's dark outside. This feels like an overreaction even after her encounter yesterday. They won't even see us. Is she hiding something? No. I'm the one with the secret. I saw what happened. I have to trust her. "How do you live like this?"

"I don't."

We move the food to the end of the kitchen island. Familiar plates and cutlery from the times she brought food to campus wait for us. The cloth napkins are the same as well.

"Ready to try?" Humor dances in El's eyes.

"You can't scare me." I cut a piece of chicken and start chewing. It's bursting with flavor. The taste buds on my tongue absorb the avalanche of heat the peppers bring to the bite. I hum in appreciation. El takes a sip of water and waits.

The spices don't mellow. The pleasant level rises to the point where my sinuses burn. I rush to swallow before I have to blow my nose. The chicken slides down my throat and coats it in a prickly itch of three kinds of pepper. I cough. I grab the napkin and ball it in front of my mouth and nose to protect the table in case that chicken decides to cause trouble. I cough some more and reach out for water.

"You need milk. Hang on."

El dashes to the fridge and brings me a glass of milk, which I chug to the relief of all the soft tissues inside my body.

"That is spicy." I sound like a sick frog when I say it.

She reaches over, takes my piece off the plate, moves it onto hers, and then gives me her untouched portion. "Try this one. I went gentler on it. I had a hunch."

I eye the chicken. "Maybe rice and salad will be enough."

"You'll be fine. Trust me."

I do. The new piece is still spicy, and I still get the burn, but I'm not worried for my intestines.

"You don't have to try to be someone you're not with me."

"Wait." I pull out my book and pencil out of my pocket and flip to the page I was scribbling at most of last night when I couldn't sleep, thinking how the only freedom El has is when she's in disguise.

"What are you doing?"

I move closer and show her. "I started a new song based on our experience on stage. What you said fits in here, see?" I point to the lines I already had and the new one I just added.

She purses her lips and gives her head a little nod. She runs a finger under the words I wrote and mouths them as she reads.

"Can I ask you something?"

Her eyes meet mine.

"And you don't have to answer. It's . . . It's just that you say you have trouble with words, and I—"

"I have trouble reading sometimes."

I search for a sign this conversation makes her uncomfortable. She's putting another scoop of salad on her plate. Not the cool and collected El I thought she was before I met her, but confident.

"Don't get me wrong. I can read. It just takes me a little longer. The letters, they don't make sounds quickly." She meets my gaze. "Especially new words. If you say the line first, and I know that's what you wrote, the sounds and letters merge together faster. Even rhyming doesn't always make sense."

"Oh. Only with words? Not with notes?"

"Mom started me on the piano before I could read, and notes, rhythm in music, pitch—they always made sense to me. You'll laugh, but I can see the notes when I hear them. They dance in front of me in a different way. The microwave beeps at G-flat, and when you tap your fingers like you are now"—she points to where my digits are drumming against the countertop—"you tap out either a sixteenth note groove or a half-time shuffle."

I had no idea I had rhythm. "Sick. What else do you hear?"

El shrugs. "Music is everywhere. The hum of the elevator at the studio—"

"What's that sound like?"

"It's a bit like Ravel's Bolero. Do you know it?" I shake my head, and she hums a melody. "As we cross each floor it loops like that."

"You're amazing."

She covers her face with her hand, hiding what might be a blush. "Right." She doesn't believe me. I wish the world could see her like I do. Someday they will.

Both of our plates are empty. I put the napkin on the table next to them. "So, what do you do for fun around here?"

Her eyebrows stitch together.

"If we can't go outside, there must be something fun we can do inside."

"You don't want to work on a song?"

"Sure, but we have all day tomorrow to do that."

Her face lights up. "You're staying?"

"Only if you have a ridiculously soft bed for me to sleep in."

The bed in the guest room she leads me to is not big. It's gimongous. Yet another wall of floor-to-ceiling windows dominates the space, decked out in pale blue and tan, like ocean and sand. I can see some light. "Is that the beach?"

El flicks off the lights. "There's a special film in the glass, so people can't see inside." She walks to the corner and pulls a handle on the glass. The whole wall shifts, and the sound of the ocean rushes in. I walk out onto the balcony, but El doesn't join me.

"Does your room face the ocean too?"

She shakes her head. "Three of the guest rooms, plus Mom and Dad's have this view. I'm on the other side. Wanna see?"

El did not just invite me to her bedroom.

"We don't have to."

"No, I want you to."

Is there a hidden meaning behind her words or does she invite everyone to her bedroom?

"You don't need to show me the lack of view."

"It has a view. Just not of the water. It's cozy. You'll like it."

She pushes a finger into my shoulder, as if she can move me in the right direction that way.

Her bedroom is down the end of the hall and up a few steps, away from everyone else. Is she separated from everyone everywhere? There is no canopy bed or pink frills. Fuzzy purple pillows decorate her regular sized bed. Nope, not looking at the bed. I walk to the window. Can't see much in the dark, but it looks like a tree.

Tall shelves filled with rows and rows of album covers bracket a desk empty except for a silver laptop. On either side of them there are two doors. Bathroom and . . . closet, I guess. On the opposite wall is a circular piece of art, which, when I look at it closely, is a collection of photos. A young El making a sandcastle on the beach, El at the piano, El and Rocker surrounded by a group of young kids, huge grins on their faces.

"Not many people know, but Dad does more than give money to charities. Twice a year, we take a group of inner-city kids camping for a weekend. This was last year." She tilts her head at the photo. "He's great with the kids, always wanted one of his own." Her eyes fall. Is she thinking about her soon-to-be baby brother?

I don't want to talk about her father. Don't want to think about him taking care of other kids. I point to a picture of El in a fancy dress, with two other girls on a red carpet. One of them might be the girl from the video at the park.

"Those are my cousins, Zoe"—El places a finger on the girl—"and Bailey. On my mom's side. Bailey lives in New York, and we went to the Met Gala last year. Zoe's into fashion."

I stuff my hands in my pockets. Sarah made me promise to ask El to be my plus one at the Starlight Foundation event. "You like going to those things?"

"With the right people, they can be fun. Sometimes I only do the red-carpet event and then slip out the back door. But the best is when I sneak in the back door. When no one knows I'm there."

Might as well get this over with. "So, Starlight has this posh award show thingy we all have to go to. We get to bring a guest, and since I don't know anyone here, Sarah thought you might want to come. You know, as part of the team. We're all going as a group. Nick's even talking about renting a limo."

Stop talking, Wil. She's not impressed by a limo. The girl rides around in a fucking powder blue Rolls Royce.

"That sounds fun."

I blink. "You'll come?"

"I want to. If I can sneak in the back."

"We'll make it happen."

"We will, will we?" She grins at me, and I have to turn away.

Twenty-Eight

Wil's guest bedroom is far enough away from the kitchen that I don't have to be quiet or worry about waking him up. Just as I thought, there are no blueberries in the fridge. Can't make his birthday blueberry muffins, because going to the store is not an option. I inspect the ingredients I have on hand. I've got everything I need for the red velvet cupcakes I promised Sven. It'll have to do.

I omit the red dye and adjust the cupcake recipe to a muffin one. A bit more baking powder and a higher temperature should do the trick. I've never had chocolate muffins for breakfast, but Wil's birthday is a great reason to rectify that. Sven's file on Wil did mention his birthday, but it was not important when I read it. And I forgot. How did I forget?

I mix the batter and pour it into the tulip baking cups I cut out of parchment paper. A small-batch recipe I found yields six muffins, which is a perfect amount for the two of us and will leave some for Wil to take with him.

To counteract the sweetness and lack of protein in the muffins, I start making bacon and eggs.

"What's this?"

I swallow. "Happy birthday?" I don't know why it comes out as a question. I should've heard him walk down the hall. "Let me grab a candle for you to blow out."

Wil grabs my wrist to stop me. "No need. This looks amazing." He gestures toward the confetti sprinkled around our plates and the food I've already made.

He lets go, and I relax. His hair is damp from his shower, and it falls over his forehead. I have this urge to reach up and push it back, but I resist. "I didn't have any blueberries, so the muffins are chocolate."

"I can't believe you got up early and did all this. You shouldn't have."

"I wanted to make your big two-oh memorable."

"It already was going to be." He puts his forehead against mine. "Thank you. For listening. For doing things for me. I haven't felt this welcome in a very long time." He steps away and grabs one of the muffins from the muffin tin.

"Careful. They're still hot."

"Should I make coffee?" He eyes the espresso machine on the counter.

"No, you're the birthday boy. I'm going to play the barista today. Do you want café au lait, latte, or a cappuccino?"

"Someone else making one of those fancy drinks for me sounds too good to be true. But black is fine."

I pull two mugs from the cupboard and set the machine to espresso. "Did you sleep well?" I'm not winning a perfect hostess prize any time soon, but I have to try.

Wil shakes his head. "I might want to marry that bed. Beats the lumpy excuse of a mattress I'm sleeping on at Mateo's frat."

Right. Living on campus. Another thing I know nothing about.

"When are your parents due back?"

And just like that, reality breaks through our little bubble. The weekend is over. Wil has to go back to his regularly scheduled life. Me—my existence. "Mom texted they're on their way. Maybe six or seven. Depending on how many times they have to stop for bathroom breaks."

Wil's eyes widen. "Um . . ."

"But Sven will be back after lunch. If you save him some of that bacon, I bet he can give you a ride home."

The slice of bacon he snatched off the plate hangs suspended in midair. "Won't the, ah, reporters follow him?"

"Sven is a pro at ditching the press. I think he secretly loves the thrill of outsmarting them. You might make his day."

"You and Sven are pretty close."

Zoe keeps asking me if Sven and I are secretly dating. And no matter how many times I emphatically say "no," I don't manage to convince her. "I get what you're thinking."

Wil holds up his hands. "I'm not thinking anything."

"There's nothing going on between us." Sven's secrets are not mine to tell. How to explain to Wil? "We . . . have a lot in common. And it's not like I have a lot of friends."

"This world of yours blows." He shakes his head. "I used to think it'd be cool to be the kid of a rock star. All this money, and it doesn't do you any good."

"Money isn't everything."

"Yeah, but it sure helps."

"I guess."

"It'd help my Mum."

"With her health?" I look away, feeling like I'm prying into something private. "You mentioned she has some . . ."

"She's got this autoimmune disease. Rheumatoid arthritis. At first, it wasn't too bad, but the recent flare-up was the worst. She couldn't walk, her knee joints were so bad. And the treatment they gave her, the meds messed up her liver and kidneys. She's in remission now."

"Oh, that sounds rough." I've heard the name but never thought it was that bad. I should look it up. "Is there a cure?"

"I wouldn't say cure. There's this new treatment. Biologic drugs that are supposed to affect the part of the immune system that impacts RA. But it's very expensive, and because Mum doesn't qualify as extremely sick, we have to pay out of pocket. If she gets selected. She's on a list, and it's a waiting game now."

"But it could help?"

"The doctors think so. They've had success with other cases."

"I hope she gets in."

"Me too." Wil puts down his fork and pushes the plate away, either full or talking about his mom's illness made him lose his appetite. I shouldn't have pushed. He jumps off the stool. "Shall we work on that new song?"

Today I bring my wide-brim beige fedora and the Versace glasses Billie Eilish made popular. Wonder if Billie would love the caramel dress with the two pockets I'm wearing. Zoe knows how to make a girl happy—add pockets. It's on the short side but the thigh-high boots she insisted I borrow, plus the belt from her personal collection, make me feel like a star.

Maybe a bit too much like one, because I catch a lot of glances on my walk to the market. Maybe the dress is too short. Maybe this was a mistake, and I need to blend in, not stick out like a sore thumb. But with Zoe on board, it's such a relief to talk to someone about my busking and the Devil's Martini gig. Plus, the dress she dropped off last night for the gala is to die for.

Of course, she wanted me to go total glam, but I managed to convince her I am not trying to attract attention like she is. For once, she listened to me. Still, when I slipped on the one-shoulder, floor-length gown and spun for the mirror, the ice-blue made me grin. Even without the clear high heels, the dress somehow made my runner's frame look curvy in the right places. I can't wait to wear it tonight. Sit with Wil as we wait to see if our collaboration wins in the Best Original Song category. Somehow, I know it will.

It's perfect. Today is going to be perfect. My life finally feels like everything is possible. I can taste the hope in the air. Or maybe it's the fresh citrus samples I'm passing by. The world around me sounds orange and is bursting with possibilities.

"You're the orange of my day, the flavor of my life, the fresh ingredient that I've been waiting for."

The hoppy melody builds itself from the laughter and haggling in the stalls I walk by but today, it has words attached. The sunglasses are not coloring the world around me; the explosion of color comes from my full, happy heart. The joy of the market and the cooler end-of-September weather lighten my steps. I want to twirl and pretend I'm in the middle of a flash mob where everyone suddenly drops whatever they are doing and sings and dances around me, filling the street with the music of my soul.

"Did you bring any of those happy pills for me?" Wil's eyes match my orange-hued day perfectly. His tan skin and the sun above him make him the final note in my journey.

"Ooo-o-o-ooo-o-o-o," I riff.

"Yep. I most definitely want some of that. New song?"

"Just came to me. I'll write it down and send it to you. I even got some lyrics for it." I drop my phone in his messenger bag. "I think it's going to be about an orange world and the power of us coloring our life in the shades we want it to be."

"Dope. Good to sing *Our Lines* and *Don't Give Me Comfort* today?"

"I'm ready." I twirl because I can't not twirl. "Do I look ready?"

"You look—" Wil's eyes slide across every inch of me and when they linger on the stretch of my exposed thigh, I'm glad I'm wearing the short dress and the boots. Zoe deserves all the accolades and a bubble tea. I'll pass them along, but right now I bask in the glow of Wil's stare. I feel whole, and beautiful, and powerful, and alive. This is what living is supposed to be like.

"You look like you're about to burst into a song and dance." Wil shakes his head.

"You're in my head again. How do you do that? I was just thinking about that scene in *La La Land*. I wish I could be in your head right now."

Wil looks away. "Happy to oblige." He picks up the guitar and starts strumming *Happy* by Pharrell. "Wanna sing and dance?"

I grab the mic and channel my exuberant cheerfulness into the verse, singing to Wil and then to the people in the market. Once I hit the chorus, I let myself bounce around without a care in the world, and I watch the small crowd around me follow suit.

Some are waving their hands in the air, the kiddos pirouette and jump, and when my hat falls on the ground, I don't care.

I keep singing and skipping and imagining the future where this is not me in the middle of a market but me on stage at an open-air concert with thousands of people jumping and waving their arms around me to my song. They'll join me in my orange world, and we will be bursting with joy together, under the bright sun of whichever country I'm in. I can hear them chanting my name, "Melodie. Melodie."

"Melodie." It's not my name. I'm El.

But I'm also Melodie. My heart stops. The metal curtain falls and the windows close, hiding the light. The sun disappears as Sven blocks it. The name, my name is coming from him. He stretches out his hand, it's holding my hat, and plunks it back on my head, permanently hiding the sun's rays. "Let's go. Now."

"Sven?" His hand closes around my arm, and I'm propelled to the left. He drags me alongside him through the crowd that parts for Superman, no one insane enough to stand in his way. "Wil?" I turn my head to Wil, and the silence of our little circle of equipment. He takes off his guitar and starts following us.

"Don't." Sven's looking at Wil too, and the command he issues leaves no room for argument. "Later." Wil wobbles on one leg, he stops suddenly. Even I know Sven is serious.

"I'll be okay," I shout to Wil. "I'll see you tonight. I'll be fine."

Wil stands between the people who whisper and move away from him. Not going to earn much today. My legs struggle to keep up with Sven's giant strides, and I'm stumbling. "You can let go of me now. I won't run away."

"Don't trust you."

"Come on. It's not a big deal." I do stumble, and he stops to catch me. I try to capture his eye, but he won't meet mine.

"It is a huge deal. And if you're too selfish to see it, I'm not sure I know you that well after all."

He's overreacting. No one knows me like Sven. He understands what all this means to me. I'll explain, and everything will be okay. "It's just singing. Practice."

"In public."

"I sing in public at the bar. It's the same thing."

He stops, turns to me. I can't see his eyes behind the reflective sunglasses, but his lips are pressed together so tight they are almost white. "Not at all. I'm there. Watching."

I swallow. Something in his tone sets my heart racing. "It's just a farmers' market." The lips press together even harder. I try again. "I'm five minutes away from Rocker, Inc."

"Alone."

I almost say "Wil is with me" but decide against it.

"It's perfectly safe. I've been doing it for months."

Sven lets go of my arm at last and takes a tiny step backward. Now, I want his hand on my arm again. "Months? This isn't the first time?"

"I—"

"Months, Melodie?"

People on the sidewalk are looking at us, and causing a scene is the last thing I want. I lean into him.

"Can we do this not in the middle of the street?"

Sven grinds his teeth, and I can see how hard he's working on not saying anything to me. I follow him through the door into the office, up the stairs into one of the empty conference rooms.

"Sit." He points to an empty chair. "Your dad's looking for you. He's been calling you. Nadine called me in a panic to find you." Damn, it must be bad if Sven and Nadine are talking.

"Is everything okay? Is it Mom?" I start to stand up, but Sven gives me a look that makes my knees wobble, and I sit back down.

"I think so. I texted Marta, and she's with her at home. But it's not like anyone tells me anything."

"I—"

"I had to use the app to track you." Sven paces the room. "Take off that stupid hat, fix your hair, and go to his office. Smile. I told him you were downstairs at the gym." He faces me, the rage evident in his balled fists. "We'll talk about what's next, once Mr. Rockerby is happy." He points a finger at me. "Do not leave this building by yourself. I'll be at the security desk waiting for you. And don't try anything else. We're done. Go."

"What?" What does he mean, we're done? "You can't—"

"I can, and I just did." He points to the door. "Go."

I open my mouth to protest then close it. It's no use. Sven won't listen to me in this state. I need him to calm down. I do my best to settle my nerves and then leave.

The hallways of Rocker, Inc. are lined with framed images of artists on stage, taunting me with their big smiles. I could detour up to Nadine to see if she can give me a heads-up on what's going on. I glance back and see Sven watching me. No. Better not risk it. What if she's mad at me as well?

I smile at Mandy, Dad's executive assistant, as I walk by, but my hands shake. I repeat my mantra in my head. Everything is going to be fine. If something was wrong with Mom, Dad wouldn't be sitting in his office, he'd be wherever she is, holding her hand. The pact Dad and I made is that we only see each other at work if there is a reason. No popping in and saying hi or checking in on me. I'm just a worker bee like the rest of the staff. No preferential treatment.

The office is the same as always. Black leather couches, platinum records in the glass case by the bar. Dad's on the phone, his Doc Martens propped up on his desk. He waves me over and signals I should sit.

"Excellent. And you can get them there by say"—Dad looks at his watch—"six?" He grins at the answer on the other line, all the perfect pearly whites. A tiny coil releases inside me. He's in a good mood. "Great."

He hangs up, sweeps his feet off the desk and rubs his hands together. "At last, you're here. I've had a great idea."

Usually, I enjoy his great ideas. Dad's got a spontaneous streak in him, the whole rock star impulse thing, that serves him well on stage. Trouble is, sometimes we pay the price. Everyone else's plans—the collateral damage to his well-intended gestures.

"Oh, yeah?" The dread from earlier creeps back in. The last time he had a spark of inspiration, Mom and I got just two hours to pack, and had to guess where we were going and for how long.

We ended up in Cinque Terra, Italy, for the weekend with world-famous chef Nonna Maria, who never leaves her hometown anymore.

"Don't look so scared. The jet is not on standby."

His stupid smile reminds me of Wil when he's teasing me. Wil, whom I left standing in the middle of the farmers' market with all our equipment. My stomach twists at the thought. I'll apologize at the gala tonight.

"That's good. Nadine would be mad if I disappeared. We're in the middle of building an ad campaign."

"She can live without you for an afternoon." Dad stands up and puts his arm around me. "We're leaving work early. I need your help in the kitchen."

"Are we cooking something?"

"Oh, yes. Are you up for it?"

Do I have a choice?

TWENTY-NINE

"DON'T YOU CLEAN UP well."

Nick stands in front of a white stretch limo. He's decked out in a similar black tuxedo as me. We rented them together. A bloody waste of money if you ask me, but the rest of the team insisted. I feel like I'm going to some lame American prom, not an awards show that may determine my and my friends' fate.

"Hey, I look good in anything. Even this penguin suit." I slap Nick on the back. He shakes his head but punches my shoulder back.

"Your chariot awaits." Nick swings the door open, and I climb into the back and join Bri on the bench seat. They're decked out in a royal-blue pantsuit with an ostentatious broach holding the jacket together keeping their breasts from spilling out, as the outfit has no top underneath. Beside them sits Riyaz in a light gray version of a tuxedo. Bloke had to be different. Nick slides in beside Sarah, who is wearing a sliver of silver material that covers the essentials—barely—and Siobhan is covered head-to-toe in gold.

"Where's El?" Bri asks.

"She's meeting us there."

The ride to the venue is less than twenty minutes, hardly worth the money we spent on this gas guzzler, but it is fun. Music blasts through the speakers. Teal hair bouncing, Siobhan dances in her seat.

"Oi, open the sunroof," she yells again at the driver. "I want to stand up."

"You can't open it when we're moving." Sarah grabs her shoulders. "We aren't stopping. We can't be late for this one."

"You're such a buzzkill." Siobhan wiggles out of Sarah's grasp. "That's what the limo sunroofs are for." She manages to open a window and sticks half of her body out.

"Woohoo! Team Indigo for the win," she shouts to the outside world, and we join in. "Team Indigo for the win!"

We jump out of the limo like rock stars. It's chaos. Who knew a Thursday night event had the power to attract so much press? I guess any day of the week will do, as long as they can get photos of their favorite celebrities. Everybody has bills to pay.

There's an actual red carpet, lined with clusters of people jostling cameras, lights, and microphones. Up ahead, a couple stops and poses for a photographer. Flashes burst like strobe lights in the clubs back home. They turn to the left, more flashes, then right. It's exactly like it seems in the movies.

Nick takes Sarah's hand, and they make their way down the parade of people, a mix of my fellow Starlight competitors and actual movie stars. Is that Asher Menken? I'm not into rom-coms but have watched a few of his with Mum. She adores Asher. Any way I can get his autograph? Or a picture with him? That would cheer Mum up.

It sucks El can't be here to experience this. Then again, she's probably done this many times. I push my way through the crowd, anxious to get inside and start this night with her. A whole night where we don't have to look over our shoulders, worry that the hour is up, or endure Sven's watchful eye. This is the one time Sven's job is a bonus and not an impediment for me to see El. Without his security guard connection, El wouldn't be able to sneak in. Not that she'd be the only one using that entrance. According to her, it's a thing lots of celebrities do.

The lobby is overflowing with sequins and silk, high hair, and even higher heels. The Starlight Foundation's logo, a gold star with a tail, dominates the wall of the theater, posters, and even the tiny glasses the servers are circulating on trays. They are full of champagne and a fruity red concoction for us under-agers. I pass, grabbing two waters instead. One for me, one for El.

"When's she getting here?" Nick looks at his watch. Bri makes a beeline for their fellow costume designer friends as soon as they see them, and Riyaz just disappears. I won't miss his mysterious ways. Sarah went to the bathroom, and Siobhan went too because women have to go to the loo in pairs.

"Soon." She was supposed to be here already. Guess there's traffic or something. I pull out my phone and shoot her a quick text. When I lift my eyes, Asher Menken is standing right in front of me. "Hey, mate." Brilliant, Wil.

The movie star meets my eye. "Which film is yours?"

"*Indigo*. I'm Wil Peters, the sound engineer. Also recorded a song."

"*Our Lines*. Right?"

I nod. Wow. He's heard our song. I can't wait to tell El.

"It's my favorite," he says. For some reason, I believe him. Either he's a phenomenal actor or he genuinely means it.

"Yeah, my friend sang on it. She's gonna be a superstar."

"I bet. She has a haunting voice"

"I hate to do this, and I know you get asked this all the time, but my Mum is a massive fan. She's . . . feeling a little under the weather these days. Can I get a picture with you? It'd really cheer her up."

"Just a picture? I think we can do better than that. What's her name?"

"Hanna."

"Okay, pull up your camera." Asher puts his arm around me like we are best friends and looks right into the screen on my phone. "Hey, Hanna, it's Asher Menken, and I'm here with your son, Wil. He's quite the impressive young man, but I'm sure you already know that. I expect big things from him. Take care of yourself." He winks, and his huge movie star grin splits his handsome face. "I hope she feels better soon."

Me too.

A man in a red velvet suit sidles up to us. "Asher, I thought I might find you here." The smile on Asher's face slips a little. "I wanted to talk to you about my script." This man steps in between Asher and me.

"Ladies and gentlemen"—a woman's voice, professional and prim, comes over the speakers—"welcome to the fifth annual Starlight Future Filmmakers Foundation Gala. Please, make your way into the auditorium."

I turn back to Nick, who is now rubbing his chin like he's trying to wear off his stubble with friction alone. While all the films are up for the grand prize tonight, they announced other award categories a week ago, like at the Oscars. El's rendition of *Our Lines* is up for Best Original Song. Nick is one of five up for best director. And Sarah got a nod for best screenwriter. It might have taken me a while to warm up to them in the beginning, but now I can see Sarah and Nick as a potential power couple.

Speaking of—Sarah struts down the hall toward us and when she reaches Nick, she tugs on his lapel. What would I do if El did this to my jacket? Nick obeys and bends down to Sarah's level. The tiny tyrant I've come to respect plants a kiss on his lips, and Nick's shoulders relax. The tension in my spine grows. I scan the foyer for any sign of El, but come up empty. Sarah runs her thumb across Nick's lip to remove the trace of lipstick left behind. Is this what affection looks like?

Nick observes at the steady stream of haute couture-clad bodies streaming through the doors into the auditorium. "We should grab our seats."

Sarah elbows Nick in the stomach. "El's not here yet, honey."

"But the ceremony's about to start."

Sarah puts a hand on my arm. "We'll head in and save your seats." I scan the thinning crowd. No sign of El. The hand on my arm squeezes. "She'll be here."

I text El: Are you close?

A girl beside me giggles and points to a retreating Nick. "Is that Shawn Mendes?" Yeah, like he'd be here tonight. People see what they want to see.

THIRTY

El

MARTA'S SMILING. DAD'S BEAMING. Mom's replacing the sun in her yellow maternity dress. I'm hating myself for not enjoying Marta's birthday party. I rub my temples. Birthdays are important in our family. It's the one thing we depend on. We celebrate together. No excuses. No exceptions. Being present is the present. Dad said his father missed too many birthdays too many times.

I shove the last ball of Brazilian cheese bread into my mouth. The warm sticky middle is the best part, but it brings me no joy.

"Never thought I'd say that, but you pulled it off, Mr. Rockerby. Your Pão de Queijo is at least as good as mine, if not better." Dad and I did an excellent job recreating Marta's top five, in our opinion, best recipes without her knowledge.

"Well, this coming from you, Marta, feels better than hearing I won another Grammy." Dad walks around the breakfast bar and gives Marta a hug.

"It really is wonderful." Marta waves for Mom to join the embrace. "Keep this up and you won't need me around anymore."

"Don't joke." Mom wraps her arms around both their shoulders. No one expects me to be part of this hugging extravaganza. "We wouldn't survive without you."

"Melodie walked me through the hard bits." Dad's praise kicks at me. It's rare he has time to take an afternoon off to spend with me, and I've used the entire evening trying to come up with a scheme to ditch him. To ditch my family.

I stop my fingers from playing with my hair, tighten my grip on the plate instead, and throw a glance at the clock on the oven. Seven. The ceremony starts in an hour. I clench my jaw. My head is starting to hurt, but I'm not a princess like the lyric in my song. I can figure this out. There has to be a way. With the red carpet and schmoozing before the event, I might have enough time to get there before the doors close.

I need my phone. Or a better memory. Or live in the last century when people wrote each other's phone numbers on paper. Wil's number is just as lost to me as my phone. Is it still hidden in his messenger bag?

Dad steals a canapé from my plate and bumps my shoulder. "Isn't this great?" He grins at the small gathering.

"Marta seems to think so." This would be great, if I weren't supposed to be upstairs slipping into the dress Zoe made for me to wear tonight. I plaster on a smile to hide the turmoil in my stomach. The effort of pulling the corners of my lips wide sends pangs into my skull. If I come up with a reason to cut the cake now, and put my makeup on at the stop lights in the car, I might be a bit late, but I can still make it.

"And this is just the beginning." What? My mouth goes dry. Dad can't be doing this to me. My stomach lurches, and my blood pressure spikes. "I have a surprise for all of you." Tonight, I don't want any more surprises. They mean this party will drag on with less chance for me to disappear and get to the gala.

Dad claps his hands above his head and draws the attention to himself. "Time for a surprise."

"No, Mr. Rockerby. This was already too much." Marta's objection holds no weight. Dad has something up his sleeve.

"Today I want to celebrate not only Marta's birthday, but the fact that she's been an integral part of my household for ten years." Dad finds his way to the middle of the living room. "Marta has been here through the most memorable times of my life, and I hope will continue to be part of our growing family for at least as many. This house"—Dad spreads his arms wide—"is not just a reflection of us but has so many touches that Marta brought in to make our lives special. So"—Dad drumrolls on the sofa table—"we're going on a Marta-themed scavenger hunt."

The guests are gasping, clapping, and I'm dying. The tension in my head is going to kill me. No way this thing can be done in fifteen minutes or less.

"Divide into teams of two, and we start on the side deck."

Marta waves at me. "I'd like Melodie to be on my team." Her eyes shine with warmth and excitement.

"Yey! Team M&M is back," I shout with what I hope sounds like enthusiasm. My mind is not on Marta, but on Wil. I need to come up with some way to contact him and let him know what's going on.

"Bathroom break and I'll join you." I plant a kiss on her rouged cheek. "Be right back."

I run down the hallway to the guest bedroom. There's a land line there. I snatch the receiver. My hands shake as I punch in Sven's cell: the only phone number drilled into my head in case of emergency.

"This is Sven." His curt greeting cuts through the static on the line.

A string of tension eases between my shoulders. Sven will help me. "Sven, its Melodie."

There's a pause. "You gave me a heart attack. I thought the house was under siege."

"No everything's fine." Everything is most definitely not fine. "Could you do something for me?"

"Are you hurt? Where's Rocker?" The cheese swirls in my stomach.

"No, no, I'm fine."

"Is it Marta?"

"No." I practically yell. He's not listening to me. No one listens to me. No, Wil does. I can't let him down. "It's me. I need you. I need you to go to Starlight Foundation Gala. Wil's—"

"You're kidding, right?"

I freeze in place. The vinegar in Sven's voice burns through my brain. I've never heard him talk like this. I hit the middle of my forehead as if it'll release the mounting pressure of trying to please everyone. "I . . . it's an emergency."

"Has Wil been bitten by a poisonous snake?" His words are full of snark and prick at my skin. "Do I have to deliver the antidote?"

"Stop this."

"Do you have the secret code to stop a bomb?"

"This isn't funny."

"Couldn't agree more."

"Sven, please."

"Go back to your party." The line goes dead and so do my hopes of getting to Wil. A tear rolls down my cheek, and I wipe it away.

"Melodie? Marta is waiting." Dad's summons mocks me, reminding me I don't have control over anything.

"Coming." I throw the receiver against the wall, and the battery pops out with a crack that echoes the invisible fracture splitting my head. My temples throb. My vision swims. I close my eyes, and the memory of the vacant surface of the lake seeps through the fissure. My biggest failure. The last place where I saw Papa. The image I refuse to face. No matter how hard I try, I keep failing.

Thirty-One

Shit. It's 8 o'clock. The ceremony is starting, and no word from El.

Me: Stuck in traffic?

No dots. I wait five minutes and text her again.

Me: The ceremony is about to begin.

Still nothing. She has to be here. The staff ushers in the stragglers. The foyer is empty. Maybe I missed her slipping in the side entrance, and she's already at our table. I tiptoe inside and stand at the back scanning for El.

The room of dolled-up men and women lacks a red head or even a fake blond wig. The small sliver of hope dies inside my heart. The reality of her not coming pushes its way into my chest, replacing the sense of excitement at what tonight could've been. Should've been.

I give up and plop into the seat beside Sarah, weary of appearing like a loser stood up at prom. I avoid the vacant spot to my left, where a napkin formed into a flower mocks me. One last try to contact the only girl who has the power to crush me.

Me: They closed the doors. I'm on the far left. Text, and I'll let you in.

Sarah taps on my shoulder, "Still no word?"

My phone mocks me with a row of one-sided texts. I slide it her way. "Nothing."

She ignores it, angles me to face her, and catches my eye. "What if something happened? She must have a good reason—"

"Sticking up for your friend. Good for you." Why does she always meddle? It's her fault I invited El in the first place. "Don't come up with excuses. She has a phone. She can use it. She chose not to." I stand up and let Sarah's hands fall away.

Mateo waves from the Green Team's side. I've had enough of "Camp El" at my table. An empty chair next to him offers refuge.

"Where's your date?"

Not him too. "The fuck do I know?"

"Did something go wrong? Something happen? Need to—"

"Not here for more excuses." I push off the seat to leave.

"Hey, mein freund." He opens his coat jacket and takes out a bottle of water. "I got you. This will take the edge off."

I collapse back into the chair and give Mateo my questioning face. He unscrews the lid, the seal already broken, and motions for me to sip. I take a gulp and nearly spit it out. Vodka. Mateo laughs at me.

Another gulp. I've been drunk before, and even though it's been a while and vodka is different from beer, I know I need more than a handful of shots. The burn feels good. It matches my mood. Princess couldn't even be bothered to text to say she wasn't coming. One more gulp. It's not like tonight was important or anything. It's only our fucking song up for an award.

Booze is my friend. Another swig scratches my throat. The alcohol floods my veins and drowns the fantasy of an evening with El by my side.

Julia, a girl from my sound editing class, turns her head and looks at the bottle Mateo and I keep passing between us. The red dress she's wearing, or should I say is wearing her, matches her full lips. I slam back another shot and extend the bottle to her.

The smooth fire of the alcohol mixes with the rippling tide of my disappointment. I've been betting on the wrong person. El's up in her castle on the hill, and I'm only playing dress-up. Take off this penguin suit, and I'm an ordinary bloke, not some prince.

I never should've invited her, trusted her. What was I thinking, falling for her excitement about the event, believing it genuine? That was my first mistake. She's been to lots of these. This is nothing special. I'm nothing special. She forgot about me and that's what I need to do. Forget. And alcohol is the fastest route to oblivion. I take the bottle away from Mateo and fill my mouth with the liquid that no longer burns. I'm past the feeling stage, and I'm thankful for that numbing mercy.

"The Starlight Award for Best Song goes to *Our Lines, Indigo*." The name of our song brings me back into the room that explodes with applause. Everyone at the table stares at me.

"More reasons to celebrate." Mateo slaps me on the back. The motion sends my head into a spin. I lean forward and stare at my plate, trying to regain my focus.

"You need to go." Nick's voice is close, too close. What's he doing over here?

"Nick?" I don't risk moving my head to see where he stands. "Join the party." My tongue is too big for my mouth. It's hard to form sentences when the world refuses to make sense. "We're celebrating."

"You've done enough celebrating." My chair jerks, but I hold on, scrambling to keep the room from shifting sideways. "The host is waiting for you." The ghost of Nick drones on.

Another sip is sure to make this version of imaginary Nick go away. I raise an almost empty plastic water bottle, but it doesn't make it to my lips.

Mateo snatches it and keeps it out of my reach. "They're waiting for you. El or no El, you deserve this award. Go get it."

El. Why did Mateo have to mention her? I almost forgot the pain the lack of her causes. Mateo's words do what the moving room didn't. Bile rises into my throat. "I'm not going there alone. I wasn't supposed to do this alone."

"You're not alone. We're all here." Sarah's hands me a glass of water. "Drink this, and we'll help you."

"I don't want any help."

"This is not about you. This is about *Indigo*. About our team." Nick's reminder cuts through the haze. I'm part of a team. "We're depending on you. You're messing it up for all of us if you don't get up."

They are depending on me. If my team needs me, I gotta get up. I can do it for them, even if I don't care about it. I push away from the table, and the reception hall tilts. Sarah threads her arm through mine and stabilizes me. Nick's on my other side, and the three of us stumble onto the stage.

I don't remember much after that.

THIRTY-TWO

El

I CAN'T LIE HERE anymore. For the twentieth time, I glance at the darkness behind my window and try not to think about Wil. The sun refuses to rise, so I do. I click on the light and find my watch. Four forty-five in the morning. Hours until I can safely escape.

Every time I closed my eyes last night, thoughts of the Starlight Gala denied me any sleep. Did *Indigo* win for best movie? What about our song? But most of all, my mind played scenarios of Wil all alone. Disappointed with me. Mad at me. Hurt I didn't show up. I called the venue and left a message for him but who knows if they gave it to him. I cling to the hope they did. I don't want to be the reason Wil's big night was spoiled.

Marta's surprise party turned out great, and I'm glad Dad organized it for her, but what was a magnificent surprise for her turned into a nightmare for me. My attempts at swaying Sven to take me to the gala for just long enough to talk to Wil and come back to the festivities were met with Sven's new favorite answer: No. I never meant to put his job in jeopardy or hurt him. He has to know that.

It's no use. I have to do something. Dad's go-to when he's stressed somehow turned into mine. Slippers on, I sneak downstairs to the kitchen. It's not even a question of what to make. Flour, baking powder, salt, stir. Cream the butter with the sugar, add the egg. I open the fridge and search for the most important ingredient. Blueberries.

The second batch in the oven, I sneak across the lawn. Three muffins and a coffee the way Sven likes it, two creams, no sugar, tremble on the tray in my hands. I balance it on one knee and knock on the door of the guards' quarters.

"Sven?"

I hear a loud thud, heavy steps, and the door bursts open.

"Yes?" Sven's voice is clipped. His chest heaves. I've interrupted his workout. Again.

"Muffins?" I raise my offering his way.

"At what cost?" He doesn't move.

"Why would there be a cost?"

"There always is with you."

"No fair."

"Do I need to rob a bank? Steal a plane?"

I shove the tray into his chest and watch the hot coffee spill over the rim onto the plain white saucer. "I have to see Will."

"Serious?"

"I am. I have to apologize."

"Wil gets an apology, and I don't."

I meant to hide that I was busking, not destroy his trust. "I'm sorry. You're my friend. I never wanted to hurt you."

"Be ready in thirty minutes." He shuts the door in my face.

The aroma of the second batch of freshly baked muffins fills the kitchen when Dad walks in. "Trying to give Marta a run for her money?"

"Had a craving. Love how blueberries go well with lemon." Dad and I made last night's dessert of Lavender Lemon Blueberry Cake. He plucks one of the fifteen muffins cooling on the rack and stuffs half of it in his mouth before I can offer an espresso.

He makes a face like he's never eaten anything this good. I grab my satchel hiding Wil's portion.

Mom runs into me at the kitchen door. "Off so soon?"

"I promised Nadine I'll be there early today to make up for leaving before we finished the recording yesterday. You don't want me to get in trouble with my boss?"

"I'm her boss," Dad says through the muffin in his mouth. "Or the boss of her boss, but that means I'm your boss, and I can tell her you had breakfast with us."

"As if people in the office don't already think I'm treated differently."

"Let her go, Bill." Mom rubs Dad's arm. "She's being responsible."

I tap my foot, waiting for Sven to get into the car. Any other day, and he's pushing me to leave. Today, he's pretending to be a sloth, everything he does is in slo-mo, and I don't dare say anything. Whenever I do open my mouth, his stare reminds me I hurt him. He's upset, and I'm lucky he hasn't told my parents about my selfish escapades.

"I'm sorry." Not even a cold stare this time. This is getting worse by the minute.

I can't blame him. But he's not who I'm worried about right now.

Wil is my priority.

Sven revs the engine.

"I'm sorry." I can't stop apologizing. "There was no way you would've let me busk."

"You didn't even ask." Sven spews. "Have I not supported you? I offered you money to pay for the video in the first place, but you had to do it your way. Every week, I sneak you out to the Devil's Martini, cover for you, so you can practice and write your songs."

His words scratch me like thorns from the blackberry bush in the back of Gran's garden, tearing at me, leaving me bleeding.

"Do you know what it would mean if your father found out? I'd never get my business off the ground."

I'm a horrible human being. Tears threaten to break through. I should've trusted Sven. He trusts me. Trusted me.

"All this, and you still lack faith." Sven slams on the brakes. "Fifteen minutes."

"I *am* sorry, Sven." I grab the bag off the floor and run into Wil's building.

In the living room, a guy is eating Cheerios from the box. Loud battle cries from an anime's fighters cover up his crunching.

"Where's Wil's room?" I have to wait for him to finish chewing the mouthful. Crunch, crunch, crunch like the ratchet in an orchestra. He points to the ceiling. "Second on the left."

A woman in a fancy red dress passes me as I take the stairs two at a time. The outfit is beautiful but completely inappropriate for this time of day. Perfect for a fancy event like the gala last night. I turn to look at her fleeing form and catch a glimpse of a gold statue of a star, the logo for the Starlight Foundation, in her hand.

The beige hallway is empty. Too early for students not doing the walk of shame to be up, I guess. I find what I hope is Wil's door and knock. No answer. A door across the hall opens and Mateo walks out, stops when he sees me and squishes up his face. He's dressed in a bathrobe, towel over his shoulder. "Ah, hey, El."

"Morning. Is this Wil's room?"

Mateo nods.

I turn and knock, louder this time.

Mateo slides in beside me. "You're gonna have to be louder. Wil had quite the party."

My stomach turns at his words. What does he mean? "Is he sick?"

Mateo shakes his head as he pounds on the door. "Nothing a few aspirin can't fix. Man, I knew Germans could drink, but he set a record last night." He purses his lips. "Boy knows how to party."

I'm about to bail on my mission when the door flies open.

"What the fuck?" Wil stands before me. Half-naked. I think. All I see are abs, chest, abs. I want to look away. I can't look away.

"You have a visitor." Mateo walks off.

Wil rubs his forehead and scoffs. "What do you want?"

"I . . . I—" The words won't come. I manage to drag my eyes away from his bare chest. He looks terrible. His face is pale, and there are bags under his eyes. Eyes that are dark and stormy, lacking their usual warmth. Isn't he cold standing there in just boxers? "Are you okay?"

"Like you care."

What is it with the men in my life today?

"Sorry?" I feel like I'm missing part of this conversation.

"Sure, princess."

That word again. It's a knife in my heart. He hasn't called me that since we became friends.

I hold out the bag with my baked goods. Wil looks at the brown paper like I'm offering him poison. "I made you muffins for breakfast." He doesn't move. "A peace offering for last night. I—"

"Got a better offer?"

"What? No. I couldn't leave the house. It's Marta's birthday today, and Dad decided to surprise her last night. He cooked dinner. I didn't know, and I couldn't leave. Marta is family."

"*Normal* people"—he emphasizes "normal," and I flinch at the term—"oh, I don't know, have the decency to at least text an excuse why they're bailing on plans. Or am I not good enough for that? Good ol' Wil won't care."

"Wil." I step back from the onslaught. "That's not—"

He scowls. "Don't worry, I found other ways to entertain myself."

My heart is a target for his words, and every one hits a bullseye. Running my fingers through my white streak is supposed to help, to sooth me, but the image of the girl in the red dress, award-in-hand, finds its mark. Another knife to slice me open. I might be standing in an ordinary hallway, but inside I'm bleeding. I'm the stupid heroine who fell for the wrong guy.

How can he have no faith in me? I almost lost Sven because of him. Risked my freedom over and over to be with him. And the jerk slept with the first girl who caught his eye, while I tossed and turned in bed awake all night.

I clench my teeth and rip the blades out of my heart. He doesn't get to hurt me anymore. The girl in the red dress can have him. Time to get what I need and leave. I shove the food at his perfect chest. Screw him.

He crumples the bag before it falls, just like he's done to my trust. "They're blueberry, by the way."

I elbow my way past him, into his bedroom, scan the space, trying to ignore the pile of clothing on the floor, trying not to imagine how they got there. Over by the window I spot his messenger bag, dive toward it, unzip the inside pocket and pull out my phone. Wil stands there watching me.

"This"—I shove my phone with the crest of Malta in his face—"is why I didn't text, you jackass." I push my way out the door and call over my shoulder, "You had my phone."

The hallway is fuzzy as tears swell in my eyes. I rub at them, almost giving myself a black eye. I swore I'd never cry over a boy again. I'm such a fool.

A wall of muscle stops me in my tracks. I try to sidestep Wil's bare chest, but it moves in tune with me, not letting me by.

"El. Stop."

I swing left, but he follows. His hands are on either side of my face, and I freeze.

"I—" His voice fades away as he drags his thumb across my cheek, removing a tear that betrayed me and escaped. "No, don't cry." A warm tingly feeling spreads through my skin at his touch, at the soft tone his voice takes on.

"I'm not crying." It's a lie. I'm so crying. I try to jerk away from his hands, but he holds tighter. His touch burns me as he presses his forehead against mine.

"Please." Hot breath puffs on my cheek as he speaks. I try to find my voice to say something, but I can't speak, my mind confused by the nearness of him. Why am I so hot? And it's not hot with anger . . . The whirlpool of lava picks up speed, and I'd much rather it didn't. Anything I feel around him comes back and hurts me in the end. Why is my media training not working? Why can't I be the cool and collected Melodie I've mastered so well?

"I didn't know. I'm an arse." Another soft stroke on my cheek. It nearly kills me. A moment ago, he was a beast with a sore paw and now he's, I don't know, remorseful? Happy?

We stand like that, breathing in sync. The little puffs move down my cheek until his lips are a hair away from me. If I tilt my head a little—

Sven's ringtone cuts through the air, making my ears hurt. I jerk away and hit answer.

"So, you found your phone?"

"Yes." That's all I can say, my stare on Wil. His arms are crossed as he leans against the wall, eyes down.

"Do you want to be late for work?"

"Yes." Why won't Wil look at me? Then Sven's question hits me. "I mean no. I'm on my way now."

I hang up. "I have to go. Sven is waiting, and he's mad at me too." I move toward the stairs and Wil catches my wrist.

"El."

I glance back at him. "Yes?"

He opens his mouth to say something, then purses his lips together. When he does speak, it's not what I was expecting. "Will I see you at the bar tomorrow night?"

His hand is hot around my wrist, and his grip is tight. I have to pull to release it. "Of course." I turn and run down the stairs.

THIRTY-THREE

"TOLD YOU SHE HAD a good reason." Mateo leans against the frame of his door.

"You heard all that?"

"Front row seat, just like last night."

I run my hand over my face at the memories of the event, the ceremony, the after party. At a certain point, they're more like snippets, flashes of images. Nick on stage, Sarah kissing him. Siobhan flirting with Asher Menken. No, that can't be right. A red dress.

"Julia." Her face close to mine. In my room. The sickly sweet stench of her flowery perfume I can smell around me now. I didn't. Did I? "Bloody hell."

"Get over yourself, mein freund. You're not the only one around here capable of pulling in the ladies." Mateo pushes off the door frame and smirks. "Just so happens, she likes the Latin blood more than the alcohol-soaked stuff streaming through your veins last night. You were a mess."

I feel a mess.

"She helped me get you back here and then, well, that's really none of your business. But she just left, so you can draw your own conclusions." Mateo looks down the stairs, where El ran away from me moments earlier.

El. I follow Mateo's gaze, as if she might reappear there. My stomach is rolling, and I'm not sure if it's because of the hangover or the thought of how wrongly I judged her. Never even considered she couldn't get away. Didn't remember she always left her phone in my messenger bag. Didn't have faith in her. I'm such an arse.

I look at my hands, the thumb that brushed away her tears. I close my eyes to concentrate on not vomiting. I made El cry. The thought rolls around in my head like a battering ram. Why didn't I give her a chance to explain?

"Did I hear there were muffins?"

"Might be muffin crumble." I pick up the bag, take a handful of mushed up breakfast and put it into my mouth. The pastry is still warm. Did she make these fresh this morning? Gooey blueberries, tart with a hint of sweetness just the way I like them, explode on my tastebuds.

Mateo eats half a muffin in one go. "Better than the stale stuff you bring from Blend."

"Shit, what time is it?" I find my phone and exhale in relief. "I still have time to shower before Nick starts texting me about being late."

"Hold up. I was going to talk to you last night"—he eyes me up and down—"but you know how that went."

"Later? I gotta clean up."

"Sure. But the peeps need an answer on when you're outta here. Other people are asking about the room. We agreed on two Sundays from now. Is that still the plan?" Mateo cocks his head to the side. "Or are you taking my advice and signing up for the class I found for you? Today's the last day to register."

"Give me a minute to think." Think about what just happened. Or almost happened. What I want to do. Do I want to stay? I close my eyes and see El's face. Am I ready to walk away from the money singing with her brings in? "Let me shower. Can you wait that long?"

"Go for it. Maybe even brush your teeth. Twice. You smell like a distillery."

In the solitude of the bathroom, I try not to throw up. Shite. I made El cry. I can't do this anymore. Can't hurt her like this. I lock the door and dial Opa.

"Hello?" It's the middle of the afternoon there. I can't have woken him up.

"I need to talk to you."

"Who's this? Speak up. Can't hear you."

I raise my voice a bit. It's not like people here speak German. "Opa. It's Wil."

"The prodigal son, at last. Your mother's planning a special Sunday roast for your return. I'm not supposed to tell you, but there are no secrets between you and me."

"That's what I wanted to talk to you about. I want to stay here."

"What do you mean, stay?"

"Spend a semester here. At UCLA."

"Need more time to talk to you know who?"

"Yes." I hesitate. "No. I've got a better way to get the money. I don't need anything from him."

"I didn't know I raised a quitter." His insult grates across my splitting head. In my twenty years, I've rarely disappointed Opa. He's not a soft man, no hard crust with a gooey center like me. But he's honest, and every ounce of praise he gave me felt earned. Every reprimand like losing my right hand.

I strum my fingers on the porcelain of the sink. "I'm not going to lie and beg and—"

"Take what is yours?"

"It is not mine. And I don't want it, even if it was. Not for the price I might have to pay." I catch my reflection in the mirror. I look like shit. I still look like him, and I don't want that either. "I like my life, and I've seen what being famous because of your parents is like. There're other ways. Like you said, America is the land of opportunity. I'm making good money here. With some more time, I'll get enough for Mum's treatment. I promise you. I will find the money, but it has to be my way."

A knock on the door. "Bathroom ain't for personal calls, bud. Talk to your girlfriend in your room."

Opa grumbles in my ear. "I disagree. It's a mistake. He owes her. You."

"Opa—"

"Asshole, get out of the bathroom, already." The voice from behind the door shouts and jiggles the handle. Opa hangs up before I can finish my sentence.

Mateo is dressed and waiting for me when I get back. "I thought you drowned or ran away. Wasn't sure what was more likely."

"I'm staying. How much will that cost?"

Mateo slaps me on the shoulder. "Wunderbar. And don't worry about the rent. We will figure something out."

I pull my black jeans on and search for my green T-shirt—the only one that doesn't smell. I need to do laundry at some point. "About that. Any way I can earn more cash? In addition to rent?"

"What are we talking?"

"That offer to DJ still on? I've done parties, events, or I can play the guitar." Mateo knows half the people on this campus by now, he has to be able to find me something.

"Sing?"

"Not me. That's El's thing."

"Will she be part of the gig as well?" I don't like the glint in Mateo's eye.

"After this morning, I'm not sure she'll be part of anything that involves me."

"She'll come around. No one can stay mad at you for long."

I type my tenth message this morning to El. I've erased all of them so far. I don't know what to say to her. So much for being the words person.

I haven't written anything in my black book since Thursday, either. Strange.

I have to text something.

Me: Do you have my water bottle?

I know she does, but I don't know what else to write.

It's hours until we go on stage, and with no busking on Fridays because El has a standing lunch with Zoe, it feels like forever since I've seen my singing partner. I went to the farmers' market at noon yesterday to grab lunch just in case her plans got canceled. Hot sun, fried pork, and a hangover are not a good combination.

El: I'll bring it tonight.

Bloody hell. What kind of an answer is that? Where's the saucy comeback? And I don't want it, really. I kinda like the thought of her taking care of it.

My chest hurts. I give up. Will talk to El when I see her, easier to read her mood that way. I screwed up yesterday—I rub the heavy spot along my sternum—well, Thursday and yesterday morning. Despite months of learning about her world, about her, I forget even the basic things can be hard for her. Why didn't I remember her phone was in my bag? I hit my solar plexus, trying to dislodge the dead weight of regret, but it lingers. Of course, she didn't have a chance to get it when Sven tore her away from me.

The big guy looked pissed, and that's saying something. I didn't think anything would ever crack his shell. I brace against the wall, and free my fingers to race over the cracks in the patched plaster. We weren't doing anything wrong. I was careful no one would recognize El. I would never let anything happen to her. No, I just make her cry. I hate myself.

Except it's not El that walks through the door to the bar. It looks like her, wig hiding her true hair. The disguise is flawless. But where's the smile? Her lips stretch into some imitation of it all right, but it's all wrong.

"Hi. Ready to go?" This El is cool, formal. A perfect match to Melodie Rockerby from the interviews I watched before I met her. Reporters—asking the same question over and over, her—controlled and emotionless. Distant. Her emptiness is heavier than her anger was, and every ounce presses down on me.

My gaze drops to the toes of her brown boots. "Sorry about yesterday. I—"

"No worries. I'm glad you had fun at the gala."

"Fun? Oh, you mean because our song won. Yeah. That was great." I barely remember it. Nick made the acceptance speech. Sarah propped me up while on stage. "I'm not sure what happened to the award though."

Pauline is on stage, announcing us. There's quite the crowd tonight, and the applause charges the air with expectation.

"Maybe the girl you slept with took it. As a memento."

Slept with? It takes a second to grasp what El said.

"I—"

El's already walking on stage, guitar in hand.

Wait. She brought her guitar?

Is she playing tonight? We haven't practiced anything with two guitars. Is her hand healed enough to play? Does she not want me on stage with her anymore? Well, she's not getting the chance. Pauline is paying both of us, and I need the money, more than ever now.

I stride on to the stage and stand beside El.

"Thank you for coming out to see us. We love you all." El addresses the audience. "Let's kick things off with something fun. This is an oldie, but I'm in the mood for a little girl power. Here's Whitney Houston's *It's Not Right, But It's Okay*."

What is she doing? I don't know this song. There's nothing for me to do but watch El strum the guitar, singing words about surviving a cheating boyfriend. I pull up a stool, sit on stage, and wait for El to finish her power anthem.

The crowd claps and before El has a chance to take control again, I launch into one of the songs we have practiced. She has no choice but to follow. I feel smug, but it only lasts for a moment. Her heart isn't in the music, there's no spark. It's like she's going through the motions of the song, hitting the notes, but she's not singing with me.

I hate it.

What is going on?

"So, a little bit about us." El's voice is chipped, not the girl having fun like we've been having for months now. And she won't look at me. "Let's see. I like to bake, and Wil's favorite color is red."

What is she talking about? My favorite color is blue. Where would she get the idea I like red? Bloody hell. Julia. Mateo said Julia left before El got there. Did she see Julia leaving and assume she came from my room? That's why El thinks I slept with someone.

I step up to the mic. "Actually, you have me mixed up with our friend Mateo. He loves red. I'm a fan of blue, myself." I point at the helio design on my black shirt, the same one I wore the first night we met.

Her eyes, the perfect shade of my favorite color, widen. She gets my meaning. That's right, El, I didn't sleep with that girl.

Halfway through the next song, I can't suppress my grin. El Vella is jealous.

The audience doesn't want to let us go. We play an encore, and another one, and Pauline has to come out on the stage and free us, to the boos and "Make them sing" heckles from the bar. It's almost perfect. Almost, because when I reach to grab El's hand for our final bow before we escape backstage, she doesn't let me. She doesn't push me away but moves her fingers around my searching ones. She can't still be mad at me. Can she?

El walks over to the blue bag she lugs her stuff in, and I half hope there are more muffins for me in there. She turns back, and it's not a muffin. It's my water bottle.

"Here. Sounded like you needed it." She shoves it into my hands, but I don't take it. The bottle clatters to the floor and rolls toward the stage. El bends down to grab it before it gets too far. "I'll just leave it here." She puts it next to my foot and walks back to her bag.

I snatch the damn bottle off the linoleum, catch up with her in two steps, take her hand and press the bottle into it. "It's yours. I don't need it."

She doesn't let go of the bottle like I did. "Why ask about it then?" Her eyes move between mine, searching for an answer I refuse to give. But I have to say something. I'm the words person.

"It was dumb. I was an arse. I didn't know what else to say. You sounded off. I was checking in on you, that's all. Keep the bloody thing. Please. I'd love for you to have it."

El pulls the bottle to her chest, unscrews the lid, and takes a sip. "I'd love to have it. No backsies."

The sass I was missing reappears, easing the burden of my mistakes. The scuffed walls of the backstage regain their charm and the world is back to normal again.

"Did our song really win?" El's voice is small and hesitant.

"It sure did." I remember the applause that rocked the room when we won. "I wish you could've been there, on that stage, accepting the award." I lift my gaze to hers and relax under the familiar sparkle of her ocean eyes.

"I wish I could too. I did plan to come. I had a dress and everything." El leans forward. "And it was your favorite color." She whispers into my ear.

The smell of beach, waves, and El mingles in the air, and I need her closer.

"Blue?" The squeak in my voice betrays my yearning.

"Yup. Zoe made it. It's a one-shoulder, and I was going to wear heels."

My mind conjures the fantasy of me running my fingers over the exposed skin revealed by the dress.

"I'd love to see it someday." I place my hand on the curve of her lower back and inhale once more. I can't get enough.

She bites her lip. Her eyes flicker to mine, the spark sending shivers down my spin. "There'll be another event we can attend. And I'll make sure to wear it for you."

The door opens, and applause ruptures our bubble.

El steps out of my grasp.

"I'm looking forward to that." I scramble to get the words out before she disappears. She nods, smiles, and leaves me alone with dreams of a blue dress and possibilities.

THIRTY-FOUR

El

ZOE WALKS ACROSS THE carpet, lowers one shoulder of her jacket, and gives me a look over her sunglasses. We are inside my room, but today it's a pretend runway for her to come up with the final looks for her show.

"And I was thinking silver earrings with this." She picks up a pair of dangling flamingo-shaped ones, puts them in, and strikes the pose again. "So they graze the shoulder and swing when she poses. That'll totally be hot."

"Yep." I glance up at her and get back to the last text I got from Wil. I wish we got into the habit of sending each other selfies. Or some kind of photographic evidence. But all I get is his Instagram, and that has become ad central for Wil the DJ.

"And I will have them wear cat tails."

The images don't outright promote the fact he's working the parties. That's apparently not legal according to the student visa, but he's making sure that anyone who checks his profile out knows he can make a just-okay party into one every age group gets up and dances at.

"And I will make them hop like bunnies."

"Yep." From the look of the smiling girls, everyone is having fun. I know he's only posting those photos for marketing, but I hate that I can't be one of those girls. See him DJ, dance to his playlists.

"Mel." Zoe walks over and grabs the phone out of my hand. "What can be more important than my show? You're a horrible adviser." Her eyes widen as she scrolls through Wil's Instagram. "Hold up." More scrolling. "This may be more important." She plops down on my bed beside me. "Are you planning a party?"

"Give it back." I grab for my phone, but she keeps it out of reach. "First, I'm your music adviser, not a stylist. If I were any good at fashion, I wouldn't need you to nudge Mom into buying me the 'right' purse."

"I like this DJ StoneHelm. Is he a friend of yours?"

I laugh. "That's Wil."

"Wil Wil? The one you've been singing with?"

"There's only the one."

"And he's a DJ as well? What does he not do?"

"Apparently, not much. Can I have my phone back?"

She hands over the device and flops back on the bed. I match her, staring at the stars on my ceiling. I put them there when we first moved into this house as a way of keeping some normalcy in my life. The stars are always in the sky, no matter what part of the world Mom took me to. At some point, I started creating my own constellations and adding them to the room I slept in.

Zoe grabs my hand. "I have a brilliant idea."

"I expect nothing less."

"You know my party next week?"

"Of course. I had to beg your mom to talk my mom into coming because she wasn't going to let me go without her."

She waves that off like it was no big deal. Except it is a big deal. This pregnancy has turned my I'm-worried-about-you mom into the I-don't-want-you-out-of-my-sight mom. And Dad is no help. It's like she's infected him as well. I can't breathe these days.

"Yep. Congrats. Back to me." She turns on her side. "You know I have to have the best. And from the looks of those pictures, your friend Wil knows how to make a party pop."

"Zoe . . ."

"Remember that favor you owe me? I'm calling it in. Let's hire Wil to DJ my party. Get some sick beats, and I finally meet the man who's taking all your attention away from me."

"Isn't it a pool party?"

"Well, not everyone likes the water like I do. People like you, for example, can enjoy the music, dance, while people like me will enjoy showing off my new bikini."

"I don't know." Is it a good idea to have Wil around Zoe? She might say something with Mom around. I turn to look at her. "Aunt Patti will be okay with that?"

"She gave me a budget." Zoe laughs. Like she's ever stuck to a budget. When Zoe wants something, she gets it. "What does he charge?"

"I'll have to ask him, but you'll have to do cash."

Zoe makes a face. "Who does cash anymore?"

"He's not technically allowed to work off campus. And you can't tell that to your mom. Or tell her I know him. And most definitely nothing about Wil to my mom."

"All right, all right, no telling anyone anything." Zoe winks at me. "I guess I can use that money Mormor sends me every year. She's so old school. I never get to a bank to put it in an account. Not a biggie."

"That works."

Zoe bounces on the bed. "Let's ask him now."

I groan. I want to think about this. But Zoe wants this, and Zoe gets what she wants. "Please, please, please."

I pull up Wil's phone number.

El: I have an idea how you can make some extra cash, but it's not exactly above board.

I tap my foot as I wait for Wil to respond to my text. He's probably in class right now. I should have waited until after four.

Wil: Do tell.

Me: My cousin needs a DJ for her birthday party. And you being a DJ and all, maybe you'd want to do it.

Wil: When?

"What time do you need him there and for how long?" I look at Zoe bouncing her shoe on the tip of her foot.

"Party starts at two. He should get there a bit before. And he should plan to stay until at least midnight. If I need him longer, I'll pay extra."

Me: Next Sunday at one. Will take all day. Zoe can pay $$$

Wil: Are you going?

Me: It's my cousin, so yeah.

Wil: I'm in.

Zoe's Calabasas home has been a place of one too many birthday parties that culminated in sleepovers, and most of them ended with us ditching the guests, piling into a car, and her chauffeur dropping us off at the white-and-orange awning of Jeni's Ice Cream. We'd try the latest flavors, buy the same old favorites we always got, and giggle on the bright yellow chairs until the store clerks shooed us out to close up at ten.

Today, there's no sleepover for me. Mom's opinion is that Aunt Patti is too careless and not responsible enough to keep me on the grounds. Safe. Coming along with me to ensure I'm not running off to Australia (her words, not mine) is Mom's way of loosening the grip so I don't have to skip my cousin's nineteenth birthday party.

"The Birkin we gave her last year was her first one, but one is never enough." Mom hands the sizable box her assistant wrapped in white paper topped with a silver glitter bow to the gifts attendant. Mom's obsession with high-end bags began with the first classic Chanel clutch her mom gave her for her fifth birthday. Nilsen women have closets full of them. We could probably feed a small country for months if we were to ever sell them.

"You know the rules. Stay on the property." Here she goes treating me like a five-year-old. "Do not leave my or Sven's sight. No drinking. No drugs. No talking to strangers." Her finger is wagging like a metronome with each rule. "You never know who might be paparazzi."

"It was one time, Mom." A reporter got pictures by posing as a server at Aunt Patti's twenty-fifth anniversary party. Ever since, Mom's lack of faith in my aunt's security has been a constant.

"Be polite to anyone you don't know but say you need to go check on something and walk away."

I've heard a version of this speech so many times, I don't have to listen. Instead, I take in the crowd. Seems more guests than last year when the theme was Pretty in Pink. The white tent dominating the left side of the lawn houses a long glass bar and a smattering of tall tables. Tucked into the farthest corner from the house is a small stage with the DJ station behind.

Everything is silver and white—this year's theme. The pool at the other side of the house features white star-shaped floaties with bunches of white and silver balls bobbing around them, creating constellations in the aqua water. A couple of dudes, who must be the male models Zoe told me about wanting to hire, walk around the edge in tight white shorts. One is blowing up the remaining floaties with an electric pump that's several decibels louder than the music trickling in from the speakers. Shouldn't they have been done with it before the party started?

"I can't even imagine what Zoe's wedding will be like. Patricia doesn't consider a party successful unless she has to redo the lawn afterward." Mom lifts her sunglasses, squints at the groups of guests creating a collage of the whites and silvers stipulated on the invites, and puts them back down when she spots Aunt Patricia and her husband Robert by the gazebo. The structure is festooned with waves of white and silver ribbons, matching balloons, and a garland of lights. "Keep your phone with you at all times. I'll text you when it's time to go."

Mom heads off one way, and there's no mistaking who's in charge here. I hope Dad makes it today. He dulls Mom's edges like no one else. She's less of a sharp object around him. Today, her outfit accommodates her growing belly, but there's been no softening or losing the cutting quality I'm eager not to be the focus of.

Zoe is easy to spot. She's wearing a white bikini with a transparent silvery sarong wrapped around her toned thighs. The girl knows how to make the men notice her. She's the only woman in our family who crossed the five-foot-six threshold and towers over us, resembling her dad's side of the family with long legs and olive skin.

I cross the makeshift dance floor and pinch her slender waist. She twists my way, scowls like I stole her favorite earrings but quickly switches to a perfect smile. We hug, and I see who she's been talking to—Wil.

He's wearing a white shirt with the top three buttons open, revealing a peek-a-boo of the chest I saw outside his room that day. The sleeves of the shirt are rolled up, and every time he moves equipment from the floor onto the table, the tendons in his forearms move. He fits in. While the guys by the pool couldn't have been mistaken for guests, Wil's confidence shines. I know he's the hired help, but if he stepped from behind the turntables and mingled with the party goers, they wouldn't have a clue. How does he do this?

"He's delicious," Zoe whispers into my ear. "I can't believe you've been keeping him to yourself this entire time."

"I haven't—"

She lets go of my waist, and with the shield of her body gone, Wil spots me. His professional smile brightens into the real one I've come to know as genuine Wil. We're in the shade of the gazebo, but we might as well have been standing in full sun.

"Fancy seeing you here."

I know it's a joke, and not only because I organized this gig for him, of which I'm getting ten percent, because fair is fair, and I still need the cash, but because I'm familiar with this tone of voice. It might sound like your average sentence to the people who've not been around Wil, but I'm in the inner circle. He's toying with me. Testing my mood.

"Fancy, indeed."

"I was beginning to wonder if the legendary Rockerby family was ever going to put in an appearance. And here you all are."

"Mom's trying to explain to Zoe's mom"—I elbow my cousin a little too hard in her exposed midriff—"why I'm not allowed to stay for the sleepover."

"Rocker's not here yet?"

"He's going to try. At least, that's the plan. With international flights, it's out of his control."

"I'll check in on you before the dancing begins." Zoe jumps into the conversation like she's the center of attention. Which I guess she is, being the birthday girl and all. "Oh, and please, no Rocker songs. He'll either come and perform live, or we'll skip that part of the program."

"I've got it written down." He lifts his tiny black notebook and waves it in the air. Now that I know what he puts inside, I wish I could have a look-see at the latest collection of words he's added to the lined pages.

Zoe saunters to the pool, leaving Wil and me alone. He pushes his sleeves up farther, and I stare at his long fingers. "Need anything?"

"No, all set."

"Well . . ." I don't have any reason to stay here. "I'll be over there if you need anything."

THIRTY-FIVE

I PUSH THE VOLUME lever up, mixing the beats from the classic vinyl to bleed into the next song on the turntable to my left. The early fall gets a reminder that summer here in LA will unofficially last a bit longer. This moment. My brain insists on capturing it. To empty my mind, I scribble in my little black book and hide it under the table by my wallet.

Bodies begin to move to the beat of the song, and a more festive vibe spreads through the crowd. The tunes weave across decades, the songs stringing one to the other without breaking to catch a breath. I'm good at this thing.

My eyes halt at the sight of red hair bouncing and the shoulders below moving, as her hands pull off the ivory wrap dress to reveal a white bikini with silver stars. Her skin isn't as tan as I'd expect a SoCal Malibu-dweller's to be. The sunscreen I smell on her all the time might be responsible for that. The top of the bikini has no straps and wraps around her body, the edges covered in some sort of black stitching. The matching bottoms sit low on her hips with the details repeating, accenting her shapely ass.

"Shea Marie." El's cousin Zoe slips in beside me.

I don't see any other women where she's pointing. I do see a group of pool-decor posers in white shorts swarm around El and move to the music I'm considering turning off. They look hot. They might need a break. "Who are you talking about?"

"Not who. What. The swimsuit. Shea's my designer friend. Loves stars. More like a mentor, actually. I'm going to launch a swimwear line of my own." She points at her swimsuit. "You like?"

Her body is a good example of a runway model's physique. Anything would look good on her but, with her attitude, even if it didn't, she'd make everyone believe it did. I move my gaze back to El, who's surrounded by the dancing mannequins now. "Or do you still prefer Shea Marie?"

I don't reply.

"Message received." She takes a step away. "You should take a break. Grab a drink." She nods toward the bar where glasses full of white liquid are lined up like little snowmen at the Christmas Markets back home. "The bartender can make you whatever you want."

"Thanks." I choose a playlist that should keep the guests' ears occupied for at least half an hour, sync my phone with the speakers, and, hide it in my messenger bag. I find my way to the bar halfway between the gazebo and the pool. "A seltzer." The bartender puts ice into a tall glass, adds the fizzy water, and decorates it with a slice of lime, a mint leaf, and an umbrella. Even water is fancy here.

A hand on my back. "You made it."

I turn to meet blue eyes reminiscent of El's, but in a face plastered with makeup surrounded by sunlight for hair. Goosebumps race up my neck. Her mother. Sylvia Rockerby. The woman carrying my half brother in her womb. I take a step back. Her pupils dilate, and her red-stained lips part. "Sorry, I thought you were—"

There's a shriek behind us followed by a splash, and the face before me pales. Her head whips in the direction of the pool, and she screams, "Melodie!"

The panic in her voice seeps into me, her grip on my shoulder like a vise. I turn and search out the white bikini with silver stars and the black border, my feet moving in the direction Sylvia runs. I don't see El.

Two wankers in tight white shorts are pointing and laughing at the aqua water of the pool, which stops frothing from the flails of a girl with pale arms and red hair. There she is. I let out a breath.

And then take another, a pounding rises in my ears. Why is she not treading water?

I watch in horror as she sinks beneath the surface. Swim, princess. Why the bloody hell doesn't she?

Somewhere someone, I think Zoe, yells, "She can't swim, you idiots."

The taste of chlorine hits my lips. Everything is wet in an instant. My shirt is too tight to get a proper stroke in as I glide through the water to El, my jeans like lead weights wrapped around my legs. I reach out for her armpits, flip on my back, and kick us both up to the surface. She's no longer moving, her eyes closed, like she's given up, resigned herself to sinking to the bottom of the pool. I have to resist the urge to open my mouth, tell her to fight, I'm here, anything to wake her up.

She's not fighting me, which can be the hardest part, when the disoriented drowning person struggles against the lifeguard trying to save them. My training kicks in, and I locate the closest wall. I use my feet to propel us to it, closer to the shouts, and closer to the hard surface where I can start CPR.

Two of the wankers, who might've been the ones who pushed her in, help me lift her out of the water. I pull myself up onto the ledge, give her two rescue breaths first, and begin chest compressions to the song in my head our instructor drilled into us during my initial lifeguard training. Coach insisted all crew members were trained in CPR and encouraged us to get certified as lifeguards. El's eyes open, and she starts gagging. I turn her to the side and let her clear her airway.

When she stops, I pull up the wet bottom of my shirt and wipe her mouth.

Her red-rimmed eyes meet mine. "Wil?"

I press my forehead against hers, reveling in the feeling of her skin against mine. "You scared me."

"What happened?"

"I guess you fell in the water."

Her body stiffens in my arms. The serenity of the moment washes away when she sees the pool next to us. She pulls her legs up to her chest and pushes me away.

"Let me go. Let me go."

"El, it's okay. You're fine. I got you."

"No, no, no. Let me go."

"Baby girl." Her mother shoves at my shoulder, and I fall backwards.

The woman grabs at El's shoulders, wipes the wet hair off her face.

"I'm all right." El breaks free of her mother's clutches and gets up. Her eyes turn to the circle clustered around her and dart between the party guests, her cousin, the idiots who laughed at her. They land on me. I jump to my feet and take a step forward. She matches my movement but away from me, turns, and runs across the lawn.

I look at Sylvia, expecting her to go after her daughter. Crumpled on the pool deck, her slumping shoulders shake, and small whimpers accompany the tremors of her body. What can I do?

Sylvia's sister beats me to it, kneeling beside her. She pulls El's mother close, cocooning her in an embrace.

I run after the girl I just had in my arms.

Zoe's right behind me. If she thinks she's going to stop me, she has another think coming.

She steps in front of me and pulls the glass door open. "She'll be in the music room. Down the hall on the left."

I stare at her.

She pushes on my back, propelling me forward. "Go."

The dark silence of the mansion swallows me. White marble is everywhere in the enormous kitchen that's bigger than my house. My bare feet splat against the tile floor, my shoes at the bottom of the pool, if I didn't chuck them when I dove in. Water drips off my clothes, leaving a wet trail as I skip to the other side where the hallway leads farther into the house.

The door to the only room at the end is ajar. I push through to a space with a curved wall of windows that flood soft afternoon light filtered through tall trees onto the gleaming hardwood floors. In the middle of the room sits a white grand piano, vacant and silent. No El here.

I turn to go, but a sniff from behind the piano stops me. I circle around and find her sitting on the floor almost underneath the massive instrument, arms wrapped around her legs, chin resting on her knees. Her eyes dart up when she hears me.

"Go away." She shifts farther under the piano.

I don't listen, bend down, and sidle up beside her. My jeans cling, still wet from the pool, and it's hard to cross my legs. I half expect her to scoot deeper in again, but she doesn't move. We sit there a moment. I search for something to say or do to make it better. Words don't come, so I put one arm around her waist.

Her skin is cold and damp. I tug her closer to warm her up. Water from her hair drips on my shoulder. Her head rests on my collar bone, nose touching the base of my neck. Before I know it, my other arm encircles her, pulling El even closer until she's pressed against me, her hand over my stuttering heart. She trembles, her own pounding against my chest like we are trying to make an epic drum and bass mix. I need to make it stop, need to make her okay again.

We sit like that, waterlogged cloth against soft skin. We wrap the curtain of timelessness around us until her heart rate returns to normal and the shaking fades into a memory.

"I was ten when it happened." Her voice scratches my neck. "I watched him die."

What the fuck?

She answers my silent question. The magic of wordless communication we share on stage extends to this moment. "My dad. We were on Lake Como in our speed boat when another boater cut us off. We hit a rock and . . ." I feel her swallow and tighten my hold.

"You don't have to—"

"I know." Her cheek rubs against the sodden collar of my white shirt. I'm supposed to be comforting her, but she's the one making me feel better. "Both of us were thrown from the boat. I had my vest on, but he hated wearing his. He was an excellent swimmer. It didn't help him. He had a . . . gash on his arm, bleeding. I think he got worn out, slipped under the water but came back. I tried, I did, but I couldn't hold him up."

I imagine a little El trying to save her father.

"He promised everything would be fine, to head to the nearest shore. Help was on the way. Told me he loved me"—a sniff—"that he'd follow behind. I did what he asked and started kicking. I didn't hear him anymore and turned back. I searched for him, but he wasn't there. He wasn't behind me. He wasn't where I saw him last. I shouted, cried, swam back, but I was alone in the water."

Her body is in this room with me, but her mind is lost in the grief of eight years ago. The little girl losing her father. Helpless herself, yet thinking about him. That was El then. That is still El now. She puts her life aside to save the people she loves.

"If only I'd stayed. What if I'd given him my vest? He—he might still be alive. He's dead because I left. Bad things happen when I leave."

Fuck. Fuck. Fuck.

THIRTY-SIX

TIME DIMMED THE PICTURE of my father's face telling me he loved me. It returns in high res in my dreams.

For years reporters have hounded me for the story of the accident, his death. My survival. Every interview, even though they agree beforehand not to bring it up, someone has to skirt the rules, try to get me to tell the story. Only close family and my therapist know it. Maybe Rocker. I never discussed it with him, but Mom must have.

And now Wil.

"I don't remember anything past that. I woke up in the hospital with a gash on the back of my head. They thought the adrenaline kept me conscious, and the vest is the reason I'm still alive." His hand is in my hair, gentle strokes on my scalp—looking for evidence.

I move his hand to the strands that stand out. The coarse hair devoid of color, of life, marks the moment my life changed. "Here." Wil's touch is gentle, as if he could take away the visible scar.

"I'm afraid of geese."

"What?"

"Can't stand the bloody creatures. When I was seven, my mum took me to a petting zoo. It was a big day out for us. I remember being so excited, up close and personal with these animals." He rubs his chin on my forehead. "Mum gave me a handful of bird seed, and the second I entered the pen this massive white goose ran toward me. Thing had to be twice my size."

I suppress a smile, and it's like he can feel it. "I'm serious. It was ginormous. I can still remember its yellow beak bearing down on me. I almost pissed my pants." I rub my thumb on the patch of skin it somehow found in his open shirt. "Thing clamped down on my arm like I was its last meal. Mum had to whack it with her purse to get it off me."

He shivers. From the memory or the wet clothes he's wearing, I'm not sure. I don't want to move, don't want to leave the safety of his strength. But I don't want him to get sick, either. I force the separation between our bodies. "We should find you something dry to wear."

"Sorry?"

I crawl from under the piano, get up, and look down at Wil. His soft eyes on mine send a chill through my body. It's not related to the drying Lycra of my bikini. I hold out my hand. "C'mon." He takes my fingers and comes to his feet.

We walk back through the house toward the kitchen, and our linked hands ignite a steady current that recharges me. I open the door to the guest bathroom, pull out two plush white robes, and hand one to Wil. Next is the laundry room, two doors down. I point to the dryer. "Put your wet things in here." I nod at the door. "I'll be out there."

The soft terrycloth of the robe feels good against my skin, and I wrap it around me with a tug on the belt. I go to the fridge, grab two bottles of water, and wait for Wil to emerge. I hear a bang and a "bloody thing." I poke my head through the laundry-room door to find Wil standing in front of the dryer, dressed in the white robe.

"How do you start it?"

"Bob, start dryer." There's a low hum as the machine stirs to life.

Wil squishes up his nose. "They call their dryer Bob?"

I shrug. "Most things in this place are voice activated. My uncle's name is Robert and my aunt thought it'd be funny to use the name Bob for the system. Says this way, at least, he does stuff around the house."

"That's . . ." Wil shakes his head and backs away from the machine like it might come for him next.

I hand him one of the water bottles and jump up on the counter opposite the dryer.

He leans against the white marble slab I'm sitting on. "Thanks."

"Thanks for"—I study the silver top of the water bottle—"for back there."

"Hey, I was dying to go for a dip."

I try to laugh at his joke, but it's too soon. "It's so embarrassing. Everyone must be talking about me out there." I point my chin to the window and the sounds of the party filtering through from outside.

"Who cares?"

I study the white fluffy belt in my hands, an "I do" on my lips.

"Let 'em talk. You are getting ten percent from the gig. Nothing like the DJ diving into the pool for entertainment value. But I'm not saying we add a dramatic rescue to our stage show. One-time deal, okay?"

"Don't worry. I usually stay away from water."

"But you live by the ocean?"

"You saw my room. Now you know why I chose that one."

Wil takes a long sip of water. I watch as his Adam's apple bobs. More like stare. How can such a simple act look hot? I pull the robe around me, wishing it were his arms instead, but thankful for the warmth.

"You're really good at the DJ thing."

Wil twists the lid back on the bottle. "You expected anything less?"

Ah, there's the Wil I know. This time I do smile. "Zoe's impressed. She's already talking about hiring you for her next party. And I saw the pictures on Instagram you posted. You make it all look so fun." I clench my teeth, not sure how to ask what I want to. We've never openly talked about it. We dance a lot around the concept of money, but I know it's a sensitive topic for him. I just want to know he's okay. "Are the extra jobs helping?"

I brace for the smart remark. Instead, he inches closer. "Mateo has hooked me up with some great gigs. One bloke tried to stiff me at the end of the night, but we worked it out. I did my best Sven impression." His face hardens, and he stares at me with dead eyes.

I can't help but giggle. "Nice try, but you need less emotion." I straighten my back, suck in my cheeks, and give Wil my best glare, thinking of not being allowed to go to a party.

Wil holds his hand up. "You win. You've mastered The Sven."

"I've had lots of chances to study under the master himself."

The dryer's hum fills the silence. I put my hand on the edge of the counter, and my pinkie brushes against his. I keep staring at my robe. His pinkie moves over mine. My hand tingles; heat travels up my arm and neck, to my face.

"Melodie?" My mom's voice rings in the air—treble-C, perfect pitch. Nothing less from her. "Are you in here?"

Wil steps back to the window. His hand leaves mine, and I miss it.

"Yes, Mom."

The laundry-room door opens wider, and my mom's eyes swing from me to Wil and back to me. "Hi."

"Mom, this is Wil Peters." I rush to introduce him.

"Peters." She says the name like she's trying it on for size. "Nice to officially meet you."

Wil raises one thick dark eyebrow, and they stare at each other. Mom breaks the silence first. "Melodie, can I talk to you for a moment?"

"Be right back," I say to Wil, hop off the counter, and follow Mom out into the kitchen.

"How are you?"

"Fine."

She puts a hand on each of my arms, rubs them up and down. "I'm sorry I didn't help you out there. I was . . . It—"

I cut her off. "I'm sorry I freaked out. It was—"

"Perfectly natural." She pulls me into a sideways hug, accommodating her growing belly, and I let her. "All I care about is you."

"I know, Mom. I love you too."

Her hands run over my body like she's checking for injuries. This one time I let her. I prefer Wil's embrace but doubt I'll ever get a chance to experience that again. Did the other girls he's held feel the way I did in his arms? I don't know how they could walk away, not ask for more.

"Who is this Wil? How do you know him?"

This is exactly what I didn't want to happen.

"I met him at Blend." I spill my prepared answer. "You know, the coffee shop Dad likes? He's a barista there and a student at UCLA."

"And a DJ?"

"He has to earn a living and support his mom."

"What about his father?" Mom tightens her grip on me. Hug time is almost over.

"He left before Wil was born."

"I see."

I can feel her judgment through the embrace. "It's not his fault he doesn't know who his father is."

"I didn't say that."

"But you thought it."

She squeezes me again. "I promise you I wasn't thinking that. You should invite him over for dinner sometime. Meet Bill. He'd love to meet the young man who saved his daughter."

"Really?"

"Yeah, I think that would be a good idea."

Behind me, Wil clears his throat. I turn, and he's in his clothes again, his white shirt crumpled. "I should get back to"—he points to the backyard—"the music."

"Oh, okay." I wiggle out of Mom's arms.

"I'll see you out there?" Wil catches my eyes.

"Actually," Mom interjects, "I think Melodie and I are done for the day." She looks at me. "Time to go home."

"What about Dad?"

"He texted. Won't be able to make it. Stuck in Atlanta, of all places." She turns her performer smile at Wil.

Wil's gaze falls to the floor, his fingers doing that drumming thing against his thigh again.

The car ride home is silent. Mom's stuck inside her own mind. I hate that I dragged up bad memories today. We eat a conversation-less dinner and Mom, drained, goes to bed early. The house is empty, and I don't know what to do with myself.

I'm texting Wil before I even know it.

Me: How's the party?

Wil: Not the same without you.

Wil: Your cousin might be drunk. She's making the underwear models carry her around like Jasmine on a star-shaped blow up.

I can picture the scene in my mind. Zoe loves being the center of attention.

Me: It is her birthday. She deserves to be treated like a queen.

Wil: When is it your turn?

Me: No interest in underwear models parading me around, thanks.

Wil: No. To be treated like a queen.

Me: You offering?

Shit. I should stop saying or typing what's on my mind when Wil Peters is involved.

Me: I'd rather be treated like a normal girl.

Not a wonderful cover, but it'll have to do.

Wil: Agreed.

I crawl into bed and resign myself to the fact that my nightmares will be back full force tonight. The antianxiety pills my therapist insists I use when I need them stay in my medicine cabinet. I hate the way they make me feel the next day, and the dreams are inevitable. Best to let them run their course.

I do dream. But not about me trying to hold Papa up against the crashing waves. I dream of a golden-eyed boy who held me together.

Thirty-Seven

THE PARTY GOES UNTIL three a.m., and there aren't any whispers about El, but I don't get to spend much time away from the turntables. Sunset brings the older folks to the dance floor, and I spin the remixes of seventies, eighties, and nineties.

With midnight, the requests change to the latest hits and the faces get younger. I bring some of my favorite sets I performed at the parties in Berlin, and the response is just as enthusiastic. The pool posers change into white pants and silver shirts, and their dance skills are much stronger than their lifeguard skills.

When the last of the guests leave, the lawn is littered with leftover party rubbish. A couple of women in uniforms carrying black garbage bags scour the premises for discarded napkins, deflated balloons, and stuff I'm not sure I want to identify. I pack the turntables I rented and find my way to the gate.

"Wil." My heart jumps at the male voice that comes from the bench in the small front garden. The giant shape moves my way, and it's either the Hulk or Sven. Sven steps into the light. "I'll take you to your place." This feels a little like kidnapping. I put a smile on my face, but I hear blood pumping in my ears.

"It's okay. I'll get a taxi." I keep walking, but Sven steps onto the path in front of me.

"El sent me. We need to talk." Not a phrase I want to hear from this giant. The talk sounds like a code word for "I'll break your nose if you don't follow me."

"Do I have a choice?" I raise my head to meet his gaze.

"I'm afraid not." He turns and heads to the roundabout where three cars are parked. The Rolls is not one of them. Maybe not the best car to smear my blood all over. Sven gets into the driver's seat of a silver Toyota and pops the trunk. I stuff the case with the equipment into it and join Sven in the front of the car. If he needs to wheel my body somewhere to dispose of it, I brought my own giant container with me. He won't even need to chop me up.

"Still the same place?"

"You can drop me off on campus by Blend."

Sven starts the car, and the mansion disappears in the rearview window.

His phone rings, and "Lisa" pops up on the car's console. Faster than I thought possible, he hits cancel and returns his hand to the wheel. We drive through the least congested streets of LA I've ever seen.

"I'll be coming to busk with you." Sven doesn't move his eyes off the road. "I'll take her there. Stay nearby. Any sign of danger or recognition, we pull the plug." I open my mouth to say there won't be any problems, but Sven isn't finished. "She stops the moment she has enough money, or if Mr. and Mrs. Rockerby get suspicious. She never leaves my sight, or she's under house arrest."

Like she isn't under it already. She lives in a multi-million-dollar fortress with zero agency of her own. A beautiful doll that no one gets to play with.

"Do we understand each other?" Sven's voice sounds like he is asking me about the weather.

"Yes."

"Good." I feel the heft of his hand on my shoulder. "What you did back there. The pool. Thank you."

The trees of LA don't change much, but everyone knows it's the end of October because temporary Halloween shops pop up, bags of mini candies flood the stores, and the walls on campus sport posters for Halloween night get-togethers and scare fests.

I knock at Mateo's door and pop my head in. He's at the desk, hunched over a piece of orange paper, lettering something with a Sharpie. The room smells like he's been using the Sharpie for a while.

"Hey." He turns his head my way at my words.

Mateo lifts the page and shakes it at me, his face that of a proud parent showing off his kid's work. "HallowRade at Lambda Sigma." He probably thinks it's clever. Words have never been his strong suit.

I hand him the envelope with the latest repayment of my debt. Zoe paid me in cash before she left the dance floor. It's made a good dent in what I owe him.

"More ones from the show with your girlfriend?"

"Stop calling her that. El's just a friend."

"Just, or for now? Last time I clocked you at the farmers' market, you did not look like 'just' anything to me."

"You should look into this thing called acting. When performers pretend for the sake of the public."

"Your acting skills are not that great, or your team would've had a chance to beat us."

"Gloating does not look good on you, mate."

"I'm not gloating. I'm glowing. Your English is not supposed to get worse." He shakes the handmade flyer in my face. "And you're supposed to ask me why I am glowing."

"Because you get to sniff Sharpies all day?"

"Because I'm hosting the party next Friday and you, mein freund, are going to be my ace in the hole. Well, you and El. Perform at the bash, and I'll forgive the rest of the money you owe me." He points at the line on the bottom of the flyer: "Exclusive performance of WE—the *it* band of the campus this season."

Although El could use the extra cash too there's no way Sven will let her come on campus to perform at a frat party. "That's a sweet deal, but can it be just me?"

"Exclusive performance by W does not sound as appealing. It has to be both of you. I promised the frat it'll be both. You don't want me to get in trouble."

During our first busking with the three of us it was painfully evident Sven wasn't joking about El not leaving his sight.

If I were a paparazzo, I'd find out who El's babysitter slash bodyguard is and follow him instead. There's no hiding Sven and his crew-cut with disguises. It's like putting a baseball hat on a bear and hoping people decide he's one of them.

But it's better than not seeing El again. When we're performing, I have permission to put my arm on her shoulders, sing into the same microphone, feel her eyes fill with triumph every time we nail the song, and the audience showers us with noise. I know it'll end soon, when the money we divide gets her closer to her goal and helps me pay Mateo back for my classes and rent.

The next time we're at the farmers' market, Sven stands off to the side in his baseball cap, not fitting in but thankfully not scaring away our customers. He's watching everyone. One eye on the crowd, one eye on El.

"I have another gig for us," I whisper in her ear as we are packing up. Her eyes light up, and I can't resist smiling back at her. I love how she loves performing. She's come so far from the girl with stage fright all those months ago. She's going to be a superstar someday. The thought makes my chest swell with pride. "There's a Halloween party at the house, and Mateo wants us to be the house band."

The light in her eyes fades a smidge. "Um." She looks at Sven. "I don't know. It's one thing to do this, but won't I be recognized?"

"It's Halloween, silly. We can go in costume. Say, Shawn Mendez and Camila Cabello. No one will know."

"Nick looks more like Shawn than you. But Sarah is the opposite of Camila." I can see she's thinking about it. Another look over at Sven. "It would be fun to go to a real party. But . . ."

"I'll talk to Sven. If you're in."

A little bow of her head makes the brim of her hat flap, and the smile is back. "A real crowd. We could try out the new song we've been working on."

Playing our own music. Writing *Our Lines* for *Indigo* was electric, playing it at the bar is great, but to perform our songs in front of a crowd of people our own age? That would be awesome.

Now I just need to convince the big guy. We're friends now, right? I give Sven the single nod. "Hey, mate. So . . ."

"No."

"I haven't even asked yet."

"Don't care."

"Sven, it's important."

He lets out a breath that would knock over a small child. "What?"

"So, there's a party at the frat house—" Sven stiffens, and I hold up my hands. "Wait till I'm done before you say no."

The Viking relaxes a little. If you didn't know him like I do, you wouldn't notice. It's in the shoulders, they lower a millimeter.

"It's this Friday. They want WE to be the house band."

"No."

"Sven."

"Wil." He glares at me. "I can't go to a frat party. I'll stick out like a sore thumb."

"Yep. You're not coming."

"No." His voice is louder, like he's talking to a child.

"It's Halloween. She'll be totally in disguise—head-to-foot costume. No one will recognize her. She deserves a chance at something normal, and what's more normal than a party with people her own age? And I won't leave her side. I'll protect her." Ah, that gets a response. Another millimeter of shoulder drop. Sven looks over my shoulder to where El is counting our tips for the day. Time for the clincher. "You'll be free to take out Lisa."

If looks could kill, I'd be dead. "Lisa?"

"Bar? Saturdays? The girl who doesn't need blush when you're around?" Pink tinges Sven's cheek bones. "See? Like you're doing now."

The big guy rubs his face. "What about her?"

"You tell me. You've been less grumpy lately." Sven lifts his hat, runs his hand over his brush cut and pulls the bill down lower as if to hide his eyes. "And in the car the night of Zoe's birthday party, the call."

"Wil . . ."

"Imagine time with her . . . all alone—"

"Stop."

"Let El come to the party."

Sven looks over at El again. "Promise you'll never let her out of your sight."

I give him my signature smile. I've won. "Never."

THIRTY-EIGHT

El

I'M AT A REAL college party. It's hot and sweaty, and someone spilled beer on my mother's yellow baroque dress, which I stole out of her closet. I'm in heaven.

Tonight, the microphone is an extension of me. I look around the room of gyrating bodies, eating up our original *Don't Give Me Comfort* we are dishing them, and I belt out the chorus. The room grabs my energy, amplifies it fivefold and showers it back at me. I'm charged, no fear, no hesitation. Wil's presence is a bonus, not a crutch. I don't need him to protect me from myself, from the demons in my head who told me I'd crumble and cry if I become the center of attention, that I wouldn't be able to support that load.

I stand up straighter and let the lightness run through me. I could've missed this, not known how performing in front of others is draining and refilling at the same time. The synergy that started with Wil and me, when he pumped his confidence into me and made me not afraid, has expanded. The surety comes from every person dancing, screaming, and waving their hands at me. They feed me, fill me. I don't need food. I can survive on this explosive electricity, powered by the vibe, the love, the connection.

"That riff you added at the end. Let's keep it."

I know exactly what Wil's talking about. The freedom I felt made me reach for the notes I wouldn't have imagined before.

"Let's hope it's not a fluke."

"It's not. You are that good."

His words give me exactly what I need. No idea how he manages that, but I'm grateful and always long for more.

We finish the last song in the set and do an encore, then another. *Our Lines* from *Indigo* is a huge success, and the higher octane *Don't Give Me Comfort* Wil and I perfected during our busking had several students, I assume they are all students, come and ask where they could download it. Even the new songs *Orange Mood*, *Telepathic*, and *Don't Need the Ocean* we just finished writing are well-received. Wil's right, we should put them out on SoundCloud and YouTube.

Maybe I was trying to do this thing backward, starting with a music video filmed by a hot-shot producer when I was afraid to set foot on stage, and hoping it would somehow get me noticed. That was the old me, hiding behind my money and pretending it didn't matter. Here I am, saving $10K to shoot a slick video as if it's something every eighteen-year-old could do.

Wil was right too. I didn't know the value of money. Still don't, but I'm getting there. Mateo brings me a refilled water bottle and takes the microphone out of my hands.

"Let's give WE a round of applause." The room erupts in noise, and I smile wider and harder than ever in my life. "We'll let El and Wil here have some rest." There's a boo from the crowd. "Hold up, people. They'll be back. And Wil's set up some tracks for us, so the paaarty does not have to stop." Grateful woohoos pop around the room. Wil puts down his guitar and goes to a laptop he set up nearby. The sound of an electric guitar peels out of the speakers, and a new wave of dancing commences.

"Want to eat first? Or dance? Or drink?" I raise former-ly-his-and-now-my chipped metal bottle of water. He smiles. He's gifted me with so much: finding my confidence on stage, a way to have words and music flow together, new friends, but this metal thing is a physical representation of how much he cares. He can pretend to be the high-and-mighty know-it-all and behave like nothing ever bothers him, but I see past the bravado, the cocky smiles, and infectious brashness. The real Wil cannot hide from me behind those things. I see the real guy. And I love what I see.

"Dance. I want to pretend I'm a student too." I'm not going to regret not taking the GED exam. Maybe a little. Wil puts his arm around my shoulders and brings his lips to my ear.

"Today is a perfect night for pretending. You can be whoever you want. There's no Sven, no paparazzi, no rules. Try out what freedom feels like. Even if it's only for one party."

Wil puts me in front of his body, and we find our way through sexy nurses, Greek gods. A Scooby-Doo tries to separate us, but Wil does something behind my back that makes him step away. Three pirates, one with a painted-on mustache, form a circle around us and shout "Ho-ho-ho" until we break through their chain. There are dogs, cats, an octopus, witches, and super-heroes from both the Marvel and DC universes all jumping up and down to the music together. The madness of it all is better than I ever imagined, the music vibrating through the floor into my body, the crush of sweaty skin brushing up against me.

I turn and step closer to Wil, avoiding the girl covered in leaves in all the right places beside me who is grinding against a tall boy wearing not much more than a spotted loincloth. This could be a music video—Tarzan and His Wild Jane. I want to be wild. I copy the girl in a mad scientist costume on our other side, and I jump. It's awkward, and it's not liberating. Wil jumps too. He doesn't stop. His elbows bend, and he pumps his fists in the air. I used to do that on the trampoline Zoe had in her backyard.

"Let your body feel it," Wil shouts over the music.

My feet leave the ground, and I find the rhythm. I have to grab the fancy white updo wig and diadem before they slide off my head. The ruby necklace I stole from Mom's jewelry box bops up and down on the shelf of my boobs pushed up by the corset.

Wil's hair flops around. It sort of goes with the Elvis imper-
sonator jumper he has on, but his eyes are not his usual shade
of honey. They turn into the Irish whiskey Dad collects but
doesn't drink anymore. Wil's eyes shine in the flashing lights,
matching the drums of the song. I don't recognize this track,
but I like it.

Next time I come to a party like this, I'm not wearing a wig.
I'm done with them. I want to let my hair do what Wil's longer
strands do. I want to do a hair flip. Maybe run my hand through
it. Maybe someone else will run his hands through it.

The song changes, and the high-octane revving that flailed
everyone around us evolves to languid beats. They slow my
blood to molasses and send the smorgasbord of costumes into
slow waves. It's another one I've never heard before. I reach up
and shout in Wil's ear. "Who is this?"

"Måneskin."

"Never heard of them. So many European groups I know
nothing about. I have so much to learn." I lean in to make sure
he can hear me.

"I'll be happy to teach you." We are talking about music, but
then we aren't. His lips almost touch my temple, mine almost
touch his neck.

"I'd love that." And I'm not thinking about records or
melodies, it's the flavor of his skin I'm most curious about.
Another inch, and I would know. How close is too close?

"Me too." The side of his head touches mine and stays there. I'm half an inch away from the vein pulsing at the base of his throat.

Jane and Tarzan are doing what I've imagined happens at every college party. They're making better use of the slow dance than Wil and I are. We shuffle side to side, our hands hang limply along our sides, our heads remain linked, neither of us making an effort to step away.

It's harder to breathe now than when I was jumping around. I let myself take a bigger gulp of air and when my chest touches his, it's an accident. One causing a need, an emergency. More air is the only way to remedy it. I breathe deeper, and the contact between the front of my Marie Antoinette corset and the deep V of his white jumpsuit is deliberate this time. We linger in the contact. I will pass out if I don't exhale, but I choose to hold it a little longer.

Tarzan's shoulder knocks the wind out of me and separates us. Wil's hand springs into action and shoves the giggling couple away. It does not return back to his side but finds a spot on my waist. Thank you, Jane, thank you, Tarzan.

"You, okay?" Wil's voice is gentle and raspy.

"Mmhm." I nod in agreement, regretting my outfit choice. If I were wearing one of the options the sexy nurses were sporting, his hand would be resting on my bare skin. But I take what I get.

"You wanna leave? Just say the word, and I'll take you home."

"There's no way I'm leaving because a couple of kids bumped into me." The next song begins, and it's a remix of a K-Pop group I recognize. Not the words, but the tune. It's catchy and light, and I'm waiting for Wil to remove his hand, but he doesn't. I'm relieved he doesn't. Just like that, I can breathe again.

I notice my cheeks hurt, and it's because the smile that started on stage never left. I must look deranged, but this once I don't care. I'm free. Free to relish the cramping cheeks because I can't stop grinning, free to admit I don't know something, free to enjoy the messy house and the loud strangers, and free to get a little bit more of Wil for myself.

I raise my hands, wrap them around his neck, and let my face rest on his chest. Not the bare skin part, I'm not that brave, but oh so close to it, he must feel my breath. His heartbeat matches the beat of the music. Mine matches his.

A hand on my back. Tarzan again? No. Mateo. He yells in my ear. "There's a dude here to see you."

"What?" I didn't hear him correctly. No one knows I'm here. Except Sven. It can't be time to leave already. We have another set to play.

"Blond Viking?" Wil shouts back at Mateo, his eyes scanning the room behind me.

Mateo shakes his head. "Dark hair. Jason Momoa wannabe."

I don't know who Jason Momoa is. Mateo leans in. "I think he said his name was Taylor."

All the warmth from being in Wil's arms drains away. "Trevor?"

Mateo nods. "Yeah, that was it."

"Who's Trevor?" Wil asks.

This is not good. If Trevor is here, that can only mean one thing. One bad, bad thing. "Where is he?"

"In the hall."

I push my way through the crowd, aiming for the door. Wil follows behind me. "El, who's Trevor?"

Thirty-Nine

Who the fuck is this creep?

The music from the party is dulled here in the hallway, but I can't pick out the words El's burbling to this mysterious Trevor in a hushed voice.

She leans into him and rests her hand on his leather-clad elbow, her face pale in the muted glow of the mood lights strung along the wall. Is he supposed to be a biker? That's the world's lamest costume—black leather jacket, white T-shirt, and black jeans. The jacket is too big on him, but it doesn't hide the muscles. So, he works out. Big deal. Don't we all? His long black hair is tied back, and his day-old stubble creates dark shadows on his face. Menacing might be too strong of a word, but Opa would've called him trouble.

He, Trevor, is whispering in her ear but eyeing me. He puts a hand on her shoulder. I've had enough.

"El, I need to talk to you." I step to them and take her free hand. Wide eyes meet mine, swivel over to Trevor, and return to me. After far too long, she moves away from him.

"Don't move." I throw the words at Trevor.

He sneers. "Whatever, Elvis."

I walk her a few steps down the hall, put myself between her and the intruder. "What's going on?"

She takes a deep breath, as if buying time.

"Talk to me." I take her hand in mine, squeeze it. Let me in, El. Let me in.

Her eyes flicker over my shoulder. I think she's going to stay silent, and it hurts. It fucking hurts. She lets out a slow breath. I thought she trusted me.

"He's Sven's little brother."

Sven? He has family? It's not like I thought he sprang from Zeus's head fully formed or anything. But it never occurred to me that the man had people related to him. "He doesn't look anything like Sven."

"Different fathers. Half brothers."

The baby in Sylvia's stomach will be my half brother. El's too. Will he look like me? Have red hair like her? I don't want to think about that right now. Or ever. "What does he want with you?"

"You have to promise not to tell. No one can know." I nod. "Sven's in jail."

"Jail?"

It's El's turn to nod. "I'm not sure. There was a fight, and Sven stepped in to stop it." She looks at Trevor again. This time, there's a hint of anger on her face. This I like better. Be mad. At him. "Trevor needs money to bail Sven out."

And there it is. It's always about money. I knew this loser wanted to use El for something. I could just tell. "So he came to you?"

"Trevor doesn't trust many people. We're friends."

That word again. Friend. I dismissed it at first. Everyone has friends. But with El, the word takes on new meaning, a depth I never considered before. El would do anything for her friends. I'm her friend, aren't I?

"I have to help him." She steps closer, her face taking on that determined look I adore when she's about to fight me on something. "Sven can't have an arrest on his record. It'll ruin his career. We need to bail him out and get this other guy to drop the charges."

We? Does she mean her and me, or her and Trevor? I don't care what she means, I'm not leaving her alone. I promised Sven. "Where are you going to get the money from?"

She lifts her chin. "You know where."

And it hits me. The money she's been saving for her video shoot. The one only a few weeks away. "No." If she dips into those savings, she won't have enough. She's barely going to make it as is. "You can't."

"I have to. It's over a thousand dollars. Trevor doesn't have anywhere near that much."

I drum my free hand against my thigh. There's gotta be another way. I can't see it, but there has to be. I stall for time to think. "So, what, you're going to go home and get it? You'll get caught. Then what will Sven do?"

"Wil, I have to help him. He's my—" El's going to say it again. Sven's a good guy. He's my friend.

"—friend. So you keep telling me." The door to the party opens, music blasts into the hall, and the poster on the wall promoting "HallowRade: the Most Epic Halloween Bash Ever" flaps against the wall. The party is over for El and me. I hate Trevor even more for ruining El's one chance at something normal, a night of fun. We barely got a chance to dance. And we had a whole other set lined up to play. Mateo will be pissed. He charged a cover for this party, promising them a show from WE.

"I have a better idea. Come with me." I tug El back down the hallway. "You"—I point at Trevor—"stay there."

I spot Mateo over by the drinks table chatting up two girls dressed like slutty nurses. Playing doctor is going to have to wait. "Hey, mate, I need a word."

"Ladies, hold that thought." He follows us back to the hallway.

I've asked so many times, it's almost easy now. Almost. "Can I borrow more money?"

"How much?" Mateo pulls his wallet out of his back pocket. "Is a hundred enough?"

"Two grand."

Mateo's hand freezes midair. He looks at me, at El, and whispers. "Is that dude blackmailing you or something?"

I follow his eyes to Trevor slumped against the wall, typing on his phone.

"As if I'd let him. No. It's an emergency." I side-eye El. Mateo crosses his arms, and I know I'm going to have to use my power of persuasion. "I wouldn't ask otherwise. I know you have the cash. The cover charge to get into this party of yours was ten bucks. There has to be a hundred people out there. Plus, you have what I gave you this week."

"No, Wil, we can't use your money." El pulls on my white polyester sleeve.

I turn to her. "We'll pay him back." I look at Mateo. "Tomorrow."

"I don't know, man. You, I trust, but how do I know your friend here is good for the money? You don't have a good track record with women." I want to punch Mateo. He's referring to the girl who broke the window back in our old dorm. But El doesn't know about that. Still, I don't want her thinking I hang out with other girls when she's not around.

I open my mouth to make something up when El lets go of my sleeve. Damn it, Mateo. Your comment is ruining my . . . whatever El and I have. I don't want El mad at me. I don't want her to have a reason to push me away, go back to the goon leaning against the wall.

She doesn't leave. Instead, El raises her hands behind her neck and undoes the necklace I thought was a nice addition to her Marie Antoinette costume, if maybe a touch over the top. The giant red stone sinks into the gap between her dress and the pale skin of her breasts. The breasts which said dress was highlighting too much for my eyes not to return to them all night. The breasts she pressed against me when we were dancing before Trevor ruined everything and I thought I might lose it.

El holds the bauble by the chain and hands it to Mateo. "Take this for collateral."

"No offense, lady, but a bit of costume jewelry is not gonna hold much weight."

"It's not costume jewelry. It's real."

What? I look at the necklace. The red of what I think is a pearl-drop shaped piece of glass now shines like a ruby in Mateo's hand. If it is real, that thing must be worth thousands. I feel a little sick at the thought of what people would do if they knew the value of it. And she wore it to a frat party. This woman.

El pulls out her phone, taps a few times and shows the screen to Mateo. "This is Sylvia Rockerby. She's—"

"Bill Rockerby's wife." Mateo cuts her off. His dark eyes are like saucers as they yoyo between El and the phone.

Bloody hell. Did El just out herself? I grab the phone. On the screen is an image of the woman I saw at the pool party in some glam ball gown at some posh event, the ruby necklace dangling from Mateo's hand prominently displayed around her neck.

"You're Melodie Rockerby?"

El nods. This is not good. Mateo is a loyal mate. He's helped me get out of a few situations. But he doesn't always play by the rules, treating the law as something he could bend, especially if he can make money as a result. He could expose El. Sell the story to the press. WE would be ruined. I'd never see her again.

I grab him by the front of his cowboy vest. "You can't tell anyone. It's important. I'll make it worth your while."

"Calm down, mein freund. I get it. Be right back." He removes my hands from his chest and runs up the stairs. He returns with a thick, dark yellow, folded-over envelope. "Hope it works out."

FORTY

Trevor tosses the keys to El, and she gets in the driver's seat; her tall wig brushes against the car's roof. Sven's baby brother goes for the front passenger door, but I beat him. "No way, dude." Yep, backseat for you.

I don't know how we're going to find the money to repay Mateo, but that's tomorrow's problem. Right now, it's about saving Sven. A quick search on my phone, and I find a number for the LAPD. One call and I learn which police station is holding Sven.

El takes a corner, and the centrifugal force pushes me against the car door. "Spill, Trevor. What happened?"

"I was only helping someone out. I needed Sven to talk to this guy. The dude put his hands on my friend, and Sven started throwing punches."

I snicker. "Doesn't sound like Sven. He's all about control."

Trevor scowls at me. "My friend is a girl."

"Oh." El and I say it at the same time. Sven would totally hit a guy if he thought the girl needed rescuing. Even if he only suspected it.

The way El drives, I fear for all our lives. I had no idea my princess knew how to handle this vehicle, never mind weave it in and out of traffic like it's child's play.

"Next thing I knew, the cops were everywhere." Trevor crosses his arms. "Sven lied to protect me. Told them I had nothing to do with it and got himself arrested instead."

Now I really don't like Trevor. "What about the other bloke?"

"Yeah, they picked him up too."

El takes her eyes off the road, and I try not to cringe. "Do you know his name?"

"Yeah, Tony Monroe."

I spot a small parking lot two blocks from the police station, and El eases the Rolls into an empty spot. Best to not flaunt the car in case anyone recognizes it. The last thing we need tonight is some reporter catching El in a cop shop.

The walk over is bizarre, late enough on Halloween that all the munchkins are already at home in candy-induced comas, leaving drunken teens either going to or from parties. We pass a group of superheroes, and Trevor points out a girl in a Wonder Woman costume to El.

"You wore it better."

Great. Trevor gets Wonder Woman, strapless top and high boots, and I get a long dress and lace, most of El covered in cloth. Except for her neck and—not going there. That ship has sailed. We're on a new mission now.

I hold the door to the police station open for El and Trevor, but he looks at me like the ground would burn him if he crossed the threshold.

"I'm not going in there."

"But it's your brother."

Trevor looks at El, and she sighs. "Stay here. Don't go far." He shrugs and retreats across the street. Good riddance, I say.

The police station on Halloween night is not a place I ever want to be again. There's no way of telling if the blood and gore on the people around me is the real deal or part of a costume. The trick-or-treaters gone wrong and party goers who didn't get charged with a crime litter the area dominated by an officer behind a plate glass window decorated with a sparkly pumpkin that does not fit the monochrome space. I don't let go of El's hand.

She whispers, "Everything's going to be fine," on repeat, as if her saying it enough times will make it true. As if she needs it to be true; I need it to be true for her.

To the left of us a scantily dressed woman chews her nails as she waits for the officer behind the glass to get off the phone. She eyes El up and down and then me, eyes widening in interest, and my skin crawls. Not in a million years, lady.

The policeman gets off the phone; we wait for the officer to finish with the lady in front of us. It's stuffy in the station, this October 31 warmer than usual, they say. I study El, make sure she's okay. I wish El could take off the ridiculous wig she's wearing. I miss her red hair. The real El. Dress-up isn't much fun anymore.

"Happy Halloween." The olive-skinned man behind the glass is in a way better mood than I expected anyone working on devil's night should or would be.

El steps forward. "Hi, Officer Brahn, is it?" The officer grins like he got a full-sized chocolate bar in his candy bag. "We're here to post bail for my friend, Sven Anders. Is he here?"

"Let me check." The officer taps away at a keyboard, nods, and whistles, "Battery, huh. Lots of those tonight. Full moons on Halloween bring out all the crazies." I'm insulted on behalf of Sven but hold my tongue. "It's thirteen hundred to spring him. Cash or charge?"

I take out the money Mateo lent us and start counting out the bills. Most of it is in ten-dollar bills, so it takes some time. Officer Brahn takes the whole thing in stride like it's perfectly normal to pay in small chunks. El grimaces at him. "Sorry."

"Not a problem. Money is money." He leans closer to the glass. "I've seen it all. Had a lady in here last week, bailed her husband out with rolls of quarters. Had to get special boxes to carry them all."

I shove the stack of bills his way, and he recounts every single one. I tap my fingers against the windowsill, and El puts her hand on top of mine to stop them from drumming. "Everything's going to be fine."

I put my arm around her and draw her closer. "I know."

"Alrighty, then. Looks like we're good. Here's your receipt." Officer Brahn shoves a paper under the glass partition. "Mr. Anders should be out shortly."

"Sir." El smiles at the officer. "The ah . . . gentleman that came in with my friend, Mr. Monroe. Can you tell me if he also made bail?"

"Friend of yours?" More tapping on the keyboard.

El's not good at the whole lying thing, so I do it for her. "Yup. My brother."

Officer Brahn shakes his head. "Well, your sister over there"—he points to the lady who was eyeballing me—"just posted bail, so you might want to talk to her."

Bullocks. "Thanks."

There's nothing left to do but wait. I guide El to a bench as far away from the crowd as possible and sit down beside her.

I see Sven before El does. Shuffling along the long hallway to the waiting room, head hanging. There's a stain on his shirt. It might be dried blood. I squeeze El's hand, and she looks at me then follows my gaze.

"Sven." Her exclamation turns heads of half the police station.

His head shoots up, feet halt, shoulders slump. There's a cut over his left eye, maybe the source of the stain marring his light green button-down. These things look worse than they are. One of my rowing crew whacked me with a paddle above my eye once. I thought the bleeding would never stop, but I didn't even need stitches.

Sven hasn't quite entered the waiting room when El slams into him, wrapping her arms around his waist. I ignore the pang at how easy it is for her to touch him. It takes what seems like hours in her presence for me to get to brush her hand, and he gets a hug right off the bat. Extenuating circumstances.

"You shouldn't be here," Sven growls into the top of El's head, which is plastered to his chest. Yet, he engulfs her in his arms, one hand holding a small clear bag with his belongings. He closes his eyes for a heartbeat then lets go of El, pushing her away. "How?"

"Trevor." Sven stiffens, and I fight the urge to pull El away from the big guy for fear he's going to hit something. The logical side of my brain knows Sven would never hurt El, but I'm afraid of collateral damage. He steps around El and barrels through the door. I move to follow, but El stops me.

"Give them a minute." Her hand is warm in mine, and the red I saw before my eyes dissipates. She brushes the side of my palm with her finger. "Besides, we're not done here."

I don't understand.

She nods toward the next man lumbering down the hallway from the holding cells. Dressed in a black suit and what was once a white shirt, this bloke could definitely give Sven a run for his money. Bald and big, muscles straining against the fabric of his slim-fitting outfit. I wouldn't want to meet him alone in a dark alley.

"We have to get Mr. Monroe to drop the charges."

FORTY-ONE

El

I STARE INTO THE cold, gray eyes of the man who could ruin Sven's life. My life too. This is about more than protecting my bodyguard, my cheerleader when I doubt myself, my supporter when even my family didn't want me to try. This is about my friend. My family, not by blood but by choice.

I have no idea how I'm going to convince the mafia-esque hulk in front of me to drop the charges against Sven. I only know I have to do it. Wil offers me his strength by holding my hand, and I take it. Together, we can do anything.

"Mr. Monroe?"

"Who are you?" His words are heavily accented. Reminds me of Papa's family in Malta.

Wil steps closer. Backs me up. Literally. I can feel the warmth of his body against my back. "I'm a friend of the man you had an encounter with tonight."

"Friend. Right." His eyes trail down and linger on my exposed chest, and I sense Wil bristle behind me. I press my hand harder into his, willing him to calm down.

"Crazy night?" I pretend I'm in control and know what I'm doing. "I'm here to improve your mood."

The ogre's eyes get a glint I didn't mean to put there. "Aren't you a little young?" His concern for my age doesn't prevent him from staring down my dress some more. Without the partial cover of Mom's necklace, and under much brighter lights than at the party, my boobs are on full display. My rapid breaths don't help.

"She's offering you money." Wil sounds too pissed to help in this negotiation. Baldy's face changes. I can almost see the dollar signs in his eyes.

"Five hundred."

"Four and you drop the charges," I say.

"Six hundred."

That's the wrong way. We don't have more than seven hundred. "Five-fifty. In cash. Right now." He looks at me and I don't know how, but I know I have him.

Ten minutes later, Mr. Monroe is signing a piece of paper erasing this night from Sven's record, and I have my arms around Wil, happy in my triumph. Wil's hand is running up and down my side. I lean into him, and his warm chest sends giddy joy all over. The Elvis jumper he's wearing doesn't smell like him, but his touch is undeniably Wil.

Playing dress-up was fun for a while, but I'm sick of disguises. I can't wait to get out of here, get this wig off, and get back to normal. Tired of pretending to be someone else all the time, I want to stop the sneaking, the hiding.

Outside the police station, the streets are still crowded with revelers. Malibu does not do Halloween like downtown LA. I've been missing out. Well, that's a given.

Mr. Monroe takes the lead, in the opposite direction of where Sven and Trevor stand. We walk two buildings down, out of sight of the police station, and dip into a dark alley.

"Give me the cash." Wil hands over the envelope with the last of our money.

"What did you do?" Sven's booming voice makes me jump as Mr. Monroe flees the scene.

"Saved your ass," says Wil.

I step in front of Wil. I doubt Sven would actually hurt him, but better safe than sorry. "What Wil means is we came to help."

But Sven is not looking at me. He's glaring at Wil. "You were supposed to protect her, not drag her to a police station in the middle of the ni—"

I pull at Sven's stained shirt and make him look at me. "He didn't have a choice. There was no way I wasn't gonna be here."

Sven's eyes have that storm-a-brewing look in them. Wil moves to step in between us, but I put a hand on his chest. My thumb lands on the skin exposed by the deep V of the one-piece suit he's wearing. His skin is warm. Wil is always warm.

"It was nice not being the damsel in distress for once." I raise my chin. "Oh, yes. And you're welcome."

"Melodie." The storm quiets, and sweet Sven is back.

"I know."

"Well, this has been a fun evening. My first Halloween in the US is one for the books."

I laugh at Wil's joke, and the tension of the last hour ebbs away. I'm suddenly aware that my hand is still on his chest. I better remove it. "I guess it's too late to go back to the party."

Wil glances at Sven. "Pretty sure Sven wants to go home."

"Where's the car?" Sven barks the question at me.

Wil points in the direction of the parking lot. "If it hasn't been car-jacked, we parked the Rolls out of sight of any reporters that might be sniffing around."

"Good thinking." Wil looks shocked at the praise from Sven. Sven holds out a big paw. "Keys."

"Oh, I don't think so," I say.

Three pairs of eyes turn and stare at me, shock on all their faces.

"No time for joking, Melodie."

I head to the car. "Not joking." I know I shouldn't push it, but when do I get a chance to play chauffeur, never mind drive the Rolls? "Besides, you're in no condition to drive, what with that eye and all. Can't get in an accident after the effort Wil and I went through to save your ass."

"I—"

Trevor backs me up. "She's right, bro. You owe her." I look to Wil for the same.

He holds up his hands and walks backward in front of me. "I'm so staying out of this. I like all my limbs attached."

I slap him on the arm. "Chicken."

We drop Trevor home first. Sven walks his brother to the door of his apartment building.

"I still can't believe Sven has a brother." Wil shakes his head.

"Family's complicated."

"Tell me about it."

I take the long way back to the UCLA campus. Sven slumps in the back seat, eyes closed, and Wil and I are almost alone. His forearm rests on the armrest. I'm thankful I don't need two hands to drive. I settle my elbow inches away from his. The street in front of me is dotted with a series of red lights, and I'm happy to hit the breaks at every one of them. The distance between his skin and mine shortens on every stop, until we touch. Too soon, I park at the cross street nearest to his dorm.

"Sorry we didn't get to finish our set." Wil's amber eye glow in the low light of the dashboard, a breath away, just like his lips.

"There'll be more sets."

One corner of his mouth rises, and he leans away. "I'll text you tomorrow."

And then it's just Sven and me on the road back to Malibu.

"How much did it cost you?"

Damn. He knows I can't lie. "Thirteen hundred for the bail and another five hundred and fifty to get Mr. Monroe to sign."

Sven scrubs his hands over his face. "Do you think he recognized you?"

"Trust me, he was too busy checking out my chest to spend much time on my face. I think we're good."

He tosses his head against the headrest and groans. "Shit, Melodie. I don't have the money. It's tied up in—"

"I know. It's not a problem. I have it covered."

"Don't tell me you're going to use the money for the video."

"Okay, I won't tell you." I do my best to keep a smile on my face. "Are you sure you don't want to go to the hospital? Get that eye looked at? It looks nasty."

"Had worse. I have what I need at home to clean it up."

"Okay."

I maneuver the Rolls into the garage, return the keys to Sven, and steal across the lawn to the kitchen door. The house is silent as I climb the stairs to my room. I close the door and finally take off the wig. My hair is a mess, stuck to my forehead, and I want a shower desperately.

But first, I open my closet and remove the bag with the cash I've been saving for the last few months. I count out the two thousand dollars I need to give to Mateo. With one gig left at the Devil's Martini, there's no way I'm going to be able to pay Leonard Astor to direct my music video. Again.

FORTY-TWO

THE WORKOUT IN THE morning should've helped me with staying still, but my body is in go mode, demanding action. Standing in the wings of the Devil's Martini, waiting, is not that, but there's nothing else I can do.

"We're on a tight schedule. Have you texted her?" Nick is standing six feet away from Sarah like she has the plague. Must have something to do with Nick showing up at the house after the Halloween party and sleeping on our couch. He almost bit Mateo's head off for joking about fighting with Sarah. Mateo needs to know everything, but I like my head attached to my shoulders.

"She texted an hour ago that she's on her way. She should be here by now." Putting this together has been a mad rush of calls, driving around with Mateo, and endless chats with Nick and

Sarah. The pieces are in place. We're as ready as we could be in such a short time. All I need is her, and it'll either crumble or come together. I have my bet on the latter.

"We've got this." Sarah walks over to me and places her hand on my shoulder. "We have the script, the equipment, the people. We'll pull this off." She stares at me, and no matter what's going on between her and Nick, I'm bloody lucky to have her on my side. I wouldn't have had the slightest idea how to approach this without her help.

"It's not like her to be late. What if it's a repeat of the Starlight Gala?"

"She texted you. She'll be here." Sarah rubs my shoulder, and some of the tension leaves me.

"What if she couldn't get out of the house?"

"What if it's LA traffic?" Her ponytail swings as she shrugs. "She'd find a way. Wouldn't miss this." Sarah walks to the opposite side of the hallway, as far away from Nick as she can. "It's your last night on stage."

Sarah's reminder hurts. WE's last performance. Pauline promised to give us recommendations and said several R&A reps were in the audience over the last month. Maybe I can find a Christmas Market or a coffee shop where we could sing that'll meet Sven's approval.

There's a gust of air as the door opens, and El walks in, all smiles. The room brightens, and my doubts ebb away. She's here. This is going to work. "You're late."

"Hello to you too." The scent of her sunscreen calms my nerves. "Had to drive here myself," she says. "Sven was the only one on the security team who didn't eat the prawns. He's allergic to shellfish. So he's stuck with Mom and Dad at the Camps for Kids fundraiser." Her face scrunches up. "Why are Nick and Sarah here?"

"Team." I wave them over. "Who wants to tell El the good news?"

El's eyes narrow. "News?"

I bite the inside of my cheek not to smile, and Sarah hits me on my forearm. "Tell her already."

"El Vella, are you ready to make a music video?" I hold my arms open.

Her face falls. Not sure what I expected her reaction to be, but this was not one of the options.

"Not funny." She puts down her guitar case. "What's really going on?"

"He's not joking." Nick's looking a little more in the land of the living, now that he has a task to do. "I've got the camera set up. Wil's recording the sound. Sarah has the script. Mateo's coordinating the next location. We have a plan."

El moves her eyes from him to Sarah, who claps and says, "You'll love it." Sarah pulls her phone out and starts reading. "We'll shoot at the bar here first. Frank has the small studio for us, for the scene on the floor. And the frat house for the mattress scene. The fellows stacked a bunch of them for us, so we're ready to go. The last location is a bit of a drive, but I promise it's worth it. Have you been to Griffith observatory?" She doesn't pause for El to answer. "Picture it. You and the backdrop of LA, sort of the new horizons, the world at your feet."

"Why?" El's question hangs in the air. Nick and Sarah look my way; El does too.

"We owe you." I stare into her eyes and don't say the rest. I don't say that it's because I'm here for her, and I want to see her dreams come true. Because I want to hear her laugh again and if this is what makes her happy, it's the least I can do. My fingertips tingle, and I brush them against the short hairs at the back of my neck. "You can still do something with Lenard Astor, but at least you'll have a video."

"What he means"—Sarah steps in front of me—"is that this is the least we can do after all the hours you put into the song for the movie. And we're friends. That's what friends do. We help each other."

El's hand—once bound with a splint—flies to her mouth. Her slender fingers healed now, able to strum the guitar, play the piano, hold my hand.

"What she said." Nick leaves his corner and comes over. "Are you in?"

El's gaze flits across the room and lands on my face. Our eyes connect, and she telegraphs her hesitation. I dig my nails into my skin, my fingers itching to reach out and transmit back that her success is as sure as the beating of my heart. But it's her decision to make.

She drops her hand, raises her chin, and nods. "What do I do?"

I let go. Of worrying for her, of worrying I couldn't fix it. The half-moon indents on my palms are a small price to pay. I can't hold back the smile anymore. And why should I? El's in, and everything is going to fall into place. My fingertips prickle awake as blood flow returns. She'll have the video she wants to kick off her singing career, and I'll . . . I'll get to be a part of history. The first person to mix the voice of the famous El Vella. I'll make it perfect for her. I roll my shoulders to erase the last bit of tension. We are doing this. She is doing this.

"You do you." Sarah fluffs El's hair and straightens the collar on her white shirt. "Oh, before I forget." She picks up a sparkly indigo bag. "This is yours."

The satin ribbon of the handles stretches over El's fingers, and she gauges the gift as if it has the power to transform her from rich girl to rockstar. She pulls out a gold statue: the Starlight Foundation's award.

Her gasp sets off a circle of drums from my hands, to my head, to my heart. "Every winner got one." Joy reverberates through me. My star now has her own star. Now, she has physical proof of her talent.

"Thank you," she whispers. El drags her thumb over the inscription *Best Song: Our Lines, Indigo*, and a crease forms between her eyebrows. "Are we singing *Our Lines* or only the covers?"

"WE are not singing." I point to her guitar. "El Vella gets her own set tonight."

Her eyes widen, and the crease on her forehead deepens. "But . . . I don't have enough material."

I shake my head. "Pauline agreed to have a shorter set with you singing some of the covers first and then your two songs. You'll sing *Don't Give Me Comfort* last." The song responsible for exposing the true El. The girl I find far more attractive than the glossy image the press loves to portray.

El keeps her gaze on the statue, and the room fills with her unsaid reservation.

I lean in so only she can hear me. "You can do this."

"You think so?" El bites her bottom lip.

"I know it." And I do.

El doesn't need me anymore. She's a different person from the weak princess I assumed she was the first time she walked out onto that stage. I'm not sure she ever needed me, would've found a way to do this on her own; she's that strong. The sweet-and-sour mix of emotions doesn't spoil my mood. I'm glad I got to go on this journey with her. Wouldn't have missed it for the world.

I hang her guitar strap on her neck. "And you know, I'm always right."

She places her cool hand over mine. "Thanks."

There's something about the way she looks at me that makes me think her gratitude is about more than my pep talk.

My heart splits in two. The selfish part of me wants to say more, to keep her here in this moment, just me and El, before it's El and the world. The rational one knows she needs to go. Tonight is going to change everything. I can feel it. For a long time, I've known she's going to be a superstar. Now, I'm certain it'll happen sooner rather than later. I can't wait to see her dreams come true. I'll stay behind when she walks onto that stage. Alone.

Pauline strolls in holding two silver balloons with "Congrats Grad!" decorated in red and blue rhinestones. "For my singers leaving the nest." A pang of regret joins the onslaught of highs and lows and dashes any hope of controlling my reactions. I yank the balloon out of Pauline's hands and focus on the slippery string as I twist it around my finger.

"Let's go and introduce El Vella to the audience." Pauline points over her shoulder.

She puts El's white strand behind her ear. "They'll like the new hair. Sets you apart from WE. And you are a much better redhead than you were a blonde." She strides onto the stage.

"Red?" El touches the ends of her hair. How did we not notice? Her hands fly to her head. "Shit. I forgot my wig."

"A round of applause for El Vella." Pauline beckons El to her side under the spotlight.

My girl straightens her back, the move I've grown to recognize. She's made her decision.

We wait for the audience to settle as El sits down on a tall bar stool and adjusts the mic. Nick makes his way to the camera set up on a front-row table. Sarah's using a handheld to film from the side of the stage to capture a second angle and outtakes. I've got my camera and my phone ready.

El strums the guitar and hums the beginning of Leona Lewis's *Bleeding Love*. I've heard her sing it so often I lost count, but it still feels like she's opening a wound each time.

The fear I saw in her the first day we got onto this stage together is nowhere in sight. She owns her voice and the space around her, demands the audience's attention with the confidence I feel for her. The bar becomes her personal playground.

The listeners are at El's mercy. She toys with them, takes them to quiet places of her heart then throws them to the height of a diva run, coloring the room in all the shades the palette of her voice possesses. I'm with them, mesmerized by this perspective. Usually part of the show, on stage beside her, I don't see her like this. See her so far away, yet so close.

She sings about hungering for a touch in her haunting version of The Righteous Brothers' *Unchained Melody* and looks off stage. Looks right at me, offers a sly smile that makes me suck in my breath as I hold her stare. And then she's gone, back to the adoring audience, telling them her story of time and needing their love.

Sarah pans across the bar, getting audience reactions. I follow her motions and peek at the packed room, patrons crowded around small tables, cocktails forgotten as they drink in the magic El is weaving. Pauline slides in beside me but doesn't say a word. We both know our roles in this part of the voyage are over. All we can do is witness the results.

Our first night, El told me the names of now-famous singers who got their start here. Pauline can add another name to the list. The last note of *Don't Give Me Comfort* floats over the mesmerized bar and fades into silence. The type of silence that is ripe with tension. The silence before an explosion. It ripples across the bodies as they stand up one by one, and the applause sweeps over the tables, then the shouts and the whistles come.

The chants start. Not, "WE, WE" this time but, "El, El, El."

I make sure to capture the ruckus, if not for the video, then to play it back to El anytime doubt reappears in her eyes. Because I knew from day one, she's the real deal and, tonight, every person in this establishment agrees with me.

There's nothing to stop her now.

FORTY-THREE

"SOMEONE HAS TO KISS her." Sarah puts her fists on her waist and shakes her head. Four hours should've been enough to get us through all the locations, but we are on hour five, and we only just arrived at Griffith Park.

"What?" I can't see her face well in the low light of the parking lot. Is that her way of getting back at Nick? I look at him but, as usual, he only has eyes for her.

"What?" El echoes me, but her voice is low and unsure. Bloody hell, we were having fun. The blokes in the frat carrying El around on a mattress like a queen had everyone in fits of laughter. I know it won't make it into the video, but the out-takes are going to be something to keep forever.

Nick played back the shots he took in the studio, stunning us with what he did using barely any equipment. Lying on the floor gazing into the camera, El dominated the screen, demanding the viewer's attention. I thought he was crazy for attaching his phone to a measuring tape and standing on a ladder to point down to El. But when he played the recording back, the camera zooming in on her beautiful face, tears shining in her eyes, her red hair spread out on the gleaming pale wood floor, I got goosebumps.

"It can't end like this. All this romantic tension and there's no payoff. A kiss does that. And the viewers'll eat it up." Sarah turns to Nick. "Right?"

I groan. Everyone knows Nick is going to agree with her. "Yup, definitely."

Called it.

"So, who's going to do it?" Sarah looks at me and raises her eyebrows.

El twirls the white streak of her hair around a finger. She does not look comfortable with this.

"Doesn't El need to agree to this first?" I turn to her. "Are you okay with this?"

She gives a small nod. "Sarah's usually right."

I shake my head. El's not wrong, our scriptwriter has good instincts, and they've all been spot on so far. But this? It's too much. Sarah looks at Nick and then back to me. Her eyes narrow, and my stomach clenches. She's up to something. "Guess I'm in charge. Mateo, sounds like a job for you."

"No can do. I promised to help clean up the mattresses." He takes his keys out of his pocket and jogs to his car.

Sarah turns her back to me and faces her boyfriend. "Nick?"

"No." The word bursts from my mouth. Three pairs of eyes turn to me. I pick El's, suck in air, and hope she doesn't choose Nick. It's not logical. Yeah, Nick needs to film the scene. "I'll do it."

El's eyes don't leave mine. "That works." No doubt or hesitation in her voice.

"Good." Sarah pats me on the arm like I'm her pet dog that just learned to roll over at her command. She moves toward El. "All you have to do is stand here, look over the city like you're searching for him. We'll make Wil do all the work."

Nick gets in on the action. "That's good. Wil"—he points down the pathway—"you start from there. Run up to El with the view behind you." He's in full director mode again. "We'll let the city be the dramatic cinematography of the scene, all soft and woozy so we can focus on you and her. You guys'll be silhouetted, no worries about being recognized. And then, you know, you kiss her."

I stuff my hand in my pocket, so I don't punch the grin off his face. Pressure builds in my stomach like I'm a bottle of champagne ready to pop. I holler at El, "Are you sure?"

She's walking to the spot Nick's pointing to and gives me a thumbs up. I wish I could see her face, know she's not freaking out about this like I am. Neither Nick nor Sarah seem to worry. All part of the movie-making process.

The actors on our set kissed on demand tens of times in a row for Nick to get a perfect take. I walk out of the shot. Kiss El. Can I do that?

I run my hands over my cheeks; at least I don't grow facial hair at the speed Nick does. This is El, my friend. Steps away, Sarah adjusts El's position, takes off the leather jacket I insisted El wear to ward off the cold winds whipping around at this height. Sarah leans in and whispers something in El's ear. I can't see her reaction, but she stays perfectly still.

The minute stretches as Sarah walks back to Nick, stands behind him, and places a hand on his arm. Sarah's right. A kiss is the pull-at-the-heartstrings people will connect with. This has to happen. I put my hands in front of my mouth and breathe into them. What did I eat last? Some mints would be nice.

Nick yells, "Action," and I start running. In the wrong direction. I should be running away from this, down the hill, back to Germany, anywhere. But El needs this video, and we've come this far. If this is what it takes, I'm in.

I halt before El, grab her face, and press my lips against hers. They're cool. Is she still cold? I'll make Sarah put the jacket back on. I count one, two, three. That has to be long enough. I drop my hands and step back.

El's eyes find mine. Is she sad? "What's wrong?" Her stare is telling me something I'm not getting. Like I messed up.

"Yeah, good first try. But let's do it again," Nick shouts from behind his camera. "Pretend you actually like her."

That's the last thing I need to do. El still hasn't said anything. I make a face and shrug to make her laugh. She only nods at me.

"Are you cold?"

She shakes her head, turns away from me, back to the city that's supposed to represent her future.

I consider telling them to stop, so I can pull El aside and ask her to talk to me. Sarah and Nick are watching me, us.

"Anytime now," Sarah says. I take back every nice thing I've ever said about her. Sarah's evil. I immediately regret that thought. She's the opposite of evil. Her heart is always in the right place. There's a reason Nick is madly in love with her. I glance at the pair of them, standing together, supporting each other. They're polar opposites, tall and tiny, dark and light. Yet they work, fit, no matter what happens, they find each other.

"Give me a minute."

I walk back to the starting point, get ready to go again. El's back in position. What do people think when they look at us? Two friends who are different but also have a lot in common. Sometimes I feel like El knows parts of me no one else has ever bothered to discover. Has made me understand parts of me I didn't know existed. When we're on stage, no, even when we're not on stage, one look from her, and I know what she's thinking.

Except now. That stare haunts me. What did I do wrong?

"Action!"

My heart beats in my ears. Maybe I was too fast last time. I stop in front of her and make sure to catch El's eyes before I lean in and kiss her. No counting. We're locked in a stare and a kiss, with as much space between us as I can manage and still do the kissing part. I don't know what to do with my hands.

"Cut."

I jump away. "Better?"

El juts her chin out. "Perfectly adequate."

The awkwardness between us breaks. I laugh. I can't help it.

"I mean, I might've uncovered the real reason you've never had a girlfriend." The cold wind blows El's hair like fairy dust around her heart-shaped face. "Or maybe this passes for kissing in Germany. Here in the United Stated of Ameri—"

My hands find her face first, my lips are a close second. I catch her mid-sentence, and this time, I feel the heat of her breath as she exhales and doesn't move away. I open my mouth wide enough to cover hers and linger there. My tongue moves across her teeth and when she separates them and I feel her tongue graze against mine, I stop pretending I like her.

I slide in farther and let myself taste her. No butter tarts. But her flavor is superior to any sugary treat, like I dreamed it would be, only better. Another part of myself that I didn't know existed takes over. The part that needs this, craves her, wants more.

My hand welcomes the freedom to touch her, moves with intent down her back until I find my way to her waist. She's too far away; I tug her closer, pulling her against me. Her hands grab my shoulders, and I revel in the feel of them there, holding me.

We are all movement now: mouths, fingers, hair flying in the wind, my knee between her thighs, her chest against mine. Lips. Teeth. Noses. Hands. Hips.

This is not right.

This is so right.

FORTY-FOUR

I CAN'T THINK.

I can't remember my own name.

I have no idea where I am.

That's not true. I know I'm with Wil. I know his lips are on mine.

Wil's kissing me.

Not that lame excuse of a kiss from a moment ago, or was it a lifetime? I can't remember, more like a duty he had to perform, void of anything. No, this, this is unbelievable. His lips soft and alive. A question asked without words, an invitation to let him in, and I do. I open my mouth, and I offer myself to Wil Peters. I give him my heart. Taking everything he's sending my way and wanting more.

I hear music. Not like the song playing on the radio in Mateo's car earlier tonight. Not from somewhere out there in the city below me that was twinkling, thriving, pulsing. No, it's something here between us, between Wil and me. A melody we're creating.

Not a mere guitar or a single piano track. It's a symphony. My beating heart is the drum, driving the refrain. Strings, woodwinds, brass in perfect pitch and harmony.

Kissing never felt like this. With Dillon it was exciting, maybe more about the danger of being caught than anything else. This is fantastic. Addictive. Delicious. Hot. He's so warm. How have I existed without this?

You just have to kiss the right person.

I grip his shoulders as his hand travels down my back, lands on my waist. The fury of want and desire I never thought I was capable of feeling swirls in the cage of my ribs and travels to my fingers and toes. I run my hands along his shoulders, trace the hard muscles there, find the back of his neck, pull him closer. Can't get close enough.

"Cut. Cut." Nick's shouts enter the tangle of us. "We can't rate this mature."

I ignore our director, focus on soaking up more of Wil, chasing the rush, trying to meet his tongue, but his lips leave mine.

He stops.

And it hurts. The separation is unbearable. I suck in air; my lungs are screaming for it.

"Mmm." I'm half full or half empty. The kiss was the amuse-bouche and it was delicious, but it only whetted my appetite. I want the main course. I have to see what the rest of Wil feels like. What his lips can do when they find their way down.

"I think we've got it. Let's pack up." The wind carries Nick's command to me and hits my exposed shoulders. I'm colder than I was when the shooting started. It's not because of the wind but because the heat of Wil's body and lips made me forget where I was. The inches between us form a canyon, and I imagine myself leaping across it, finding Wil's face, and kissing him not because of Nick shouting, "Action," but because that's what I want to do. Because I choose to.

One step is all it takes for me to close the distance.

"El." The husky low B of my name warms me.

"That sounds so much better when you say it." I slide my hand up his arm, grab onto his shirt, and stand on the tips of my toes. I'm going to do it.

"Melodie Maria Vella Rockerby." A part of me registers the voice; the sharp tone slices through the sliver of space left between Wil and me. That is not the name or the voice I want to hear. I don't want to look at the source, look away from Wil.

But I do. My world shifts. From the promise of warmth to the dread of cold.

Dad's gray form is more menacing against the darkening sky than I've ever seen before. The white of his tuxedo shirt a ghost of the jovial attitude he had when he left the house earlier with a wave and a wink. Now his eyes are slits, and his mouth is pressed into a hard line. "You need to get in the car."

If I thought he was pissed when he came to get me in London, he sounds ten times worse now. One hand on the hood of the Rolls, the other in his pocket. I feel Wil's fingers dig into my waist. I'm caught between staying where I want to be, here in Wil's arms, or doing what Dad wants, which means leaving Wil's side.

I let go of Wil, turn to Dad. Not because I want to. Because I owe Dad an explanation. He deserves to know everything, why I went to London in the first place, the singing, Wil.

Dad needs to meet Wil.

"Is this him?" Wil's voice is steely.

Wil needs to meet Dad.

Cars enter the parking lot, followed by a motorcycle. The previously empty—but for Sarah's car—lot is now sporting five vehicles, and I can see the headlights of more coming up the hill.

"Dammit, Melodie." Dad never swears around me, never. "It's the press. We gotta move."

I take a second to glance at Wil, hoping to use the telepathy that works between us on stage, but he's not looking at me. He's looking at Dad as if he's seeing a monster. "It's okay, I'll text you." I brush Wil's hand with mine but get no response. He's frozen in place, cold, and not a version of Wil I've ever encountered before.

"Now, Melodie." Dad breaches the invisible line between him and us, and I run to grab his hand, one that welcomes me. Dad throws a protective arm around my shoulders, and we jog to the car.

Flashes pierce the dark, and I see stars. Dad ushers me into the back seat and closes the door behind us.

Inside the car is quiet. Sven peels off and maneuvers the car around the haphazard press. The car's engine and the closed windows muffle their words, but the flashes of the camera continue to blind. The car swerves again and again to avoid the onslaught of paparazzi, and only when we make it off the mountain and merge into regular traffic, do I remember I left all my stuff with Sarah. My bag with my phone and wallet in it, my guitar, my balloon, Wil's water bottle that I consider mine.

"You made your mother faint." Dad's tone bears the full weight of his disappointment in me.

"What? Where is she? How is she?"

"Marta's looking after her." He stares out the window. "She's resting. Worried but resting."

The reality of what has happened hits me. Mom's worried; Dad's here. I look at Sven.

"How did you know where I was?" I didn't even know where I was going to be tonight. Wil surprising me with the video shoot still stuns me. It was all going so well. I search the car like it has answers. I find Sven's eyes in the rearview mirror, and my stomach sinks. The app. Sven is how he found me. I'm deleting that app as soon as I get my phone back.

Dad shakes his head and looks down at his hands. "Not a question I hoped to hear again."

I swallow, trying to figure out how much Dad knows.

"Your little stint at the Devil's Martini made the rounds on social media. You're Twitter famous. Or should I say El Vella is?"

"I can explain. It's all for a good reason."

"Great, 'cause I can't wait to hear it." His voice is low, but the words cut into me like little steel pins. "Going across town at night without a bodyguard? Lying to us? Betraying our trust after we barely started to relax after your London stunt? What's going on?" He faces me, eyes lacking the warmth I so often see there. "Your mom's sure you're reacting to not being the only child anymore, but I can't believe we brought you up to be that immature."

"I'm not." I hate the whine in my voice. I calm myself, hold on to the surety that what I'm doing is right. I belong on that stage. I know it now. "It's not the baby. It's the same reason I went to London."

"Dillon? He's back? Was that him on the hill next to you?"

"Dillon?" The boy seems a lifetime away. Me—another girl then. "No. It's never been about him. It's about my music video."

"A music video? What for? Why?"

"For one of the songs I wrote."

"You're writing songs again? Another thing you've been lying about?"

"I tried to tell you." I look away, focus on the headrest in front of me. "But you don't listen to me. Won't let me do music. Neither of you."

He opens his mouth to protest. I know what he's going to say. I hold up my hand. "Producing doesn't count. That's your dream, not mine. The safe option you and Mom agreed to—without consulting me." I find his face, determined to show him I'm serious. "I have to sing. Be in the music, not on the outskirts helping someone else make their dreams come true. I can't not do it. It's part of me. I will die if I can't have it in my life."

"Die. Don't be dramatic." He closes his eyes and bangs his head against the headrest. "You will most certainly not die if the spotlight isn't on you."

My fingers find the familiar thicker strands of my hair. I have to make him understand. "Dad, it's—"

Dad talks over me. "Producing gives you plenty of access to music, to be creative, to foster talent in others but saves you from the dark side of the life. It's not all fancy recording studios and kids playing at make believe. It's a dangerous world, and you could get hurt. Or worse. I don't know why I'm still alive, because I've made all the mistakes you can possibly think of. Didn't kill anyone, but that's just luck. And you might not be that lucky."

He takes my hand in his. "It's a hard life, Melodie. On the road for months on end, away from family and friends, never knowing who to trust but forced to trust someone. It looks fun, parties everywhere you go, but they get old fast. Fans breaking into your hotel room, stealing your toothbrush, trying to get their hands on you because they know, just *know* you are singing for them and them alone. People always want something from you. No privacy, no honesty—" He squeezes my hand. "Your mother and I, we don't want those temptations around you. Why not learn from my mistakes?"

I pull my hand from his, cross my arms. "Because I am not you. I am not related to you. I am responsible."

Dad huffs.

"I am. And I wouldn't have had to sneak around if you'd take me seriously. Treat me like an equal." I twist in my seat, make him look at me. "I've been nothing but responsible. Nadine says I'm great at work. I've never missed a day. Done everything you asked with a smile on my face."

He nods. Maybe he's getting it.

"On top of that, I've made my own money, doing what I love." I put my hand on my heart, feel the solid beat there. "I'm an adult. I am not a child anymore."

"You will always be my child. Blood or no blood. My marriage vows were not only to love and cherish your mother until death do us part, but to love and cherish you. I love you, Melodie. I will do everything in my power to protect you."

"I don't need protecting."

"I beg to differ. I'll be your father whether you want me or not, and that includes doing things you won't like me for. Being without music will not kill you. Being shot up full of substances, not remembering the name of the person you wake up with or waking up to someone choking on their own vomit next to you, or you being the one choking on it. That will kill you. I've seen it. Lived it. Watched that life kill many of my friends. It nearly killed me. There's no way I'll let you go down that road."

Dad turns back to the window; his face reflects on the glass. "I'm keeping my vow. I'll keep you safe."

FORTY-FIVE

HE WAS RIGHT THERE. A few feet from me.

I couldn't move.

My body is stone, and my mind is too weak to move the rock I've become. I watch the brake lights from the Rolls Royce blink on and off as it swerves to avoid the men and women running to it, shouting, breaking the night with the fireworks of their flashes. I hope Sven's driving. He'll protect her. Rocker's car disappears from view, but the voices don't stop. They get louder, closer, blocking my vision, assaulting my ears.

It's a repeat of what I saw happen to El on Labor Day weekend. But I'm their target now, the object of these reporters' curiosity. There're so many of them, some running toward me, others speeding off after the car that took El away. In front of me, another flash goes off, and the world goes white; for a moment I'm blind. In the void, a faceless voice hollers, "What was Melodie doing here?"

A hand grabs my arm and pulls me forward. "Move, Wil. Now." Nick's dragging me forward, but I can't see, the negative of the flash still hurting my eyes. "Wake the fuck up." He pushes me into the back seat of Sarah's convertible, onto our gear and bags, and jumps in next to her.

"Do you know Rocker's daughter?"

"Who are you?"

"What's your name?"

"No comment." Sarah shouts as the roof of her convertible hides the stars from my view. I'm out of the wind that was whipping around us on this hill, but a chill runs up my spine. What just happened?

"Hold on." Sarah guns the gas, and I slide sideways. I need to find a seatbelt. I need to sit up. Instead, I close my eyes and replay the scene of the man who ruined Mum's life now ruining El's. I didn't get a good look at him; it was so dark. More of an image. Tall frame, dark hair neatly trimmed, not long like the photo of him on stage at the benefit concert I first saw after Opa told me about him. Was he wearing a tuxedo? No, that can't be right. He only wears leather pants and shirts that never have enough buttons done up.

It was his voice all right. Same as the interviews I've watched. Just harsher. Biting out El's name, her full name, demanding she go with him, leave me. Leave her own video shoot.

Anger stirs inside me. He doesn't get to do this. Not again. I have to help them both. Mum. El. They didn't deserve the way Rocker treated them. I pull myself up. I fasten the seat belt.

"You alive back there?" Nick cranes his neck to check on me, his hand braced against the dashboard.

"Dandy."

"What happened?" Nick barely fits in Sarah's car with the top up. "Why did you freeze? Star struck?"

I don't reply. The tripod is jabbing me in the ribs, and I shove it over to my lap and push the legs in one by one. Click. Click. Click.

"Can you find my backpack? It's blue."

Like I haven't seen his backpack before. I lift the bag with the camera, move the Pelican case with the lights, and I see my old water bottle. The one El's been using. I rifle some more, past the pack Nick wants, and find her guitar case, and her big blue bag. My hands shake. It must be here. I dig around, find Sylvia's ruby necklace, push it aside, and my hand feels the familiar shape, the embossed gold of the crest of Malta brushes against my fingers. I pull El's large smartphone out.

She needs her phone. I have to talk to her. I can't text El if I have her phone. Can't make sure she's okay. This is all so wrong. Tonight shouldn't have ended like this. We were having fun. We were . . . I don't know what we were. She was there, where she was meant to be, and now she's gone.

I squeeze the device that's full of melodies El has played for me, cradle in my hand the words we wrote together. It holds parts of El I want to know more about. This is my way in.

The home screen comes to life. It's a photo I forwarded to El that Bri took of her at the viewing of *Indigo*. And in the top left corner there's half of my face, my eyes trained on her.

"I'll wait here." Sarah parks her car on the side street. "You have her stuff?"

I lift El's guitar case and her big blue bag. Our water bottle, her phone, and her Starlight trophy for winning Best Song are safe and sound. Sylvia's necklace Mateo traded in exchange for the money we borrowed to save Sven lies in a Ziplock at the bottom. How can this be everything I have of El?

"Say 'hi' if you see her."

Speaking has become difficult. I nod. Moving is hard too. But move I must. Up the sidewalk. Left. Along the street we drove down a moment ago. Another turn, and the gates I've seen from the inside of Rocker's mansion look a lot taller. There's a screen off to the left. I put down El's guitar and tap it. An image of the Rocker, Inc. logo fills the once blank space.

"Yes." A gruff male voice comes from a speaker below the screen. Not Sven, someone new. I don't know what to say.

"Hi." This is going well. "I'm here to see El. Melodie. Melodie Rockerby."

"And you are?"

"Wil Peters."

"Is she expecting you?"

"Yup."

"Hold up." The screen goes blank. For hours. I tap my fingers, waiting. The logo pops up again, and the metallic voice is back. "Wait there."

I breathe again. She's coming. Everything is going to be fine. My hands grab the handle of her guitar case, and I stare at the smaller gate on the other side of the iron bars. I stare and imagine El's face in place of the metal grid.

There's a squeak as light cracks through the opening door. She's here.

Disappointment stabs at my chest. A scowl greets me instead.

"Sven."

"Wil."

"Where is she?"

The big guy sighs. "Is this her stuff?"

"Is she okay?" The big guy's eyes drift to the floor. Bloody hell, she's not okay.

"Her parents aren't too happy right now."

"Do they . . . what happened?"

"Someone recognized her at the Devil's Martini. Tweeted about it."

A knife twists in my chest. The wig. She didn't wear her disguise. If only I'd taken a moment to find her a hat. No one noticed El for months at the farmers' market.

This is all my fault. If I hadn't insisted on making a video, this whole thing wouldn't have happened. Why didn't I think? Think about her? I wanted to be part of everything. I trusted my gut, thought it would all work out like it always does. But it doesn't always. I should have been more careful.

"But how did her father know where to find us?"

Sven looks away. Right.

"You used the app again?"

"Her stuff?" Sven opens the gate and advances, a giant hand aimed at her guitar case.

I hesitate. I hand over these few items and what? Is that it? Will I never see El again? This is not why I came here. "Can I see her?"

"Not an option."

I don't like the feeling of dread that raises the hairs on my neck. I want to hold on to her things. Hold on to her. "Please, Sven." Apparently, I'm not above begging now.

Sven's shoulders slump a little, and I get my answer.

"But you'll tell her . . ." What? What do I want to say to El? Thanks for the memories? Don't stop singing? Don't give up on us?

"She knows." Sven takes El's guitar case and reaches for her bag.

"Wait." I pull out our—no, her—water bottle. Something of hers has to stay with me. I give the rest to Sven.

"Don't come back." The gate slams behind him, and I'm left staring at the metal. The barrier between her world and mine sealed for good.

It is over. Really over. I'll never sing on a stage with El again. Never hear her hum a new melody, words bursting in my head, running to complement the tune. Never hold her hand. WE no more. El gone. The pain in my chest stabs at me again. Worse. This can't be it. It just can't be.

The camera loves El. I can't blame it.

Nick sits beside me in the editing booth. It's the scene on the studio floor, the camera looking down at her, her red hair framing her face. The face I've become used to brightens my world. I want to reach out, run my thumb across her cheek. But I'll never feel the warmth of her skin again. The ache in my chest is back. Hell, it hasn't left since he took her away.

My hourly texts get no response.

"I want to slow this shot down a quarter, let the screen fill with her. Look at the tear in the corner of her eye. She was amazing that night."

I turn away. Can't stand the sight of El crumbling to the floor to match the line I've overlaid on the video. Her words, her voice invading my body like her scent whenever she was near. What is wrong with me?

"You okay, little buddy?"

Nick's staring at me. "Sure. Fine. Why?"

"Any word from El?"

I check my phone in case there's a message. Nothing. I shake my head.

Nick punches me in the arm. "She'll be okay. Maybe they never gave El her phone back."

"Bloody idiots. Controlling her."

"She's stronger than you think."

"I know." I snap back at him, sick and tired of the world assuming El is some helpless princess. She has an inner force like no one I've ever met. She's taught me more than I ever thought possible.

Nick holds up his hands in surrender. "No need to bite my head off. I'm not the one keeping her from you."

"Just edit the bloody video."

Nick goes back to pressing buttons, winding the recording back and forth, El in and out.

"You know, she feels the same way."

I put my head in my hands. "What are you talking about?"

"El. She likes you too."

"I know she likes me. We're friends." Or we were. What are we now?

"More than friends."

I stare at him. "No. Just friends."

Nick shakes his head. "I was there. Friends don't kiss like that."

"Oh, fuck off. We were acting." I can still feel her lips on mine, the taste better than the butter tarts she obsesses over. My hand in her hair, on her waist. Bloody hell, I have to stop this.

"Listen, I know what it's like to be forced into the friend zone."

"I'm not in the friend zone."

"But you're friends?" Nick raises an eyebrow, and I want to punch him.

"You're twisting my words."

"I'm trying to make you see it's a good thing. You and El are good together."

"We were good together. Past tense."

"If that's what you want." Nick shrugs. "If it were me, I wouldn't give up. I didn't."

"Sarah?"

"It wasn't all peaches with us. I screwed up." Nick rubs the stubble that's always present on his chin. "She's it for me. No one else comes close. I'd do anything for her."

What would I do for El? What wouldn't I do?

"El's gonna need people in her corner."

"She has people."

"Not the right people."

Nick presses play, and El's voice fills the room. "After you post this video, her parents have to change their minds. They're both musicians. Even they can't miss her talent. It hits you in the face the moment she opens her mouth to sing."

El's voice echoes Nick, answering as she sings. "Is not what I want. To portray. In the mirror of the world's eye."

"I can't just post it. I need her consent." I shake my head. "Putting her under more scrutiny with the press without her knowledge—I won't do it to her."

"Then you need a plan."

"For?"

"Seeing her."

I'm so going to punch Nick. "I tried. Sven was very clear that's not happening."

"Try something else." I look at Nick. "Is she still going to work?"

"No go. I tried to get into Rocker, Inc. before. Security turned me away."

"That was you, a rando from the street. What if you are not a rando?"

Did Nick figure it out? Or Sarah? Do they know I'm Rocker's son?

The corner of Nick's mouth twitches. "What if you are there to deliver Blend's famous coffee to Mr. Bill Rockerby?"

I feel a spike of adrenaline. Then reality hits. "That'll only get me to the front desk."

"It can get you a lot farther. I've only done it once myself, but I took it all the way to the meeting room he was in. Stood in the same room with the man. This pretty brunette gave me the best tip of my life."

"I don't care about tips." Nick got in. The adrenaline rushes back. If I could get past security, find El. Talk to her. This might be my last chance. I push off the seat and send the chair flying into the wall. "Do you think it could work?"

"What's the worst that can happen? You get kicked out again? El's not there?" Nick rises and slaps me on the back. "What have you got to lose?"

FORTY-SIX

AN ICED CAPPUCCINO, TWO shots, with cashew milk, a pump of caramel, two pumps of vanilla, poured, not shaken, complete with a mint leaf, and a matcha latte sit on the two trays of drinks I have in my hands. They are whatever other customers mis-ordered or didn't pick up. They are the camouflage that's supposed to add to my Blend baseball cap and the brown paper bag that sports a sizable Blend logo on it, which isn't filled only with pastries. I'm either a Blend employee or a mad fan of the coffee shop, who has no reason to stand in front of the security desk of Rocker, Inc.

"Time for a pick-me up?" The bloke in the security uniform turns my way. For a second, I think it's Sven. Panic lets go when brown eyes catch mine. "Love your signature house blend."

"It's the best." I grab the tray tighter.

"She's coming down for you." The man at the security desk gives the coffees another glance.

She. Could that be El? Could it be that easy? The woman who exits the lift and waves me in is beautiful with her glossy brown curls and ultra-modern ensemble, but she is closer to Sven's age and most assuredly not El. This must be the famous Nadine El goes on about.

"No one told me about placing an order." She looks at my tray and reads the orders. "Melodie ordered one for herself but not for me? And Mr. Rockerby ordered his favorite. I feel ignored." She reads the rest of the orders. "Must be for the rock group in recording booth three. They're up on the second floor. You'll see number three there."

Nadine's phone buzzes, and I feel sweat trickling down my brow. "Wait there, and I'll be down with your tip." She points at me. "Don't let anyone touch the latte or the cappuccino. I'll let the Rockerbys know their orders are here too. Maybe torture Melodie first for not getting me anything."

The security guard laughs, and I fake laugh with him. Nadine steps around me and heads in the opposite direction, typing something on the phone.

I jab at the lift button. My luck is working, and the doors open immediately. I need to find El before security figures out something is wrong. So far so good, just like Nick said. I step in and press the fourth-floor button. After a short stint up, the lift opens on the second floor instead, and I freeze. The man who took El away from me that night meets my eye. Bill Rockerby takes a step in and looks at the collection in my hands. "Someone ordered from Blend and didn't tell me?" He surveys the tray and spots the matcha latte. "Is this one for me?"

I nod, unable to find my voice. He holds the doors open and points down the hall. "I'll show you the way to the studios." Rocker smiles at me, and he looks so normal, approachable even. No high-handed remarks; he's not ignoring me. He's going out of his way to treat a delivery boy with the polite helpfulness I'd expect from someone in the hospitality business, not a millionaire rock star and producer.

I can drop the coffees off and detour back to the fourth floor on my way out. El's somewhere above me. We're in the same building, and I just need to get rid of Rocker's unwanted company. Months of trying to get in front of the man, and now all I pray for is for him to leave. He leads me along a hallway. "Which studio d'you need?"

I remember Nadine's instructions. "Three. The rock band."

"Resorting to coffee already, are they?" Rocker rambles away by my side as we move down the hall. Like we are friends. "What's in the bag?"

Crap.

"Pastries." He reaches out, and I yank the bag back. "It's for the band."

"They won't mind if I steal one. Everyone knows I have a sweet tooth."

"No." I can't give him the bag. I brought this for El, and if he sees the contents, he'll know I'm not here to deliver coffee. I tighten my hold on the handles.

"No?" The easy-going dad routine fades, and his eyes narrow. He opens the door next to us and almost pushes me in. It's an empty studio, the sound room dark and silent. "This better not be what I think it is, or you and the band are out of here."

The band?

He snatches the bag, and one of the paper handles threatens to tear. "I have a no drug policy in this company. And no matter how much they paid you and what disguise you've used to get in here, I'll call the police."

He opens the smaller bag with pastries and tosses them on the table, shakes the pages of my little black book over the table and then tosses it there. I resist the urge to grab my book in case he might open it and read what's inside. Last night, I filled the pages with everything I've wanted to say to El for a long time. It took me forever to come up with the opening.

Dear El, I have a confession to make. You always say I'm the words person. Maybe you are right and maybe my words will make a difference this time as well. Promise to read to the end of this page before you throw this out.

My hopes of putting this in her hands fade.

"They will be blacklisted not only from my studio but from any reputable studio in town." Rocker's thick eyebrows knit together as he inspects my dented water bottle. "Okay?" He slams the bottle down on the table and the USB stick I put inside clanks against the metal. Hands used to plucking strings twist off the cap and shake the empty container upside down, as if it might contain the illicit drugs he's expecting to find. Instead, out falls the black tube with my note, El's music video attached.

"What's this?"

"It's not for you." I put the coffee trays down and try to take my stuff back, but Rocker's staring at me. He reaches out and rips my Blend baseball cap off. Heat surges up my neck, and I grind my teeth, attempting to not snatch my hat right back. I've spent months trying to get to him, and now that he's close, I just want to push him away.

Rocker's expression hardens as he studies my hair, shoulders, arms, legs, and returns his glare to my face, angrier than before. A copy of the eyes I see in the mirror every day drill into me. My cheeks burn with the hope he will recognize himself in me and the fear he won't. "You're the guy from that night. At Griffith Park."

Bugger. My cover is blown. What do I do? El's in this building. I stare back, unblinking, and try the only thing I have left. The truth. "I need to see . . . Melodie."

Rocker throws my cap onto the table and weariness laces his words. "Did you put my daughter up to this singing business?"

"No." This guy is so clueless. I almost feel sorry for him.

He sighs, as if he's heard this before. "What was the play here? Ride her coattails to get your chance at the spotlight?"

"What? I wouldn't."

"Yeah, yeah"—he waves my protest away—"let me guess, you sing too. Want to be a rock star and you thought Melodie was your ticket." The phrases sound rehearsed, like he's said them a million times before.

"It's not like that." I can feel El slipping away. The more time I spend here with him, the less of a chance I get of seeing her. Is security already on the way?

"Do you think you"— Rocker points his finger to my chest—"are the first to try to use my daughter?"

"I didn't . . ." But I did try to use her. I hate myself for it. "I'm not using her." Now.

"You know nothing about Melodie." He leans my way. We are nose to nose, and the weariness from a moment ago morphs into something more menacing. "What's good for her." He says it like I'm no good for her or anyone he cares about.

Is he serious? "I know your daughter better than you do. You're the one who's causing damage. Treating her like a hostage in her own home, telling her what career is the right one for her." He needs to hear this. If no one else dares to speak up for El, I will. "You won't listen, to her words, to her voice. Have you ever even heard her sing?"

"Of course I have. I'm her father." This man is such an arse. The pounding in my ears is deafening. His words throw gasoline on my already flaming skin. Rocker looks over my shoulder. Security must be here. My time is up. My luck failed me. I'm never going to see El again. He sneers. "You're just a nobody after your fifteen minutes of fame."

"If I wanted fame, I wouldn't need to use anyone." Everything is on fire, and I burn my bridges. "I could just tell the world I'm your son." My voice booms through the room.

There's a gasp behind me. The hairs on the back of my neck stand up. I didn't need an audience for this. I turn to face whoever is behind me and find El standing at the door. The fire that consumes me dies down at seeing her. She's here. My ruse worked. She's more beautiful than the last time I saw her. I move toward her, my fingers need the relief of her hand. To prove she's real.

Her lips are a severe line, her forehead creased, and the look she gives me is aflame with cold blue fire. Dread at what I just said crawls across my heart as the reality of my admission sinks in. My secret, my reason for being in the US that I kept from her, hangs between us. The ice storm in her eyes freezes her familiar face into a mask I've only seen her wear in front of the paparazzi.

"Right, like I haven't heard that one before." Rocker barks a laugh. "So it's money you're after. How much for you to crawl back into the hole you came from?"

I tear my eyes away from El and stare at Rocker. Months of scheming and planning all to stand in front of him and ask for money for Mum, and he offers it to me like it's nothing. Doesn't even think about it. One word from me, and all her treatments would be paid for. No more rent weighing us down. No more bill collectors calling day and night. No more barely getting by. Just like that, her life could be different. My life could be different.

I want it to be different. But not like this. I want to be with El. I want to hold her hand, create magic when I perform on stage with her, take her in my arms and kiss her.

The scent of the beach hits me. Her cold unfeeling expression smarts. El pushes by, saying, "It's always about money with you." The slam of her hand on the table might as well be punch to my gut. How can she think the worst about me? Didn't I prove I'd do anything for her?

"Don't forget your tip." The two twenty-dollar bills she leaves on the glossy surface are nothing to her. Like me. The shrapnel of her dismissal lacerates my heart. I can't guard against it. Money ruins everything.

"El." I look up for her, but she's moving toward the door. I reach out and catch her arm. I need her to listen, to hear the explanation I've prepared but never dared to confess to her. Five minutes of her time and she'll understand. She has to.

"Let go," she hisses, reminding me of the first time I met her. And just like then, I do as she asks. My fingers resist as I straighten them to release her. I can't force her to stay and listen to the truth I wrote in my message. Everything is wrong. It's backward. She should've read the note first and then we would've talked. I pick up the black notebook from the table. "Take this."

El steps back, shakes her head, turns, and disappears down the hall. I go to follow, but there's a hand on my shoulder.

"Oh, no, you don't."

I try to shake it off, but the grip is tighter, and another clamps onto my elbow. "I have to talk to her."

"You just won't take no for an answer, will you?"

I give in, stop resisting his grip. She's gone. It's no use.

"No." I turn toward him. If I can't have El, I'm going to do my best to make sure she gets everything she wants. It's the least I can do for her. "She's worth it."

"You can drop the act. Melodie's not here."

"It's not an act." I pull out my phone. "You have to see this."

Rocker's voice booms. "I've seen it all. Your kind just wants a piece of my daughter. The last boy who tried—failed. One lucrative job opportunity, and he gave her up. What offer will persuade you to walk away?"

"What the—?" I find the video Nick finished cutting last night. "Here." I shove the screen in his face, force him to watch.

El's voice fills the room. Rocker doesn't bat it away. Instead, his face turns soft, like Opa's does when we sing *Happy Birthday* to Mum. As he watches, I can see the interest in his eyes; he recognizes how amazing and talented she is. When El sings, "It awakes the pain from my past," he slumps back onto the table like all the air has been sucked out of him.

"I didn't know," he whispers when the last note fades.

"You don't listen."

Rocker pulls himself up to his full height. "Don't tell me about my own family."

Now, it's my turn to laugh. "What do you know about family? You play-act with El but hide from your actual flesh and blood."

"You are not my son." Rocker's eyes narrow. "Just because your mother slept around and had a one-night stand with a stranger doesn't—"

Pain explodes in my hand as my fist connects with his face. "Don't talk about Mum like that." Rocker is rubbing his chin, his eyes dark with malice.

"She stepped up when you ghosted her. Sacrificed everything for me." I want to hit him again. Keep pounding until he gets it through his thick skull. "Look at me." I'm yelling now, my words doing the hitting my fists won't. "I have your face, your eyes. Even your fucking talent with the guitar. Believe me, I wish I didn't." I look to the door El fled through. "I wish I had nothing to do with you."

The man before me re-scans me from head to toe and back again. This time he's not comparing me to the guy he's seen with his daughter. He's comparing me to him. His wife mistook me for him. As a little boy when I was imagining what my father looked like, I dreamt of a younger Opa not an older me. But I am like Rocker. Too much like him.

He shakes his head. "I can't have a son."

"You do."

Rocker rubs his temples, eyes unfocused. Is he going through the hundreds of women he slept with? Trying to figure out which one he knocked up? Does he even remember Mum's name? My hands ball into fists, but he isn't worth the effort of another punch.

"You know what? Mum didn't need you, and I don't either. You can take this life of yours and shove it." I grab my water bottle and book off the table, the only things in this room I care about, and leave Bill Rockerby in my dust.

FORTY-SEVEN

Wil

I'M NOT IN JAIL, but I feel like I am.

Why did she have to find out that way? The lies caught up to me when I was coming clean. I'm not the scheming wanker Rocker painted me to be. I'd never intentionally hurt El like the reporters, like those others that poser Rocker compared me to. The thought of what they did to her, what they could have done to her—it makes my blood boil.

Yes, I started out not with the best intentions, wanted his help, but it was for a good cause. Okay, maybe in the back of my mind I wanted to see what having a father would feel like. But I'm not an evil person. I wasn't robbing him, even though I could. I didn't drag his name through the tabloids, even though it would be so easy. Upload one video to YouTube, and he'd have to deal with me. His son. I dare him to deny it then.

But I won't do that. Not because of him. No. Because of her. Maybe I'm lucky because instead of finding a shitty father and his money, I found El. If it weren't for him, I never would have come to this country, never would have recognized her in the Devil's Martini, never—oh, my chest hurts at the thought of not knowing El.

Is having had El in my life for five months and losing her better than not having her at all? El who now, because of her wanker of a father, thinks I'm a dirtbag?

One thing Opa got right is that Rocker is a dirty bastard. A right proper Drecksack.

I dial my home phone. "Bill Rockerby is a Drecksack."

"Wil?" My mother's voice comes from the speaker.

"Why aren't you at work?"

"I . . . had a doctor's appointment today." There's a hesitation in her voice.

"Everything okay?" I know it's not. My head pounds. "Mum, how bad is it?"

"Luv, it's not bad news. The new treatment we've been waiting for—they have an opening. It's sooner than I thought."

I close my eyes and let out a breath. "That's good, Mum."

"Yes, but it means we need to find the money a little sooner than expected."

"I'll figure it out."

"Wilhelm Augustus Peters. This is not for you to figure out. You need to concentrate on school, your life in California. We'll find a way. We always do."

"But—"

"No buts. I will not have you worrying about me."

Like I can do anything else but worry. It's all I've done since the day she got sick. "Yes, Mum."

"Now, let's go back to the beginning of this call. I agree Bill Rockerby is a Drecksack, but I'd love to know why you think so."

"It's not important, Mum. I promise you—"

"Promise to tell me the truth."

"Mum." Her words ring in my ear. I can't tell another lie. I can't.

"How about I help? You know he's your father."

I'm on the street, somewhere between Rocker, Inc. and Blend, in between worlds. I lean against a wall ablaze with the warmth of the midafternoon sun. "Did you figure it out or did Opa tell you?"

"Mum."

"Right, Opa. I guess I should be surprised he lasted this long." I hear her sigh on the other end. "I never wanted you to find out, luv. It's—wait. Tell me this isn't why you're in the US."

"Mum. It's—"

"It is. Blimey, Wil. What else are you lying about? Is the money you've been sending us from him? Is it?"

"No, absolutely not. I haven't taken a penny from that man. I won't. I'm not a piece of shit like him." A woman walking by stares at me, and I want to give her the finger. But I don't, like Mum would know what I'm up to and disapprove. I can't take any more disappointment. "No matter what he says, I'm not, Mum. I swear."

"Wil, listen to me. No one thinks you're"—she edits my swearing—"a bad person. No one. You hear me."

I nod.

"Wil?"

"Yes, Mum." My voice cracks. I crack. I raise my hand to my eyes to block out the sun. Or hide the tears threatening to break free. How can she say this after I've been lying to her for months? How can she ever forgive me?

"And Bill's not a bad person, either. Despite what your Opa told you, he's never been bad. Misguided. Blinded by fame at a young age, yes. But not bad. He has a good heart. Like you do."

"Don't say that. I don't want to have anything in common with that man. I've seen his photos. I've looked at myself in the mirror. I know the truth. I don't want it. I don't want him."

"Luv, it's all right."

"It's not all right. I'm glad he denied I'm his son. He doesn't want an overgrown son with opinions different from his own when he's about to get a perfect little baby for himself."

"You told him about me, and he denied it?"

"Yes, he basically called you a whore and me a bastard."

"He wouldn't." I can hear the shock in her voice. I didn't mean to be so harsh. She doesn't need this. I don't need this. I need—

"He did. What do you think of his good heart now?"

"I think all I care about, all I've ever cared about, is you. My son. I love you. I've never been more proud of you. I'm sorry I couldn't give you a father."

"Don't say that, Mum. Opa was plenty of a father to me." There's a sniff on the other end of the call, and I think she's crying. I wipe at the water in my eye. The sun is blinding. "I love you, Mum. I'll find more money."

"Wil, I'm the parent in this relationship. It's my job to take care of you, not the reverse." Her voice takes on the crisp tone of determination that reminds me of El when she's made up her mind and I no longer have a choice. "I'll get the money. Promise me you'll finish out the semester and get home in time for Christmas."

I hang up with Mum and look around. I don't know what to do, where to go. I know where I want to be, but that isn't an option. Never will be. I fucked this whole thing up.

My phone vibrates and even though it's not the double buzz of El, I jab at the text in case she's using another phone. Or it's her cousin.

Nick: Did you get in?

I press the phone against my forehead, wishing it were El I was touching instead of this cold technology. Why did this have to happen?

I look at the text from my friend. Nick is my friend. Mateo too. Even Sarah. They care about me. I liked my life here. But it's over now. I'll do what Mum says, finish the semester, get my credit, and go back to Germany. If not for Mum and Opa, it doesn't feel like home is there anymore. I admit to myself I want it to be here.

A car drives by blasting a song I don't know, the singer shouting about how things sound when you're winning. Another text. I open my eyes and look at my phone.

Nick: Or are you in jail?

I don't want to answer him. I put my phone in my pocket and resign myself to walking back to Blend.

I'm slammed against the wall. I look up into the coldest blue eyes I've ever seen.

"What the fuck did you do to El?"

I try to answer Sven, but his massive hand puts pressure in the middle of my chest, making it hard to breathe. I cough, and the strength of his hand lifts me up. "Stop." He doesn't stop exactly, but he lets my feet find the ground.

"Talk."

"She deserves the freedom to be who she wants to be, and he"—I can't force myself to say his name—"treats her like a doll. They dress her up, put her in expensive cars, find her a job they approve of. It's their dream, their life. Not hers."

"Not what I'm asking about." Sven grinds his teeth. "Did you claim you're Mr. Rockerby's son to extort money from him?"

"No. Double no. I *am* his son"—the pressure on my chest increases again—"but I didn't ask him for anything." Less pressure, and I suck in air. "I was there for El. To give her a copy of the video Nick and I mastered." Less pressure. I can almost breathe normally. "The shoot you interrupted at Griffith Park was for El's song, the one she couldn't record because she spent the money bailing you out."

Sven looks at the wall beside my head. I fear he might punch it.

"I had to do something. Help her. She needs"—I think of Nick's words in the studio yesterday—"friends on her side. Friends who care about her." I clench my fists. "I care about her." There, I said it. To the wrong person, but I said it. It's out there in the world, and I can't take it back. Don't want to.

I don't know how I expected Sven to react to my confession, but completely ignoring it was not it. "Bill Rockerby has no children. Yet. And if you're claiming you are his, it means you want something from him."

"I am his son. Look at me."

Sven studies my face. I know he sees the resemblance. "Maybe a look-alike."

"Now who's lying?"

"Do you know how many people claim to be his child?"

"Would you like a DNA sample?"

"I would." Sven lets go of me and pulls out an oblong white stick-like thing wrapped in plastic. "I have one."

I gawk at the contraption in Sven's hand. He's not exactly asking. I don't have to do this. But do I want to? Maybe I'm not his son? No, Mum wouldn't lie. If this proves it once and for all, I can be done with this mess. "Prepared much?"

"Like I said, you're not the first. Open up." Sven motions to my mouth.

"Ah." I can feel the swab scrape against the inside of my cheek. He caps the item, seals it in a clear vial, and pulls out another.

"One more time."

"In case I borrowed someone else's skin for that one?"

"Open up." Sven never gets my humor.

He repeats the procedure and tucks the kits back into the inside pocket of his jacket.

"Follow me."

I could run, but I know he's a much better runner than me. Not that I care what happens to me at this point. But maybe I can persuade him to help El. He's on the inside, can at least talk to her. "Have you seen the video?"

"No."

"I can show you." We walk up to the car he drove the night of Zoe's birthday party when I convinced him to let me busk with her again. He helped her then, he has to again.

"Get in."

Sven swerves into the beginning of rush hour traffic in LA, and my heartbeat speeds up. He won't hurt me, but the unknown of what's happening is messing with my head. The drive ends in less than five minutes when he pulls up to the frat house.

"Get out."

"You don't want to see it?"

Sven grips the wheel of the car tighter. "You got enough for the video before we showed up?"

That's my cue. I pull my phone out, turn the video on, and put it on the dashboard between us. It plays scenes of El on stage, El scaling a pile of mattresses, El on the studio floor with the tear in her eye, El overlooking the city of lights, turning and smiling before I kiss her, her voice ringing out over the images. I've seen it, heard it so often, but it still gives me chills.

Sven picks up my phone and hits replay. Again. And again. And again. And again. On the fifth time, I grab my phone from his hands. He looks like a tiger who just had his favorite toy taken away. "You owe her."

Sven looks at his hands. "How can I help?"

"I need to talk to her. Persuade her not to give up. She needs to keep going. I don't have to be by her side, but she can't just stop."

"Too late." He stares out the window. "She promised her father to drop everything. He wants her to go to New York for a while."

"No. What?" She can't leave. I can't get to New York. "When?"

"After you left. She. We. I found her in the stairwell." Sven doesn't say it, but I know she was crying. I made her cry again. I punch the dashboard.

"Sven, it's not her decision. Help me stop this." I point to my phone. "Help me show her this, and she'll see she can't give up."

"I can show her."

I shake my head.

"You want to see her."

"I need to see her. Talk to her. Explain it all."

He turns to me, the stare so intense I have to resist jerking my head back. "And then you'll leave."

"I have school till Christmas."

"No. If I get you in to see her. You talk and then you leave. The country."

The idea of a life without El pierces my heart. "Why?"

"Because if you truly care about her and not yourself, you don't need to interfere. Say what you have to say and leave the rest up to her. I'll support her decision. You're right. I owe her. I pay my debts."

FORTY-EIGHT

THERE'S A KNOCK AT the door. The opening of Beethoven's Fifth.

"I told you, Marta, I don't want anything to eat."

"It's not Marta."

Wil?

I fling open the door. An arm holding on to each side of the frame, Wil stands there dressed all in black except for the arm of his hoodie, which sports a golden design from its cuff, up over his biceps and slips onto his broad chest. The color matches his eyes.

"What are you doing here?" I ask.

"Can I come in?"

"You already snuck into the house. Might as well." I stand back and use the door to steady my shaking hand.

"I need to talk to you."

"Oh, so now you want to talk to me. Done with my dad?" I throw my hands in the air. "Shit, our dad. That's not fucked up or anything."

"El—"

"You planned this whole thing, didn't you? Did you get Jeremiah drunk that night at the bar?"

"El—"

"Were you following me?" I know the answer already. I'm not as simple as Wil Peters thinks I am. Blind, but not simple. When Nadine sent me down to tip the Blend delivery person, I never expected to see Wil. I heard his voice in the hallway, and my foolish heart jumped for joy, I thought Wil was there to see me. I opened the door, prepared to defend Wil against my father.

But it was Dad who defended me. As usual. He saw Wil for who he was. Even after hearing about Rocker being Wil's dad, I didn't see it coming. But Dad did. Asked him straight up how much money it'd take to make him go away. And Wil thought about it. Actually stood there and calculated how much I was worth. "Was everything about money?"

"No." He raises his voice, and I freeze. Did Mom hear that? Dad? "Sorry, I didn't mean to yell. You need to listen to me."

"Why? So you can lie to me some more?" Did he expect me to just roll over and let him worm his way back into my heart? Of course, he did. "Oh, please, turn on your special charm and deceive me some more." I cross my arms and tap my foot. "I'm all ears."

"I'm not lying," he whisper-shouts at me.

"But you were."

He hangs his head. "Sometimes."

Ah, the truth. At last.

"How long?"

Wil crosses my room, looks out the window. The one that doesn't look out at the ocean. Shit, I told him about Papa. He could sell that story and live off it.

"The first night. I didn't know you'd be there. But I decided to use you then."

I don't know what I was expecting, but the words slice through me. Physically hurt, and I reach for the chair to support myself. Wil takes a step toward me and halts. "You don't understand. I had to talk to him. My mum needs—"

"The money. It's always about money."

"It was. But I don't want your father's money." Wil's voice cracks. He runs his hands through his hair and searches for understanding in my eyes. I can't turn away. "He tried to bribe me, but I told him to stuff it."

"Sure." I want to believe him, but I want to believe my father as well. My stomach twists. How can I trust someone who's been lying to me? I dig for the truth. "Is it because you never wanted it or because your mother's problems disappeared?"

"That's not fair. He owes her. She supported me on her own, sacrificed for me, and he got richer and more famous without a care in the world." Wil shakes his head. "That's not right."

"What about this is?" The stabbing pain in my middle intensifies. "How can I trust anything that comes out of your mouth?"

The all too familiar tapping appears, his fingers furious against his dark jeans. "But you have to."

"Actually, I don't. I survived before you. I'll survive after you've left." I walk to the door of my bedroom, grab the handle. "You can leave now. Go back home. You got what you want."

"What I want—" He scoffs and throws his hand in the air. "I want you." He crosses the room so fast I don't know what's happening, my back hitting the door at the force of his approach. Hot hands on each side of my face, his forehead pressed against mine. "I want you," he whispers.

I swallow, overwhelmed by his words. Words echoing my own heart. Did he really say he wants me? His thumb does that thing where it grazes across my cheek with the barest of touches, and the floor falls from under my feet. I breathe him in and never want to let go.

It's the first time on stage again, but the connection no longer belongs solely to the music. Yes, the creative synergy is there. Amazing. Powerful. Undeniable. Dissonance turning into consonance. An empty world into a full life. Yet, for months now, it's been more than the songs between us.

He writes the words my soul screams. I hear the meaning his beats with.

But he lied. I can't shut out my logical side, the part of my brain trying to function.

Did he though? Yes, Wil confessed his plan which, in the end, he says he rejected. He helped me get Sven out of jail, organized the video shoot for me. If his goal was to meet Dad, Wil could've pushed, had plenty of opportunities. After confronting Dad, he should've left.

But he stayed.

Why is he here? If what he's saying is true, Dad offered him money, but Wil insists he didn't accept it. It could've changed his mom's life. His life. But . . . Wil chose me. He found a way to me. Wil is risking a lot to be here. For me.

For. Me.

Wil drops his hands, moves his forehead away, and retreats to the other side of the room. "I don't have a chance, do I?"

I step toward him. "Wil—"

"I cocked it all up. So many times I tried to tell you."

I take another few steps. "Wil—"

He holds up a hand. "Don't say it. I can't take it. I'll leave."

I grasp his hand in mine, the rough calluses so familiar to me now, and take the step that puts me beside him. "Wil—"

"Why El? Why can't it be me?"

The boy with all the words won't stop talking. And I can't find the words to tell him what I want to say. So, I show him. I reach up, take his chin between my fingers and drag him down to me, sealing the mouth that won't shut up with mine.

It shuts him up all right. He completely freezes. Maybe that's not the right way? But it's the only way I can think of. Actions are my go-to. Not words. Determined, I move my lips, telling him I want him too, I want more than WE, I want us. A hand around my waist, crushing me against him, is his answer. His mouth comes alive, and I tilt my head back. It's the night at Griffin Park again. Only better. He's not acting.

Wil Peters kisses me back.

This kiss isn't our first, but it might as well be. The forcefield around us closes and amplifies every moment of it. His nose brushes against mine as he adjusts the angle, the butterfly-soft caresses of his lips transition into firm pressure, the heat of his tongue raises the temperature by many degrees. Permission granted, we follow the song our bodies create together. No longer cautious or afraid the chemistry is one sided, we draw new lines. We leave traces of our exploration on each other's skin. We make noises. We separate only to come together with less space between our bodies.

Any doubts I had before about not being able to feel lust toward a guy vanish. My body melts with his touch, and we still have all our clothes on. I want to know what it will be like with them off. We're no longer in the middle of the room but against a wall. I can feel something digging into my back, but I welcome it, because Wil's chest pushes against me so hard, I can sense the beating of his heart as it plays as fast a rhythm as mine. Boom-whoosh-boom-whoosh. Mine is a D of a timpani, and his is an E of a Conga drum. We sound good together.

Crash.

We step away from the wall, from each other, and look at the broken photo frame of me and my cousins playing dress-up. I look around my room. I'm not that child anymore, and what I want cannot be contained in this room, orderly and planned and always right.

"I'm sorry—"

I kiss the apology away from Wil. "It's just glass." Wil's hands never leave me, like he can't let go.

I loved the care my family showered me with after Papa died. Somewhere along the way their help turned into a stifling embrace that only grew tighter the older I got. I know they mean well, but what was right for a child, is not a good fit for me anymore. I want to make my own choices and my own mistakes without the safety net of my parents. It's time I learn to look after myself, and I won't get that option here.

I pick up the photo and put it on the side table. "The real memories are in here." I tap my heart. "This is my past." I put a hand on Wil's chest. "You are my future."

"I want that too." His voice rumbles against my palm. "A future, but how? You're locked up here."

"Well, if there is a Wil there's a way." The details of what to do fall into place. I smile up at his searching eyes. "You got in. I can get out."

I walk over to the door to my closet and find my yellow suitcase. I open it and survey the rows upon rows of clothes I didn't choose. Shoes I didn't expect wearing ever again. Bags that each one on their own could support me and Wil for a month financially outside of these walls. I want none of it.

Wil leans against the wall sideways, watches me. His hand reaches out and tucks a strand of hair behind my ear. The freedom to be touched, to have him touch me, is heady. I want more.

I choose my favorites, the few items I feel comfortable in, essentials because I have to wear something. The palazzo pants I wore our first night, my running shoes, the jean jacket that kept me warm in the freezing studio. It's silly, but I include Zoe's designs, the dress I wore to the farmers' market and the one I didn't get to, the ice-blue gown I want to wear with Wil by my side.

"What are you doing?"

"I can't stay here. I'm leaving."

"And going where?"

"Anywhere that is not here."

I'll figure out the rest later. I look at my laptop. My music is saved to the cloud. I can't take it, much as I want to. It's theirs as well. The tablet was from Aunt Patti, a gift. I shove it into my blue bag. My eyes go to the trophy, sitting on my nightstand. I pick it up and hold it.

"You don't need it."

"But I want a reminder singing is not a dream, it can be real."

"I'll happily tell you every day." He takes the award out of my hand and returns it to my side table. "You have me. Always."

Wil picks up the photo from the white surface of the table. "Take this instead." It's the picture of Zoe, Bailey, and me. The frame we broke when we kissed.

I take it from him, add one of my mom and dad, one of Papa and me, and the ultrasound of the baby brother, who'll have to fill the space for Mom and Dad when I'm gone.

"How will this work?" Wil sits on my bed; his fingers rap a sixteenth note groove against the wood. "Rocker will find you by lunchtime. You can't run away from them."

"I can, if I run far enough."

Wil wraps his arms around my waist and pulls me to him. "Are you sure? Think about what you're doing."

I stroke his cheek, hope it has the same effect on him as it does me. "All I ever do is think. I want to live."

Wil leans forward, kisses my forehead, then presses his there. "Okay. Let us live."

My heart skips a beat at the word us. There is an "us" now. I'm no longer alone. I don't know if it's because Wil is here or because I'm doing something I believe is the right thing for me, but I feel sure about the future. Mom and Dad will be upset; I can't help that. But I've lived my life trying to please them.

"Shit."

Wil tenses under my touch. "What?"

"Sven." I close my eyes. "I can't leave without saying goodbye to him."

"About that." Wil walks back to the door, opens it, and disappears. Is the mention of Sven enough to make him flee? I don't believe that. He strides in with Sven behind and closes the door. "He knows everything."

"Everything?" I look at Sven. Is he here to stop me from running away or . . . I can't lie to my friend. "I'm leaving, Sven. You need to pretend you weren't here. Go hang out with someone else. Get an alibi so when they realize I'm gone, no one will suspect you."

Sven steps between me and Wil, blocking my view of Wil. "Is this what you want?"

"It is. I don't want to get you in trouble because of my actions. You have Trevor to worry about." I put my hand on his arm. "You need this job, and Dad will need you when the baby is born. Everything is going to be fine."

"I can get you out of the house and wherever you need to go. Jailbreak for a jailbreak. Fair trade."

His face remains stony, but I see the change in his eyes. He's not kidding.

"Are you sure?"

"As long as you are."

My hug is not enough to express the gratitude I feel for this giant. His friendship has been one of the reasons I found my path. I squeeze his hard body, and when his hands wrap around my back our hug is complete. There's no going back. "Thank you, my friend."

His grip on me tightens, and he breaks us apart. "You have thirty minutes before we lose our window. My car is at the end of the private path past the Menken mansion. Here." He hands me the car keys. "I turned off the motion sensors, but you have to be careful. Leave your phone here. Get a burner. Buy tickets for the first flight out of the country. Do you have money?"

"Yes." I point at the bag with the almost eight thousand dollars I have left. "From the singing. Thanks to you."

"Leave all your credit cards here. Only use cash. Get someone else to buy your tickets. Do not contact me. Do not tell me where you're going. And if you can, dye your hair."

I touch the white streak and look around for a hat. I settle on the fedora I wore to the preview of *Indigo* and stuff a baseball cap into my bag. Just in case.

I swallow my fear, push the image of Dad and Mom's disappointed faces away, and focus on the one face that believes in me. Wil. I have no idea what we will do when we are no longer where my parents can rule my life, but we'll be together. I know it'll be an adventure.

FORTY-NINE

HEATHROW INTERNATIONAL AIRPORT IS one I've been to almost every year of my life. The place changed as I grew up, but what I saw as a young lad traveling to visit my cousins with Mum, and what I see now sitting at the departure gate with El, are the same. Hope. Excitement for the next months. I feel lucky to be here. I write:

Hope. Future. Opportunities.
Past and present merging.
Home sweet home.

"This mug is so cute." She picks up a cheap touristy "I heart London" one.

I close my black notebook and slide it into my breast pocket.

"Can I get it?" She's not wearing a hat, and the dark hair is nowhere as long as her fake wig was. It looks great. Mateo was right. With the new brunette color and brown contacts, no one will look at her and think she's Melodie Rockerby. "Just this one thing. I know we have to be careful with the cash we have left, but I don't think I've ever bought anything with my own money."

I put my arm around her waist, a freedom I will never grow tired of or take for granted. "It's your money. You can get whatever you want."

She pays, and we find two seats by the window away from the gate. "We have thirty minutes until boarding time. What would you like to do?"

Her arm is threaded through mine, her head on my shoulder. I miss the smell of the beach but don't miss having to find excuses to touch her.

"I have a question."

"Anything."

"Can I see your notebook?"

"This?" I pull the little black book out of my pocket and hand it to her. "It's just words."

She opens it and traces the indentations my pencil made on the lines of paper. "I love how your W's look, like they're about to fly off the page or hit the high C. They remind me of you."

"Don't think I could hit a high C even if my life depended on it."

"Not that. You always look up. Look forward. Strive for something. I admire it about you."

I pull her closer. "I admire everything about you. And you've hit a lot of high Cs since I've met you."

"Still speaking metaphorically."

"Maybe."

Her eyes travel across the pages, but she's not reading my words. She's watching them. I watch her. The announcement of the next flight to Portugal interrupts our watching party.

"Hold on." I lean down and take an identical black notebook out of my messenger bag. "This is yours." I entrust her with the words she must know. Ones I've created only for her. A secret oasis with my soul scrawled on the white pages she alone gets to discover. The essence of me no one in this giant airport would ever guess.

"Another one?" Her eyes light up.

"Oh, I go through one every month or so. But this one is for you." My hand dips under her wig, and my thumb caresses the soft skin of her neck. "Everything in it is for you."

"Sorry?"

"I brought it to, you know." I'm not allowed to say his name. We've banned all references to Rocker. Not that I want to. The luxury of it being just the two of us is something to preserve as long as possible. "When I delivered the coffee. To give to you. This is what I wanted you to read."

The pain on her face at the memory almost ruin the moment. But she shrugs it off, probably just as determined as me to keep our bubble of happiness intact.

A man running to the gate almost rolls his suitcase over our feet. I tug her closer, shrinking further into our cocoon. We exchange the notebooks. She snuggles into me and opens the first page. Her finger is not over my letters, it's under them.

Dear El, I have a confession to make. You always say I'm the words person. Maybe you are right and maybe my words will make a difference this time as well. Promise to read to the end of this page before you throw this out.

I've covered the reasons why I came to the US on our way to the airport, but those words were rushed, piecemeal between booking flights and getting the disguise El needed. The account in the notebook is worded precisely, deliberately, and expose not just the facts, but my heart.

I watch her lips move as her nail travels farther and farther down the page. My confession is complete. She knows everything; I have nothing to hide.

Eyes of the wrong color meet mine. "You finished the video? Can I see it?"

"Your dad didn't show you the video?"

She shakes her head.

"Bloody—"

"Wil. He's still my dad."

One earbud in her ear, one in mine, and my phone in between us, she presses play. I look at her and at the redhead on the screen. One day, she won't need to hide who she is. But that day is not yet here. I get to keep her all to myself a little longer.

El's hand finds mine, and she brings it to her face. My gaze follows. Her smile is wide and full of warmth and sunshine. She makes the airport brighter.

"This is amazing. The locations, the music, the kiss. Sarah was right. It's the perfect addition. And Nick's direction is better than Len Astor any day. It's hard to believe our little crew managed to pull this off."

Her face quiets, and I know she's thinking about something sad. I nudge her with my forehead.

She answers my silent question. "I wish I could thank them. Properly. They deserve credit for all their hard work."

"Someday. I promise."

El nuzzles closer to me and plays the video again. "It looks so professional."

"I remember you saying I'm a professional."

"Well, it feels good to be right. This video is better than anything I imagined. It's me. It's El Vella. It's perfect."

"You're perfect."

I feel her smile against my chest. "You have to stop saying that to me."

"I'm pretty sure I don't. It's my right as your boyfriend to tell you how perfect you are as frequently as I can."

"Boyfriend?" She lowers the phone. "I thought you don't do that kind of thing."

"I'd never met you before. I'd love nothing more than to call you my girlfriend."

El sits up and leans into me. "You do have a way with words. Boyfriend."

My lips find hers, and we laugh and kiss and do it over and over again.

"You are perfect too." She brings our joined hands to her mouth and kisses them. "Perfect for me. Thank you for the video."

"What are you going to do with it?"

"Watch it on repeat?"

"What was your plan? With Lenard Astor's video?"

"Oh, I was going to post it on the YouTube channel I created. Maybe open an Instagram page. But it's too late now."

"Why? We can do it right now. Right here."

"And what does it prove? Dad's already seen it. He's not impressed."

I try to ignore the hurt lacing her words. Rocker is a wanker, and I want to punch him again. "Stuff that. The world needs to see this. You want a career as a singer, you have to fight for it. Believe in yourself like I believe in you. What's the worst that can happen?"

"The world will hate it?"

"The whole world? Not sure you could be that bad if you tried."

She elbows me, and I love it.

"Okay, you might get some trolls, so what? That's part of the deal."

"Can we do it together?"

Ten minutes later, El Vella's YouTube channel hosts a whopping one original song video. A new Instagram account is up, and her first post is a screen capture of the shot Nick obsessed about, looking down on El. The caption reads "Hello world. I'm El Vella."

"At this time, we will begin boarding flight eighty-seven to Frankfurt. Passengers with priority seating or young children are asked to approach the gate." Between Mateo's obsession about making it difficult to trace us and the struggle to find available seats with the lowest prices, a normal twelve-hour route with one stop turned into a day's travel with three.

One more layover, and we will be home. I get to show her Bremen. I turn my face to the window and rehearse the sentences I'll be delivering to Mum and Opa when I show up on their doorstep weeks ahead of schedule, without warning, and with Bill Rockerby's stepdaughter in tow.

El hands me my phone back. "The world can meet me now. And I'm ready to meet the world."

It's snowing.

Big fat flakes that get caught in our hair and eyelashes. Everything is blanketed in white; fresh and clean, like Bremen wanted to put on its Sunday best for our arrival. It's early for a storm like this, and our fellow airline passengers are dashing about, the wheels of their luggage leaving tracks for others to follow.

Neither of us have boots or a coat appropriate for the weather. When I left for LA, I expected to be back before summer ended. I pull El closer, trying to use my body to keep her warm. I've never loved snow so much.

"Are you sure your mom won't mind me staying? I could find a hotel."

I squeeze El's hand in the back of the taxi. "She'll be thrilled."

"Has she been thrilled when you brought other girls home?"

I peep at El under her wide-brimmed hat. She's grinning. She had me worried there. "You know I've never brought a girl anywhere before."

"Just checking."

I lean in and whisper in her ear. "You can trust me."

She kisses me on the cheek and whispers back. "I know."

Two little words. But they mean everything. El's trust is something I'm not sure I deserve, but I'll do anything in my power never to break it again.

The taxi lurches to a stop. El peers out the window at the semi-detached houses as I pay the driver. "Which one is it?"

"The red door is ours."

Her yellow luggage, her guitar, and a bouquet of flowers El insisted on buying in her hand, my guitar in mine, my backpack and my messenger bag over my shoulder, we climb the three steps to the porch, and I knock on the door. "You're sure she likes lilies? 'Cause some people don't."

I go to kiss her again when the door flies open, and Opa's standing there, scowl ready to scare away any door-to-door salespeople. "What?" One German word is his idea of hospitality. He blinks, and the crusty face of the construction worker shifts into the grin of the greatest man I know. "Wil."

My bags slip off my shoulders as Opa wraps me in a bear hug. After months of being on my own in a foreign country, I relax in the arms of someone who knows me, loves me, accepts me. "Opa, let us in. We're freezing."

Opa lets go and pushes me aside. "Who's this?"

El juts out her hand. "Hello, Mr. Peters. I'm Melodie, but you can call me El."

Opa looks at me, then back at El, takes her hand and shakes it like he's greeting the queen of England. In English he says, "Nice to meet you. Come in, come in." He pulls El over the threshold, and I'm forgotten, left holding the bags. Opa always was a sucker for a pretty lady.

"Who is it? Wi—" Mum's hands fly to her face when she spots me. She looks good. Healthy. There's color in her cheeks, and she may have gained back some much-needed pounds. Mum puts down the dishtowel in her hand and beelines for me. "This is a surprise, luv." Another hug, another relief. Everyone I love is safe and sound in this house.

Mum pulls away and glares at me. "You're not in trouble, are you? Did you get kicked out of America?"

El snickers behind me.

"Bloody hell, Mum. No."

"Language."

"Yes, Mum."

Opa clears his throat.

Right. I put my arm around El. "Mum, this is my girlfriend, Melodie."

I get the reaction of a lifetime as Mum's eyes practically bulge out of their sockets. El steps forward and offers Mum the bouquet. "I prefer El. These are for you. Sorry, they're only lilies, but we didn't have time to stop by a proper florist."

"They're lovely. Lilies are one of my favorites." Mum takes the flowers and grins at El like she's the best thing she's seen since I downloaded an app that identified flowers by their pictures. "Well, don't just stand there, luv, let's get you and your girlfriend"—Mum lifts an eyebrow at me—"warmed up. Shall we? I'll put on the kettle. Do you like tea or coffee, El?"

"Both, I mean, either." And just like that, I've lost my girlfriend to Mum.

Opa slaps me on the back. "Looks like you have quite the tale to tell. But seriously, you're not"—he nods his head in El's direction—"in trouble, right?"

"Oh, I'm in trouble, all right."

Opa's face pales.

"You know how you told me you knew Oma was the one the moment you met, and I laughed at you?"

He nods, relaxing.

"I owe you an apology."

My phone buzzes. A message from Mateo. I gave him my German phone number, and he promised to only use burner phones. "El's a hit." A link to a news article pops up. *Who is El Vella?*

The internet broke watching the video of a newcomer El Vella singing her heart out in her instant hit Don't Give Me Comfort.

Has Rocker read this story? I don't doubt he's spending his fortune trying to track her. If Sven gave him the DNA swab, I might be someone he's searching for as well. I don't want him to find either of us. El needs the time to find herself, and I need the time to lose myself in her.

I don't know what our future has in store, but if my luck holds, I will find out with El by my side. I glance at my girlfriend, who's laughing with Mom as they arrange the flowers in a vase. Looks like the world isn't going to wait any longer.

El is about to be a star.

FIFTY

Epilogue

Tendrils of joyous live Christmas carols waft around us on the *Marktplaz* as I tug El in the direction of my favorite spot. I haven't been this excited about the holidays since I was ten. My chest tingles with the ease of the old worn-in comfort and the sharp pleasure of the new happiness. The joy of today is double-sided: both good. Better than good. Familiar stomping grounds seen through the eyes of El—the girl I get to call mine. We breathe in the cold winter air. The smell of pretzels mixes with the pine of the boughs over the doors and the spicy whiffs of Glühwein from the Christmas market around the corner.

El peers through the windows of the stationery store. "The notebooks are so fancy."

"Mum loves those as well."

"I prefer your black ones. I love reading them."

I love her reading them too. My fingers have no excuse to touch her, so I brush a pretend snowflake off her shoulder. My lips move into the now semi-permanent grin Mum keeps commenting on. "They fit everywhere. And I owe the owner. He's an old-time friend of Opa's and was the only one who didn't shoo me away when I started busking." I point to the maroon cover over the entrance. "I earned my first money right under this awning. Spent it on my first small black notebook the same day."

"Can we go in?" The wonder in her eyes is usually the one thing I'm unable to say no to. But today I have better plans.

For the rest of the epilogue, sign up for our newsletter.

Scan the QR Code below, and we'll get you the ending.

Wil and El will be back in WE Breathe in 2023

Add WE Breathe to your Goodreads Reading List today.

Acknowledgements

It takes a village to raise a child: same goes to publishing a book. Julie, Kay, and Kia have been excellent doulas who guided us along on our book journey and helped deliver what you see on the pages of this romance.

Judging a book by its cover: very true, no metaphors required. Maria Pena brought to life our vision for Wil and El and Books and Moods transformed our chicken scratch sketches into a colorful cover we're proud of.

Tell me who your friends are, and I will tell you who you are: our friends are amazing, what does it say about us? We were lucky to make author-friends through the Kindle Vella community. Jessica Erin, Callie Thomas, Christina Vourcos, and many others got into the trenches with us and cheered our journey along. A special thank you goes to Christine Daigle and JP Rindfleisch from the Serial Fiction Show for our first podcast interview featuring WE Blend (we were so nervous, but they are pro interviewers), and to Azrielle Lawless from Hella Vella for our first YouTube interview featuring Wil and El (she makes everything fun).

You can thank L. Hansen for keeping our German words and realities in check and suggesting German curse words for Wil.

Before any readers saw WE Blend, several trusted others gave us their feedback.

Our alpha readers, Kyra Diamantidis, Evangeline Myrtos, Estelle Kim, and Lucy MacDonald who read WE Blend while we were still writing it, and spend hours on the phone with us, giving feedback.

Our ARC readers caught formatting errors, typos, and some rather funny bits (only funny because we caught them in time).

Our Street Team for not only reading but talking about this book and maybe being the reason this book is now in your hands.

Last, but very important: Becky and Cece, our support people. Thank you for making our lives a lot easier, so we can spend more time writing.

Story time.

In April 2021, Amazon announced their newsiest venture: Kindle Vella.

At that time we'd co-written three short stories together and were thinking of continuing the trend with another one. We never considered anything more, shall we say, arduous. Kindle Vella was only available for US authors and was launching in July 2021. Gala knew she didn't have enough time to put a full-length story together on her own, so she asked D.L. if she'd like to try writing as a duo. D.L. didn't scream and run away; instead, she said hella yes.

We knew we wanted to write something in our Star-Crossed Lovers' universe, and D.L. had just written a new character into a new short story: Wil. He was supposed to be the comic relief side character. He still is. However, Wil spoke to us and said, "Give me my own story. I'm worth it." And was he ever. Wil is funny, but he's also kind, musical, stubborn, and would do anything for his family.   Wil's love interest took a little longer to figure out. However, El is the perfect match for him. They are opposites in many ways, but what they share is undeniable. We spent May and June of 2021 writing Wil and El and ended up with over 100,000 words/over 400 pages (told you it's a full-length story). When Kindle Vella launched, we were there on day one. Wil and El's sweet yet angsty story solidified our partnership, and we'll never forget that magic.

DL: To this day I still pinch myself that I have the privilege of creating characters and stories with Gala. When she suggested starting this adventure of writing as Willa Drew, I didn't hesitate for a split second. We've laughed, we've cursed, and then we've laughed some more. Thanks for putting up with my peculiarities. Special shout out to the family Gala doesn't get to see when I hog all her time.

Thanks to my mother for reading multiple versions of Wil and El's romance. I'm not at all upset this is her favorite book

I've ever had a hand in writing. No, really. My favorite moment was when I called her, eager for feedback, and she texted me to say she couldn't answer the phone because she was reading the kissing scene. By the way, did I mention my mom doesn't like romance books? Not her cup of tea.

This book is dedicated to my father, William. I got the writing gene from you, so basically this is partly your fault. To my brother, your support means the world.

Gala: This book is full of firsts. Like I would never forget my first kiss, or my first trip abroad, this book will live in my heart as the first time I completed something people paid to read. This is the first book that I co-wrote with D.L. and discovered what a difference a writing partner and friend who I can share the ups and downs with can make in my life (it got lighter and brighter).

WE Blend is the first book we went through a full round of edits with, and the first book that got a cover not made by me. The first book that, when my friends (or strangers at the store or doctor's office) asked me what they can read of mine, I can direct them to.

Fun fact: I'm forever grateful to my husband, who is very supportive of my journey as a writer. But a tangible sign of his support is him giving a voice to Wil (check out Willa Drew's YouTube channel for Wil's interview if you want to hear for yourself).

WILLA DREW IS NOT one, but two writers of fun, flirty fiction full of feels.

Lovers of emotional scenes (don't tell anyone: someone always cries as we write them), dramatic scenarios (don't blame us, the characters insisted), and the best the world has to offer like eclairs and butter tarts (don't ask us to share, but we'll point you to the recipes).

Our young adult and new adult romances have every flavor. Angst? Check. Secrets? Of course. Risk taking? You bet. Expect slow burns, heart flutters, soul mates, first loves, and swoon-worthy kisses.

Hang out with us over on all the socials @willadrewauthor or get sign up for our newsletter and get updates sent right to you.

amazon.com/author/willadrewauthor

facebook.com/willadrewauthor

goodreads.com/author/show/21818028.Willa_Drew

instagram.com/willadrewauthor/

tiktok.com/@willadrewauthor

https://twitter.com/WillaDrewAuthor

OTHER STORIES BY WILLA DREW

Star Struck – Available now

FALLING FOR THE ROCKSTAR'S DAUGHTER SERIES
WE Blend – Available now

WE Breathe - Coming 2023

FALLING FOR THE LIAR SERIES – Coming Fall of 2022

Kisses, Lies & Us
Misses, Hearts & Us
Crushes, Friends & Us
Passions, Hopes & Us
Distance, Loves & Us

SNEAK PEEK

STAR STRUCK – A NOVELLA

Siobhan and Asher's Romance

ONE

Siobhan

A cardboard tube with a shred of toilet paper mocks me. Of course, I end up in the bathroom stall that's missing the key element. My parents ran out of Irish luck when they had me: I'm the only member of the Casey clan born on US soil. "C an't open the flippin' holder." My best friend isn't her usual happy-go-lucky self. She's nervous for a reason. Months of hard work, and the possibility of writing for a big Hollywood movie comes down to tonight.

"Don't break your new nails. Just shove a bunch under the divider."

The coveted wad of white toilet paper and Sarah's undamaged red nails appear beside the spike of my stiletto.

"Got it." My voice sounds strangled, because I'm holding the bottom of my floor-length sequined dress between my chin and my chest.

"Good. Now hurry. We don't want to miss the opening number," says Sarah. "I hope we'll be celebrating more than just your birthday tonight."

The best birthday present would be hearing, "And the Starlight award goes to Sarah Connor." Ever since I met her two years ago when she moved to LA, Sarah's been the one with a plan: become a screenwriter. May have hit a few bumps (okay, craters) on the road, but my girl is making her dreams come true.

The shapewear I have on at the insistence of Mrs. Marino, my boss who lent me this elaborate golden gown worth a year of my salary, doesn't want to go back up. How do people spend all night in these things?

"We were so sorry to hear about you and Leyla," the interviewer says on the TV in the lounge part of the restroom.

My ears perk up. I'm not sorry at all. I've been obsessing over my favorite romantic star's newfound freedom for weeks now.

"Well," Asher Menken's deep baritone loses its smoothness, "all I can say is—"

"Ladies and Gentlemen"—the TV switches from the pre-recorded interview to the real-time coverage of the awards ceremony—"welcome to the Fifth Annual Starlight Foundation Gala."

For feck's sake. The world is dying to know Asher's take on his ex. Okay, I'm dying to know. Even if I get a chance to see him, it's not like I could ask him myself.

"How much longer?" Sarah can't hide her impatience. "I don't want to miss anything."

"Just go." I wave my free hand at the closed door as if Sarah can see me. "I'll be in as soon as I can wrangle this tiny torture device back onto my crotch."

"You sure?"

"Aye, go already. Nick's waiting." Probably cursing me. Boyo is also nervous tonight, and we don't get along at the best of times. "Enjoy yourself. You've worked so hard for tonight."

A few clicks of her high heels plus the sound of the door closing, and I'm left alone with my tight beige nemesis.

I tuck the bottom of the dress into my décolleté. This is bollocks. I peel the undergarment off my thighs and balance on one, then the other silver strappy sandal as I struggle to free myself. Dress righted, I take my first deep breath of the night, ball up the offending material, toss it into the bin, give it the finger, and exit the stall.

A quick check of my stomach in the mirror shows it's as flat as it was with the awful contraption. I wash my hands and ensure my hair survived the battle of the bulge. The aquamarine dye I've been using this summer is starting to bore me. Might be time for a change.

The blue corner of the tattoo on the inside of my wrist is showing. I tug the long sleeves of the dress down, causing the neckline to plunge even more. Gotta make sure I cover up my body art tonight. While highly unlikely, Mum and Da might see pictures. They don't exactly know about this version of my artwork. My tastes run more towards black ink than gold sequins, but I do rock this dress. I blow myself a kiss in the mirror. Time to get this show on the road.

I reach for the door handle when the painted wood panel flies open and smashes into my shoulder. For a moment I teeter on my heels, sure I can save myself, but this battle I don't win. I land hard on the solid tiles of the bathroom floor.

"Bloody hell," I yelp.

The door slams shut, then opens again, and a tuxedo-clad figure enters the room. "Damn it, sorry, I didn't mean to . . . didn't know . . . are you hurt?" The crisp black silk of men's trousers crinkles as the offender crouches down and stretches his hand my way.

I blink. Then blink again. Wide pools the color of whiskey I've drooled over during movie nights with the girls peer at me.

"Are you okay?" An expression worthy of an Oscar nomination graces Asher Menken's face as he scans my body for broken bits.

I wiggle my toes, rub my shoulder, and swivel my head around. "All in one piece, no thanks to you." I've wanted to approach him since I first saw Ash on the red carpet a couple of feet ahead of us, but he was in the middle of an interview, probably the one I'd just been listening to. He and my big brother

Owen are still best friends, but over a decade has passed since the superstar and I have been in the same room together.

"What can I do?" There is no spark of recognition in his eyes despite the fact that other than the long hair, I'm a mini copy of my brother. I wait to see if anything clicks, but his focus is not on my face. Rather, he gawks at my naked leg, exposed in all its glory thanks to the thigh-high slit in this fancy dress. His gaze travels up my leg and I follow, until we get to where the lace of my aquamarine thong is visible, no longer shielded by the Spanx. He looks at my hair, then my thong, and swallows.

"I still like matching things," I say.

"Sorry?"

"My hair matches my thong. Like my hair bows used to match my clothes, remember?"

His eyes narrow, and he tilts his head. "I think you might've hit your head."

"I'm Siobhan." I lift the sleeve off my left wrist and show him the tiny star, my very first tattoo. I got the memento as soon as I moved here seven years ago: my design, based on the one I drew for Ash a lifetime ago. "Réiltín?"

Another sweep of his eyes takes in more of my face as he scans me up and down, or left to right, or however the horizontal plane is looked at. "Owen's little sister?" His eyebrow rises.

"Aye."

"Unbelievable." He reaches inside his jacket, pulls out his wallet, and takes out a piece of paper. Ash sits next to me on the icy floor as I tug at the dress in a too-late attempt to cover up. He gives the paper to me. "My good luck charm."

I stare. In my hand is a faded copy of what I now have on my wrist. The original little star I drew for him when I was nine.

"You . . . kept this?"

Asher casts his eyes to the floor, and my pulse takes off. I mean, I've seen the expression before, both on and off the screen, yet up close and personal like this he's . . . gorgeous. Yes, the teeth are perfect, the chin is chiseled, and the hair—oh, how I want to run my hands through his hair to test if those strands are as tuggable as they appear. But this is more than the good looks. He's lit up from within.

I hand the piece of paper from the past back to him and will my heart to slow.

"Owen did say you lived here." Ash tucks the drawing carefully back in his wallet and puts it away. "Of all places to run into you." He smiles, and there's the "I'm sorry" smile that got him out of a trip to the police when he bumped into a car in front of us. The lady who owned the Peugeot let him go with, "What's one more scratch on this old heap of metal?" She would've berated any of my brothers for doing the same thing.

"I promised my friends not to get starstruck, but I didn't think they meant literally." I smile back. "Howeyeh, Ash? Can I still call you that?"

He nods, giving me the once over again. "Can't call you Little Star anymore. You're no longer . . . little."

My turn to swallow. The way he said little sends a shiver through me that I can't blame on the chill of the tile floor. My name is a puzzle for most people in LA. At work I heard a million attempts at my name until I came up with "she-Vaughn." Sarah shortens it to just Sio, "she." Back in Ireland my family calls me Shiv, and Mum insists on Baby Girl. But Asher's nickname for me, Réiltín, which means Little Star, might be my favorite. "I don't mind." He can call me anything.

"Réiltín it is, then." He runs his hand through the thick light brown strands he inherited from his movie star mother and rests his fingers on the nape of his neck. "We should probably get off this floor." He jumps to his feet, wraps his fingers around my wrist, and lifts me up. I wince in pain.

"Did I hurt you?"

"The shoulder is a bit tender." I lower the neckline and see a red line across my skin. Ash's thumb traces the mark from the door. His touch doesn't make the pain go away, but I'm both nervous and more secure with his skin on mine. His presence has always had this effect on me. The thrill and the comfort at the same time.

The first time I met him, my nine-year-old self didn't know what to think about Ash. He wasn't a famous Hollywood star then, just the nineteen-year-old friend my brother brought home for Christmas break because Ash had no family in Ireland to spend the holiday with. A breath of fresh air all the way from California to light up our middle-of-nowhere in County Kerry.

I fix my dress. "We should get going. My friend Sarah must be wondering where I am."

"Sure you're okay?"

"I'm tougher than I seem."

"You look"—he pauses—"great in this dress. All grown-up." His eyes stray to my cleavage.

"Yup." I straighten and push my chest forward. "Got me big girl boobs and everything."

"I didn't mean to . . ." His "I'm sorry" smile is back. "This isn't what I—"

"Just having a laugh." I tap him on the arm, like we're old pals. "Great way to start my next quarter century."

"Today?"

"'Tis."

"Well, happy birthday to you." He purses his lips, and his eyes brighten. "We could have a drink after the gala? Celebrate? Catch up?"

"Bang on." I don't jump up and down like I used to when I got to spend time with him, but I flash him my "thank you for a great tip" smile. Asher Menken wants to have drinks with me. I ain't saying no.

"Great. But"—he rubs the wrinkles between his eyebrows—"a favor? Could you check if there is a guy in a red velvet tuxedo hanging around by any chance? If he is, I'll stay here a while longer."

"Aye." I peek out of the door and see empty hallways. "The coast is clear."

Asher

Siobhan Casey.

I can't believe Owen's baby sister scared my bathroom stalker off with foul language worthy of an R-rated movie. The creep thought he was clever hiding around the corner, ready to accost Siobhan and me on our way to the ceremony. Her vocabulary, among other things, has grown. In fact, there isn't much left of the little girl with a short bob, matching hair accessories, and hand-me-down outfits from her brothers. Although the eyes, those sometimes green, sometimes blue, sometimes gray eyes of hers, and Owen's, and their Ma's. I should've recognized those eyes.

When my publicist Jackson asked me to be part of tonight's ceremony, I almost said no. I hate these types of affairs. The fakeness. The shallowness. The constant vying for attention. I never dreamed my night would be like this.

I glance out into the sea of creativity, and the rush of youthful exuberance hits me like a tidal wave. My partnership with the Starlight Foundation was the right decision. This is the perfect project to kickstart my new production company. I already got the green light for two TV shows, and this movie, with the proper amount of press, will give me the cachet to do more.

Still, the best part is the opportunity to give back, do something worthwhile with the fame I've been lucky enough to achieve. And when the tall kid accepts his Best Director award, he's genuinely ecstatic. I can't help grinning like a fool along with him.

"That's Nick." Siobhan sits down after she finishes clapping her hands raw. An empty seat next to me had been an open invitation for the opportunists looking to pitch, but now I'm glad the organizers assumed I would bring a date. "He's been in LA less than six months, and look at him. I'm here seven years and keep slinging drinks."

"You want to be in the movie business?"

"God, no. Owen is the one with the acting bug in our family."

"Why LA then?" Owen refused to tell me the full story.

"Farthest place I could escape to with my American passport that met my criteria."

"Which were?"

"Far from Ireland, fun, sunny, and not an island." She winks at me. Good to see she hasn't lost her spunky attitude. "Had a string of jobs. Let's see, I was the Belgian waffle girl at Disneyland first. Girl's gotta start somewhere. Graduated to waitressing at a fifties themed diner. Gawd, that was horrible. They put that yellow American plastic they call cheese on everything. Who puts cheese on pie?"

Siobhan has the right to judge. Her family's cheese is the best I've ever tasted. Of course, I've had the privilege of stealing the stuff fresh from the cheese fridge when no one was looking. As a teenager I preferred to ask for forgiveness rather than permission. The bonus of performing in Dublin was that in three hours I could be at the Casey farm indulging in unlimited quantities of first-rate cheese. Well, and pretending I'm part of their large warm family. Owen is so lucky.

"Anyhow, now I work at a swanky resort bartending with my girl Sarah over there"—she swings her champagne glass in the direction of a group of young people, of which Sarah could be any one of three girls—"but the hours give me time to play artist."

"Well, lucky me. You saved me from being cornered by overeager fans and wannabe writers." And she saved me before. The first Christmas I spent at her family's farm, she saw me struggle to memorize my part for The Little Prince. I was ready to throw in the towel. Maybe the acting gene skipped a generation, maybe the tabloids were right and my good looks and family connections were the only reasons Trinity's theatre program accepted me.

Siobhan didn't let me give up. She ran lines with me, jumped up and down every time I got one right, and even drew me a picture of a little star, a réiltín, for good luck. The folded piece of paper with her design was in my pocket when I first went on stage and has been with me ever since, calming me when I'm nervous. And being back in the States has me super nervous tonight.

"He deserved the tongue-lashing. Shoving his script at you in the middle of the event is the worst way to get your attention."

"Hollywood is hard, I get it. But he was going to stuff the flash drive inside my jacket if you didn't interfere. I should've just shoved him off, but that'd end up in the papers with me as the unreasonable superstar, too stuck-up to talk to his fans." I take another sip from the flute the server keeps refilling. "The guy's face matched his red suit after you told him off. You're more effective than my bodyguards."

She laughs. Not the polite tut-tut of reporters reacting to my lame jokes or the light tinkle that warmed my heart when I managed to get Leyla to break character. No, this is a roaring, full-bodied, full-of-life laugh.

And I'm laughing along with her, feeling lighter than I've felt in months. No, years.

My real smile hasn't graced my face in forever. The world thinks Leyla and I broke up a few weeks ago. In reality, we've been apart for over a year. Our publicists timed the news for maximum impact, every step calculated to advance our careers. Well, her career. It's always been about her career. Every fight, a tug of war between her need to shoot for the stars and mine to settle down. In the end, our marriage came down to one thing: I can't wait to have kids, and she didn't want any.

"Gotta stand up for myself and those I care about," Siobhan says. "You know my older brothers; add waitressing in LA, and there's no better verbal self-defense school." She curls her arm and almost spills champagne onto herself. I catch the glass in time. "I know how to punch, too, if it comes to it. Owen made sure to teach me. And I always keep my thumb out."

She puts her glass down and demonstrates the proper fist technique. "Brothers." Her eyes widen. "Oh." She holds out her hand. "Give me your phone. Let's send Owen a selfie. It'll freak him out."

I like nothing more than pulling pranks on my best friend. My phone in hand, Siobhan leans in, her shoulder brushing against mine, and I inhale a mixture of honey and something spicy. "Smile," she instructs.

Easily done.

She plucks my cell from my fingers, her thumbs fly over the screen, and in a second, she flashes our smiling faces at me. "Check out who I bumped into," is written underneath our picture.

"Bumped into, huh." I chuckle at her play on how we met in the bathroom. She sends the text.

Siobhan opens my jacket, the gesture she berated the guy in the red suit for. "Done."

My body shrunk away from the rando's touch, but with my grown-up réiltín, I savor the contact. She puts my phone in the inside pocket and adjusts my sky-blue tie. Her eyes narrow, and she runs her fingers against the dots on the smooth silk.

"This tie, doesn't it remind you of the Infinity exhibit Yayoi Kusama did with the mirrors at The Broad a few years ago?"

I nod. "Like being inside a kaleidoscope." I took Leyla on a private tour of the immersive art installation at The Broad Modern Art Museum. We spent the evening lost in the multi-reflective rooms.

"Exactly." She smooths my tie one more time. The touch of her hand on my chest does things to me it should not. "Wasn't it deadly? Blows you only got five minutes in each room."

She's deadly. Real and beautiful. And alluring.

Gone is the little girl who doodled on anything she could get her hands on. Before me sits this vivacious, gorgeous woman. Her green—or are they blue—eyes twinkle in the low light of the reception hall.

"Did you study art?"

"I take classes when I can, but nothing official. I love to explore—oils, watercolors, sculpture, loom, pottery, print—tried them all. I even thought about costume design. But I think skin is my favorite canvas." She looks down at the star on her wrist.

This woman is a bright star in the dark night that has been my life lately. I can't look away; I won't, not when there's so much to see.

Even her dress teases by covering up practically everything yet accentuating her body in a way no garment should be allowed to. But I've glimpsed the secrets the fabric hides. Thinking about her long leg and how I'd run my hand up the curves to . . . I feel a twitch I haven't felt in a long time.

What am I doing? How can I be thinking like this? What would Owen say if he saw me ogling his sister?

Hey, boyo, don't even think about touching her.

Which is exactly what I'm doing. Thinking. And that's where I'll be stopping.

"So, you've traveled the world?" Siobhan reaches for another glass from the server walking by and our hands brush.

There it is again, the little electric shock like when I touched her in the bathroom. What is she doing to me? Am I having any effect on her? It's so hard for me to tell these days, reality and fiction always blurring. Is a woman truly interested in me, or is she just caught up in my fame and fortune?

It was easy when I met Leyla. We were both unknowns at the time, just starting out in the business. When our movie hit number one at the box office everything changed overnight. I was used to my parents' fame and seeing my face on the cover of tabloids wasn't new, but with my own fame, the frenzy reached a whole different level. Leyla and I relied on each other, bonded in the fire of chaos.

Siobhan is different. She knows me and doesn't have the starstruck expression my fans get. Talking to her brings the instant comfort I associate with my visits to her family farm. She taps her glass to mine, and I enjoy another brush of our fingers.

Her skin is cool. No, comfort isn't the right word. Connection? There's something here. We're on our third glass and I should be feeling the haziness of the alcohol, but instead, everything is crystal clear. For the first time in a long time, I'm alert and aware.

Four delicate fingers brush over the back of my hand, as if she's painting me with invisible watercolors. Her pupils dilate, and I'm sure mine do too. A slender index finger wraps around my thumb and slides up, down, and up again. If I'm reading her right, my year of celibacy is ending tonight.

She touches a sensitive part at the base of my thumb. "Wanna get out of here?" Siobhan's eyes confirm her invitation.

"Yes" escapes my lips before I even think about consequences.

"Give me a minute."

As she walks away, I text my security detail to let them know I'm ready to leave and there's going to be a plus one. Hopefully, we can slip out the back door and not get noticed.

Across the room, Siobhan's talking to a short blonde in an even shorter silver dress. They hug, and my little star's walking back toward me. Her slender hips swing with the movement, glittering gold. My body reacts with more than a twitch this time.

"Where to, sir?" asks the limo driver.

"The hotel," says Siobhan.

"How'd you—"

"Know? Figured you'd be staying with your parents since you just got back. Their house is in Malibu, right? A tad too far for tonight."

She's too smart for me.

The hotel is only a short ride from the venue, and in no time we're in the underground garage. I hop out of the car hoping to open the door for Siobhan, but she's too quick for me too. Leyla would've waited, expecting a grand gesture from me in case there were any cameras around. Always a show with that woman.

This girl—woman—however, pinches my security guard's arm. "Oh, you're a tough one." The guard sticks out his chest and eyes Siobhan up and down. "Spend every day at the gym, do we?"

I feel a pang in my chest. Jealousy? I jut out my arm. "Shall we?" Siobhan slinks hers through and leans into me. My temperature rises with the contact of her warm body as we make our way to the private elevator.

The metal doors slide together and once again we're alone.

"What is it about elevators?" she asks, a hand running down my arm.

"What d'you mean?"

"They're just so damn sexy."

"You think?"

She reaches up and tugs on my tie, giving me a low, breathy, "Yes."

I'm done for. Reason, propriety, and resistance are out the window. My lips collide with hers, one hand circling her waist to pull her closer, the other finally getting to touch the soft skin of the long lean leg she's hooked over my hip. My palm travels up her thigh and cups her butt.

The sequins of her dress scratch against my thin shirt as if they are clawing to get at me. She's amazing, and so alive. Her taste, her scent, her heat invade me, send currents through my body, and light me up like no other. The twitch is now a throb.

I don't have enough hands. I need to touch more of her, but there's no way I'm letting go of this luscious ass. I tear my mouth from hers and explore her chin, her neck. I pause, pressing my lips against her pulsing artery, the thump matching my own racing heartbeat.

The soft ding of the elevator indicates we've hit my floor, but I don't want to leave our little cocoon. Siobhan has other ideas and starts backing out of the elevator, my tie still clutched in her hand. I'm happy to follow, as long as I get to keep kissing those amazing lips.

We move down the hall, and I reluctantly break the kiss. "Wait."

"What? Bored already?"

"Not in the slightest." More like alive for the first time. "My room is this way." I clutch her arm and haul her down the hallway in the opposite direction, searching for my hotel room key with my free hand. I jam the card into the reader, the light goes green, and we burst into my suite.

Before the door closes, her fingers are undoing my belt.

"Careful of the gown. It's not mine."

END OF SNEAK PEEK

Get the whole story in Star Struck, out now.

SNEAK PEEK
"KISSES, LIES, & US"
FALLING FOR THE LIAR SERIES BOOK #1

ONE

NICK

The truth is—I tell lies all the time. What's one more?

I twirl the fake ID my friends gave me for my birthday. It's my face all right, but according to the black block letters on this driver's license, my name isn't Nick, it's Shawn. The address is also not mine, nor the age. I'm newly nineteen, and Shawn's twenty-one. Old enough to drink but not too old for those inclined to question.

I catch the bartender's eye for the third time. A tingle travels down my neck.

She reaches over in front of a woman my mom's age, lays a snowflake-shaped coaster on the bar to my right, and places a fancy pink cocktail with a paper umbrella on it. Glossy green leaves frame the name tag on the pocket of her white resort uniform. The sprig of ivy is the only nod to Christmas Eve. The tag hangs down at an angle, making it hard to read her name, but it begins with an S.

"And what can I get for you?" She hands a glass of sparkling water to a server who appears and disappears to my left. Her voice rings over the smooth jazz. My pulse beats in my ears and dampens the chatter of a couple dozen patrons scattered around the small dimly lit bar.

"Old Fashioned." Dad's been ordering them at every place we've been to this week. This whole trip turned into him showing off that he's landed on his feet. He spends every day trying to get back into Mom's good graces. Bonding time with me doesn't appear to be on the agenda anymore.

"Is that your ID?"

I slide the laminated card her way, and she flicks her eyes between the photo and me. The one-corner-of-the-mouth smile I learned from my brother plus the direct eye contact should project enough confidence to calm any suspicions. I vibrate as if she raised the bass in my chest to high but don't lift my eyebrow or move into full-on flirting. That'd be too much.

"Visiting from Chicago?"

"Yep."

One of those preppy professional-service smiles reveals white teeth that amplify the glow of her sun-kissed face. Lots of hours spent at the tanning booth to get that shade, I bet.

She beams even wider, and I see that one of her canines on top is crooked. You have to pay attention to notice, but now that I do, her whole image changes, and the film of affluence the resort transferred onto her disappears. The tightly wound string inside me slackens.

The bartender hands my fake back. Her fingers are cold and. . . damp? I run my thumb over the ID to remove what I hope is water and slide the card into the pocket of my jacket.

"Sorry." She catches my gesture and wipes her fingers off on a bar towel, reinforcing the humanity behind the uniform. I relax into my seat. "Buffalo Trace or Woodford Reserve?"

What the fuck are those? I flip my phone over. Me, Nick, has no idea what she's asking about, but the twenty-one-year-old Shawn should have an answer.

"Whatever you think's best." Another thing I picked up from Dad. He's been throwing the phrase around, and Mom thinks he's matured. I hope he did. For her sake.

The bartender nods and turns around. While the bulky shirt doesn't reveal much of her body, the black pants hug her butt, and she'd get much better tips displaying that thing to the customers. More of a boob man myself, but I don't discriminate. She stands on her tiptoes to get a bottle with amber liquor from the glass shelf. I should stop staring at how cute her nose looks in profile, or wondering what she would look like in a less bulky top, or looking at her pants. I shift in my seat and try to ignore the flare of heat at the base of my spine. Definitely not looking at those. It's a slippery slope.

I force my eyes away from the perky backside that matches her whole sunny persona and survey the rows of bottles. The bar has no Christmas trees or Santas, going with a snow theme instead. Along the shelves with multi-colored jewel cases containing alcohol lies white fluffy material pretending to be the snow that doesn't exist in LA. A string of large snowflake-shaped lights glows above the top of the bar.

There aren't many things I'll miss about Chicago, but snow on Christmas might be one. I'd have to get used to people walking around in shorts, flip flops, and light sweaters. No matter how festive it is, nothing screams "Christmas" to me in LA.

The blond ponytail above the bartender's shoulders bounces when she moves to get a short tumbler with a line design cut across the bottom. Something James Bond would use. Many steps above the red plastic cups I drink cheap beer out of back home.

She grabs three bottles and sets them next to the glass. It's like I'm watching Mom's favorite British baking show, wondering what's next. I lean in. First, a bit of clear liquid goes in, then water, some dark stuff from a small container with a yellow cap, and a dash from an even tinier one with an orange label. The text on them is too small for me to read to find out what they are. I assumed cocktails could be convoluted, but this looks a bit like my chemistry class. She stirs the mixture with a silver spoon that has a long skinny handle, places one gigantic baseball sized ice cube into the glass, and pours Woodford Reserve over the ice.

Everything she does is self-assured and practiced. She shaves
a bit of orange and lemon peel, folds them, runs them around
the rim of the glass, squeezes a twist of mist over the whole
thing, and places them in next to the ice. The scent of citrus
hits my nostrils and sends me back to Yaya slicing lemons from
her garden for Psari Plaki. The bartender's tan fingers match
my drink but it's her crisp uniform, the glass, and the garnish
that make this scene look like everything I'd expected from an
overpriced bar at a high-end resort.

"Enjoy." I almost believe she means it. I bite the inside of my
cheek as she moves the glass my way.

Ah, here it is. This would be the money shot: her hand setting
the drink down as if it's in front of the viewer. The bar top
can't be wood. I'd change it to something more reflective, maybe
acrylic, so I could play with the lights and reflections.

I narrow my eyes and see the camera moving in as her hand
pushes forward with the drink. The contrast of the amber liquid, tan skin, white cuff of the shirt, and touch of yellow and
orange from the fruit peels work together to make the shot
dramatic. I could underscore this scene with some sick beats as
the glass comes toward us, and then something slow as we pan
to it.

"Something wrong with the drink?" She leans closer and the
foliage moves on the tag, revealing her name. Sarah C.

"Sarah, right? All good, thank you."

Another trick of Dad's. "Call them by their names," he told
me yesterday, "the staff appreciates it." The staff. My stomach

churns. People like him who come to places like this have staff, listen to smooth jazz, and order drinks you need a degree in mixology to make. He forgets Mom is the staff.

She's been cutting people's hair for the last ten years.

I take a deep breath and rotate the glass. How do I drink this? I've come too far to disappoint Sarah. Am I supposed to sniff it, like Mom does with her wine? I can't remember if Dad did anything special with his. I raise the drink to my lips.

The liquid burns my throat, but I think I hide it well. Lying's always come naturally to me. I get that from Dad too.

I take another gulp. Pretending. One more gulp. Fibbing.

Sometimes I forget who the real Nick is.

And another one. It burns less with every swig, but I hate the taste. Bitterness coats my tongue. I can't drink any more. The glass, however, I love. Maybe I'll buy one like it for myself one day and drink beer out of it.

Why didn't I order a beer and enjoy something I liked instead of pretending I'm sophisticated? For the sake of who? The middle-aged crowd around me? The sunny Sarah, with her big grin and bright blue eyes? Eyes that are checking me out. No. I shake my head. Checking the fancy, Old Fashioned-drinking Shawn out.

Would she like me if I didn't pretend? If, for once, I was just me?

The fake ID can shield the real Nick from potential fallout yet let me be. . . well, me. Minus the right name. I straighten, my brain lighting up at the idea. The little piece of plastic, the small lie offers a chance to not be afraid to be Nick. Be myself.

"Sarah?" I begin my experiment.

From this point on, I vow to only tell the truth.

To this girl.

For this one night.

My heartbeat tries to outrun the tapping of my foot. Bartenders are like shrinks—they're supposed to listen and keep your secrets. Right?

Sarah

And I thought tonight would be boring.

Pull a double on Christmas Eve, compliment a few drunk lonely men, and make some good tips so I can pay off my overdue cell phone bill. Maybe get back to the apartment and the swinging Christmas Eve party my roommates are holding before someone starts having sex in my bedroom. The plan was simple.

Enter this guy. He's a plot twist in the film noir that was supposed to be my evening. He's all sorts of tall, dark, and handsome dressed in a black jacket and a red T-shirt that's calling to me like a beacon in this sea of winter white.

I swish the martini shaker and watch out of the corner of my eye as Shawn takes a sip of his drink. Did he notice I put a little extra bourbon in? Probably not. Years of bartending to figure out how to pour the perfect shot, but no one notices. They just want to name drop when ordering their fancy drinks. The silver cylinder almost flies out of my grasp, I rattle it so hard. I grit my teeth and restore my customer satisfaction smile. Sometimes I wonder if they even know what it is they're drinking, or if it's just the latest fad.

Shawn rubs the condensation off the smooth tumbler of his Old Fashioned. Up and down. His strong fingers wrap around the crystal. Lucky glass.

Really, Sarah? It's been a bit of a dry spell but c'mon. It's just fingers. And who under forty orders an Old Fashioned?

Old Fashioneds aren't in right now. It's all about gin these days. Thanks, Ryan Reynolds and your millions of Instagram followers. But maybe I should change my lead character's drink from a rum and coke to an Old Fashioned? Make Wesley seem more worldly. Hmmm. Need to think about that.

Sure. I've been thinking about Wesley and my opus for two months now. How about writing for a change? That screenplay isn't going to finish itself.

Unlike this martini. I can make 'em in my sleep. Plop, swish, pour.

I turn on my signature smile and focus on delivering a perfect martini to the next customer. In return, I get the glassy-eyed response from the woman sitting next to Shawn. Seeing me, but not seeing me. To her, I'm just another California blonde. That's me, your sweet, valley-girl bartender, here to listen to your woes, offer a kind nod or encouraging word as you spend your evening getting pickled at this swanky resort my poor broke ass couldn't afford to eat at, never mind stay.

Except I'm not sweet or from the valley. No one here notices or cares that I grew up far away in the great white north, as Californians like to joke. No, really, never heard that one before. It was like a daily mantra when I first got here and people remarked on my accent, or rather lack thereof. It's plain Canada to me, where the maple syrup is sweet and people can't look you in the eye when they lie to you. Not like here.

But Shawn's brown eyes didn't look away. The sparkle I see there almost makes me believe he cares enough to know my name.

"Sarah?"

Shawn did want to know my name. I sway his way. "Yes, Mr. Old Fashioned."

He swings his head, and I watch his dark hair flop over his forehead. "You're never going to let that go, are you?"

"Well, I call 'em as I see 'em and you . . . you dug your own hole." I bite my lip.

"Seriously, what can I do to change my reputation here? I'm desperate. Give a guy a break." His puppy-dog eyes urge me to give him anything he wants. I grin.

Holy crap. What is wrong with me?

"Fine. Give me something to work with here." I roll my eyes but flash him my real smile. Will he even notice the difference? Wow. Did he just raise an eyebrow at me? I'm seeing things now. "What's your favorite song?"

It's like he struck gold. Or I did. He sits up straight, and I have to look up. The skin on my neck heats. Wow, he is tall. I like tall.

Evens out my short. One side of Shawn's mouth curls. Cute. So cute.

"That's a big question. I mean, one song for all time? Too many options." His gaze locks on mine, and his pupils grow as we enter a staring match. "You have to narrow down the playing field a bit. You can't put my latest fave and the Beatles in the same category."

I laugh. I actually laugh. Air rushes into my chest, and I'm giddy. Where did this guy come from?

I place my arms on the bar and lean toward him, waiting to see if he checks out my cleavage. I'm pretty sure he was eyeballing it earlier. They all check out my chest. Maybe I should give him the benefit of the doubt and chalk it up to an attempt to read my nametag. Yeah, right.

Shawn's eyes never leave mine. Okay. The bar behind him falls out of focus. I might need to sit down. "Okay, then. Favorite Christmas song."

Now he laughs. Crinkles form at the corner of his eyes, and the sparkle is back. "Oh, I asked for that, didn't I?'

"Yup." Who am I to disagree?

Tapping his finger—the one previously feeling up his glass—against his bottom lip, Shawn makes a face like he's concentrating hard. Goosebumps rush across my clavicle. I love that he's taking this seriously. He's taking me seriously.

"Well, you know, I like the classics. I'm gonna stay in my lane. Little Drummer Boy, wait for it"— his grin is infectious—"Peace on Earth by Bowie and Bing." He slaps his hand on the bar, pleased with himself. "Two geniuses of their genres coming together to create magic. That's Christmas to me."

"Who are you?" My mouth takes over.

The light in his eyes dims. No, no, we were having fun. Ignore my stupid question, keep talking about Bowie. I clutch the edge of the bar. My brain scrambles, trying to bring back the sun. "I love Bowie too."

"Just a k . . . guy from Chicago here for the holidays visiting my dad." He rubs the fine layer of stubble on his chin. Would the short hairs be soft, or scratch my fingers? "I'm waiting for him to finish up a meeting."

"The windy city? Enjoying the warm weather?"

"I guess. Doesn't feel like Christmas, though."

"Where I grew up, we always had a white Christmas. We'd go skating on Boxing Day."

Shawn peers at me like I have two heads. "Boxing Day?"

"Keep forgetting you Americans don't celebrate Boxing Day. In Canada, where I'm from"—I point at my chest, but his eyes don't stray— "it's the day after Christmas. You get to lounge around stuffing yourself with leftovers, watching movies, or, if you're like my mom, you throw your kids out into the snow to burn off the sugar we inhaled. I think she wanted some peace and quiet."

Why am I still talking? I pick at a snowflake-shaped coaster. I just shared more with Shawn in two minutes than I did the first six months I lived with my roommates. And I'm pouring the liquor, not drinking it. Yet. One of the perks of this job is sampling new products our boss acquires so we can recommend them. The new Japanese and Belgian beers I'm bringing to the "so you're alone on Christmas too" celebration—the impromptu party my friends Siobhan and Claudia are throwing for out-of-towners—looked promising. Is there even such a thing as a local in LA?

"I can roll with that. Not the sugar, it's not my thing, but the movie part, for sure. I'm either watching one or filming one."

"Well, you're in the right town." I wince at the vinegar in my voice. Really, Sarah, you gotta get over this. It was one bad move. How were you supposed to know it was a scam? Not everyone in Tinseltown is a liar or a crook. Newbies, like Shawn here, start off decent, straightforward, and honest, and he might even stay that way. I shrug. For most of us, this town eventually chews us up and spits us out like yesterday's trash.

"That's my plan. Move here."

Should I burst his bubble? Warn him? Nah, not my place. Shawn has family here. They'll look out for him.

"Hey, Sarah, where d'you want this?" Ryan's holding another box of the wine I asked him to bring from the storeroom. Is it number eight or nine? I'm losing count. I massage my temples. Hope we have enough to last the rest of the night.

"There is fine." I point to the other end of the bar, where the last unopened bottle sits.

"What else do you need help with?" Patience has never been Ryan's virtue. The man can't seem to sit still. "I need to get back to the floor. The VIP group needs attention."

Shit. I survey the dwindling crowd. Standing here just chatting with this Shawn guy isn't good for my tips.

"On my way," I shout to Ryan over my shoulder and give Shawn my best apology smile.

I top off the guy whose attempts at flirting irritated me before Shawn showed up but are ridiculous at this point. He's drinking Veuve like it's water, which is great for the bar, but my skin crawls as he licks his lips while not so subtly staring down the open collar of my uniform. My stomach rolls. I pull the material closed and hoof it down to Ryan to help him unpack the box.

This Icellars Winery's red is popular lately. Another thing from Canada that made it in LA, unlike me. I leave two bottles on the bar as my coworker stacks the rest underneath.

"Got a live one there?" Ryan turns his stoned smirk on me.

"What?"

"The hot kid." My partner for the evening nods in Shawn's direction.

"Him? He's not a kid." Not with that five o'clock shadow.

Ryan narrows his eyes at me like he's got a secret. "Only guy here under fifty. Besides me."

"What's your point, Ryan?" He's a little too aware of my LA loser streak. You could say, he got the ball rolling. We had a thing when I first started—another one of my mistakes. I was so green when I moved out here. All bright-eyed and bushy tailed. Good thing the thick skin grew quickly.

Still, unlike every other aspect of his life, Ryan is pretty mature about being friends. I think. He doesn't seem to mind that I'm basically his boss.

"All I'm saying, I've seen that look before." His eyes dart down the bar to Shawn. "Is he eligible to join the Sarah Club?"

I follow Ryan's gaze. Shawn's honey brown hair flops over his eyes as he studies the half-empty glass he's no longer drinking. Flutters dance at the base of my throat. Good taste in music. Check. Doesn't take himself too seriously. Check. Hands big enough to wrap around my waist. Check.

"Why not?" I scrunch my nose. "Could be fun."

"Attagirl." Ryan grins at me. The same grin that got me in trouble the first time. Good thing it holds no power over me anymore. "Get back on that horse. Ride, baby, ride."

I punch Ryan lightly in the stomach. The flutters spread to my diaphragm as I turn and saunter toward my target. Maybe this Christmas won't suck after all.

END OF SNEAK PEEK

Kisses, Lies, & Us arrives November 22 2022.

Add Kisses, Lies, & Us to your Goodreads Reading List today!

Made in the USA
Middletown, DE
22 October 2022

13291285R00283